Heat belched all around him. Brimstone bubbled just under his nose. He was afire. His smock ignited, as did the skin on his elbows and knees. He screamed at the sudden pain, and forced his eyes open to see this new attack, to get away.

The water was gone. Instead, the creek bed roiled with black, sticky tar. Huge gas pockets burped sulfur. Things charred and long dead floated on the surface. The tar was near boiling, and Candlemas was elbow- and hock-deep in it. It stuck to his face and neck, and burned where it touched. He wailed with fright and agony as he plucked himself free and grabbed for the shore.

The monster was there to meet him. . . .

The Netheril Trilogy
Clayton Emery

Sword Play

Dangerous Games
Mortal Consequences

FANTASY ADVENTURE

Mortal Consequences

Clayton Emery

Dedicated to
J.D. "Too Cool" Quick

MORTAL CONSEQUENCES

First Printing: January 1998
Printed in the United States of America.
Library of Congress Catalog Card Number: 96-60807

9 8 7 6 5 4 3 2 1

ISBN: 0-7869-0683-9
8573XXX1501

U.S., CANADA, ASIA,
PACIFIC, & LATIN AMERICA
Wizards of the Coast, Inc.
P.O. Box 707
Renton, WA 98057-0707
+1-206-624-0933

EUROPEAN HEADQUARTERS
Wizards of the Coast, Belgium
P.B. 34
2300 Turnhout
Belgium
+32-14-44-30-44

Visit our website at **www.tsr.com**

Chapter 1

"Watch it! It's a—"

The land around the pair extended for miles in all directions, flat as a white tabletop. Yet the part they'd trodden on suddenly erupted upward like a snapped rug, then twisted and curled high as a man's shoulder to engulf them.

Sunbright Steelshanks, barbarian, grabbed his much-smaller companion Knucklebones, part-elven thief, by one arm, and hurled her a dozen feet to plow into powdery snow. By the time the thief had rebounded to her feet and whipped snow from her eyes, the barbarian was gone.

Not gone, she realized, gulped down. Entrapped.

Some monster like a wide, flat rug, diamond-shaped like a manta ray from the ocean, had whirled upward from the tundra floor to snare Sunbright, then slammed itself and its prey hard against the ground.

The leathery thing was a dozen feet across, big as a

tent, and strong as a yoke of bulls. Though hard to see against snow and winter-white sky, Sunbright was wrapped like a mummy in white folds so tight that Knucklebones could see knobs marking his belt buckle, back scabbard, and the iron rings of his moosehide boots.

She didn't look for long. Whipping out a dark-bladed elven knife, she pelted toward the monster, powdery snow flying from her boots, and drove the slim blade into the creature's hide directly above Sunbright's head. As the creature jerked, she sliced sideways, fearful of scalping Sunbright. The hide was tough as a boot sole, and stiff with white hair sharp enough to pierce her hand. She heaved and sawed with her blade, parted flesh, but drew no blood, only a white ichor that froze instantly in the chilly air.

Her carving was rewarded by a brief glimpse of Sunbright's topknot and trailing horsetail, hair so blonde it was almost white, giving him his name. His face was dangerously blue from suffocating.

Sucking air as if drowning, he gasped, "My sword! Cut out my—"

The vision was whisked away. Astonished, Knucklebones saw the wound seal as if by magic. A white-on-white line glowed, then the hide was as smooth and tough as before. As impervious to harm.

Inside the rolled-up carpet-beast, Sunbright kicked, kneed, flexed, bit, tussled; all to no avail. Even his brawny arms, pinned alongside his head, could only shove the living walls away a hair. He was locked in a white chamber tighter than a coffin, lungs and stomach constricted. He would have blacked out already had not Knucklebones let in fresh air with her knife. The monster healed instantly, and would wrap tighter until he suffocated. After that, the snow lurker would take days to digest him, gaining life and warmth from his rotting carcass. Sunbright had seen reindeer skeletons with the ribs and pelvis crushed, marking a lurker's attack.

He kicked, but both legs were trussed tight, as if roped. Bucking his back and buttocks did little good, for he couldn't gain leverage against the ground. As part of its brutal attack, the snow lurker rolled over and over, humped, and flattened like a gigantic inchworm. Such gyrations would disorient and panic prey, squeeze air from the lungs. Whirled around and around, Sunbright felt his stomach lurch. He'd already banged his nose against the leather hide twice. Blood and snot were salty and bitter on his tongue, foul enough to choke him. Biting did no good, for the leather hide was slick with blood and sweat.

Strength alone couldn't save him. He could only hope Knucklebones got his message. Otherwise this hot thrashing darkness was a preview of hell.

Yet the elven thief fought two menaces. It was bad enough trying to catch the bucking lurker, it rolled as fast as she could run. Now, where the beast had left a diamond-shaped impression on the ground, there was exposed gray-green tundra moss. And from a hole in that lumpy ground issued a flood of white ants as large as her foot. Hundreds of them.

These arctic ants churned tunnels in the snow to chase the lurker. Knucklebones reasoned that the ants took advantage of the lurker's attack to scavenge left-overs. The thief got in their way as both struggled to catch the rolling monster and its prey. Ants swarmed over her. In passing, they tasted her flesh. Pincers like pliers ticked hunks from her neck and hands. The insects must have found her sweet, for some unheard signal brought more ants rushing. Within a minute, a dozen white ants big as rabbits galloped up and down her furs and gear, nipping at exposed flesh, drawing blood.

Knucklebones yelped, swore, and swatted. With one hand she grabbed the thorax of an ant, cold as an icicle, and squeezed. Brittle legs windmilled as the carapace cracked. Acrid chilly glop stained her hand, and stung in an ant bite. Another bit her ear alongside her leather eye patch. She batted it away, losing a piece of her ear to icy jaws.

Yet Knucklebones was raddled with scars from years of fighting, and could ignore pain and distress to keep herself alive in a fight. So could Sunbright, for he still squirmed within the leather folds of the snow lurker.

Pushing aside the irritation and threat of the ants—enough of them could strip her to her bones—she pursued the humping monster. The beast slowed, tiring, but was still dangerous as a kicking horse. The man trapped inside slowed too. Sunbright was running out of air.

Thinking furiously, Knucklebones tried to time the erratic flailing of the lurker, but found no pattern. It could as easily roll over and crush her legs as tumble the other way. Finally, she locked her elven knife in her right fist, blade sticking out and away, and leaped.

Though the lurker's hairy skin was slick with snowmelt, the nimble thief managed to wrap her legs around it, but only for a second. The creature reacted to the unnatural touch with new energy, humping high and slamming the earth, then rolling to toss Knucklebones off. She tapped a foot against the ground, slid her bottom along the slick skin, and stayed atop it. The horizon jumped and danced, her stomach lurched, but she only needed a second.

Slashing hard at the end of her arm, she sheared the skin along the ridge where Sunbright's mighty sword Harvester was strapped across his back. The wicked slash parted the flesh so it wept white ichor, though the ends immediately began to close. But Knucklebones's clever hands had done their work. Seizing the two-handed, leather-wrapped pommel, she yanked it free of the scabbard, a sword nearly as long as she was tall. As the heavy, back-hooked nose pulled free, the lurker's wound had already sealed around the blade, and Knucklebones cut it anew by drawing the blade.

Sliced twice, the tundra beast pitched her off with a sideways lurch. The small thief tumbled to hammered snow hard enough to jar her teeth, but she retained her grip on the huge sword.

Instantly she rolled to her feet, held the long blade high despite its great weight, and raced after the snow lurker again. The twin cuts she'd made were already invisible. She prayed Sunbright hadn't blacked out.

The lurker had enough intelligence to track Knucklebones as a threat, so it curled itself almost double and sprang to arch away. The grim thief pursued. Outlined in white leather, like a body under a sheet, she saw Sunbright's shoulders, his elbows vainly pressing against the living prison, and the thrust of his jaw. His hands, she guessed, were pinned by his ears. Bad, considering what she had to do.

Stumbling, diving, combining power and grace, she slammed the knife at Sunbright's face. The razor-sharp blade skimmed through the first layers of white hide, then parted to show tanned flesh. The snow lurker twisted away, but she pressed on, twisting as if carving a steak from a mad cow. From deep inside she heard a gasp, and took courage that her lover was still alive. With a final wrench, she hollered, "Give me your hands!"

The wound was healing fast, but Sunbright's fingers protruded through the slit for just a second. In that second, the nimble thief rammed the pommel of the great sword into Sunbright's numbed fingers. Then the gap sealed, or tried to, for the sword blade projected from inside the monster.

Exhausted by her mad dashes, Knucklebones dropped, unable to close for fear of being sheared herself. She could only pray to Shar, the God of Thieves, the Greater Power of the Gray Waste; with herself trapped in a white waste.

The lurker fought, rolled, curled, twisted, but even banging the ground couldn't shake the steel blade from Sunbright's iron grip. Through a mist of her own breath, Knucklebones watched, fascinated, as the barbarian's trapped arms flexed, pushed, unbent.

Then the great hooked sword Harvester of Blood sliced through the lurker like an axe through fog.

One second the white rolled body was whole, the next a rent six feet long slit it like a fish. From the rent spilled a gasping, blue-faced, white-smeared Sunbright, who collapsed on the snow, melting it with his body heat.

Knucklebones wept for joy out of one good eye, ran to her huge lover, and grabbed his shoulder to pull him upright. The ravenous snow lurker was already curling back, slithering, pursuing.

"Run—at an angle—to its path!" Sunbright wheezed. He was pale but smeared with blood, eyes red, throat raw. Assisted by the thief, he gamely jogged in his big boots across the trampled snow.

They ran and ran, stumbling and lurching, always at an angle from the deadly pursuer that rippled along the snow after them with the smooth grace of a manta ray swimming under water. Yet slowly the two humans pulled away, for the huge beast was tired. And finally, glancing over her shoulder, Knucklebones saw nothing.

"Wh-where did it go?"

Sunbright slammed to a halt, sobbed for breath so hard he drooled, but he pointed out a shimmering square on the snow. Knucklebones saw the white surface ripple and tremble, then lie smooth as if never trodden. The effect was all the weirder because their footprints began just at the edge of the silent square. The lurker had burrowed under the snow within seconds.

"Will it come after us?"

"No, but let's keep—walking—anyway." Plodding, trudging, they left the disturbed spot far behind. Only then did Sunbright collapse to his knees and wash his bloodied face clean with snow.

"I must be—" he rasped, "—the only barbarian to ever—escape a snow lurker! Thanks to your deft hand."

"I was afraid I'd split your skin to the skull!" she admitted. Knucklebones's knees were weak, so she sank beside him. The barbarian didn't mind the snow and cold, but she found kneeling so chilly it was painful. Born in a lofty city that drifted south in winter, she had barely seen snow a dozen times in her life. Now she was surrounded by leagues of it. She'd never get used to this frozen wasteland. There wasn't even wind to fill it.

"There were ants, too," she panted. "Big white ones that bit."

"Just a nuisance. Brush them off."

Knucklebones fingered her ear, and found bloody scabs. Her flesh was too numb to feel much pain, despite a fur-lined hood.

The two were dressed for the weather, at least. Knucklebones wore a coat of brown sheepskin with the fur turned inward and the sleeves cupped into mittens. Her legs were clad in blue wool leggings tucked into boots made of reindeer hocks with the hair still on. At her back hung an ox hide pack stuffed with jerked meat, oatmeal, and dried fruit. Her long elven blade hung on a thong to thump on her small bosom, immediately handy. Beside it was strung a yellowed knucklebone, her namesake, the hardest bone in any animal's body. With the hood up, all that showed were tufts of dark, unkempt hair, a pale nose reddened by cold, and one good eye with a slight slant. The other bore an old knife wound and a leather eye patch. Under her coat she wore woolen sweaters. Her fingers were deeply indented from brass knuckledusters—hence part of her name—but she'd shucked them because the intense cold made her clumsy.

In contrast, the tundra-born Sunbright wore little.

Red woolen leggings were tucked into iron-ringed moosehide boots stuffed with moss for insulation. A long green shirt reached to his knees, but only a thick scarf and sheepskin mantle hung from both shoulders, with a pack and Harvester's scabbard binding the mantle in place. He wore no hat, despite that his temples were shaved and his white-blonde hair dragged back into a topknot and horsetail. When the wind blew and Knucklebones's teeth chattered, Sunbright dragged the scarf up to warm his ears. Just to look at his naked forearms and chin made Knucklebones shiver.

As did looking at the naked land. For the thousandth time, she turned a circle for a landmark. Anything would do: a hill, a tree, a bush. But there was only snow-clad tundra, rising slightly in spots, dipping here, but altogether too flat. Even the horizon was a blur, white snow meeting a white sky. She had no idea of their direction, destination, or distance covered. Left alone, she'd go mad in hours, run screaming in circles, crying like a child until she collapsed and died. Or was eaten.

"Are there many carpet beasts out here?" she asked. Even her voice was lost in the wastes, like the squeaking of a baby rabbit. She barely reached Sunbright's breastbone. He could have slung her across his shoulders like a lamb.

"Lurkers? No, not many. There's not much for them to eat. And when they do catch something, reindeer mostly, though sometimes polar bears, they curl up and digest for months. My people kill them when they can. I should have been more alert, should have seen its track."

"Track?" Knucklebones said. She couldn't even trust the ground she walked on. White on white, it always looked too far or too near, so she blundered like a drunk.

"A lurker follows the vibrations of our feet. It swims under the snow, circles to get in front of you, so you step on it. Lucky I threw you clear."

Lucky nothing, the thief knew. A lifetime on the tundra had saved him. Both of them, actually, for she wouldn't last a night if Sunbright died.

"I should have seen the outline. And ant steam." To her puzzled look, he explained, "The ants are cold-blooded, but storing food underground in their burrows makes heat and wisps of steam. Ants often burrow near lurkers to pick up scraps of food, and they swarm over the beast's hide after lice. They help each other survive. Everything up here works together."

And eats each other, Knucklebones thought. "How much farther to your tribe's hunting grounds?" she asked, for perhaps the millionth time.

"Not far now," he answered patiently. "In fact, that's why I missed the lurker. I was excited about getting home." He raised his hand to shield his eyes from the sunset. The sun had only risen a hand high in the southeast, and after only four hours sank toward the southwest. Nights were twenty hours long, so they mostly traveled by starlight. Why they hadn't been eaten long ago—by lurkers or polar bears or wolves or ants—Knucklebones couldn't fathom, but Sunbright's knowledge of the land and its inhabitants had steered them around danger. Usually.

He pointed into the gathering dusk and said, "There. Where the land begins to fall again. A shallow rill feeds a frozen stream that drops off a low cliff at a rookery into an arm of the Narrow Sea. My people ice fish at this time of year, then pack the sledges and search for reindeer before spring. It won't be more than six hours on."

"What will you do when you arrive?" Knucklebones phrased the question delicately.

Sunbright rubbed his stubbly jaw, picked an icicle of blood off his upper lip, and said, "I have no idea."

Knucklebones stifled a sigh. In the few months they'd been together, he'd explained how he left his tribe, the

Rengarth Barbarians of the tundra. How his father, Sevenhaunt, a great shaman, had died suddenly, mysteriously wasting away. How Owldark, the new shaman, dreamed a vision that showed Sunbright the ruin of his people, and so demanded his death. How his mother, Monkberry, warned her only child to take his father's sword and flee. How he'd fled to the "lowlands," as barbarians called all territories south, for no single individual could survive on the tundra. And of his adventures to hell and to the future, where he met Knucklebones, then returned. How he'd conquered death. How in a few years, the boy had grown to a man, then a warrior, and finally a shaman.

But a shaman was worthless without a tribe, and so, defying the sentence of death, Sunbright journeyed home. And Knucklebones, herself cast to the winds, went with him, knowing she might be executed too. So, without a plan, and with little hope, they trudged across the darkening wastes.

After a time, Knucklebones said, "It's a long way to come for revenge."

"I don't want revenge!" Sunbright snapped. "I want . . ."

"What?" she asked, peeking around her furred hood.

"I want to clear my name, and that of my father," the shaman, staring at the dark horizon, said. "I want to find out why my father died, if possible. I want to disprove the notion that I'll bring destruction to the tribe. I want—I just want to go home. And I feel—I *know* bad times are coming. I want to be with my tribe, for good or ill."

"Do you mean the fall of the Netherese Empire? That's not for three hundred and fifty-odd years yet."

"No, sooner trouble. I've dreamt of it."

Knucklebones's sigh blew fog. "I believe you," she said. "A shaman's dreams are both a gift and a curse. Sometimes you thrash all night, then drag yourself through the day, half asleep."

The barbarian nodded grimly and said, "And sometimes dreams show the future, or distant events, and sometimes they mean nothing. Sorting them out is the chore."

"Why do it then? Why take the responsibility of being a shaman? It must be hell trying to advise folk on what's true and what's false."

Oddly, the shaman grinned in the darkness, his fine white teeth glowing by starlight. "Better to be a thief," he asked, "see what one can steal without losing a hand? Like a jackdaw waiting to swoop down and steal a button?"

"Yes, better that. Life is simple for thieves. If you can carry something off, fine. The owner should have been more careful. It teaches folks responsibility."

Sunbright laughed aloud, and swatted her fanny wrapped in wool and fur. "I'll remember that," he said. "But you were born to be a thief and I a shaman, like my father and forebears. We can't escape our destiny, we can only endure it."

Knucklebones cast about the barren landscape, which hadn't changed a jot to her eye. "I'll be glad to escape this wasteland."

"Wasteland?" Sunbright barked a laugh. "This is beautiful country! Wide open, bright and clean, sweet-smelling, sharp-edged, and simple. Either you adapt or you die."

Knucklebones saw snow and stars. "Perhaps," she mumbled. "Maybe in the summertime. . . ."

"Oh, no. Summer's a sea of mud. Bog so thick and gooey it jerks your boots off. No, in summer you're a prisoner of the land, and have to camp by the sea and stay put. In winter you can hitch up dog or reindeer sleds, or strap on snowshoes or skis, and go wherever you want. No, this is the finest time of year!"

The thief swallowed a groan.

More walking, for the tenth straight day. A rest with

cold rations, since they had nothing to burn. Eating snow for water. Walking and more walking. Trudging through fog for two days once. Darkness, daylight, darkness. Boots crunching a million times, and walking on.

Just when Knucklebones thought she'd go screaming mad, a spark glowed on the horizon. "Is that a village?" she asked.

"No. Northern lights."

The thief stared in awe. Reds and blues shimmered like rainbow curtains in the sky. The colors danced, dipped, soared, settled, jiggled, never still.

"They're beautiful!"

"You're learning," Sunbright chuckled. "Feel? The land dips. And hear that?"

The part-elf tipped her hood to reveal pointed ears. Far off she heard a jabbering, the first noise in days.

"What is it?"

"A rookery. A nesting ground for puffins."

They walked faster over snow tinged red and blue by northern lights. Gradually the land sloped, then dropped by the frozen stream Sunbright had mentioned. (And found unerringly, she noted, after ten days of walking through a void.) The slope grew lumpy with rocks where the tundra had been scraped away eons ago. Rocks the size of skulls lay beside boulders as big as houses. Scattered amidst them bobbed knee-high birds with black bodies, white masks, and fat yellow beaks. Even at midnight they were busy, waddling, gossiping, arguing, fighting, lovemaking, even tumbling and sliding on their bellies down a slick mud slope. Knucklebones laughed, "It looks like market day!"

Sunbright pointed and said, "And down that rill we'll find my tribe. They've wintered here for centuries, pulling the whitefish through the ice and salting them down. . . ."

His voice was mixed with joy and sorrow. Happiness at seeing his tribe and mother, sadness that they might be killed outright. Or driven away again. Knucklebones wondered which, for Sunbright, would be the crueler fate.

Skirting rocks, careful of twisting ankles, they negotiated the rill by starlight, then touched coarse sand. A bluff rose at their right, and the frozen arm of the sea trapped a narrow beach between. Ice floes grinding together drowned out the happy clatter of the puffins.

Down the beach they walked and walked. At every step Sunbright strode faster, until Knucklebones trotted to keep up. Finally they rounded the bluff, and walked onto a sandy spit. Before them loomed the growling, ice-packed ocean. And nothing else.

"Where are they?"

Sunbright cast about again and again. "I . . . I don't know."

Knucklebones felt a pang for him. "But—if they're not here—where can they be?"

The shaman's voice drifted away. "I don't know. I can't even guess. . . ."

Chapter 2

The gulguthhydra was hungry. It was always hungry. Now it sensed food approaching.

The cavern was black, so its many heads couldn't see. The gulguthhydra was also black, though its dozen eyes would shine dull white in any light. The monster looked like a hill of black thorns that sprouted necks studded with scales like chips of volcanic glass, and atop the necks were fang-studded mouths, pug noses, and short, sharp ears. Too, the beast sported a pair of tentacles. All these writhing organs roved over the walls and floor of the cavern incessantly, scouring the stone so often it was worn smooth as far as the beast could reach. Centuries ago, the black hydra had been captured by the pit fiend Prinquis, and rooted in this corridor by magic. Over decades, it had scraped the walls clean, caught the occasional rat or bat or lesser imp, growing a tiny bit at a time, reaching a little further with tooth and tentacle.

But always it was starving, and here came food.

The creature picking along the corridor came with a heavy tread. The monster was taller than a tall man, naked but for an ugly, lumpy, flinty hide formed of something stronger than stone, for its jagged feet scratched and nicked the polished stone floor. In light, the flinty hide would have glistened slightly, so dense were the minerals that made up its skin. It had hands and feet like a human, but no eyelids, so its blue eyes were round and staring and frightening. No hair, no fingernails or toenails, no marks on its body except the dense flint.

It talked to itself in a gravelly voice like steel on a grindstone. The gulguthhydra perked up, stilled its lashing heads and tentacles to wait until the flint creature was close enough to seize. This being would make a fine meal.

"Out. This must be the way out. Must be. Outside, finally. Out . . ."

Closer trod the crusty feet of the monster. The hydra lunged.

Three heads struck as one. One dived from the right, one from the left, one straight down, like three fingers snatching a morsel. Toothy mouths clamped onto the flint creature in the same second, biting hard and gnashing fast to rip the prey to flinders, to reduce it to bloody gobbets before it could escape, or even limp away wounded.

The flinty fiend was knocked to its knees under the triple assault. One arm and one shoulder were pinned by mouths, and its head had been sucked into the maw of the largest head. Yet fangs broke on the stony hide, so the gulguthhydra's mouths filled with chips and black blood. Champing furiously didn't tear the stone skin, or even dent it.

Then the human monster struck back.

From one fist lanced a long white beam like a sword

of moonfire. The blade exploded through the roof of one mouth and pierced the tiny brain and scaly skull so the head snapped back, then hung loose, dangling. From the other fist poured a rain of acid that smoked hydra flesh in a thousand places. Black blood shot in jets to stain the walls and ceiling. From the flint creature's mouth shot a bolt of pure energy like venom. The invisible arrow-shaped jolt sliced through the biggest head, shearing it open like a rotten melon, then plunged deep into the hydra's writhing, hilly shape. The thorny body was torn open, the many-chambered heart sundered.

With a scream from four mouths, the hydra whipped heads and tentacles in a frenzy until suddenly it stopped cold, and collapsed into a heap, stinking like charred garbage.

Spitting out scales and tooth chips, the flint monster arose, mounted the sodden, sundered carcass, climbed over, and moved on. If Prinquis, lord of this hell, had anchored the hydra here, then this passage, ". . . must be a way out. Outside. Got to be. Chance to get out . . ."

But half a mile on, the flint creature bumped into a rockslide. The roof had collapsed, leaving a cavity of solid stone, and time and heat and pressure had sealed the whole tight. The monster screamed, wailed, pounded with blocky fists that cracked boulders. Yet it could never dig free, never escape this way.

Turning, the monster retraced it steps. Its rage still burned white-hot when it reached the dead hydra. Screaming anew, the monster kicked the carcass so chunks of black flesh rebounded from the walls. Tearing with stone claws, it ripped more hunks loose, bit through them, slammed them down, hurled them away. It raged and ranted and revelled in gore until the hydra was nothing but a black smear studded with teeth and gristle.

Only then did the black-spattered monster continue on, like some misshapen parody of a man or woman smeared with offal. As its great heavy feet scratched along, it muttered anew.

". . . Not the way out. There must be. Must get out. Revenge . . . that's all. Death to everyone I hate.

"But first, must get out . . ."

* * * * *

Onward they trekked. Winter waned as Sunbright and Knucklebones searched from the Channel Mountains in the east, north past the fork at Two Rivers, then westward along the edge of the High Ice, where even polar bears didn't go. Nothing did they find.

Sunbright patiently explained that his people always followed this route, for as the snow retreated, the reindeer came after, cropping the soft moss of the tundra, until the herd reached the High Ice and turned westward. Yet there was no evidence of any tribe. Disturbingly, Sunbright noted the reindeer herd was thinner, the animals gaunt. The moss was thin, and the tiny purple blossoms he remembered from his youth were sparse.

"The land is weak," he told Knucklebones. "Even the deer's bones are flimsy. All these skulls of infant reindeer means they're stillborn, which means their mothers are sickly. The life of the land is being sapped somehow."

Spring turned to summer, until Knucklebones stripped to leathers by day, though she was never very warm. As the shaman had foretold, the soft earth of the tundra turned to bog. Muddy wallows under the moss formed a gluey trap that pulled Sunbright's boots off, made their legs throb from the weight of mud, slowed them down, and finally stopped them.

So they abandoned the search for the summer. They had reached the edge of the tundra at the west anyway, and faced high cliffs topped by the Cold Forest and the icy mountains of the Dementia Range in the distance. Skirting the Bay of Ascore, Sunbright sought work in Sepulcher and Arctic Rim. He found it easily, for the towns were starved for meat. Even townsfolk saw that the once vast herds had thinned, and few would enter the trackless bogs for food. So Sunbright hunted, and sold venison, wild boar, even bear meat. He gave the money to Knucklebones, for he had no use for it. The thief, with shrewd bets and quick hands, doubled and tripled their coins gambling with sailors and loggers and fishwives.

"I still don't understand," Knucklebones told him one night as she stacked coins by candlelight. They'd rented a small cabin along the water, in sight of the Barren Mountains. Sunbright found this ironic, for there he'd begun his adventures, years ago. "How can the tundra be weak? How can any land so cold and icy and muddy suffer? It's the people who live there who suffer!"

Sunbright rolled over from a doze. Hunting for miles from dawn till dusk, dragging back heavy game, tired him out. "The tundra is a hard country, but a fragile one, though it seems contradictory," he told her. "It only supports a few beasts and birds, so they rely on one another to survive. Reindeer eat the moss and leave droppings. Birds pick out seeds and bugs that live in the droppings. The birds in turn carry the seeds far and wide. That spreads the moss, keeps muddy spots from growing barren. The new growth attracts musk oxen, who churn the soil with their hooves and leave more manure, and so on, in a closed circle. If one part is removed, the circle falls apart. If the weather grows too warm, as happened once, lungworm sprout in the musk oxen. Too many worms kill the calves. Then the soil isn't turned over, barren spots spread, water erodes the wallows so the earth is scarred, the moss grows thinner, the reindeer starve—"

"All right, all right. I believe you," Knucklebones cut

him off, tugging up her eye patch to rub sleepy eyes. Revealed was her blind eye, a milky white. At Sunbright's grimace, she hurriedly tugged it down. "I don't want the natural history of the world, but why is just the tundra weakened, or drained of life, or whatever you call it? Why not everywhere?"

"It *is* happening everywhere," Sunbright yawned, and lay back by the tiny hearth fire. Golden flames reflected on the white skin of his scarred and muscular chest. "It's just the effect shows first in a fragile area like the tundra. Candlemas spent months fighting a blight, a wheat rust, that spread through grain crops. He couldn't find any logical cause. The crops simply couldn't fight off normal diseases. As someone with measles will die if exposed to whooping cough, while a healthy man or woman shakes it off. This mysterious drain and as a shaman, I sense it more than understand it—affects all life. Eventually, it may cause—"

Nodding at the table, Knucklebones jerked awake at the sudden silence. "Cause what?" she asked.

"Disaster. Famine. Possibly for years. Deaths in the thousands."

"No." The small woman rose, stretched like a cat, unlaced her leather vest and trousers, and said, "I was born in the future, remember? There were no great disasters. Not that I ever heard of, anyway."

"I'm not sure you would have heard," Sunbright said. He sat on their thinnest blanket and stared at the fire. By the hearth, his great longbow and heavy-nosed sword softly gleamed. "The Netherese run this world, and write down history as it suits them. They've never shown compassion for starving peasants. Commoners are fit for farming and mining and hunting—as prey— and nothing else."

Yawning, Knucklebones lay beside him. Fire reflecting on her body showed more scars than the barbarian's. The thief had grappled in knife fights since she was a baby. Lifting a thin arm, she cooed, "Come and lay your head on my shoulder, country mouse. You need to rest, not fret. Summer will end soon, and we'll travel on, won't we?"

But Sunbright didn't listen to her words, only her tone. Laying his big white-blonde head on her shoulder, he murmured, "You sound like Greenwillow."

Knucklebones stiffened, said, "And why her?"

Sunbright closed his eyes. "You called me 'country mouse.' That's what she called me. Curious, isn't it?"

"I suppose," Knucklebones said, her small bosom heaving in a sigh. "It's not mete to mention one woman while lying in the arms of another."

The barbarian opened his eyes, looked straight into her one good one, and said, "I'm sorry. I didn't think. I love you, Knuckle', and only you now. But Greenwillow was a boon companion, and I loved her once. She died saving my life, and was trapped in a corner of hell as a result. Somehow, some day, I'll get her loose of it, if her soul survived."

Again Knucklebones sighed, but wrapped her skinny, scarred arms around his head. "Your life would be easier if you busied yourself with daily tasks," she told him softly, "and people close by, not insurmountable problems that span the globe."

"Easier if I had no conscience, or honor." He kissed her white shoulder, licked her pointed ear as he spoke. "Perhaps you should marry a fishmonger or cobbler. They could give you a home, get you eight or nine children, make you fat and gray. Would that suit you better than tramping the world beside a dream-haunted barbarian?"

Knucklebones chuckled and kissed his forehead. "You're full of odd notions, Sunbright, and silly besides," she said. "Go to sleep."

And he did, as she watched the fire and caressed his thick hair.

* * * * *

Come the first cool day of autumn, when the hills burned red and gold and orange, Knucklebones knotted her sack of cash, Sunbright shouldered his sword and bow and satchels, and they left the summer cabin. Embarking on a small caravel with lateen sails, they were ferried down the Narrow Sea, past Vandal Station, past Northreach, past Frostypaw and Coldfoot, and through the Channel Lock. At Harborage the two asked after the Rengarth Barbarians, but received only blank looks. All summer Sunbright had asked everyone he met, travelers and locals alike, for the whereabouts of his tribe, but none knew. As far as the northwestern reaches of the empire were concerned, the Rengarth had vanished, and their ancestral lands stood empty. Wondering, and growing more fearful all the time, Sunbright had decided to sail into the eastern arm of the Narrow Sea and inquire there. But even at the crossroads of Harborage, they found no trace.

Over time, learning nothing, Sunbright's face grew longer, his eyes haunted, his demeanor bitter. Even with Knucklebones his answers grew short, until they passed days without speaking. They sailed on, clear to the east, to Janick near the river called The Alley, and found naught. There Sunbright disembarked, and stood on the docks, and stared at the sea and land for hours.

Finally Knucklebones said, "Perhaps we search too hard." Worn down by constant travel, she perched on a bird-stained bollard. All around the harbor ships and boats tacked and rowed, delivered supplies and people and fish and sails and water. They were the only ones idle, and they felt out of place.

But no place was home now, and Knucklebones, not even of this time, found herself saddled with a gloomy companion, and nowhere to go.

"Eh? What?" Sunbright said, turning from his daydreaming. "How can one search too hard? How else shall we find my people?"

"I don't know, but wandering blind isn't working, and you're unhappy," she said, desperately trying to think of any alternative. "Perhaps—perhaps if we set another goal, temporarily, we'd have luck. That might lead us in the right direction. When the way of mortals fail, it's best to trust in the gods."

Sunbright turned back to the harbor, as if to see over the horizon. "Perhaps you're correct. Perhaps the gods have other tasks for us."

Absentminded, the big barbarian rested his hand on the warhammer tucked into his belt. The long head bore a parrot's beak and crushing face, a tool for war, more a dwarf's weapon than a man's. "I've carried this a long time, with a pledge," he said. "I told Dorlas's brethren in Dalekeva that I would one day return the hammer to his kinfolk. I could return it now."

"Capital! A wonderful idea!" The thief exclaimed. Encouraged by the change, Knucklebones hopped up and kissed his chin. "We can journey to the south, where we haven't been before, and learn the news. Perhaps we'll find word of your tribe. Strange roads often lead to treasure!"

Without further ado, the barbarian walked off the dock and turned his back on the Narrow Sea, stomping down the first muddy street tending south. Shaking her head at his obstinate nature, Knucklebones scampered beside him.

A ghost of a smile creased Sunbright's face as he told her, "You realize this is just another quest, another foolish need to satisfy honor."

"I understand, but your honor is all you have. Feed it to keep it strong," she laughed. "At least, going south, we'll be warm."

"Sticky, muggy, buggy, and hot."

Sunbright tramped steadily past wagons and workers and shops.

"Warm like the sewers of Karsus," Knucklebones corrected. In celebration, she reached into her pockets and dug out her brass knuckles, slipped them onto knotty fingers.

"Anticipating trouble?" the barbarian asked, arching an eyebrow.

"Wherever *you* go, there's trouble," she chuckled. For the first time in days, Sunbright chuckled with her.

* * * * *

"I knew we wouldn't be warm for long," Knucklebones groused.

"It's not cold." Sunbright flicked snow from his eyelashes as he said, "It's . . . *bracing.*"

"I need to brace myself, all right." Knucklebones said. She clutched a cedar bush jutting from the rock face to her left. "Else I'll be blown clean off this mountain."

"You could dance on the head of a pin, you're so nimble," Sunbright chided. "I'm the one slipping and sliding, taking two steps up and one back."

The two were again wrapped in sheepskin coats and mantles, tall boots, and wool leggings. Their boots slipped often, and Sunbright needed to catch rocks and roots to climb the steep mountain path. They'd climbed for three days, leaving the steppes and the last village far below. The vista to their right had yawned wider with every step, miles of wintry valley dark with pines and sheltered meadows dotted with sheep. A storm rushing over the Iron Mountains pelted them with snow and blotted out all vision except their path.

"It's not far now," Sunbright called. "It can't be."

"How can you know?" Knucklebones sniffed. Her furred hood was rimmed with white flakes that set off her shadowed face like a halo. "We could step to the moon."

"They said in the village the dwarves live below the

treeline. We've climbed almost to where the green stops and the rocks are bare. And this is the only path, ignoring a few forks, so we can't be lost. Any minute now we'll probably smell smoke, or spook a sentry—*whoa!*"

The travelers stopped in shock. Around a bend, looming through the hissing snow, a trio of black-eyed cow skulls stared at them.

Knucklebones whispered a charm, Sunbright grunted. The skulls were huge, from oxen he supposed, bleached white and heaped with snow that trickled down the muzzles, one of which bore deep axe marks.

"What are they?" Knucklebones asked. "Warnings, or just markers?"

"I don't know," he said. Yet without thinking, he drew Harvester from the back scabbard with a low moan.

"Is it wise to bear your sword? Won't the dwarves, these sentries you speak off, take that amiss and shoot first?"

"It is foolish to bear a sword when coming in peace . . ." Sunbright pulled the scarf clear of his ears and nose to track sounds and smells. "But something else is up here. I feel it."

Knucklebones tugged off her hood to free her elven ears, keener than the human's. "Besides dwarves," she started to say, "what would—*Hark!*"

"What?"

The small thief grabbed the warrior's arm, and tugged him into a niche crammed with snow-laced bracken. She whispered, "I heard a jingle of harness, or a leper's bell."

"Bell? How—*look out!*"

Both whirled as an avalanche crashed down. Sunbright and Knucklebones had a vision of huge hoofs, gray, hairy muzzles, thick horns, and gray rags wrapped around tremendously wide shoulders. Carved wooden staves pointed like nocked arrows, then they were attacked by magic, staff, and fist.

Crowded, Sunbright hollered a warning to Knucklebones. There were three or four enemies, but he could see little with snow in his eyes. Rising within arm's reach, they must have crouched in the rocky niche, lying in ambush. For them, or for dwarves?

No matter. The barbarian slapped his free hand onto Harvester's pommel and stabbed straight. The long sword was unlike any other seen in the Rengarth tribe, won by his father decades ago in the southlands. The blade curved slightly from the pommel, then widened so the nose was fatter than the shank. Yet metal had been cut from the tip's back to form a wicked barbed hook. Thus the sword could stab, chop, or tear on the back draw. Sunbright tried all three attacks now.

But so close loomed these gray, shaggy foes, and so hindered was Sunbright by waist-high bushes, that the blade was batted aside. Before the shaman could recover, a wooden staff smacked him alongside the head. White lights exploded behind his eyes. He staggered at the knees, and dimly saw the shaft rise. To do what? Stab him? Knock him onto the snow-slick path and lever him off the mountain? Either way, his stunned brain couldn't focus.

Then the end of the staff erupted with red light. Sunbright felt a burn sear his neck, then he fell or was tripped. He crashed in snow.

To one side, slick as an eel, Knucklebones shed her coat and satchels, scrunched low as a hare and leaped high. She popped up almost in the face of the huge enemies. To her astonishment, they proved to be shaggy beasts like upright cattle. Horns jutted from the sides of their heads, and from some dangled tiny bells on leather thongs that jingled. These cow-beings possessed the bleached skulls along the trail, then. Their long hands bore blunt, black nails, and all carried curved wooden staves.

Surprised by her rush, a yak-man shrank back to aim the end of his staff. Knucklebones gave him no chance. Doubling her fist of brass knuckledusters, she slammed the yak-man hard on the nose. The cow face jerked, and bright blood spurted, so Knucklebones knew he or she was hurt. She smacked the same spot, and saw blood erupt from twin nostrils. Good, their noses were vulnerable.

A blistering red light erupted at her. She heard Sunbright grunt and fall. Another yak-man aimed a staff at her.

She ducked just in time, for a blast of alien wind blew leaves off the tough cedars that ringed them. Knucklebones was shielded from the tiny tornado by the hulking yak-man in front of her. Deciding to stay put and keep his protection, she closed again. She couldn't defeat them all, but could pound hell out of one, and hope for the best.

The yak-man grabbed his nose so blood ran between black-nailed fingers. Crowding her luck, Knucklebones stooped and aimed a savage uppercut at his long chin. Brass knuckles batted his snowy goat's beard, bashed thin bones underneath. A loud crack announced a broken jawbone. She wanted to yell for joy, for the sheer thrill of battle. Instead, she slid even closer as the yak-man tumbled backward.

Meanwhile, Sunbright had fallen below the brush, and so saved his life. The yak-man wielding the magic staff blasted again, but the searing flame only blasted snow into steam. Ignoring the throbbing burn on his chin and neck, Sunbright bulled aside brush, glimpsed a hairy, crooked leg ending in a rough hoof worn from mountain climbing. That small target was all he needed.

Gritting his teeth against pain, he snaked Harvester past tough roots and hooked the barb behind the yak-man's hock. A savage yank severed the tendon, and the creature was ham-strung. He toppled into a compatriot with a bawl like a slaughtered ox.

Knucklebones heard the cry and took heart. Together they might subdue these queer people and escape. Pressing one hand against the bloody-nosed yak, she slithered around his wide ribs after another foe. She found one shorter and slimmer than the others, probably a female, but the cow saw her at the same time, and whipped up a staff topped by a tiny hourglass. Knucklebones had only a second to wonder what it was—

—then she was standing in the village in the valley. Beside her, Sunbright asked a milkmaid where lay the path to the dwarves' high caves. The milkmaid had blue eyes, and rubbed the tip of her nose. Knucklebones saw freckles on her hand, smelled manure, and bread baking in a cottage, and heard milk sloshing in the pail.

But how could this image be real? What happened to the mountain and yak-men and snow? The sun was warm on her neck. The maid's dog snuffled her hand, and she felt its warm tongue on her fingers. How had she been transported three days into the past, and many miles distant?

The staff bore an hourglass, she recalled. Some magic time spell? Had it sent her mind into the past?

Images and thoughts tumbled in her mind, then a staff smacked the top of her head with a fierce crunch. The milkmaid's farm winked into blackness.

* * * * *

Sunbright saw his lover struck down, saw her drop as if lifeless. Rage overcame sense, and he reared upright with a roar. Bushes and snow flew as he hoisted Harvester in the air, slung it far behind to shear at the bull neck of the nearest of the four yak-men, but was undone again. All four turned on him. The tornado-spewing staff aimed, puffed like a dragon, and the barbarian was blown backward to sprawl on the snow-slick path.

His head slammed stone, his burned neck sent jolts of lightning coursing through his frame. Before he could rise, the yak-woman stamped forward with her staff, and knocked Harvester from his numbed hands. A tremendous hoof stamped on his chest, and drove out his wind. Through a gray fog loomed the calm, deadly face of an otherworldly executioner. The yak-woman drew a curved scimitar, and coolly aimed to split his throat.

Sunbright bucked against the hoof, got nowhere, gasped, and drew no breath into his squashed chest. He flailed his arms uselessly. He'd die now, and Knucklebones next. So ended all his mad quests.

Obscured by snow, the curved blade topped its arch, came whistling around—

—and three crossbow bolts buried themselves to their feathers in the yak-woman's breast.

Chapter 3

Pinned by a hoof, stunned by a head blow, half-blinded by snow and pain, Sunbright saw the yak-woman's brown eyes roll white as she died. A thin trickle of blood stained her round nostrils—sign of lung puncture—then she slumped onto the snow and collapsed in a heap. Her curved sword landed in the snow without a sound.

Another yak-man cast right and left for danger, whipped his staff through the air, rumbled a gurgling command to his two comrades. A black crossbow bolt slammed into the side of his neck and cut his orders off. His black-nailed hand grabbed the shaft.

Glimpsing this in seconds, Sunbright rolled, scurried on knees and elbows to grab Harvester of Blood lying on the narrow path, its imprint outlined in snow. Keeping low, he shouted, "Knuckle', watch for arrows! Someone's killing them!"

There was no answer, and a spasm of fear clutched

his heart. Was she just being silent for the fight? Or had she been killed, or pitched off the mountain? Perhaps she lay bleeding. He must—

A brawny hand clamped onto his shoulder from behind, and he was hurled flat, so hard his spine rattled. Etched against a white fluttering sky surged figures like short brown bears bristling with weaponry. The bear-beings swept to either side. One leveled a crossbow, let go with a *slap* and *clack* of string and bow. Another hoisted a long-faced battle-axe and hollered a cry like a condor making a kill. In a furry wave, the newcomers roared, and fell upon the surviving yakmen.

Half-seen through snow, Sunbright winced at the slaughter. The yak-man with the bolt in his neck turned, one hand still clutching the shaft, and tried to rip free his scimitar. A screaming dwarf—for such were their rescuers—hopped in the air and swung his battle-axe so hard the cow-being's arm was severed at the shoulder. Blood spurted over attacker and attacked. Before the yak-man could take another step, the fur-clad dwarf chopped savagely at a backwards-bent leg. Cut down like a tree, the yak-man tumbled over so fast the dwarf had to fend the shaggy body aside.

Sunbright crawled toward where he'd last seen Knucklebones; he didn't want to rise in front of a crossbow. The other two yak-men were hacked to pieces. Smashing through snowy brush, a dwarf lanced a bolt into a yak-man's jaw, pinning it to his skull. Another stabbed upward with a short spear under broad ribs. Driving the spear deep, the short one shoved so hard the yak-man's horns clacked on the rock wall behind. Again the dwarf shoved, until the shaggy body was slammed full against the stone, then again, so hard the shaft snapped, and the dwarf stumbled against his dying foe. The last yak-man raised his staff over his head sideways, a sign of surrender, but died. Two dwarves with mattock and falchion slammed blades into the beast's bowels, so it doubled with a cry of agony, and a third dwarf smashed down on the broad head with a warhammer square between the horns. Even then their ferocity was unquenched, for other dwarves swarmed around the fallen creatures to hack them limb from limb.

Steering clear of the battle-crazed warriors, Sunbright found Knucklebones lying on her side in her woolens atop smashed brush. The tiny woman was already half-covered by snow, unconscious. The shaman scanned her with his hands, found a crease in her skull and blood matted in her dark hair. Gently for such huge gnarled hands, he lifted her eyelid to peer at her pupil. One way to gauge brain damage was to compare a victim's pupils, check they were the same size, but Knucklebones only had one eye. Then snow settling on her eyeball made it twitch. Relieved, he guessed she'd recover, once he got her warm.

Brushing off snow, Sunbright fetched her shed coat and wrapped her tight, then hung her satchels on his shoulders. He hoisted Knucklebones in his arms, but even her weight, light as a lamb, made him dizzy, for he'd also been head-bashed by a curious staff. He leaned on a rock until his head stopped spinning. Too, a burn alongside his left ear and neck itched and throbbed abominably, and he knew lymph and blood wept from the wound to soak his shirt, chilling him. Gritting his teeth, he wondered what the dwarves had in store for them.

The mountain men were busy. Savage fury abated, they resorted to their usual industrious ways. With an axe they methodically hacked off the four oxen heads, then propped and wedged them amidst stones to dry and collect snow. Continuing, they sliced off the gray rags that passed for the yak-men's clothing, chopped off hands and cloven feet and threw them off the mountain, then hoisted the still-warm bodies to split the bellies and dress out the guts, which they left in a steaming pile along the trail. Finally, dragging the dressed carcasses, booty of satchels and staves and swords, they stamped free of the brush and trooped up the trail with their burdens.

The last pair faced Sunbright, who was fighting fatigue, cold, and dizziness while clutching Knucklebones, who hung limp as a rag doll. The barbarian blinked when he realized the dwarf with the thick, braided hair was female, for she had a thick beard, and her face was craggy and seamed as an old shoe. Sunbright hadn't known there *were* dwarven women. Legend said dwarves grew from the rocks like golems and ogres.

The frowning, blood-spattered woman paused, a thick falchion at the ready, and said, "Why have you come here?"

"Uh . . ." Sunbright groaned. The abrupt question flustered the shaman. "I seek the Sons of Baltar. I have—something to give Drigor."

He was never sure if his sincerity or the promise of a gift turned the tide, but the dwarven woman muttered to her companion in a voice like grinding rocks. The other growled back, then the first said, "Follow me."

Blinking against snow and exhaustion, Sunbright nodded gratefully. The two dwarves, no higher than his belt buckle, stumped up the slick path, and the barbarian picked after, hoping he didn't faint and tumble a thousand feet.

* * * * *

The trail got worse for the suffering Sunbright toting Knucklebones, for eventually the dwarves turned from the path and mounted steep steps hacked from stone, then entered a pass no wider than his shoulders. The narrow chasm was dozens of feet high. Silhouetted against falling snow were crouched sentries with crossbows. Stumbling and slipping, Sunbright kept up with the sturdy, sure-footed dwarves, and eventually passed into a black slot where warm air gushed into the barbarian's face.

After that he saw little, for he had to hunch over. The ceiling was so low, and stretches were entirely black, though all the caves were gloriously warm. After a while he saw torchlight, and a faint glow from rough paint splashed here and there on the walls, paint infused with some magic luminosity. The dwarven woman turned once to say, "Go in there and stay put," then marched off after the rest.

Ducking double, Sunbright blundered into a rough-cut room. There was no furniture, just a single iron pipe with a spigot running along the craggy wall and daubed with glowing paint. He thanked the gods he could stand upright. Cradling Knucklebones, he shucked off his heavy coat and made a bed for her on a crude stone shelf. Testing the rusty spigot singed his hand, for it was scalding hot. He guessed all the caves were heated by boiling water springing from the earth. He used his sleeve to turn the spigot, soaked a rag, and cleaned Knucklebones's scalp wound and face and hands. He drank some of the water, flat and reeking of iron, then cleaned and bandaged his neck wound. Sitting, he straightened his tackle, honed his sword back to razor sharpness, and—ordered to stay put—sat beside the sleeping Knucklebones. Lulled by the delicious heat, he nodded off.

He awoke to heavy stamping and jumped off the shelf with sword in hand, quick and lithe as a panther, but groggy in mind. So, weaving and clutching a sword, he greeted his frowning hosts.

The dwarf was old. His wrinkled face was framed by a bushy white beard and eyebrows, with six silver rings braided into his drooping mustache. He wore a tunic of rough-out gray leather with a shaggy hump behind his neck, and Sunbright supposed the hide came from a yak man. A kilt of goat hide, much stained by rust and pitted by burn marks, hung to battered boots stiff with tar. Somehow, he looked familiar.

"I am Drigor," stated the dwarf. Of course, Dorlas's father resembled him. "What have you to give me?"

"I am Sunbright Steelshanks, of the Raven Clan of the Rengarth Barbarians." If they still exist, he thought dismally. "I bring you—bring you—"

But the old dwarf's deep brown eyes had already spotted the warhammer holstered on the barbarian's belt. Without words, Sunbright pulled the weapon and handed it over.

With hands marked by crooked fingers, inch-thick callouses, and burn scars, the dwarf cradled the hammer as gently as a baby. The hammer had always looked and felt big enough to slay an ox, but in those hands it looked like a toy. Without any visible emotion, Drigor said, "We heard. But you were there? Tell me how it came to pass."

A little civility would be nice, Sunbright thought, a please and thank you for risking his and Knucklebones's life to visit these mountains to deliver a hammer. But the old man—if dwarves were men—had just been reminded that his son was dead, so Sunbright could stifle his irritation.

"We were bodyguarding a caravan, and almost to Dalekeva, when the Hunt caught us . . ." Still groggy, and hungry, Sunbright sat on the stone shelf beside a sleeping Knucklebones and told the tale. How within sight of the city walls, a hunting party of decadent Neth on golden mechanical dragons and birds swooped down. How Dorlas discharged his duty by sending the caravan's merchants ahead while the bodyguards fought from the woods. How, eventually, the forest was ignited, so they ran for the city gates. How Dorlas, wounded, fell behind, and insisted they run on. How a huntsman pierced the dwarf with a golden lance through the belly but, incredibly, Dorlas hung onto the lance, jerked himself up it, yanking the shaft through his own guts, to crush the metal wolf mask of the huntsman and kill him first, before the dwarf died himself. How Sunbright and Greenwillow were saved by Dorlas's sacrifice.

Though he was an excellent storyteller, like all tundra dwellers, Sunbright didn't embellish the story, for Dorlas's deeds needed no exaggeration. All through the tale, the eyes of Drigor never left the shaman's face, and Sunbright felt burned anew, as if he'd been pierced to the guts himself, cut open to expose any untruth.

"A good death, and brave . . ." The old dwarf talked mostly to himself. "We own little here in the Iron Mountains, we Sons of Baltar. Scanty food, iron used up, little coal to burn. So, for generations now, our children are our resource. We train our sons and daughters to war, and send them into the world of men to fight as soldiers and bodyguards. Many never return to this, our ancestral home. So with Dorlas."

Sunbright was quiet at this epitaph, feeling that, rather than floating a coffin down a river, he'd finally helped bury Dorlas, who'd been a friend in the short time the barbarian had known him. He murmured, "I'm sorry."

"Sorry is nothing," pronounced the dwarf, obviously an old mountain adage. Then surprised him with, "I owe you, Sunbright Steelshanks. I, Drigor, son of Yasur, owe you a favor." He tipped the warhammer, then left the stone room.

Sunbright sat on the shelf and stared at the empty doorway, wondering what next? A quiet stir made him turn.

"A dwarf owes you a favor. Better than money in the bank."

Sunbright looked into Knucklebones's single eye and asked, "How long have you been awake?"

"Long enough. As a child, I learned to wake silently. You make powerful and lasting friends, country mouse."

"I meet a lot of people, true, though some I must kill. How's your head?"

"It hurts. What are you looking at?" she murmured, almost against his chin as he loomed above her.

"It's a shame you've only the one, because it's a pretty eye," he whispered, then he planted a big juicy kiss on her eyelid.

"Yick! That's not where they go!"

He kissed her small, firm mouth.

"Better?"

"Much better," she murmured.

* * * * *

Sunbright and Knucklebones spent the night huddled under two blankets and the glowing iron pipe. The stone was hard, but the warmth wonderful. In dry clothing and with breakfast (their own rations) under their belts, they felt better, if sore.

Drigor walked into the room shouting, "Are you better?"

Noise made Sunbright's head throb, but he answered civilly, "Yes, we're better, thank you. This is my friend, Knucklebones, by the way."

The dwarf only puffed a wisp of ring-braided mustache from his mouth. "It's well you can travel," he said, "for you must leave."

"Leave?" The word was jerked from Sunbright.

By the glow of luminous paint the dwarf's face looked like old parchment. He nodded glumly, brooking no argument, and said, "We have nothing to offer you, and you nothing to offer us. Your mission is accomplished and you may go. We conserve food and fighters because of yak-men. What you saw yesterday was another scout party. The yak-men covet our mountains. They push in from the east, and we are busy killing them. This takes food, and we have barely enough to feed ourselves."

"More folk on the move . . ." Sunbright pondered aloud. "Tell me, do you find the animals fewer, and sickly, even plants not thriving?"

Drigor frowned, and said, "Yes, perhaps. The elk and goats did not climb as high this autumn, and even the high-dwelling chamois have moved to lower meadows to scratch moss. Scouts tell us the lichen and gorse is thin on the highest peaks, and not recovering from their graze. Why ask?"

"The high mountains are another harsh territory, but fragile, like my tundra. I sought my people in traditional lands for months and never found them. They've moved into new territories, unless they're all dead, which I don't believe. Now you tell me yak-men press in from the east, outside the empire. I wonder if they too find their land can't support them."

"I care not." Drigor waved a craggy hand as he said, "These mountains can't support them either, and we kill all they send. But our best fighters are away soldiering, and the yak-men are many. Sometimes I think . . ."

The pause arrested Sunbright and Knucklebones, but the dwarf never finished, only changed tack. "Never mind. You must go. Gird yourselves. A guide will lead you out." He spun on his heels and stamped away.

"The rotten bastards!" Knucklebones snapped. "The lousy cheapskates! Pitched out into the storm without so much as a by-your-leave! Why not just hurl us off the mountain, for Shar's sake?"

"Or charge us for the room and hot water," Sunbright sighed. "It would be kind to give us some of the yak-men's rations. They had food satchels."

"I'd like one of those carved staves." Knucklebones groused. She rammed clothes into her ox hide pack, yanked the straps tight, and slammed her blanket roll atop. "They're probably worth a fortune! And we earned them, for we engaged the enemy first."

"We would have died if the dwarves hadn't attacked," Sunbright reminded her.

"They still stink, the penny-pinching shrimps. I hope their mountain collapses around their ears."

She shut up as a dwarven woman, the same who'd led them here, clomped through the doorway. Crossing her arms, the dwarf waited impatiently for them to strap on their tackle. Silently, the humans complied. Without a word, they followed her through corridors black or illuminated, searing hot or just warm. Knucklebones craned her head around, for she'd seen nothing when carried in. They heard bursts of coarse laughter, smelled cookfires and food, glimpsed rooms where dwarves repaired gear or stoked charcoal fires for forging. Once she heard a snatch of lonesome song like a coyote's cry. Deliberately she dragged her feet to slow them.

For Knucklebones found this mountain enclave enticing. The winding dark tunnels with jots of light, so warm, reminded her of home, the sewers and tunnels of the floating enclave of Karsus. And too, the hustle and bustle and busyness reminded her of the thieves' community with its quiet secrets and bold camaraderie. Visiting the dwarven warrens made the city-born orphan feel homesick, and yet at home.

But they were ejected. A wave of cold air gushed, and made Knucklebones draw her sheepskin coat close to her neck. Her breath fogged, misting the picture of the outdoors, though she knew it was sunny. By the time her one eye had squinted open, they stood alone at the mouth of the pass, the dwarven woman having turned back.

Sunbright huffed in the clear mountain air. After last night's storm, fair weather brought blinding sun reflected from a million icicles and knobs and patches on gray, naked rocks. Far in the distance, beyond lesser peaks, lay some blue-gray and green land to the south.

Knucklebones sipped chilly air and waited for the barbarian to begin the trek down, but he stood stock-still. His lover realized he seethed inside, furious, the insult of being thrown out finally fanned to a white-hot rage. Yet he breathed deep, swallowed his anger, and finally summed up, "A hard life makes a hard people. But still, they could have . . . But never mind. Let's go." He tramped off, going too fast on the icy slope.

That was a contrast between them, Knucklebones thought. While her anger flared quickly, and quickly died, Sunbright took a long time to anger, smoldering low but hot, perhaps for days, then exploding.

Meekly, Knucklebones picked after him. She reflected that Sunbright too was hard, for the tundra had made him so. And being driven from his tribe, surviving on his own, had hardened him more, until he was tough as tempered steel. But even steel could shatter under tension, and the constant disappointments galled him, she knew. Seeing Dorlas die, losing Greenwillow, being dragged to the future against his will to be chased and abused, failing to find his tribe, being refused hospitality by dwarves he'd pledged to visit. . . .

"Hard lands and hard people, yes," she murmured, "just please don't turn bitter on me, Sunbright. Don't harden your heart. . . ."

* * * * *

The casura hung in the air, dozens of mouths working; scores of eyes glaring; spidery hands threatening, pitching rocks, sticks, bones, and shafts and blades of broken weapons. The ghost argued with itself, for it was composed of many, many creatures thrown together by violent death, and they hated one another.

Yet the sound of scratching feet stilled it. The casura turned to the noise, for that meant life, and more than anything the collective ghost hated anything that lived.

Onto the littered floor of the cavern trod the flint monster. Its horny feet, sharp-edged as granite, crunched underfoot a hundred bones, hooves, horns, jawbones full of fangs, rib cages, segments of tails without flesh. That hundreds had died here meant nothing to the monster, for it was obsessed with its own goal.

". . . This way out. Must be the way out. Must be. Need to get free, and kill my enemies . . ."

The monster glanced around, sniffed through nostrils that were mere slits in its stony face. With the stirring of the high ghost came a graveyard reek, dead flesh and turned earth. Too, the dark air of the cavern resounded with sinister rattling, knocking, scratchings, and skittery, uneven footsteps. Yet none of these warnings deterred the flint monster, for it sought only a way out of the endless, winding caves.

Suddenly, in the darkness, loomed a host of eyes, all sizes and shapes and colors, all flaming with hatred. Their baleful glare was so intense the cavern was bathed in yellow-white light that flickered along the broken walls like firefly glow. The casura was nothing but eyes and mouths and rootlike, spidery hands, the whole flung together like chopped grasshoppers caught in a threshing basket. The gathered ghost stretched thin in spots, held together as if by fish glue, while other parts were clumps of eyes and hands and mouths. The fiend was a sticky web dancing in the air, clinging to the walls, touching the floor in spots. An awful and impassible barrier.

The casura's burning glare sparkled on the monster's flinty hide, yet the monster's round, staring eyes showed no fear. The flint monster hated with a deeper passion than even the ghost, for it hated all souls: living, dead, or in between. Without eyelids, the exposed eyeballs were a shocking blue in its dark carapace.

Yet there was recognition here. Ages ago, it seemed, the casura's many dead creatures had been an unholy army: imps, ghouls, ghasts, blind giants, barbed fiends, things without names. Together they'd battled the enemies of Prinquis, arch-fiend of these pits. Until treachery brought down the balor of the Abyss, ancient, deadly enemies who'd descended with joy and crackling whips to slay everything moving in this vast throne room.

And the flint monster had been one of those enemies. And still was.

A howl echoed from the casura's hundred gibbering mouths. Writhing hands snatched rocks, skulls, and broken blades, and flung the lethal lot at the flint monster. Yet nothing harmed it, not the missiles, nor the stench, nor the screaming noise, nor the rolling waves of hatred. The flint monster had lived with pain for so long, nothing outside could hurt it.

Raising two long, misshapen arms, curling fingers like shards of glass, the monster retaliated. From one hand exploded bolts of pure darkness, shafts blacker than moonless night, that stabbed amidst the spiderweb ghost. Eyes popped into jots of gore, twisted hands were splintered to fragments, mouths had teeth smashed out and knocked to the four winds. From the monster's other hand spun a whirlwind of blades sharper than steel. Propellers of dweomer sliced through ectoplasm like water, ricocheted from stone walls, and went on spinning. Phantom blades ripped through the undying spirits of fiends and imps and giants, who screeched in protest as they were killed yet again. They howled too because they knew they would heal again, slowly, in agony, never dying, never cured, again hanging in this chamber to die anew. For such was the nature of this pocket hell, that all the denizens suffered, died, and were resurrected to suffer forever.

Before long, darkbolts and whirlwinds of steel ripped the casura into shreds like a sundered cobweb. Ichor and blood and snot and ectoplasm dripped in a ghastly rain onto the antique bones and weapons of the dead below. Ghostly beings shriveled, died, retreated, shouted, hated one another and themselves, almost forgetting the flint monster in their midst.

For the monster passed on. Down another long tunnel it scuffled, searching. Its dark-bred senses were attuned to the air, the rock, the dust and decay, constantly seeking any sign of outside life.

And far down, where rocks had collapsed the tunnel to a hand's height, the monster sniffed a trace. Rusty water, far off. The merest trickle, yet a hopeful sign, for nowhere in this corner of hell was there any standing water, for thirst was another form of suffering, and the arch-fiend who ruled here liked his subjects to suffer.

Any water, no matter how foul, came from outside.

"My enemy, she sealed us in. But not all. Sloppy work, sloppy. I shall be free, outside, at last. Free to wreak vengeance. To kill . . ."

Scrabbling with hands hard as diamonds, the flinty beast dug at crumbled rock.

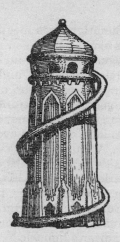

Chapter 4

"That's it! Put up your fists!" bawled Delmar.

"If that suits you!" Sunbright shot back.

Both men swung while everyone else hollered.

Delmar was Sunbright's height but broad as an ox across the shoulders. He had dark skin, dark, curly hair and a beard to his chest, a tight blue shirt hacked off at the shoulders, and woolen breeches above rawhide boots. His arms and fists were hard as oak stumps from a lifetime of hauling baggage and wrangling horses, and he knew how to brawl, which was more than Sunbright could boast.

But the barbarian was furious, having fumed for weeks at the jeers Delmar pitched his way. It was inevitable that tempers would explode into flame.

Dark Delmar stamped his heavy boots down near Sunbright's toes to distract him, or else cripple him given the chance. The barbarian danced nimbly backward, but Delmar added a savage right hook at

Sunbright's ribs. Sunbright was rocked half off his feet by the tremendous blow.

Merchants, bodyguards, cooks, and others—including Knucklebones—circled to watch and cheer and slap down bets. The caravan came to an abrupt halt on the woodland road, a good fight livening up an overcast summer afternoon. The only one not thrilled was Knucklebones, who held one hand over her mouth and tried not to scream. At Sunbright.

Crooked to one side by aching ribs, Sunbright guarded his left and whirled to present his right. He learned fast, and as Delmar repeated his trick of stamping before punching, Sunbright beat him to it. A fast right smashed into Delmar's brow and glanced off, dinging a swatch off the barbarian's knuckle.

Delmar had flipped his head aside, missing most of the blow, but his bruised eyebrow and eyelid began to swell immediately, cutting off vision in that eye. "Lucky!" he sneered, and made to stamp again.

He changed tactics, so his off hand strove for his foe's brisket. The wooden fist slammed into Sunbright's belly, but that was hard as iron plate itself and did little damage. Rather, the barbarian hammered both fists onto Delmar's neck and knocked the man into the dust.

Delmar crashed, but he didn't stay down, vulnerable to kicks, for long. Flailing his hands blindly, he caught one of Sunbright's moosehide boots, hooked his fingers into the iron rings, and yanked.

Upset, the warrior crashed on his rump. His long red shirttail flew up, entangling his fists. Humping on his belly, Delmar tried to punch Sunbright between the legs. The barbarian barely flicked his knee sideways, kicked and flopped like a fish ashore, and rolled over his shoulder backward to get away. By the time he was upright and shaking dust from his face, Delmar had risen and charged.

The wrangler's shoulder slammed Sunbright across

the hips, cannoning him backward. Hoisted in the air, Sunbright rammed a horse's ribs with his spine. The frightened beast whinnied and hopped, almost stamped Sunbright's toes with iron-shod hooves. Delmar dug his toes in the road to slam his shoulder tighter into Sunbright's breastbone, crowding and mashing his foe while he pounded hammy fists into the shaman's guts again and again. Sunbright could barely keep his feet as the horse danced sideways, unpropping him. If he fell, Delmar would land on top and pound his face to jelly.

Tightening his gut, Sunbright felt berserker rage flooding his mind, and, for once, let it come. He was glad to be clobbering someone after weeks of ragging and teasing from Delmar and his friends, was thrilled to get in some abuse of his own. Aiming with savage glee, he bashed Delmar's ears, jaw, and temples, almost popping his own knuckles on both hands.

Then someone grabbed the horse's reins and tugged the beast to safety. Sunbright reeled backward with Delmar still punishing his breadbasket. Both men tripped and tumbled. Sunbright managed to shove Delmar to one side while he fell to the other. He landed hard on one cheek, rattling his teeth and jolting his spine, but curled and spun and whirled to face his attacker immediately.

Just in time. Sunbright almost snapped his own neck ducking his head, and felt a thunderous fist scrape his cheek. Since Delmar was leaning right, Sunbright threw out his right arm to bowl the man further. Yet Delmar hooked his hand around Sunbright's neck, latched onto his long horsetail, and yanked viciously. Neck creaking, Sunbright's nose was mashed against Delmar's hairy forearm. Not wasting the chance, Sunbright bit on ropy muscle with keen, white teeth.

Delmar howled, tried to yank the horsetail again, but had to let go for pain. Losing his temper further, the wrangler drove the heel of his free hand at Sunbright's face to break his nose.

But the barbarian ducked, relying on nimbleness to save himself against the heavier man. Lashing out with both hands pointed, he struck Delmar's throat with fingertips like blunt spears. The big man's howl was cut off as he gagged. Yet he resisted doubling over into more blows; instead he snapped his head back. That suited Sunbright, who rammed the heel of his own hand upward from near the ground. Catching Delmar's chin, he banged the man's mouth shut with a frightful *clack* of bruised teeth. Stunned, the wrangler took three awkward steps backward, and crashed on his back.

Still raging, Sunbright hopped after him, and landed with both moosehide-booted feet on Delmar's belly. Shouting a war whoop, he jumped viciously on his fallen foe's belly, and nearly ruptured the wrangler's guts. Despite being stunned, Delmar folded in half around Sunbright's big foot, but the barbarian kicked free, hopped back, and aimed to kick the man's head off. Dimly he heard his lover cry, "Sunbright, *no!*", but he never paused.

Nor did he complete the kick. A noose sailed from overhead, dropped around his shoulders, snuggled around his elbows, and snapped tight. Someone strong tugged hard, and he crashed on his rump for the third time, and found it sore. He was dragged backward as if hitched to a horse, then someone grabbed his horsetail and slammed his head to the ground. A painful jolt shot through his skull as gravel bit his scalp.

Struggling to get loose, Sunbright found a large boot pinning his chest. Aselli, caravan mistress, was silhouetted against the gray sky. In her hand bobbed an axe handle, inches from Sunbright's forehead.

"Lie still and settle down, northman," Aselli growled, "or I'll crease your skull, and leave you for the wolves."

Helpless, Sunbright laid still. Knucklebones crouched

beside his head, searched for permanent damage, but she wouldn't look him in the eye for shame.

Actually, now that battle-rage had left him, he was ashamed of himself. He shouldn't have been prodded into a brawl. Fighting for pride was stupid, and for the moment, so was he.

Aselli stamped off, ordering Jun to plant his boot on Sunbright's chest. A moment later, the caravan mistress returned, lugging Sunbright's satchels, sword, and tackle. She dropped them in the dust, fished in a purse, counted out seven silver crowns, and sprinkled them over the pile. Her white-framed face was grim. "We'll go on, but you lie quiet. If we see you follow, we'll play at target practice. I've stomached your stiff-necked pride and bristly hide too long. We're close enough to Quagmire that I don't need a pigheaded bodyguard who picks fights."

"It wasn't I who sneered—"

"Save it! If I want an argument, I'll visit my daughters-in-law. Give me back my rope, and don't act cute, or I'll coldcock you."

Relieved of boot and rope, Sunbright remained lying in the road with elbows propped. He and Knucklebones watched the dazed Delmar muscled up and across a mule. Aselli called, "Get 'em goin'!", and the caravan plodded down the road. No one looked back at the barbarian and thief.

When the wagons rounded a bend under green, leafy oak trees, Sunbright picked himself up, and dusted himself off. Limping from hammered and sprained muscles, he trudged to a roadside stream, washed his face and hands, and slaked his thirst. Then he strapped on his tackle.

"I hope you're happy." They were Knucklebones's first words in a long while. "We don't get pitched out of enough taverns and marketplaces and towns, and now you've been chucked off a caravan. What's your object?

To aggravate every human being in the empire so you can become a hermit in some mountain cave?"

A slight exaggeration, but only just. Since leaving the Iron Mountains last winter, the pair had wandered north, and worked as needed. Sunbright had gathered game, split wood, hammered rock in a quarry. Nimble-fingered Knucklebones had gambled, assisted a jeweller, told fortunes with knucklebones at fairs, and cut purses from the belts of rich folk when Sunbright wasn't looking. Gradually they'd drifted toward the Narrow Sea, barrier to the tundra, but often dallied rather than face the fact that they couldn't find what they sought. And now they were bereft again, and alone.

"I didn't start anything. Delmar and his cronies have been mocking my accent and clothes and weapons for weeks."

"Stop it," the thief snapped. "You whine like a child. If you were among your tribespeople, they'd probably cut out your tongue."

"Well, we're *not* amongst my people! And we never will be!" Sunbright roared back.

That was the problem, of course. In all their travels, asking everyone they met, they had found no sign of the Rengarth Barbarians. Cut off from his people and heritage, frustrated by not being able to return, though he risked death in doing so, Sunbright had grown increasingly irascible and taciturn. He would brood the day long, and never speak a word to Knucklebones.

And she? She trod alongside, steadfast and quiet, usually biting her tongue, but occasionally lashing out. Though she never said so, if anyone should feel cut off from their heritage, it was she, who wouldn't even be born for over three hundred years yet, and had seen her beloved city crumble to dust, utterly and irretrievably lost in the dim future. Sunbright at least had a tribe, even if they were lost somewhere in the wide world. She had nothing, not a friend besides him, not a relative, not a home or hope of one. Sometimes, late at night, when the barbarian was asleep, she wept, not for lack of love, but for loneliness.

Sunbright tugged the last of his straps tight, and slung the blanket roll to his shoulder. "Never mind arguing. Let's go."

"Go where?" Startled from her reverie, the phrase popped out. Unable to stop, Knucklebones lifted idle hands at the empty road and woods. "Where shall we go? Where in the whole world is a place for us?"

Sunbright stared around gloomily, then let his blanket roll fall to the dust. He had no answer.

* * * * *

Deep in a steaming swamp, where the slimy water ran so deep even the giant lizards couldn't walk on the bottom, a hissing and boiling commenced.

Eels and bass stirred from the muck at the bottom, sensed the water heating unnaturally, and finned away. A heron flapping lazily overhead swooped to spear a perch, but found the thing dying, parboiled. The white bird sheared on thermals rising from the water. Other birds scattered from cypress and pine trees at the disturbance. A troop of dimetrodons sunning in shallow water plucked their feet from mud, lowered their rainbow sails, and swished out of the water, leaving wavy tail marks behind. Some creatures spiraled in, for where there was distress, careless animals were apt to become food. Ravens flapped in to watch, and smaller dinosaurs with foxy manners minced over ferns to wait, and pounce.

The water at the center of the bog swirled and churned, until a fountain of boiling water rose the height of a man. Ripples shook the water so hard that an errant bog hound, created long ago for some lost purpose, stirred in nearby reeds, tried to creep off from its secluded day bed, but stricken by sunlight, reverted to a lifeless pile of straw and mud that crumbled back to the earth.

Higher the boiling column rose, until it was three times the height of a man. Murky spray scattered rainbows. Birds lifted from trees and wheeled away. The dimetrodons turned droopy eyes upon the phenomenon, but made no other move except to twitch their tails from the hot water. Fish killed by heat floated to the surface, and flies swarmed onto them.

Then the water column abruptly collapsed. Murky water swirled in contradictory patterns, then settled. A streaming **V** marked the progress of something plodding through muck and weed, aiming for shore. The **V** narrowed gradually, and the creature's head broke water.

A skull: dark as flint, no hair, no ears, no eyelids, no lips, no nose, a block of stone poorly hacked into the shape of a human head. A thin neck of stone glistened wetly, then a wide-shouldered frame that canted to one side as if made misshapen. Prominent ribs and a pinched waist, bony pelvis without genitals, matchstick legs. Arms were two different lengths, but both sported long, black claws harder than diamonds. Feet were splayed lumps.

The flint monster gained the shore, and sank ankle-deep in ooze from its great weight. Water dried in the hot sun, but its hide still glinted and sparkled from impacted minerals. Below staring blue eyes, the gash of a mouth, like a ragged cut in steel, opened to breathe. And chortle for the first time in ages.

"Free! Finally free!" A croak like a tortured hinge. "Free to gain revenge . . . to slay my enemies. To slay anyone who opposes me!"

Casting about, the monster pointed a long-fingered hand at the sleepy dimetrodons, who looked on unimpressed. There came a flash and a crackle, and an icicle flew from its fingertips to lodge in the ribs of the nearest dinosaur. The stung animal hopped, bellowed, and roared. It snapped its head around to bite at the offending missile, but the ice spear had already melted, leaving a wound that bled furiously. The stricken animal mewed.

"You like that?" cackled the flint monster. "Here's more!"

Pointing mismatched hands, the fiend made icicles fly into the hapless dinosaurs, who hooted and mewled in pain and outrage. Icy lances thudded into ribs, flanks, and necks. Rainbow sails arching over gray-green backs were punctured in a dozen places so blood ran down their spines. One big bull that snapped at the attacker had an icicle fly down its throat, puncturing its lungs and heart. The monster kept conjuring icicles and sending them into the dinosaurs' bodies until the animals were reduced to heaps of green scales, spattered with blood that drew flies.

Still, the horror hadn't killed enough. Raising clawed hands, it sent a blast of darkbolt sizzling into the top of a red pine that exploded needles in all directions. A hawk circling nearby dropped as a gobbet of burned feathers. Insects, an old tortoise, primitive rose bushes, all were frozen or burned or blasted into scraps.

And above all the noise, screams, and crackling of flames scratched the creaky laugh of the monster. "Yes, death to all that oppose me! Death to all that live! But death to Sunbright and all the rest first!"

* * * * *

The end of summer found Sunbright and Knucklebones standing under a line of drowsy birch trees where the river known simply as the Watercourse had undercut the bank, so some trees hung precariously with their tops brushing the rippling water. The river spilled into the Narrow Sea a few leagues north, and that was the last barrier to the tundra. Yet Sunbright hadn't the heart to go on, so they'd camped.

"But where next?" asked Knucklebones, though she knew the answer.

"Nowhere," was the gloomy reply. "Or anywhere. Being free means you can go wherever you wish. Like a child's kite rising on the wind. We wander just as aimlessly."

"We need lodging for the winter."

"Pick a direction."

Knucklebones sighed. How much more lassitude and despair could she stomach? His heartsickness was contagious, and her days were gloomy. She loved him, would stay for good or ill, but lately her mind betrayed her own heart, whispered she'd be better off by herself. Somewhere else. Alone.

Sunbright looked out over the river, watched a kingfisher dive like a spear and spring back up. The struggling bird and flapping fish spiraled up over the forest. Idly, Sunbright tracked them.

"That's a male kingfisher living in those elms. The sunfish school in the shallows, feeding on minnows come sporting from under the bank to seek sunlight, for blue flies hover over the water. The water's half salt and half fresh, so the two cultures mingle here before us. Handy things for a shaman to know, no? Would I could tell my tribe."

"It's not good enough to talk to me?" Knucklebones was bored enough to pick a fight, and hurt that his idle thoughts excluded her.

Sunbright sat on the grassy bank with his back to a birch. "No," he told her, "I enjoy talking to you, but you must be powerful sick of my useless chatter."

That statement struck so close to the heart that Knucklebones blinked. To cover her confusion, she fussed with her brass knuckles, shining them with spit and her thumb. "No," she said, "it's just—Aren't there other tribes of barbarians?"

"One. The Angardts dwell on the plains below Redguard Lake, near the Far Horns Forest, but we split from them ages ago. They adopted magic, taboo to my people. The feud ran bloody and long, and finally they retreated south. Were I to approach, I'd be skinned alive. Funny, considering how I've learned to use magic."

"I thought shamanism wasn't magic, but—I don't know—a gift from the gods?"

"From the Earthmother, and the land itself. A little magic is acceptable, such as healing and blessing weapons and homes and crops, but were I to conjure a storm, say, many would take it amiss. I could be stoned to death, or buried alive, or staked out and sacrificed. Still, my father could call the spirits of the dead, even elementals. My grandfather could shapeshift to mimic Brother Seal and Grandfather Walrus . . . but I ramble."

"It's interesting," Knucklebones insisted. "It's just—it's been so long since you talked at all."

Sunbright nodded absently, plucked grass and sucked the stem, and said, "You bring out the best in me, Knuckle', though I've been poor company lately. It's just that I need my people. Without them I can't get on with my life. I'm as dead as an uprooted tree. Not much comfort for you."

Knucklebones refrained from chiding, just tried to keep them talking. Yet she had no plans of her own, and his were frustrated, so there seemed little to discuss.

Then the man blasted the mood by adding, "Greenwillow was good for me too. She kept me level-headed and busy, applying and testing myself."

"I *don't* want—" Knucklebones's temper flared, but she bit her words back. She was tired of his singing the praises of a dead lover. Still, better he talked, and she suffered in silence. "Tell me about her."

"Well . . . she was a lot like you."

"What?" This was news. "How can she, a high-caste elven warrior from the forest be anything like me, an orphaned sewer rat with one eye?"

Sunbright shook his head. "It's not outward appearances, it's inner. Greenwillow had courage, not only to face terrible odds, but to face herself too. To force herself into battle, or the dark, or the unknown. As you do. I so admire your spirit. I can face polar bears and ice storms and ice worms and starvation and cold, yet I was raised by my tribe and taught these things slowly, and coddled when I made a mistake. How you managed to survive, abandoned and alone in the underworld of Karsus, I can't imagine. You must have a core of steel, and an undying heart to boot. Greenwillow was the same way."

Knucklebones glowed under the compliments, wondered. Maybe Sunbright loved her not as a pale imitation of the elf maiden, but because she had mastered a dangerous environment. For the first time, the thief felt sympathy and interest in this elven warrior she'd never met, but she'd still prefer he concentrate on a live lover. But so did people pine for things they couldn't have.

Like a tribe. And a home. Or any clue where to go—

"Behold. The geese and the enclaves fly south for the winter."

"Hunh?" Knucklebones craned her head around, scanned the sky where Sunbright pointed. High overhead drifted an inverted mountain studded with buildings, a floating city. Enclaves drifted north in summer and south in winter. "Oh. That's Ioulaum," she said. "It's easy to recognize." In three hundred years it hadn't changed much.

"And in three hundred and fifty-five years," Sunbright added, "it'll fall and shatter, scattering buildings and people like an anthill kicked apart."

Thief and shaman watched the city drift. It went slower than the wind, for the massive mythallar, the dweomer engine, could drive it in any direction decreed by the archwizards and city council.

The pair watched the city-mountain float, and Sunbright mused, "Too bad we can't get up there. Perhaps we could see the whole world, look down and see my people waving. Or at least shooting arrows at it." He joked because memories of floating a mile high in the air in Castle Delia, and then Karsus Enclave, set his stomach churning. He'd never been comfortable in the air.

Knucklebones gazed wistfully on the city, for sometimes she found Sunbright's "groundling" world too wide. She often longed for the cozy confines of the city, its varied buildings and parks and houses, the tangled caves and tunnels and warrens that honeycombed the former mountain.

As Sunbright's jest penetrated, the woman mused, "That's not such a foolish notion . . ."

"What?" Sunbright frowned. "Looking down from the city to see my tribe is impossible. And the guards would never let us board an airboat."

"But you *can* see the world from up there," Knucklebones insisted. "Not directly, but some ways, and getting up is no problem. Every door has a key. Trust a sewer rat."

"No! No, I say!"

But it was too late, Sunbright saw the floating enclave reflected in Knucklebones's one eye. He wished he'd kept his mouth shut.

Chapter 5

"I can't get my head out!"

"Let me help."

With small, strong hands, Knucklebones grabbed Sunbright's chin and forelock, and jerked. The barbarian yelped as his ears scraped between stacks of grain bags.

"*Aggh!* Lady of Silver, *I* could have done that!"

Gingerly he felt his ears, testing for blood.

"Cheap bribe, bad ride," she told him flatly. "Now hush up."

"I can't hear you. My ears are shredded. How do we get out of here?"

Knucklebones pointed to a tiny sunlit window high up in the deserted warehouse. "Scale the wall," she said, "slip through, and hope there's something soft to jump on outside."

"Pandem's Pain, what fun. Go ahead."

Sniffing, Knucklebones led the way. She felt cocky

and happy now that they'd made it onto a floating enclave. Home, for her. Asking in Quagmire, she'd found a tavern, then a boatmaster with a shipment of grain bound for Ioulaum. There were many shipments as the city stocked up for winter before drifting south. The tipsy boatmaster had agreed, after haggling over the "fare," to pack them in a hollow behind sacks of rye. Sunbright had clamped down on his stomach as the airboat lifted into the night sky, drifted, tacked, dropped and lurched in capricious air pockets, and finally docked, a mile in the air, at the spidery airdocks of Ioulaum. After his boat was towed into a warehouse, the boatmaster wandered off—after finishing the requisite paperwork—leaving the boat temporarily "deserted."

The thief scaled the wooden wall with fingers and toes, chuckling at how easy and familiar it felt, slid out the window, and circled to open a door so Sunbright could walk through. "Sissy!" she teased.

"Sewer rat!"

"Hush up! I smell guards."

Then she was flitting down damp, dark alleys like a moth while Sunbright splashed and stamped and huffed to keep up. As she listened at a corner, he asked, "You've never been here before, correct? So how do you know your way around?"

"There are maps of all the enclaves in the libraries. When things got hot we studied them, trying to decide if moving was practical."

"But where are we bound?"

"Thieves' Quarter."

"How do you know there *is* one?"

She laughed, low and melodious. For all the aggravation, Sunbright was glad to hear her happy. It had been a long time since she'd laughed. Regrettably, that was his fault. He'd have to make up for the grief he'd caused her. For now, he plodded along without complaining.

It was dodgy, though, to stay calm. He was a creature

of the earth, a groundling, and being a mile in the air unnerved him. Too, he couldn't banish the picture of Ioulaum shattering to fist-sized chunks from his mind's eye. True, the island wouldn't be destroyed for over three centuries, but still he felt it hung by a thread.

Through the warehouse district they tripped, avoiding city guards and night crews and dogs, sometimes skirting so close to the city's edge that Sunbright felt the yawning gap kiss his quaking knees. But finally they turned inward where lights and roistering marked taverns and food shops where workers wended after hours. Knucklebones told Sunbright to sit tight while she scouted. The barbarian propped his rump in a niche, folded his arms, but left his ears awake, and napped.

Cat-quiet, Knucklebones faded through shadows, circling buildings, and hunting the darker spots. Her part-elven night vision was sharper than a human's, and since mostly humans inhabited the enclaves, she had an advantage. Sure enough, she spied prime targets, two sailors drunk and lurching. They passed an alley perfect for ambush and, as she expected, were hooked into the shadows like dazed trout. Scanning for onlookers, Knucklebones skittered along a building front, down the side and around, to catch the assailants in the rear.

The thieves were good, she noted. They'd dumped the sailors in the alley, smacked them with sacks of wet sand just hard enough to stun them—killings roused the city guard—rifled their purses and boots in seconds, then charged down the alley, quick to flee before anyone sought missing comrades.

Knucklebones would have been plowed under if she hadn't hissed from the dark, "Heads up, fasthands!"

"Eh? Split, Littledark." The thieves, a husband-and-wife team, plastered themselves against the walls lest this was a trap and crossbow bolts came flying. They rattled Thieves' Cant so fast Knucklebones could barely grasp it.

"Just hatched, turtles," Knucklebones whispered. "Where pillow?"

The thieves exchanged the lowest murmur, then decided to entrust Knucklebones—whose cant was correct—with the location of a den, but warned her not to follow. "Toe to Elkan's, hooks and hods, Blue Cobbles, west, two, one, two, Kibbe. Fog."

"Misted."

And like fog, Knucklebones faded away in the dark, stamping unnaturally loud so they heard her leave.

Sunbright jerked awake at her touch. "Whoa!" he grumbled. "I didn't hear you."

"Piffle. If I were noisy, I'd have died at two. Come, I know where to go. Elkan's, hooks and hods, Blue Cobbles, west, two, one, two, Kibbe."

"Those are directions?"

"Elkan's must be an ironmongery, selling pothooks and bricklayer's hods, in the Street of Blue Cobbles on the west side. Knock twice, then once, then twice, and say Kibbe sent you."

Sunbright scratched his sore ear and asked her, "How do we know we won't drop through a hole in the earth? Or as a joke we're sent to knock on the city guard's barracks?"

"We don't," she said casually. "That's what makes thieving so exciting."

Sunbright straightened his tackle and followed her tiny, dark form through more alleys. They traveled light in summer, with Knucklebones in her laced leather vest and breeches and no shoes, her black elven blade at her waist, and only a thin blanket roll with her comb and such tucked inside. Sunbright wore a long yellow shirt and iron-bound boots of moosehide, his back scabbard holding Harvester and a longbow and four arrows beside, a blanket roll and canteen and haversack of rations. Ever since returning the dwarf's warhammer, he'd had no other weapon except a long knife on his wide belt.

He opined, "Spearing killer whales through the ice before they can burst through and eat you is exciting too."

"Belt up, country mouse," she whispered over her shoulder.

"Yes, milady."

Flitting through dark streets, Knucklebones occasionally touched a wall, setting it aglow with her cold light cantra—everyone born to the empire knew some magic—to study how paint had faded on public buildings. From this information, she figured out which was the western side of the city.

Sunbright objected, "But if the city engineers rotate the island, how can there be a west side?"

"Silly. They rotate it at varying speeds. The Netherese consider it lucky to view the dawn, so nobles favor the eastern side to build their homes. So the western side is less prosperous, and houses are smaller. The paint fades at a different angle and rate. There are signs in a city, same as a forest."

"I'd need another lifetime to learn them."

"No need" she said. "You have me." From the dark, she squeezed his craggy, calloused hand with her small, cool one.

Knucklebones found the ironmongery by the smell of rust, lampblack, and grease. Crouching along the foundation and sniffing, she whiffed sweat and wine and moist earth. "A *deep* cellar."

Hunting found the entrance, a building away at the end of an alley. Sunbright had to crouch to negotiate a wet-walled passage that Knucklebones said was guarded; lined with murder holes with cocked crossbows behind. At the end she knocked twice, once, twice, and whispered, "Kibbe!"

A greased door yawned open, cool air hinted of wine. A doorman closed the portal, pointed to a turning, downward-sloping passage, twinkling with light. The fearless Knucklebones tripped on. Sunbright had to stoop because Harvester's pommel scraped on stone overhead. He groused, "Why not take an hour and raise the ceilings?"

"If guards come raiding, they have to bend over. Slows them down."

Or maybe all thieves were short, Sunbright supposed. Living in caves must stunt them. The big barbarian didn't know what to expect, but was surprised to arrive at a table with a clerk behind it. Knucklebones had already warned him to keep mum, so he listened to a conversation of gibberish.

By candlelight, the clerk was old and gray, and his palsied hands shook. A retired thief employed by the guild. He nodded at Sunbright and said, "Purse?"

"Blood," Knucklebones replied. "Fisted or palmed?"

"Palmed. Ferrets sent some flying home. Half up front, half after. Cutty?"

"Latch booster, mostly. Peeler with bigarm here."

"Bones're clean, but suit," the old man said. "Clink."

Knucklebones demanded of Sunbright, "Give me your purses. All of them."

"I only have the one."

"Shut up and give!"

Meekly he handed over his lean purse: Knucklebones usually carried their money anyway. The thief produced three purses from her leather vest and breeches, and dumped out a meager pile of coins. Methodically, the old clerk sorted them, weighed some on a small scale, bit others, then returned exactly half. Asking for names, Knucklebones gave "Butterfly and Ten Pound."

The clerk jotted glyphs in a small book, and finished with, "Keep your stone honed." Knucklebones nodded and circled the table, then spiraled down toward the torchlight.

"What is this hole?" asked Sunbright. "Why does it loop?"

"Don't know. Enclaves are mostly hollow, to save weight so the mythallar doesn't have to work so hard. When they build one, they drill all sorts of tunnels in odd shapes. Some have uses right away, like sewers or grain storage or water pipes. Others are for future expansion, or just a whim."

"What did he call me back there? A purse?"

"A victim, someone with a purse to steal. I said you were a blood, a blood brother. I can't pass you off as an assassin because you don't move like one. I asked if the guild were fisted or palmed: closed to new members or open. It's open because the ferrets have killed some folk lately. Am I a pursecutter? No, a burglar—a latch-breaker—mostly. And a scavenger looting warehouses with your muscle. The guild fee is half what you carry to join, then half what you make after. Keep your stone honed means keep your knife sharp for good luck. If your blade snags while you're cutting purse strings, the pigeon might notice and object."

Brain reeling, Sunbright thought of a dozen questions. Why a ferret, which was a brown weasel, for instance? "What happens if you don't join the guild?" he asked.

"And go about thieving? The guild saws off your hands and feet. While you watch."

"Hunh. Why give your name as Butterfly?"

"Would you have me give Knucklebones?"

"Why am I Ten Pound?"

"You carry a ten pound tool, don't you?"

"No. Harvester weighs—oh. A joke." Sunbright huffed as they clumped down and around the spiral ramp. "Why all this obscure cant? Why not just talk?"

"Cant is quicker in an emergency. And it confuses guards if you're in their clutches."

"Are thieves captured often?"

"And robbed by the guards, yes. Usually they're forced into labor gangs on the ground. Unless you hurt or kill a guard. Then they fly you home."

"Home where?"

"Earthmother. They pitch you off the island to 'fly' to earth."

Sunbright's stomach lurched. "But why does the city tolerate thieves at all?" he asked. "Why not make one big purge and wipe them out?"

A shrug of narrow shoulders, and Knucklebones said, "Catching thieves gives the guards work. What would you have them do, arrest mages? Besides, many rogues are only part-time. Otherwise they toil at the docks, or black boots, or dig graves. Which lets them pilfer leather, cut purses, and loot the dead. Besides, when I pay half my 'winnings' to the guild, the guild pays half to the authorities."

"What?" Noise from below had increased, so Sunbright no longer whispered, "You mean the *city* takes bribes from the thieves' guild?"

"You're learning, country mouse, but they're not bribes. They're taxes, gifts. It costs to be a citizen."

Sunbright sighed. "None of this makes sense."

"Neither does spearing killer whales through the ice."

"Hunh? That's easy."

"Uh, hunh."

The spiraling ramp finally ended, and Sunbright was amazed by a virtual village at the bottom. In a catacomb bored from stone ran tunnels and passageways and balconies filled with smoky taverns, shops, a smith, a washroom with hot and cold water, niches with beds, and a common room where three dozen roisterers cheered a wrestling match among two women and a man. The air reeked of sweat and ale and smoke and ham and soap and drain water, and rang to the sound of hammers, laughter, jokes, creaking bellows, laundry slapping, and children splashing one another.

"Are these all thieves?" asked the tundra man.

"Oh, no." Knucklebones grinned, her usual aplomb giving way to joy at finally being home. "Those with the

gloves in their belts are stevedores. The aprons mark
housekeepers. And those blokes in the tight pants are
prostitutes. And see there? Rich snots seeking thrills—
you met some like them in Karsus. Isn't it grand?"

"It's not very secret."

"Don't fret. Hungry?"

Knucklebones laughed to see Sunbright salivate. She
handed him coins and told him, "Order something at
the bar while I check bolt holes." She faded away, leaving Sunbright as awkward and out of place as a polar
bear amidst these ribald strangers. He bought bowls of
mutton stew, mugs of frothy harvest ale, and black
bread at the bar, found a not-so grimy table, and
plunked down. He'd eaten all his before Knucklebones
returned.

"Found the exits," she said. "There are seven, but five
one-way only. That's good."

Sunbright watched her eat hungrily, so she gave him
more coins for a refill. The wrestling done, a man with
a lute sang a long, sad romance. Finally the warrior patted his belly and said, "What next?"

"Already done. A mage named Bly can scry what we
need. She lives in the Street of the Faithful Protector on
the east side. What does that tell us?"

Sunbright thought. "If she lives on the east side," he
said, "she must be prosperous? Good at her work?"

"Excellent!" Knucklebones said, licking gravy from
her lip. Her one green eye shone with happiness at
being home. "But she'll be expensive. We'll need money,
or else must strike a bargain. I don't know what to offer,
but mages are always arse-deep in intrigue, so—"

"*RAID!*"

Knucklebones didn't even look around. Grabbing
Sunbright's wrist, she hurled the table aside and
yanked him out of the chair. He stumbled to one knee.
She shrilled, "Come on, sluefoot!"

Men and women hollered, shouts rebounded and

echoed from stone walls. Children scurried underfoot like rats and dived through doorways and down chutes and up ladders. In the tavern, bartenders doused torches in dishwater. In darkness, the cat-eyed thief slid past panicked people, upset furniture, and spilled flagons and plates. Towed by one hand, Sunbright banged every item with knees, shins, and toes.

As Knucklebones dragged him around a corner, the barbarian glimpsed a horde pounding down the ramp in blazing light. City guards in polished lobstertail helmets and yellow tunics emblazoned with I for Ioulaum carried silver-tipped maces and I-shaped shields with gasglobe lanterns bolted to the upper bar. As they surged into the crowd, a mix of workers and young nobles, they methodically clubbed down the working class, breaking collarbones and arms and cracking skulls, while letting the nobles stream past and up the ramp. That rich snots escaped harm while average people suffered lit Sunbright's temper, but Knucklebones soon towed him into a dark tunnel after other escapees.

Yet light flared ahead. Someone yelped before being clubbed down. Curses and screams and thuds resounded.

"They've come two ways!" Knucklebones chirped, and immediately tacked against the stalled crowd.

"Get behind!" Sunbright yelled, hoisted her bodily, and plunked her in back of him. "Which way?"

In spinning darkness and a milling crowd, the small rogue latched onto his belt, and tugged sharply left. "Go! But for the love of Kismet, don't kill anyone!"

Good advice, the barbarian recalled. He'd killed guards in Karsus, and whole teams with sniffing golems had tracked them to Knucklebones's lair, and wiped out her gang. Pointing his arms as if swimming, Sunbright cleaved into the milling mob, but gently.

And too late. Lights sparkled before Sunbright's eyes as three guards in a wedge smashed and trod under a half dozen people. The big barbarian became their target. In the glare of shield lamps, he saw three maces raise as one.

Tilting back on one leg and mashing Knucklebones against a wall, Sunbright raised a moosehide boot and lashed out, hollering, *"Ra-vens!"*

His high kick smashed a lantern atop an I-shaped shield. Glass and a silver-wire cage crunched, and the globe winked out. The mighty blow snagged an inside corner of the shield and wrenched it from the guard's arm. The man rocked back with a curse, his hand sprained. He fumbled his mace and dropped it.

The other guards were quick, though. One flailed for Sunbright's head, missed. The other slammed at Sunbright's knee. Even though he retracted the leg, searing pain like a bone saw sang up and down his leg.

But not crippling pain. He stamped the foot flat, missed crunching toes, ducked low then drove high with his shoulder. His broad frame collided with both shields. The owners were shoved up and backward, off-balance. The barbarian roared, and hammered them again. One guard flopped on his bottom. The other, a woman, raised her mace, but found her wrist snagged in a grip like a vise. With a massive twist, Sunbright slammed her hand across the top of her own shield. She cried out as the wrist sprained or snapped. The shank of the club rapped the gasglobe so it winked out. The barbarian was encouraged. To douse the lights would give Knucklebones the advantage, and they could escape.

But the last guard danced back, leveled his shield, and took aim. From the corner of his eye Sunbright glimpsed a flash of silver. He made to throw up his right hand, but his sleeve fetched on a corner of the shield. Too late he realized the I-shape, with its sharp angles, was also a weapon. He ripped his sleeve loose, but too late to keep the mace from braining him.

Yet the mace barely flipped over his head, and

bounced off his back. A streak of black had flitted by, and Sunbright realized Knucklebones had hurled her elven blade. Hadn't she ordered not to kill?

The trio of guards were down, and the flood of people stampeded over them. The guard with the cracked wrist rolled on the slimy floor, whimpering in pain, but someone had already swiped her silver-tipped mace. A child kicked her ribs, sawed through her belt, and jerked away her belt buckle.

Sunbright felt a dig in his ribs. Knucklebones barked, "Move your bloody big feet! Ha! Drop it!" A woman had stooped for the dark elven blade. Knucklebones stiff-armed the woman on her duff, and snatched up the black hilt wrapped with silver wire.

"I thought we weren't supposed to kill!" Sunbright recalled.

"Who killed? I flipped it backward!"

She waggled the hilt under his nose, showed the dia-mond-shaped skull-popper. The guard had been beaned on the forehead.

The mob pilfered the guards bare. Then the last gas-globe was stomped and the catacombs were plunged into blackness. It was stifling hot with so many frantic bodies, and sweat stung Sunbright's eyes. The tunnels grew more chaotic as folks ran in two directions at once. Evidently there was trouble at both ends.

True. A roar, a wash of light reflected on steel weapons and stone ceiling, shrills from the common room, and another wedge of brutal guards charged. The thud of ebony wood and silver on skulls and shoulders was sick-ening.

"This way!" Having sheathed her blade, Knucklebones planted both hands on Sunbright's midriff and pushed. Sunbright walked backward, shov-ing smaller folk aside like a bow wave. Before long, she called, "*Duck!*"

He crouched, and backed through a doorway into a

small room with only a few people. Knucklebones poked his belly, and slid under his arm.

Cold glow striped the walls. Sunbright saw long pipes fitted with shelves, jars and crocks atop. A pantry. A handful of thieves and dockworkers screamed at a man by a stout door in the opposite wall. The man was thick through the body, bald, and adorned with enough earrings to make a bracelet. He yanked an iron handle, thumped the door with his shoulder, panted and sweated and thumped again. The door didn't budge.

"Open the damned thing, Senon!" someone yelled. The crowd sweated, cursed, glanced for oncoming guards, but Sunbright blocked the doorway.

"I can't! It must be glyphed!" The fat man slammed the door with his shoulder, hammered with his fist. "We're trapped!"

Chapter 6

"Hogwash! He's lying!" The shout came from Knucklebones, to Sunbright's surprise. She whapped his elbow. "Go! Pound him! Knock him aside!"

The crowd mashed against pipes and shelves, creating a corridor for the two men. Without a clue why, Sunbright advanced, hands poised to grapple or brawl. Instantly he saw that Senon had been exposed at some trick, for the fat man's face changed from helpless fright to rage. Whirling from the door, he snatched at a boot top, and yanked up a triangular spike four inches long. Enough steel to pierce a heart through the ribs. Bellowing like a bull, the man charged.

Sunbright yanked his belt knife, thin and a foot long, and caught it tightly in his right hand. He wished he could unsheathe Harvester, but he had to stop the fat man's rush.

Hollering, Senon bunched an arm thick as a hog's leg to stab straight. His left he put on guard, but he counted on Sunbright quailing and falling back.

Sunbright didn't budge. Rather, the tundra-born fighter rotated both hands in circles to distract his foe. And when Senon closed, the barbarian attacked from an unexpected corner.

As Senon lunged to strike, Sunbright's left foot snapped up. Senon's fat knee smacked into Sunbright's sole, jolting him to a halt, but the fat man stabbed wildly, hoping to land a lucky blow.

Luck was no part of Sunbright's fighting. Skill and instinct drummed into him by training saved his life. As the deadly spike slashed by, he snagged the fat wrist in his free hand, locked his wrist, and twisted cruelly. With his arm crooked backward, Senon stumbled helplessly. Sunbright neatly slipped his blade into the pudgy elbow and severed the tendons. Blood erupted to spatter a half dozen folk squashed along the walls, who winced and yelled. Dragging Senon like an ox to slaughter by his trapped wrist, Sunbright inverted his own wrist, and bashed the stag horn pommel on the fat man's temple. Thin bone popped, Senon's eyes flew wide, then slammed shut. Sunbright kicked the falling body against the far wall. Senon's flopping head bashed the door frame. A fountain of blood soaked his clothes.

Amazed at the cool savagery, the crowd whispered and gasped. Knucklebones squirmed past them all, and rattled the far door's handle. It opened easily onto a wet cave smell. "Come on!" she called.

Sunbright sheathed his belt knife, and straightened his shirt. "He'll bleed to death!"

"Let him! He's a ferret!"

That word again. Rather than shove, Sunbright let thieves rush by. Finally, the impatient Knucklebones grabbed the barbarian's thick wrist. "Let's *go!*" she said.

They scurried into wet darkness that echoed like wide-open chambers. "What's a ferret?" Sunbright finally asked.

"A crawler. A squealer. A spy in the pay of the guards." Her panting voice led him on. "I saw the door wasn't locked because he was pulling it shut. You could see the muscles in his arm work, and the handle couldn't be glyphed, or his fingers would have been singed. He must have thought us stupid gulls!"

"Quick of you to spot that in a second." Sunbright's voice was warm with admiration.

Her voice floated back, "It's nothing." But he imagined she smiled.

"Where are we bound?" he asked. The dark made Sunbright's neck ache, for he feared bashing his skull.

"Wherever this leads. We've lost everyone else. They went up at the fork, but I suspect a mousetrap awaits there. South by west will get us out, I hope."

Sunbright had known they jogged alone. Now cold light glowed as Knucklebones striped her vest. Underfoot ran dirt and gravel and creases dappled with water that reflected silver. The passage opened overhead, and he heard bats squeak, a comforting sound because it promised an exit. Abruptly the trail slanted, and Sunbright had to hold Knucklebones's shoulder to keep from overrunning her. She trotted as confidently as a cat until her foot crunched something hollow.

"*Whoa!*"

"What is it?" he said. "That sounded like—"

He squinted at more light. Knucklebones stroked a round rock aglow, but it bore eye sockets, an underslung jaw, and yellow fangs. "Skull of an orc," she said.

"Orcs," he corrected. "Look."

What looked like yellow sand around them was actually bones. Knucklebones lobbed the luminous skull, and they saw that the boneyard extended farther than the glow could reach. Thousands, perhaps millions of bones littered the cavern.

"I don't . . . understand . . ." murmured the shaman.

"Sure you do," Knucklebones hissed. "Remember? In

my time, the cities warred, and prophecies came true? The Rain of Skulls.

"An explosion hit Ioulaum's underside, and bones spilled out in the millions. The legends recalled Ioulaum was sheared from one of the Unholy Mounts, Redsnow or Bloody Hill, where an orcish army was wiped out. This is that cavern."

"Yes . . ." Sunbright squinted upward. "I keep forgetting the natural caves lie upside-down so we walk on ancient ceilings. But all this death. There should be—" He swallowed the word "ghosts" before it escaped. No sense in conjuring the spirits of thousands of slain orcs.

"Come. Quickly," she said. Even steadfast Knucklebones was spooked, and led him by the hand. They couldn't walk without stepping on bones, so they closed their ears to the crunching and grinding. They made for the far end of the cave.

A quarter-mile on, dawn light sparkled on cave walls. They reached a grate where the thief pronounced, "*Wisht!*" to pop the rivets. Rattling it aside, they crawled into a culvert and up to the street. Merchants called to their friends and neighbors, clucked to ponies, and lugged their wares to the marketplace.

Sunbright was bewildered by the abrupt transition from death to life, but the city-born Knucklebones was already towing him into the crowd, saying, "Come on."

"Where?"

"East side. Street of the Faithful Protector. Bly's. To have her scry what you've sought so long."

* * * * *

"It's no good, Cholena. It's foolish to fight the yakmen."

"Oh, so, Drigor? Ayaz died for nothing? And Ridon and Nodin, their deaths were meaningless? Best their ghosts haunt your nights until all turns black before your rheumy eyes."

"Berate if you will, woman. I only speak from three hundred years' experience. That counts for nothing, I suppose."

Deep in the Iron Mountains, Drigor and Cholena, his sometimes wife, worked at a stone bench littered with crude axe heads and blades. The weapons had been puddled in antique molds. By candlelight reflected from copper and brass holders, the dwarven artisans worked with craggy hands to etch the old designs deeper: entwined dragons, bold kings, noble steeds, and fierce sailing vessels. They polished or darkened the swirls and whorls, and brought a glittering luster to all. They argued as they talked, an argument years old.

"We must defend our homeland," Cholena chided. "The Sons of Baltar have inhabited these mountains for centuries. It's—"

"Aye, centuries," Drigor interrupted, "but not forever, not since the first dwarf sprang from a glacier by the breath of Igashum. I've lived here all my life, three centuries, but my father, Yasur, came from the Rampant Mountains, which tall men call Gods' Legion. If my father could leave his homeland—"

A scream cut him off. Not a scream of pain, as someone scalded by molten metal at the forges, but a scream of terror, pure fright. Drigor and Cholena grabbed a mattock and stabbing spear, clumped in tarry boots, and thundered down a wide tunnel toward the foundry.

Lights sputtered like sparks from a forge. Above the screams of the mortally wounded the dwarves heard a screech like a dragon's.

"Where is the bright-haired one? Where is my enemy? I smell his tracks! He must die! You will die for sheltering my foes!"

Drigor and Cholena burst into a scene from hell. The cavernous foundry, lit by red and yellow fires from iron slotted doors and smoldering heaps of charcoal, was crammed with a writhing mass of black tentacles. A dozen dwarves were snared in hundreds of slimy arms that grew before their bulging eyes. The slither and rustle of these thousand arms was deafening, like the crash of surf in a storm or the roar of an avalanche. Kicking dwarves hung ten, twenty, even thirty feet in the air. Tentacles coiled around them, sliding into their clothing, wrapping arms and legs, circling their necks, as if the plantlike assassin had a mind and a will.

Centermost in the room, in a hollow the roots avoided, a tall scarecrow of stone shook misshapen fists and screamed. "I'll destroy you all! I'll rip the flesh from your bones, then crack them and suck the marrow! I'll rend your children before your eyes unless you tell me where lies my enemy!"

Drigor went for roots, Cholena for the monster.

A dozen feet high, Cappi and Pullor hung upside down. They kicked and writhed, yanked at the vines around their necks with powerful, work-worn hands, but couldn't squeeze even a finger under the tendrils. Only the solid muscle of necks and chests kept them from being suffocated, and Drigor saw they couldn't hold their breath forever. Slinging his keen-edged mattock over his head, he scraped the blade within a hair's breadth of a stone wall, and sheared through a dozen dark roots. The devilish web sagged, and Cappi's boot thumped Drigor's shoulder. Savagely the old dwarf yanked his comrade down, towing a snarl of roots along.

Deft slashes of a worn knife freed Cappi from the thickest vines. The young dwarf sucked air like a bellows, and retched from a raw throat. Turning to the wall, Drigor leaped, chopped, tore magic vines, and tugged Pullor free. The dwarf's face was white, and Cappi had to bang on his chest to get him breathing. By then Drigor had waded deeper, hacking at the jungle growth toward Oredola trapped farther on. The stink was terrible, for the slimy vines reeked like something dead and rotten raked from a river bottom. Drigor gagged on the stench, spat, but kept cutting.

By reddish hell-light he saw scuttling movement and cursed freely. The black roots he'd sheared curled in the air. Not alive, but not dead, they clung again to the wall, and spawned new vines from bare rock. Cappi yelled as vines twisted around his boot, and he had to stomp them loose while dragging Pullor clear.

They'd never defeat this spell, Drigor could see, but he cleaved valiantly, and called, "Hang on, Oredola! I'm coming!"

All the time, the monster screeched madness. "Where is my enemy? I'll punish you all! I want the bright-blond barbarian! These caves will be your boneyard!"

Cholena didn't know what this flinty monster was— golem or crypt servant or wight or troll—but few creatures could stand a thrust of dwarven steel. Charging head on, stifling a war cry rather than warn the fiend, Cholena bunched her arms to stab straight and hard. The fiend turned from its ranting too late, and the hand-forged blade jarred its spine just above the cockeyed hips.

Yet the monster must have been true stone, for the hollow-ground blade only knocked loose a shale chip. Red blood flowed from a jot no bigger than a dwarf's hand. Cholena was shocked at the toughness of the hide, and how easily the blade had skipped off. Frantic, Cholena stamped to set her feet, slashed upward with her stabbing spear to strike again at the small wound. Only by prying it open could she hope to kill the fiend.

But the flint monster whirled with clawed hands, fire flickering in its blue, staring eyes. "You *dare?* You would harm *me,* who crawled alone from the depths of hell to gain vengeance? You would halt my quest?"

The last thing Cholena saw was twin tornadoes issue from the unmatched hands of the fiend. Then she was blinded by the hundred-mile-an-hour winds that erupted before her. Blistering, killing winds roared over the dwarf, tearing away her eyes, ripping loose her hair, then the scalp from her skull. Hissing zephyrs like a basket of knives stripped the unfortunate dwarf to shreds in seconds, until hair and flesh and bones and then chips of bone were scoured to splinters and blown in a gory trail across the floor of the foundry. The spear was flung away to clatter in a corner.

Drigor looked up at the first shrill of wind, and howled like the tornado himself as Cholena died. He'd dragged Oredola free of the death-dealing vines, was cutting his way to the next dwarves, so enwrapped he couldn't tell their identity. Whirling winds filled the cavern with noise and destruction. Backlash from the tornadoes whipped around the monster so magic vines were wrenched from the walls. The flint creature became a center of snapping, flailing tentacles that spattered into slimy fragments or else wrapped around their creator like seaweed around a shipwreck.

Drigor howled in outrage, and champed on his beringed mustache over Cholena's death. Yet even in grief the old dwarf analyzed the enemy, and saw that the monster had made a mistake.

The dark roots sprang from stone, and now they'd touched the monster's frame. On the stone-like skin, they took root and grew anew. Vines sprouted across the monster's back, on its bald head, on the backs of its knobby legs. Within minutes, the rampaging fiend was festooned with vines thick as hedgehog quills. It screamed and slashed at the onslaught of its own magic, gibbered as it raked the vines from its skin with obsidian claws.

Elsewhere the vines curled and writhed and thickened, but a large hole had been blown in the jungle growth, and several dwarves wriggled free. They hit the ground running, sprinting on stumpy legs past the weedy monster. Yet three still hung in vines, and kicked more feebly, or hung limp as rag dolls.

Drigor hacked at roots until even his famed strength began to fail. Freed dwarves and others came running to chop and flail. The vine-wrapped monster screeched, blathered nonsense, and sputtered like a rabid wildcat.

Finally, in an eye-smarting blaze, it scorched the air with a shifting spell and vanished. The only things remaining were a blackened patch of cave floor, the reek of charred vines, and a forest of slithering vines that fell still, then withered and died. By the time the dwarves had cut the last three dwarves free, the vines were dried stalks, no thicker than burned hay.

But the three victims were dead. Strangled, they lay in heaped stalks with bulging eyes in blue faces. Many dwarves, unused to showing emotion, broke down and wept at the loss to their tribe.

While someone stoked the coal forge, Drigor rested his mattock head on the ground and leaned on the shaft. Death coming to young ones made him feel uncommonly old. And the death of Cholena, who'd given him a son years ago, tore at his heart like iron fingers. Red firelight glistened on tears dripping from his pouchy face, like icicle melt from the crags of a mountain in spring.

Yet even his grief was interrupted, for one young dwarf blubbered, "This is the fault of those humans! The tall barbarian and the one-eyed part-elf! They brought death to our house!" Others agreed, anger and resentment growing to a muffled outrage.

Drigor cut them off. "The upperfolk could not know this monster pursued. We would have read their faces, heard fear catch in their throats. They are ignorant of this fiend's quest for revenge, and I owe the big man a boon."

"Owe?" Cappi's voice rasped from near-strangulation. "You'd return a favor to a *human?* After your tribe has suffered?"

"I would," stated Drigor. "For in times of crisis the

trivial burns away and important matters lay bare, as grease burns off iron in the forge, as winter winds scour dirt to bedrock." Images of wind brought pictures of Cholena ripped to flinders before his eyes. "This visitation is an omen."

"Omen?" echoed a dozen.

"Just before the attack, I talked with Cholena about how these rooms have sheltered our tribe for centuries. Centuries, but not forever. She bade me stay. Then the gods sent us a test. I survived while Cholena was killed. An omen of blood is strongest of all."

"I don't understand," squeaked Pullor. "You blame the gods for Cholena's death? And you'd go where? For what purpose?"

Drigor just shook his head, and with aching arms shouldered his beslimed mattock. "I don't presume to know the gods' will, nor the heart of a woman, nor my own. I only know to go forth and seek what needs to be found. And to warn the barbarian, Sunbright Steelshanks of the Raven Clan of the Rengarth Barbarians, that a deathdealer comes calling."

* * * * *

From a mile in the air, Sunbright and Knucklebones watched the dawn light flare on the horizon. Edged by the saw-toothed peaks of the Abbey Mountains, brilliant light filled the sky and washed the clouds golden, so the tundra-dweller and thief saw why the Netherese worshiped the sun, and paid a premium price to welcome it. With the caroling of choirs in temple belfries, the trill of birdsong in gardens, the cry of vendors of oysters and shoes and sharpening echoing from the walls, the wicker of horses and laughter of children at games, the empire could be seen as a glorious and happy place—providing the visitor could ignore memories of marching armies, oppressive taxes, wasteful practices, and the blind and stupid disregard and neglect of any non-Netherese "undermen."

The Street of the Faithful Protector sported a statue of Tyche where it branched from a roundabout. The goddess—more capricious than faithful, Sunbright knew—was tall and willowy with a clinging gown. The statue was etched from some iridescent metal, or else enspelled, so dawn light scintillated across the surface like a rainbow. One outthrust arm of the goddess arched down the street as if to point their way.

It was warm, so Knucklebones wore only leathers and knucklebone pendant and knife, with a rucksack slung over one shoulder. Sunbright wore a shirt of washed-out yellow and tall boots, and lugged weapons, satchels, and their blanket rolls so he looked like an itinerant peddler. As they passed along the street of square white stone buildings with particolored doors, the big man asked casually, "Do they erect statues to the god of thieves in the enclaves?"

"They try," Knucklebones said as she counted houses, alert for a red and green door. "They erect statues to Shar with big purple agates for eyes, but thieves steal the eyes, leaving her blind. It's a funny tribute."

"The only one of your gods that makes sense to me is Kozah the Destroyer, lord of storm and wildfire and rage. Or Vaprak the Destroyer, god of ogres. To brave the tundra, you need a tough god. Clingy-Robe back there would freeze her melons off in my country."

"Which is why the empire leaves your country alone, I suppose," Knucklebones joked. "Who wants frozen melons? Ah, here!"

The door of Bly the Seer was indeed red and green, as they'd heard, and decorated with a glaring eyeball surmounted with bat wings. Knucklebones tripped up the stairs and rapped sharply on the eyeball. "Perhaps I should steal this. I could use a spare," she said, and winked at Sunbright with her one good eye.

A servant looked them over, then admitted them down a long hall glittering with gold mirrors and candelabra to the rear of the house, where they descended a short stair, passed outside through opulent gardens, and entered a two-story workshop against a high fence of white brick. Climbing to the second floor, they found the workshop of Bly lined with books and racks of odd cards in wooden holders, with sheaves of herbs hung from the rafters. Centermost was a table so black it absorbed light like a square hole gaping to another world.

Bly was so old her white skin was like parchment etched with unreadable writing. Drawn-back hair was white, and her face was painted on. She wore a quilted gown of silver and blue that failed to hide a rail-thin figure. Sunbright reflected that, if these archwizards could sustain life for centuries, Bly must be near the limit.

Knucklebones introduced them, her cultured accent and easy poise marking her as Neth-born. Bly stared at Sunbright until the thief wondered if she wasn't dotty and man-crazed. When they explained their wish, Bly creaked, "You seek the whereabouts of these Rengarth? And this man is one? Simple, then. Let me work."

Plucking a sprig of sage from the rafters, the archwizard walked circles around Sunbright, bidding him stand still as she brushed the herb up and down, from topknot to toes. The barbarian frowned, but the thief shook her tousled head. Finally, Bly stepped to the black table.

There was nothing on the tabletop, yet Bly bid them stand back. Raising her skinny hand, she dropped the sage. It struck the table once, bounced, then sank from sight, as if into water. The visitors gasped. Without touching the table, Bly bent over and peered deeply, all the while crooning some ancient air. Then she smiled and said, "Look you."

Sunbright and Knucklebones craned. Below the surface of the table, as if seen through polar seawater, he glimpsed a shaggy head. The man wore his hair like Sunbright's, shaved at the temples, with the distinctive roach and horsetail of the Rengarth.

"Rattlewater! He's a cousin, many removed! Who else is there?"

Slowly the image widened, until Sunbright saw Rattlewater talking to Leafrebel, his wife. The two argued, it was clear: the man stabbing the air angrily, the woman shaking her head, tight-lipped. Behind them Sunbright saw a reindeer hide painted with a raven, totem of his clan. The picture widened further, and he saw other folks sitting around the common house fire. He recognized Forestvictory, and thought he saw Archloft. The picture lit up as the fire itself was revealed. A copper pot of cornmeal bubbled at its side, and Sunbright could almost smell it. The familiar sights sent a pang through him, a wistful stab that almost stilled his heart. He hadn't known he was so homesick until he saw home. It took all his willpower not to leap into the black tabletop and see if he could plunge into the scene. The picture widened, and he held his breath, for there was his mother—

A scrawny hand slapped the table, and the vision vanished.

Wrenched from his waking dream, Sunbright cried, "Don't! Let me see! Please! I must know—"

"When I'm paid," Bly said simply. The archwizard's mouth was prim and dry as a parrot's beak. "You know I can locate your tribe. As we widen the sphere of the scrying spell, you'll see some landmark you recognize. Then you'll know the way home.

"*After* I'm paid."

"What do you want?" Sunbright babbled. "I'll get you anything, find anything!"

Knucklebones tsked, rolled her one good eye at his hopeless non-haggling. Promise the moon to this rich archwizard and she'd demand it. The way her rheumy eyes assessed Sunbright, Knucklebones disgustedly thought she knew part of the payment.

But oddly, the archwizard gathered her silver-blue hem in one claw and waved toward the stairs.

Bemused, thief and barbarian followed the sweeping train down the stairs, past the first floor, to the cellar. Knucklebones knew that, since the enclave was honeycombed, the archwizard might have any number of basements or storage rooms beneath her estate, as many as she wished to pay for.

One vast cellar matched the lot. Bly spoke a word to make the ceiling light. Along the outside wall a locked door obviously gave onto thin air. The room was packed with crates and heaps and furniture under dusty covers. But also two vehicles they recognized. Sunbright groaned.

"Oh, no! Not flitters!"

Chapter 7

"I hate these things!" Sunbright groaned.

"Anyone with sense does," Bly replied. "That's why I need flyers. A team. I've had a standing wager with Lady Fayina for months now—we contest ownership of a building on the north side—but we've been unable to secure flyers. Too many have been killed, and the new ones are incompetent. She's hired two airboaters from Buoyance and challenged me. And—Lady of Luck—in walk you two daring freebooters! Surely Tyche favors me, and all who adorn her street!"

"How do you know we're 'daring freebooters'?" Sunbright asked dully.

"No one could acquire so many scars without sojourning after trouble," the mage reasoned. "And you're still alive, so competent. Have you flown before?"

With a ghost of smile, Knucklebones nodded. Sunbright groused, "Once, for the merest moment, and mostly straight down."

"But you survived. Splendid! This won't be any more complex." She turned to go upstairs.

"Wait!" Sunbright called. "We crashed in a tree! Knuckle's still got a scar over her eyebrow—"

"Don't bother," the thief put in. "She's set on us flying this beast. We might as well accept it." Shucking her battered rucksack, Knucklebones walked around the two flitters, grabbed the overhead bar of one and oozed into the seat. She cheerfully tested the twin steering bars, watching the tail and wings tilt and straighten. They'd flown a similar vehicle from Karsus, in the future. These primitive gliders were simpler, with shiny gossamer wings overhead and to the sides, and an upright fishtail, all painted with an ornate **B** and connected by brass tubing, steel struts, and numerous wires bearing on rollers. The seats were wicker with no floor. The thief nodded.

"This one's in fine shape," Knucklebones said. "There is one difference, though. That later flitter had wards to protect you in a crash. This one doesn't."

"Ouch," Sunbright joked. "You seem a presumptuous expert, having flown once and cracked your pate."

She craned one eye as if winking, and said, "We wouldn't have crashed if you hadn't crumpled the wings."

"It wasn't me! It was a guard dog!" his voice echoed in the cellar. "We were under attack. Otherwise, I never would have set foot in the damned contraption! And speaking of feet, why is there no floor? My boots will fall off!"

Knucklebones pursed kissable lips and said, "You launch by holding the frame around your waist and running off the edge. Skids on the bottom there let you slide to a landing."

"Run off the edge . . . ?" Sunbright closed his eyes, held his stomach, and groaned, "*Why* must we do this?"

Knucklebones slithered out of the seat, lithe in tight,

buffed leather, to inspect that wires and fixtures ran smoothly. "We've nothing else to offer. She could see that by our clothes," she told him. "We have little money, not near enough to pay for scrying. Thirty thousand crowns wouldn't buy that spell, I'd guess. Any tasks we might perform for her—thieving or brute strength work—she can buy elsewhere.

"But there're always foolish bets amongst the rich, and she needs two fools to launch this butterfly. We're big fools in need. You want to find your tribe, don't you? This is how."

A wave of homesickness washed over the barbarian, and weakened his knees. He made to lean on the flitter, then thought better lest it crumple under his hand. "But what's this 'other team' tripe? What are we supposed to do, outfly them, or outrace them?"

Fiddling with wires, Knucklebones huffed, "My guess is we tear them from the sky—make them crash. She was eyeing your tackle, especially your longbow. The Neth favor blood sports."

Now Sunbright held his head. "Wonderful," he grumbled. "And if we don't shoot them down like ducks on the wing, they shoot us?"

"Absolutely," Knucklebones said as she straightened. "But don't fret. We'll win, because you'll shoot, and I'll fly. I liked it last time!"

Sunbright stared through thick fingers at her grin. "Traitor."

She stuck out her tongue. "Sissy."

Knucklebones had guessed correctly. After a while Bly returned and announced that the duel was set. Lady Fayina's team would launch from her mansion, three blocks hence, and Lady Bly's team from here. Their opponents were a man and woman in a flitter marked with an **F**. By common consent with the other "gamers," no other flitters would launch at that time. The object was to knock your opponent from the sky.

They could shoot the flyers, tear or ram their wings, grapple on, or use any other method. There were only two rules: no magic, and they mustn't crash themselves or their opponents *on* the city. The opponents were not to meet, or spy on one another, until the duel. Nobles would gather in the late afternoon to watch and cheer, judge, and lay sizeable bets. "So put on a good show," Bly commanded.

"Good show," Sunbright groused. "We're pitted like dogs on short leashes."

"Such are commoners to the high-born," Knucklebones nodded. "Good for work or play, to live or die or suffer, as long as we do as we're told."

"No wonder this empire crumbles," the barbarian complained. "If it treats its people, the foundation of its wealth, like animals—"

"Animals eat better," Knucklebones interrupted, then stretched like a cat. "We should pillage the kitchen, build up our strength."—Sunbright held his stomach—"I'll eat. You fast. We don't want to knock the enemy from the sky with puke."

"You're . . ." the barbarian hunted for a word, ". . . unkind."

Knucklebones smiled and sashayed up the stairs. Sunbright stared bleakly at the flitter.

* * * * *

"It's time. Get in. And don't step through the wing. We need it."

"I'd rather just jump off the edge of the city and get it over with," Sunbright said as he climbed carefully through bars and wires and finally squeezed his big frame into the small wicker seat.

In three hours, Knucklebones had rummaged through the cellar and garden shed, and cobbled some tricks. Tied with thread across the front of the cockpit were a dozen long arrows with heads a foot wide. The thief had scavenged rake teeth in the hopes these T-shaped arrows would shear through gossamer fabric and disable a wing. Another addition was a long scythe blade spot-welded to the nose of the flitter like a mosquito stinger. And lastly, a length of light chain with a long hook nestled between them on the seat.

How they'd ply these Sunbright didn't know, or care. "We're doomed, and that's plain," he said dramatically. "I was born on the tundra, an earth-dweller. I don't belong in the sky."

"Hush, and do what I say, or you'll visit the earth sooner than you'd like," Knucklebones scolded. "I intend to land us whole and hale. And stop whining. You'll jinx our luck."

"If we had luck, we wouldn't—I'm not *whining!*"

From the entrance to the cellar, a maid heard a signal from above and called, "They're ready!"

Knucklebones grunted, "Drop your feet, country mouse. You're a country bat today."

Stiff as a zombie, Sunbright planted his boots, caught the edges of the flitter, and marched forward. Servants had shot the bolts and unlocked the outside door, and it did indeed gape upon nothing but blue sky and blue hills in the vast distance. The barbarian closed his eyes as the thief called, "Run, run, run, run—*here we go!*"

A hop, a stomach-lurching drop, a sickening tilt toward the ground, and a prolonged scream from Sunbright. . . .

Swearing a steady streak, Knucklebones twisted and yanked and shoved the twin steering bars until suddenly, as if by magic, the wings scooped wind and the flitter buoyed on air currents like a boat. Quick experimentation and fast hands leveled them.

Knucklebones hooted with laughter as she hauled a bar to her belly, made the nose of the glider climb, then level again. The framework vibrated like a balky horse at a run, the wings and wires hissed, gusts of air slapped their faces and mussed their hair, but she hollered, "I've got it! I can fly! We're saved! Open your eyes, damn it!"

Unsquinching his eyes, stomach, and bowels, Sunbright peeked, and gasped. His boots dangled over a mile of sky. Spread in all directions were summer-yellow fields giving way to dull green forest and blue hills. Far to the north he saw the Narrow Sea like a squiggle of quicksilver. "Lord of War!" he screamed. "Beyond that's tundra!"

"True! But we need to spot the other flitter! Look around!"

Head hunched between his shoulders, Sunbright craned until he saw the city. It was a blur of white buildings atop a blurry mountain to his watering eyes, but his keen tundra vision picked out—

"I see them! White wings marked with an **F**!"

"Tell me something useful!" Knucklebones yelled back. "What are they doing?"

"They're . . ." he said, straining to sort out the picture. Between the jiggling and dipping of their craft and the other, they might have been two drunken dragonflies. "They're coming after us, I think!"

"They're supposed to be good! Arm your bow, and I'll loop!"

"You'll *what?*" he screamed. "*Aagh!*"

Cranking twin bars in two directions, Knucklebones hooked the craft in midair as if yanking reins. The wings shuddered and Sunbright hurled prayers, but when the thief snapped the bars back, they were level and pointed at the floating enclave. Bearing directly for them like a war chariot was a white-painted flitter marked with Lady Fayina's emblem. Knucklebones bit her lip and aimed the craft like a spear.

"When we're close enough, shoot! Then arm again, but wait till we're close!"

Sunbright broke threads to pluck a T-headed arrow, and nocked it. He had trouble drawing the tall bow in the cramped cockpit, and had to lay the wood sideways. Knucklebones pulled her head back as the string kissed her nose. The man grunted for holding the draw. "You're steering right at them!"

"Aye!" the thief yelled above the hissing wind. "We won't kill them from afar!"

"But aiming right at them?"

"Let *them* veer aside!" she yelled. "*Shoot!*"

The craft were so close together now Sunbright saw freckles on the female flyer's nose. Both flyers were dressed in green, both redheads, and the barbarian realized they were brother and sister. The woman's mouth worked as she shouted, and her brother leveled a crossbow with a big, barbed bolt. Before the other could shoot, Sunbright loosed. He had the satisfaction of seeing the arrow slash through the cockpit, but it only spanked off the metal frame, and did no damage.

"Shoot the wings, damn it!" called Knucklebones. "Watch out!"

The redhead shot. The barbed bolt sizzled over Sunbright's head, punched a hole in the overhead wing, and stayed fast. The barbarian reached to yank it free, but the bolt jumped as if alive, almost slashed his fingers, then tore free and tumbled away. The two craft had overshot, and nothing showed ahead but city.

An amazed Sunbright heard Knucklebones yell, "They tied a thin line on the bolt! He ripped it free to reel it in! Look!"

Sure enough, down and left sailed the flitter. The red-headed woman had indeed dodged from Knucklebones's dare. Below it trailed a black bolt on a silvery line that the man was reeling in. "They can shoot at us all day like that!" he exclaimed.

"Arm your bow!"

Fumbling, Sunbright nocked as the thief threw them

into another gut-churning turn and spin. As they steadied, the enemy flitter was ahead and side-on. He called, "Why don't we spiral all the way to the ground, like a maple leaf?"

"We ride the hot air a bird. Hawks soar for hours, don't they?"

"Oh, yes," Sunbright grunted as he strained to draw. His initial terror was dissipating in the thrill of the game. When they were close enough, he shot. The T-arrow slapped through the end of one wing, splitting a gash as long as his arm. He saw the craft begin to flip until the woman wrenched it aright, and the barbarian growled with satisfaction, "We can knock them down!"

"Arm!" Knucklebones answered. "And hang on!"

Throwing the levers over, Knucklebones made Sunbright urp as she dived at the enemy. Her goal was to spear their flitter's fishtail with her "mosquito stinger," but the white vessel lurched and bucked and squirted away.

Cursing, Knucklebones cast about, banked to rise, and the shaman called, "Where are we bound?"

"Back toward the city! They want a good show, and we're too far away!"

"What do we care?"

"They won't pay!" Knucklebones said, irritated.

A quick anger flashed in Sunbright's mind, made him grit his teeth and mutter about bloodthirsty bastards ruling the empire. Yet he'd swallowed the bait and tried to kill two strangers as if life and death were a game. Everything the empire touched it corrupted, including himself. Emotions churning, he spoke aloud, "It's too confusing!"

"It's simple. Kill them or get killed! Aim! They're crawling up our backsides!"

White flickered at the corner of Sunbright's vision. The flitter, surprisingly large in this vast sky, soared at an angle to intercept them. He glanced at his lover, saw the muscles writhe in her thin arms riddled with scars, and realized it took all her strength to control the craft. Knucklebones spat through her teeth, "*Shoot!*"

Sunbright didn't like the angle and rushed the shot. The arrow flew wide by six feet. Then the enemy flitter rose, so they rose to keep above it. A black bolt flashed, sheared into their wing, was ripped loose to leave a long, flapping scar.

Knucklebones grunted as she yanked the steering bars. For a second, Sunbright thought they'd crash wing to wing, then their flitter bucked above the enemy's. They shot off in two divergent directions. Knucklebones hooked to steer after. The floating city filled their horizon, but they didn't have time to study it.

"Once we get over them—Once we're over—"

"Look out!" yelped Sunbright. "They've got a—something!"

The redheads below raised a hollow brass tube. Flame flickered in the dark end, then a flash scorched a hole in the overhead wing. The gossamer flared briefly before snuffing out. Sunbright yelped, "A fire rod! That's magic! Cheating!"

"What'd you expect? Help me pitch—*ugh!*"

Doing it herself, Knucklebones snatched a hand at the chain nestled between them on the seat. Threads broke, then it rattled through the bottom of the cockpit. Nocking another arrow, Sunbright felt the thin chain brush his leg, and saw the hook dangle below. The enemy flitter appeared in the foot hole. He couldn't shoot through it, so he craned out of the cockpit to aim. Part of his mind screamed that he was crazy to hang outside, but a cooler part hunted a target.

Suddenly, with a savage grunt, Knucklebones threw both bars over so they closed on the enemy flitter. Below, the redheads blasted another ball of fire upward that plowed through the cockpit. Sunbright felt flame lick his thigh, smelled burnt wool and wicker. Then the dangling hook snagged on a strut of the flitter beneath.

For a second, the two craft were tethered together like a mad horse and cockeyed cart.

Then Knucklebones snapped the bars the other way. With a splintery crash, the top wing of the enemy flitter tore free. Sunbright glimpsed two surprised faces topped by red hair, and felt his own craft lurch from the added weight and the pinwheeling of the hooked wing. He yelled, "We won! We won! You did it—"

Fire-damaged wires under the cockpit snapped: one, two, three. The bars in Knucklebones's hands stopped jerking—because they were free, unattached.

Unfettered, the flitter banked, stalled, hung, then dived nose-first for the city of Ioulaum. In flashes Sunbright saw a wall, a building corner, a garden, a treetop—

—then an explosion of green and brown and brilliant light. Then nothing.

* * * * *

Voices split Sunbright's skull, hands tore at his flesh, and fire seared his eyeballs. Lurching in midair, he grabbed for support and heard a man yelp. His back slammed earth.

Gradually pain subsided, though his head hummed like a hive of bees. Someone rolled back his eyelid and peered close. It was Knucklebones. She wore a split lip and blood was running from her forehead. "Sunbright? Can you hear me?"

Over the buzzing, he roared, "Yes! Let go of my eyeball!" With a grunt from pangs and twinges, he rolled to his knees, pushed against the grass, and staggered erect.

Nobles in fine gowns and capes and hats, and servants in house colors and aprons filled someone's yard. Maids and serving boys were smeared with blood: Knucklebones's and Sunbright's. Besides her scalp and lip wounds, the thief had a lame arm stuck in her belt.

Sunbright checked, found numerous scratches, scorched skin, and a leg game from a wicked bruise. Cable was still twisted around one ankle. The wreck of the flitter hung in an elm tree. Cardinals and squirrels skittered over it, investigating. Servants had tugged them out of the trees, and Sunbright groggily thanked them.

Lady Bly was neither thankful nor quiet as she berated Knucklebones. ". . . told you repeatedly not to crash in the city! This is not my tree, it's Lord Kyle's, and I must pay damages! If you'd *listened*—"

Knucklebones sniffed, closed one nostril, and blew blood, making Bly jump backward for fear of staining her clothes. In a scratchy voice, the thief asked, "What of the redheads?"

"They're not my problem!" Bly snapped. "They're Lady Fayina's charges! And they ruined a dining hall belonging to Lord and Lady Greatas! Their blood has *soaked* the carpet—"

"So they're dead?" Knucklebones groaned.

"Don't interrupt me, you saucy tart! I don't care if they're dead—they knew the risks—and if you think I'll pay after you—"

Quicker than a mink snatching a chick, Knucklebones's one good hand flicked her long, black blade from her belt. The crowd gasped as the knife tapped Lady Bly's upper lip. Ever so gentle, ever so threatening. The archwizard froze.

"You'll pay us," Knucklebones hissed quietly. "We flew your craft, killed the other crew—who cheated like you, you skiving parasite—and won your bet. It will take you seconds to scry for us, and you will, or you'll be Lady No-Nose until they regrow a new one. And I suggest you other 'nobles' refrain from employing any magic. It might jiggle my hand. Let's walk to your workshop."

"Certainly," squeaked the archwizard. Her eyes bulged to see the blade under her nose. "Howsoever you wish."

Knucklebones slid behind the mage, prodded her, and waggled at Sunbright. The three left crowd and garden behind.

It was only two houses to Lady Bly's, and Knucklebones made the elderly mage skip. On the stairs, the thief ordered, "Sunbright, block the door! Pile furniture against it. They'll have guards immediately. You, milady, make magic. And be quick, or you'll snort your own blood! Brush Sunbright with that sage—"

"No need," the archwizard said, standing ramrod straight with the knife under her nose. "The table remembers the last enchantment. Let me just touch it." Leaning forward, she brushed the night-black surface, crooned softly as if putting a child to sleep. A faint gray blur formed on the tabletop, then widened and clarified as before.

"Sunbright, hurry!" called the thief.

Still weaving from being knocked out, Sunbright nevertheless had dumped crates, books, chairs, and a table against the door. Now he crawled upstairs for fear of pitching backward. Knucklebones watched Lady Bly while Sunbright peered at the scrying table. Blood dripped from an ear, splashed the black stone, and sank without trace.

As promised, the same scene appeared, the common house, but time had lapsed, and the dim room was empty except for an elderly couple who huddled by the fire and gazed into smoky depths.

"Iceborn and Tulipgrace! Oh, Mother Reindeer guide me! I need to see more!"

"Patience," gargled Bly. "The image grows."

As if the viewers were birds taking wing, the old couple grew smaller. The picture changed to a scabby rooftop made of brush. Sunbright saw that the ground around the common hut was oddly littered with bones and offal and trash. His tribe had always kept their camp neat. Higher rose the view, until they saw more huts of bark slabs and brush, or sunken homes of stone, haphazard and slovenly. He didn't have time to study the camp, for the scene shrank rapidly. Soon they were a bowshot in the air, and details were obscure. Across a broken plain of rocks he saw a village—no, a whole town! His people had never camped near towns before! Then a flash of silver. Sunbright recognized the salt waves of the Narrow Sea. He'd seen them a thousand times. His tribe was camped near the sea, and a town, in summer?

But that put them on the wrong side of the sea! Why . . . ? He caught his breath as a trio of mountains swirled from the distance. "I know them!" he said. "The Channel Mountains! The last we call the Anchor! They're northwest . . . The town must be Scourge, and my people south of it! But *why?*"

He blinked as the image went black. Lady Bly had touched the tabletop and ended the scrying spell. Poised once more, she ignored the thief's blade and commanded, "You have it. Now leave."

"You can find them?" Knucklebones asked her lover.

"Aye, I can . . ." Lost in thought, the shaman barely heard himself say, "But why *there?*"

"We'll go ask them," Knucklebones snapped. The shattering vision had left Sunbright more stunned than any bang on the head, so she took charge. "Watch her a moment."

Jerking a leg from under her, the thief tumbled Lady Bly across her own magic table. The old woman squawked. Pinning her hands, Knucklebones tugged down twine used to bind herbs and lashed the woman's thumbs together, passed the twine under the table, and lashed it to her ankles. The archwizard cursed, but the thief conceded, "You won't lie here long. Your precious city guards—may the gods rot their livers—will come hunting us criminals. Rest easy, and be glad you survived trying to weasel out of a bargain. Come on, Sunbright!"

Knucklebones flew to the stairs and spiraled down. The barbarian clumped after, entered the cellar. The thief dumped their satchels and weapons onto the remaining flitter and lashed them tightly. "Open the doors!" she said.

"We're not flying again, are we? We've crashed twice!"

"We've had practice, then. Get the doors while I check these wires. The guards will break down her doors soon enough, so there's only one way out. Besides, your tribe's at the Narrow Sea, aren't they? We saw that from the air."

Sunbright was glad to be groggy, though the haze was hardening into a throbbing headache. Maybe he'd black out in flight. Shuffling, he pried open the doors, and felt his guts clench at the sight of the nothingness outside. Knucklebones yelled for him to climb in. A banging and clattering sounded from the stairwell, and an odd screeching like an animal in pain. "What's *that?*" he asked.

"We don't care! Pick up!"

Together, lugging the tubular frame and gossamer wings, they hopped forward toward the gaping hole crisscrossed by clouds. Wind blew in their faces, and Sunbright closed his eyes.

The cellar floor was suddenly gone, and the barbarian's boots dangled. Then they plunged nose-first into naked sky.

* * * * *

On the top floor, Lady Bly called for help, then stopped at the smashing and crashing downstairs. The guards had finally arrived. Good, except they should be gentler with her property. She'd sue the city for damages. And sue—someone—for the indignity of being trussed by a gutter rat in her own workshop. What did she pay taxes for? So the city could let thieves break into peoples' houses?

"Hurry up, you dimwitted nincompoops! Get up here and untie me! I command it!"

Silence below. No answer. Another crash, a chair tossed aside. Scuffling on the stairs. Odd sounds, scratchy and uneven, as if the walker limped. Bly had expected the tramp of boots. This animal skittering made her nerves crawl, as if rats came creeping . . .

No, something far more horrible. Too awful to look at. The thing topping the stairs was tall, misshapen, rail-thin, covered in a shimmering carapace of stone that glinted with minerals. Hands were hooked claws. The bald head had eyes a startling, staring blue, quite mad.

It rasped, "Where are my enemies? I smell them! Tell me!"

Bly the Seer had lived a long time. As a scryer, she'd spent decades hunched over her magic table, seen sights from around the world and beyond, but never, in all her visions, had she beheld a monster like this one. Trembling overtook her, and a low moan escaped her lips.

The monster scuffled to the black table and touched the midnight surface with a crooked claw. "My enemy was here. What does this do? It scries!" the fiend hissed, more to itself than to the trembling mage stretched across the table. "Show me!"

Shivering as if frozen, Bly pronounced the words that opened the vision. Bulging blue eyes watched the picture, and murmured, "The bright-haired one goes there. But far. Too far, too sunny, too open . . . But I have many enemies. You will find one. Polaris is its name. And another, a fat mage . . . Make magic!"

With a claw it severed the twine binding Bly. Numb with fear, the archwizard slipped off the table to the floor. Quickly the monster caught her hair and wrenched her upright, then banged her face on the table so blood spurted from her nose.

"Scry out my enemies!"

With no physical element, like the sage and the scent of the barbarian, and with Bly clumsy with fear, the scrying went badly, but finally the monster croaked, "Yes, yes! There is one I seek! I'll kill him, flay his flesh from his bones and suck the marrow! Yes, I go to kill, to avenge!"

Bly closed her eyes. She was banged up and near fainting, but if the monster left—

Suddenly her face was caught in obsidian claws that cut her cheeks and throat. She screamed, but claws strangled her. Helpless before the monster's crushing strength, Bly felt herself dragged into the air. Piercing, white-hot pain ripped through her hands and she swooned.

Slapping her face brought her around. Her hands felt afire. Glancing up, she saw the monster had bent open an iron hook that held herbs and—Scribe of the Doomed!—impaled her hands over the hook before crushing it shut! Writhing only ripped flesh and ground the bones, so she hung still. Her world was pain.

The monster rasped, "You aided my enemy, so you become one! All my enemies must die!"

Stepping back, the monster extended both craggy claws. Fire flickered from their tips and washed over the room. Herbs, books, papers, paint, walls, and Bly's gown all crackled with eldritch energy. And burned.

Bly screamed long and hard before smoke choked her. Then she fell limp, and never felt the flames around her legs. The monster disappeared, hissing of revenge. The black table went with it.

Chapter 8

Wind rushed in their faces until their cheeks were numb and their eyelids swollen. The breeze made them thirsty, and Sunbright was hungry, for Knucklebones hadn't let him eat before their aerial duel. The barbarian was cramped from sitting hunched in the wicker seat under tubes and wires, and he ached from crashing in the treetop. Yet there was one consolation to all this misery. Fatigue and battering had expunged his fear of flying. In the hours they'd banked and soared, Knucklebones had even let him steer. Later he'd even dozed off, exhausted, while Knucklebones wrestled the steering bars with one good and one lame arm.

Yet he jerked awake with a cry, making Knucklebones jump. "What's eating you?" she asked, irritated. "You're moony as a hammer-struck calf!"

The barbarian shook his bright-blond head. "Someone's after me, I think. Cursing my name, hounding my dreams. Evil, and mad, and angry."

"Not just imagination?" Knucklebones's voice was hoarse from shouting over the wind. Far below rolled plains with a glint of sea in the north. All were slanted with black shadows, for the sun was setting, ending the long summer day.

"It could be," Sunbright sighed. "When I'm tired, who's to know if I dream or hallucinate? Sorting truth from fancy is hard enough in this world, never mind the next."

"We'll have the world in our laps soon! We must land before the sun drops. We can't land in the dark."

Sunbright hadn't considered that even birds bedded before sundown. He squinted ahead. The Channel Mountains looked larger, tall as his hand. "Land east of the mountains," he advised. "Walking with them at our left hand, we'll find my tribe south of Scourge."

The thief banked east, until the flitter's nose slanted across the mountains. "We'll fly until I think it's too dangerous."

Sunbright felt a familiar looseness in his bowels. Launching, Knucklebones had pointed out, was simple as falling off a cliff. Landing was like diving headfirst into an eagle's nest without cracking any eggs. Sunbright called, "Let's get it over with. If we're hurt, we'll need daylight to patch up."

The small woman didn't argue, simply tipped the bar, and pointed them down. Sunbright gulped, and clamped down on his stomach.

The plains were glossy with summer grass. As they sank, antelope and bison and skulking wolves fanned out before them. Knucklebones slowed the flitter by hauling the wings back while pointing the tail down, though the landscape swept by alarmingly fast. Finally, at spitting height, the thief called, "Hang on!" and shoved the nose down.

Sunbright gritted his teeth as the land leaped up like a tiger. But the clever thief flopped the craft on its belly skids, and they slithered over grass for seeming miles. Sunbright yanked his knees to his chin, felt chaff and grass stalks snap and tickle.

Then it was still. Grass billowed all around, except for the flattened track behind. Knucklebones pried stiff hands off the bars, massaged her scarred forearms, and chuckled, "I could get to like this!"

"You can have it!" Sunbright grabbed bars and hauled himself out of the flying coffin. Unlashing their supplies, he hung his great sword Harvester of Blood across his back. His bow and arrows were lost, but he kept the empty quiver, and hung his food satchel and both blankets around his shoulders, ready to march.

Knucklebones tossed her rucksack over one shoulder. "Shouldn't we scavenge wires and such? You made snares last time," she said.

"I just want to get away," Sunbright began, "but you're right." With their knives they cut away loose wires, lengths of tubing, and fabric from the wings. They never knew what might prove handy.

Looking at the wrecked flitter, Knucklebones asked, "What will the coyotes think of this?"

"A bird skeleton picked clean," he mumbled, then faced north, where a sentence of death awaited. "Let's get this over with, too."

They walked where the evening shadows of the Channel Mountains touched the tall grass, and, gradually, darkness overtook them.

* * * * *

After three days' walk—the last across rock and shale—they breasted a low hill. Sea wind carried salt to their nostrils. Sunbright stopped dead. "That's them!" he cried. "But it can't be them!"

Knucklebones just stared. In the distance winked the Narrow Sea, a silver so bright it shone white. At its

shore, and surrounding the toe of the last Channel
Mountain, the peak called the Anchor, lay the villainous
town whose name had become Scourge. Punished by
hard winds off the sea, the town saw any steel mysteriously rust away within weeks. Since industry could not
prosper, the town had fished until the fish thinned out.
Good people left, the desolate stayed. Them, and
plagues of rust monsters. The idle population turned to
thieving and infighting, until Scourge gained its name
as a place to avoid.

And here, on the outskirts, amidst sand and rocks,
where no humans would venture, Sunbright found his
tribe.

The camp was lumpy huts of piled stone, or caves cut
into hillsides, or mere holes in the ground covered by rotting hides. The only wooden structure was the common
house, a ring of rotted aspen trees dragged from the
mountainside, the roof thatched crudely with brush. The
disordered camp was rife with garbage, droppings, bones,
ashes, and trash. The smoke of a few fires trickled into
the brassy sky. At midday it was hot here on the rocks, as
it would be cold by night. A few women trudged through
camp with fagots or bundles of meager food. Men slept in
the shade or lay with feet jutting from canted doorways.
Dirty children crept at quiet games, or else turned over
rocks, hunting salamanders and insects for food.
Buzzards picked at garbage, unmolested.

Sunbright stood with his mouth agape. "I had a
hint . . ." he said, his voice heavy with shocked disap-
pointment, "when I glimpsed the village in the scrying
table . . . but how. . . . Where are the reindeer? Where are
the dogs? How did this happen?"

Knucklebones only shook her head. She'd grown up in
poverty, in the sewers of a mighty city where every
scrap was stolen or scavenged. But even she was
shocked, having heard time and again of Sunbright's
proud people. This motley bunch looked like trolls.

After a long time the barbarian picked up his feet—a mighty effort, as if they were glued to the ground—and descended the slope.

At first there was no sign they'd arrived, as if the pair were ghosts. Children looked up curiously with big eyes, and retreated around rocks. A woman glanced up, for strangers never came from the south, and rubbed her eyes. Without a word she slunk into a hut. A man peeked out and frowned. Other folk noticed the odd couple, one small and one tall, and trailed them. Sunbright kept walking, watching everywhere, but not believing his eyes. His goal was the common house. By the time he reached it, thirty ragged barbarians had trickled from shelter to see him enter.

Sunbright ducked under a reindeer hide so old it was white strings. Knucklebones slipped after, quiet as a cat. Inside hung rotted hides with faded totems, but nothing else: neither animal masks nor enemy scalps nor ancestors' skulls. The old couple seen from afar, Iceborn and Tulipgrace, huddled under thin blankets by a smoky fire. The old man turned blind eyes, demanded, "Who is it?"

His wife, Tulipgrace, woke with a start, peered at them with red eyes, and asked, "You are . . ."

"Sunbright Steelshanks, son of Sevenhaunt and Monkberry," he said flatly. He almost added: of the Raven Clan of the Rengarth Barbarians, but these were the same folk, or had been.

"Sunbright . . ." Tulipgrace said, awed. "You fled, were banished in absence. You're sentenced to death."

"Unwrap the wolf masks then, and sing the death song! Kill me if you can! I've yet to see a man or woman in this village bear a sword! By the Teeth of Kozah, what's happened to my *people?*"

The elders didn't answer, only turned back to the fire. Knucklebones cleared her throat, an explosion in the awesome silence. She noted that once Sunbright had set

foot in the camp, he walked taller and spoke more bold-
ly, blood and thunder in his voice, but boldness seemed
lost on this lost race. It was as if they'd invaded a graveyard full of tired ghosts.

"Sunbright," came a mild reproof.

The barbarian whirled, hand over his shoulder to
snatch Harvester, then froze. A wizened woman peeked
from the doorway.

"Mother!"

In three steps the warrior-shaman became a small
boy, stumbling as he hugged his mother. Barbarian
emotions never lay deep, so he wept openly, tears
streaming onto her gray hair. The woman curled
arthritic fingers around his massive, scarred arms and
patted his back like a baby's, cooing, "My boy. My man-
child."

Sniffling, Monkberry led the pair from the common
house to her own abode. It stood on the edge of the
camp, a heap of stones roofed with branches, but round
like the ancestral yurts of reindeer hide. The roof was so
low they sat, Sunbright's head brushing dead leaves,
the room so tiny their knees touched. A bed of rags was
the only furniture. A fire pit let smoke through a hole in
the roof.

Once seated, no one knew what to say. Monkberry's
face was seamed as a prune, her eyes deep-set but
bright blue, like her son's. Her hair was long and gray,
but neatly combed. She wore a simple smock of deer
hide, almost worn through at the shoulders. As the awkward silence dragged, she nodded at Knucklebones.
Flustered, Sunbright said, "Uh, this is Knucklebones of
Karsus. She's a—rogue. Good with her hands. Clever, I
mean. She's a friend." When Knucklebones shook her
dark head, he amended, "I mean, I love her."

Monkberry took the thief's small hands, touched her
scarred cheek with crooked hands, and said, "She's lovely. Elven blood so becomes a woman."

"I'm not," Knucklebones stammered. For the first time in her life, she felt shy. "I'm just an old, scarred alley cat. A sewer rat too contrary to die."

The old woman caressed her tousled dark curls, and said, "Scars are a badge of honor in our tribe, dear. You carry enough to sit at the elder fire." Then she sighed at painful memories.

"Mother," Sunbright began. "What's happened? How came you here? Where is everyone? Why don't you leave this awful place?"

Another sigh. "I prayed you'd return, Sunbright," his mother said. "In my heart and dreams I knew you'd come back. I could feel your eyes on me, hear your voice, grown so deep and manly. And it's time, for the tribe needs you desperately. Needs a miracle, or else we die out. Far worse than the gods forsaking us, we've forsaken our own heritage. But ask not, and let me speak . . .

"I don't know if you've been north, but the tundra is dying. Or sleeping. We don't know which. Perhaps it's some cycle that runs centuries, beyond the memory of our tribe. Howsoever, the Earthmother could no longer sustain us. The reindeer were scrawny, calves dropped stillborn, salmon ran thin . . ." She went on, listing small disasters that Sunbright already knew. Finally she came to, ". . . We knew we couldn't remain, so we moved south, to the edge of the tundra. But immediately the cycle of our lives was broken, and we felt uprooted. With nothing to hunt or gather, we were bereft of work, lacking any way to make a living.

"Owldark did not help. He recounted dream after dream, led us hither and yon along the southern shore, aimlessly. We were not welcome in the villages of southmen, so many mouths to feed and nothing to trade, and their harvests have been poor.

"Blown by the winds, whipped from place to place, we finally stopped here, where Owldark commanded. His next dream would lead us on, but food ran low. Our

reindeer could not walk many miles over stone and
sand, so were eaten. With nothing to feed the dogs, we
had to eat them, and carry our belongings on our backs.
After a while, the strongest men and women went to
Scourge, seeking work. They found a few jobs, the vilest
chores southmen refused: shoveling fish too rotted to
salt, breaking up old ships for firewood, wrestling and
knife-fighting for sport. The townsfolk hate us, hate
everyone, and mocked our barbarous accents and
superstitions.

"Yet we've survived so far: no children have died of
hunger. Yet none are born either, for our women's
wombs shrivel, like our spirits. And so have we lan-
guished for too long." She laid her hand on the rim of a
redware bowl as she said, "Even the water is brackish,
half salt, not fit for cattle."

Sunbright listened, stone-faced, through this sorry
history, then he asked, "What of the council? Why do
they allow this?"

Monkberry sighed and turned to the door, as if
expecting someone, but there was only salt wind. "The
council argued with Owldark, and each other," she told
him. "Some thought we must remain. The gods drove us
from the tundra, they said: our own faults and sins
brought it on. So we must linger in hell on earth as punishment. Others urge we go elsewhere, but cannot
agree. Even our ancestral summer lands lie empty and
fallow. Others would have us return to the tundra to
die, like lemmings in the sea, or whales on the beach.
Others brood over wine fetched in the village. Some
wandered and didn't return, we know not whence.
Destroyed in spirit, some women married town men
and no longer visit. Some youngsters have joined the
emperor's ranks as soldiers and been sent far away.
Perhaps that is right, for nothing lies here for anyone."

Frustrated and raging, Sunbright raised his hands,
his fingertips brushing thatch. "What of Owldark?" he

asked. "If the gods haunt his dreams, surely even he can find our true destiny!"

"Owldark tried. Despite the pains in his head, he trekked the wastes, fasting, scourging himself with thorns, beseeching the gods for an answer. Any answer. Then he didn't return, and the hunters searched. They found his bones in a ravine. Wolves had eaten him, probably after he fell. So we lost our homelands and traditions and work, and now we have no shaman to guide us."

"Not true," stated Sunbright. His mother's eyes peered. "See."

Gently, he laid his hand atop the clouded, rank water in the redware bowl by his mother's knee. Quietly, crooning an ancient winding air with a steady beat, he dipped his fingers one by one, sending ripples through the bowl. At each tap the cloudiness receded, until the water was clear.

"Mother of Magic!" wheezed Monkberry. She dipped a crooked finger in the water, tasted it. "It's sweet! You are a shaman!"

"After my father and my forebears," Sunbright smiled. "Actually, the salt is not gone, merely sunk with other minerals to the bottom of the bowl. You'll have to scoop the sweet water before the salt dissolves again."

"How? . . ."

Sunbright softened the truth by saying, "I came near death, and left my body, and descended into the earth and learned her secrets. Some. How to sort things into proper order, like separating salt from water. It's a blessing and a curse, for my dreams are haunted like your husband's.

"But I have the strength of spirit to face them. If necessary, I will brave the gods themselves and learn our fate."

"Mind your own fate!" boomed a voice at the door. Sunbright saw a familiar face. The broad, craggy features of Blinddrum, his old sword instructor.

"Sunbright Steelshanks," he said, "leave our village!"

Sunbright exploded to his feet and almost bashed his head through the thatch roof. Clambering to free Harvester's pommel, he shoved past Knucklebones and outside. Blinddrum was a huge man, taller even than Sunbright, but fell back before the warrior. Unbeknownst, other folk had gathered, returned from meager jobs in the town now that the late-summer day was ending, so the tribe looked almost populous, a couple hundred at least. Most were dressed in tall, battered boots and long shirts of either deer hide or faded cloth, and fighters still sported the distinctive roach and horsetail of the Rengarth Barbarians.

But many men looked like strangers, townsmen, with full heads of hair grown out and scruffy beards soiling their faces. Yet all were familiar. Sunbright recognized Thornwing, the other sword instructor, and his cousin Rattlewater; and Leafrebel, Forestvictory, Archloft, Rightdove, Goodbell, Mightylaugh, Magichunger, and Starrabbit.

Emotions churned within Sunbright. A wave of homesickness and relief made him want to embrace the lot, laughing and crying. Yet their stony faces chilled his heart. Some wouldn't even look at him, as if he brought shame to the village.

Blinddrum stated, "You were pronounced dead when banished, Sunbright. Leave this place of the living. None here commune with the dead."

"*You* are the dead!" Of all Sunbright's thundering emotions, anger won out, and he practically screamed, "You shuffle around this hellhole like zombies! You forsake the old ways, let them trickle through your fingers! You abandon pride to cower here like mongrels! Half of you don't even *look* like Rengarth! What say you to *that?*"

But not even insults stirred them. Blinddrum and Thornwing marched off. Magichunger and Starrabbit spat. Others looked at the rocky ground or turned away. Curious children were cuffed around and dragged off. Monkberry and Knucklebones crept forth, agonizing at how Sunbright was ignored. For a moment the barbarian wished he *were* dead, rather than see his people like this, and be unable to help them. But why talk if they wouldn't listen?

"Mother!" cried the shaman in desperation. "What do I do?"

Tears fell from Monkberry's chin as she said, "Nothing I know. We've no wisdom left."

"There must be something!" Knucklebones spoke up. "Some way to make them listen, and pay attention. I don't know your ways, Sunbright. What is sacred to them? What honor must they obey?"

"Nothing. I don't know . . ." he said. The warrior-shaman scanned the scabby village with slumped shoulders. Returned to his tribe, sought for so long, he saw only their backs. "What can you take from people that have lost all?"

Then his eyes fell on the round common house, and the trickle of smoke rising from it.

"Unless . . ."

"Unless what?" asked the thief.

But Sunbright ran like a child for the common house. Wondering, Knucklebones caught Monkberry's hand and they tripped after him.

Sunbright shoved through the retreating crowd, jogged to the common house, and ducked inside to the smoke and haze. Despite themselves, the Raven Clan crowded the entrance to see what transpired.

Madness, it seemed. Sunbright took old Iceborn and Tulipgrace by the shoulders, begging their pardon, and towed them away from the sacred council fire. Then, shouting, the young shaman drew back a boot and kicked the smoldering embers. Ashes and smoke flew in a cloud. He stamped and stomped the fire pit until his moosehide boots were scorched and sparks dappled his skin. In a minute, the fire was out.

Stepping from the fire pit, coughing in smoke, Sunbright pushed past stunned barbarians into sunlight. Sneezing, he crowed in mad glee, "There! If the sacred fire is the heart of my tribe, then my tribe is now truly dead! And since only a shaman can kindle a council fire, it will stay dead! So am I, a dead man, returned to a tribe of dead people!"

This idea, both new and old, sank in slowly. Sunbright saw confusion and shock on their faces. And for the first time, the animation of hard thinking, something they'd been denied.

Sunbright gave them more to chew on. "Think! Do the dead hear? Let me test. Hear *this?*" People fell back as he drew the long, fearsome, hooked blade Harvester of Blood over his shoulder. Inverting the blade, he used the leather-wrapped pommel to thump Blinddrum on the breastbone, then continued, "I, Sunbright Steelshanks, dead or alive, challenge you, Blinddrum, to combat! Else I name you a stinking, dung-eating, bastard, mongrel dog! Do you hear *that?*"

"I hear," Blinddrum murmured. His broad, simple face was uneasy. "I accept."

"Good!" Turning, Sunbright thumped Thornwing on her skinny chest, and said, "I challenge you! Would you be a barb-lipped, bottom-feeding sculpin picked clean by gulls, or a free and proud barbarian? Do you accept, or be named coward?"

"I accept," she said drily. "But like it not."

"I care not if you like or dislike, only that you hear! You, Archloft! Was your mother a maggot, and your father a pusworm, or will you fight me? Good! You, hold still! I name you nest-robber, and egg-breaker! Fight me? Fine!"

With a madman's delight, he poked Archloft, Goodbell, Magichunger, Forestvictory, others: anyone who'd ever wielded a sword, saying, "I challenge you all, and anyone I forgot! And why? Because I cannot leave the village until the duels are done! This custom would I have levied on Owldark had I been a warrior and shaman, but at the time I was only a boy. Well, that boy is dead, and a man returned! Blinddrum, when shall we fight?"

"Whenever you wish," replied the swordmaster. "No, wait. An hour. T'will give you time to visit your mother, and commend your soul. For after an hour, you visit the gods." With that, Blinddrum turned away, as did the rest.

Sunbright was left alone, inverted sword in hand. Knucklebones and Monkberry came forward, having lingered at the back of the crowd. The thief wept from her one good eye. "Why did you do that, Sunbright?"she sobbed. "Why come back just to die?"

Huffing with exhaustion, as if he'd run twenty miles, Sunbright sheathed his sword, and said, "In part, it was your idea."

"*My* idea?" Knucklebones shook small fists in his face. "You really are mad! You'll be killed! And I'll be left alone. What's the point anyway?"

Surprisingly gentle, Sunbright enfolded the small woman to his chest, kissed her tousled dark curls, and said, "Oh, Knuckle', if only life held simple answers. . . . Come, I'll try to explain, not that I understand it well myself."

Seated in Monkberry's hut, Sunbright shared rations and sipped water from a canteen.

"You asked what tradition I could invoke that would make them listen. Killing the council fire was one. Yet I'm still banished—unless I have promised a duel to satisfy an insult. It's the only way I can remain with the tribe.

"And I can't leave, for they need me. They need some-one—the gods must believe—and I'm the only one who's come. If nothing else, I must make them think, and return to themselves. I must rekindle the fire in their minds. Keeping alive customs, habits, and traditions— even mishmashing them when necessary—is a shaman's job. By challenging everyone, I can stay a long time and work."

"And get killed!" objected the thief. Angrily she thrust his canteen away. "You're a fine swordsman, a wonderful fighter, but even you can't fight nine dozen duels! You'll be hacked to pieces all at once, or a little at a time!"

"But in between, I can talk to folks, and think how to save us."

"Until you're dead," Knucklebones spat.

"Until a miracle occurs."

* * * * *

In their short hour, Sunbright talked to his mother about the old ways. Monkberry knew them all, for her husband had been the tribe's shaman for decades. Knucklebones listened raptly to a new world of tradition and legends and superstitions. When Monkberry finally asked Sunbright where he'd been in the years past, the shaman only smiled and shrugged.

"Around," he said. "Working here and there. Seeing the sights the empire has to offer. Meeting Knucklebones. I was lucky in that."

Dimly the warrior recalled the days when he'd first left the tribe, how he'd hungered and thirsted for revenge night and day. Then later, after sojourning in hell, he'd become a man, and known that one day he would return to his tribe, and walk amidst them scarred and powerful and mysteriously quiet, for he'd learned true strength lay within, and he could just quietly rejoin his people. And now that he'd really returned, he found himself in an unpredictable role, the preserver and savior of his tribe. Which just went to show, he supposed, how men made plans, and the gods made men fools.

"Yet it's my destiny to save this tribe from extinction." He was surprised to hear himself speaking aloud.

His mother smiled and squeezed his broad hand with her twisted one. "Yes," she said, "your destiny, and our miracle."

Sunbright smiled back. "Knuckle"?" he asked.

The thief rolled one eye, and answered, "It must be my elven blood that finds this stiff-necked barbarian pride a lot of claptrap and folderol. You need a miracle, I agree, but we'll help however we can." She squeezed both their hands.

A voice boomed across the village: "Sunbright Steelshanks! Come out and fight!"

Sunbright dropped both hands to creep outside. "Excuse me," he said to his mother. "The shaman has a patient."

Chapter 9

Dusk came early to this rocky wasteland, for the Channel Mountains cut off the sun. In darkness, Sunbright found the tribe waiting for him. Silently, Blinddrum led the way. Boys and girls toted torches with hardwood handles split at the top and jammed full of poplar bark. At the center of the crooked village, tribesfolk had rolled up rocks to make a rough arena. There were over three hundred barbarians now, including many who'd moved to town but had been fetched back by runners. The shaman smiled to see the changes. His coming—for good or ill—had already made an impact on the tribe.

Now, if he could just survive to get his message out.

Sunbright entered a ring of torches and people to stand alone. Monkberry and Knucklebones were admitted to the edge of the ring. The big barbarian shucked off his belt knife and back scabbard, tossed them aside so as to fight unencumbered. The crowd parted, *oohed* and *ahhed,* as giant Blinddrum stepped forth with only a long steel sword in his hand. The huge, craggy instructor raised his sword in a lazy salute, then took the first stance a student learned: left toe pointed, right foot and sword back. But he blinked when Sunbright lifted a bare hand.

"Wait!" Sunbright called out. "We must pray!"

The crowd gurgled a question. Blinddrum blinked again, as if his eyes were aging, and asked, "We must? Why?"

Sunbright tilted his sword down, raised his voice so all could hear, and said, "This is a formal duel, not a brawl. We needs pray so Amaunator, Keeper of Law, will oversee the fight and maintain fairness. Otherwise Shar, the Shadowy Seductress, might cast a veil over one of us; or Tyche, Lady Doom, might, on some whim, visit one with luck. To pray before a duel has always been a tradition amongst our people, has it not? Or has everyone forgotten that?"

Folk muttered. Some frowned at the interruption, but old Iceborn, blind and seeing only in his mind, quavered, "He speaks aright! It was always thus!"

Sunbright twirled a circle, raised his arms, and called out, "Rengarth, pray with me! Keeper of the Sun, please hear us! Send us truth, send us light, send us wisdom as we see these men battle for what is just! We praise thy name!" The crowd echoed, "Praise Amaunator!"

Grinning foolishly, Sunbright waggled his blade at Blinddrum. "We may begin," he said.

But the swordmaster stood still. "Your travels addled your brain, Sunbright," he said. "You grin before a death duel."

"I'm just glad to be home."

The fighter's grin had become a death's head rictus. White teeth gleamed in the torchlight.

"To come home to die is foolish."

"I could have died a thousand times in battles past,

Blinddrum, but my sword prevailed because I had fine instructors. Probably the best in the world. You and Thornwing."

The straight sword drooped. Almost petulant, Blinddrum rumbled, "You make it hard to kill you. And I don't think you came home to fight."

Children scuffled bare feet around the ring, eager for battle. Adults stilled them to hear.

"I came home to talk to my people, to make them listen and think. They will not listen, only let me fight. So I fight. Prepare!"

Sunbright Steelshanks leaped into battle. Illuminated by torchlight, Harvester of Blood glittered like a crescent moon as it swung across the night sky. The shaman's howled war cry, *"Ra-vens!"* sent a shiver and thrill through the audience.

When his blade crashed on Blinddrum's upraised sword with an awesome *clang!*, sparks scattered. The crowd roared.

Instantly, Sunbright dropped back for the parry, as he'd learned long ago. And it came, for Blinddrum scythed his sword sideways to shear Sunbright's leg or knee. The young man was not there, having hopped free, and Blinddrum had to snap his blade up to protect his shoulder from a hissing sideswipe. When their blades clashed and rebounded, Sunbright feinted a head blow, then aimed for the same spot again. His quadruple blows came so fast that Blinddrum was slashed across the shoulder. The big man grunted and stepped back.

"You learned much in the southlands."

"I learned everything from you," Sunbright panted. "And practiced it every day. Have at you!"

Blinddrum stepped back, almost into the crowd, as Sunbright grabbed Harvester's pommel in two hands and slashed sideways. The giant tilted his blade, and banked Sunbright's off. Normally a fighter using two hands couldn't poise his blade quick enough, and Blinddrum swung at exposed ribs. But Sunbright surprised everyone by whirling a complete circle and slashing again. Blinddrum whipped his blade too slowly, and was pinked across the wrists.

The giant, much older than Sunbright, waggled his blade as a shield. He puffed, "You make me recall tricks I'd forgotten!"

"Recall them then! That's why I'm here!" Sunbright shouted. "*Hyaah!*"

Two-handed, Sunbright aimed a down-angling slash, but feinted once, then twice. His blade spanked Blinddrum's both times, lightly, then he knocked it high. Leaping, he tipped Blinddrum's tunic at the breast, shearing the old hide and drawing a trickle of blood.

But the wily instructor took the nick and snapped his steel up to wound Sunbright's right elbow. Blood dripped from the barbarian's forearm as he stamped backward.

"The lion is not toothless!" Sunbright shouted over the yelling of the tribe.

"The cub is," Blinddrum gasped. "You won't kill me! You pulled that blow!"

"Prove it!" Sunbright yelled. "*Huzzah!*" Stamping forward and driving hard, Sunbright aimed a two-handed lunge at Blinddrum's belly. The instructor batted it aside heavily and swung wild, just clipping Sunbright's chin. The younger man flicked his head aside, reached too far, but snagged Harvester's barbed hook behind Blinddrum's bicep. Whipping it back, he dug a furrow in the man's bronze skin. So sharp was the cut, it bled little at first, but soon ran a river.

Blinddrum hollered, stamped and slashed, feinted and double-thrusted, but only pinked Sunbright once in the thigh. By then the instructor's left arm was spider-webbed with blood and hanging limp. Finally he cried,

"Hold!" and dropped his point to the rocky ground. "I cannot continue. I concede."

"No!" cried many. "No! To the death! Finish him! Kill the outsider!" Yet others yelled, "No death! Honor is satisfied!"

Blinddrum shook his head, handed the long steel blade to Thornwing waiting in the ring. The tall, thin woman used her hem to wipe blood from the pommel and blade, then entered the ring and saluted.

Sunbright blew like a bellows, wiped sweat off his brow and blood off his chin. Salt stung and he winced, for he was pinked in four places. He kept his swordpoint down.

"You'd make me fight another duel right away?"

"Yes," Blinddrum wheezed. "We counseled, and decided it was best to get it over—"

"You cannot council," the shaman interrupted, "for you have no council fire."

The giant demurred, corrected, "We *talked* then, and decided it was just. You must abide by the decision."

"Talk is fine," the shaman said, shaking his head, "but only the council can change the rules of a duel. True?"

Confused, Blinddrum turned to Thornwing, who nodded and dropped her swordpoint. "He is right," she said. "Tradition gives him a day to rest before the next duel."

"Saved by tradition!" Sunbright gulped. "I choose to rest." He limped to the circle, where he joined Monkberry and Knucklebones to return to the hut.

Behind, noise swelled as the crowd argued. Why didn't Blinddrum strike to kill? Why grant Sunbright a day of rest? Was the duel even necessary when Sunbright was under a sentence of death to begin with? Why not just execute him? Who would wear the wolf masks? Did they even have a wolf mask now?

Monkberry smiled in a small way, resembling her grinning son. "You're not back one day, child," she said, "yet the tribe buzzes and talks as they haven't in months. Would your father could see this."

"See people squabble endlessly?" Knucklebones demanded. "They gabble like ducks in a pond and say nothing!"

"At least they're not crying, lamenting their fate," Sunbright offered. "They discuss how their lives should run, not *be* run."

The thief shook her head. "It must be the water here," she mumbled. "Or the thin air. It drives people insane."

Sunbright chuckled in the dark as he crawled into his mother's hut. Knucklebones striped cold light on rocks and angrily prodded his wounds. Lying on dirt, his head pillowed on stone, Sunbright hissed at her touch, then sighed, "Ah, it's good to be home."

"Completely," growled the part-elf, "insane."

* * * * *

Sunbright and Knucklebones used the next day to scout the camp, identify old faces and learn new ones, climb a low hill and scan the wasteland, and walk to the mountainside to check the local resources. In a narrow cleft, fresh water spilled into a shallow, pebbled pool where they swam and made love. They spotted a few small deer and rabbits, so set wire snares, but found little else. Rocks ruled this corner of the world. Sunbright concluded, "This land can't sustain us. We must move out."

"Where? And why do you keep saying 'we?' I'm not a member of your tribe, and never will be. A part-elven thief is as different from your yellow-haired northerners as a fox from a fish."

"True." The two sat on a rock and watched mountain shadows overtake the wasteland. He put his brawny arm around her small shoulders and said, "But it's tradition in our tribe to steal wives and husbands, for we're forbidden to marry within the tribe. My own mother was stolen from the Angardt in a raid. Father said he picked the female who fought back the wildest, then just hung on. He showed me scars she gave him, bite marks that never went away. He lacked an earlobe that my mother spat out. Mostly we marry other barbarians, but some have dark hair. Note you Archloft has brown hair? He was kidnapped off a trail by a raiding party and married to Jambow."

Knucklebones snuggled under his arm, waggled her bare feet in the air, but was not comforted. "There are none of elven blood," she said, "and I am more of the old folk than human, I think. I wish I could talk to *my* mother for an hour. . . ."

Sunbright leaned forward to peer at her face. This wistful heartsickness was new, but then Knucklebones's city-tough shell had been gradually eroding under his loving attention, and by traveling where she needn't battle for her life every minute. He kissed her forehead above the eye patch.

"I don't know much, but I know your mother was beautiful and gentle and sweet and bright, for so is her daughter."

The thief surreptitiously wiped away a tear, and said, "I shall be lonely too, when you're killed."

Sunbright chuckled, "No one will kill me."

"You're a thorn in their side. You remind them of what they've lost, their homeland and dignity and traditions, and people hate to be reminded of loss."

"What's lost can be reclaimed," he said. "Come, I must prepare to fight Thornwing."

Knucklebones hopped down beside him. Her head barely reached his breastbone. She pointed at the raw wound on his thigh. Sunbright had used minor healing spells on his other cuts, but lacking traditional herbs and ointments, could not close the thigh wound, so it was bandaged, and red on both sides. Pain made him limp.

"You'll fight with that?"

"I've no choice," he said.

Knucklebones suddenly squeezed his middle hard, making him grunt. "*We* have a choice," she insisted. "We could leave! Take your mother and go. There's a whole wide world to live in. . . ."

Sunbright kissed her curls. "No," he said. "I belong among my people. Without them, I'm nothing."

"Without you," she murmured into his shirt, "I'm nothing."

He picked up her chin, kissed her small mouth, and said, "You could be a queen if you chose. An empress. Or anything else. For you're brave and smart and kind, just like—"

He interrupted himself, but she caught his meaning. "Like Greenwillow?"

"Like any strong woman of elven blood," the man demurred. "Come, we mustn't be late."

"Late to your funeral," she said, but then picked down the slope with the man she loved.

* * * * *

The torchlit arena beckoned, but tonight the air was different. The crowd didn't wait passively, but argued among themselves, jabbing fingers, recalling stories and precedents and songs, demanding to be heard. Sunbright saw his people, docile as cows at slaughter yesterday, animated as sparrows today. Winking at his mother, then his lover, he limped into the circle with Harvester in hand. The crowd stilled to watch. And listen.

Thornwing waited. The woman was tall and rail-thin, bony across the shoulders and breast, with arms and legs of wire and gristle. A fighter, she wore the traditional haircut, shaved temples, roach of hair tugged back in a horsetail. She saluted with her sword. "Pray as yesterday," she said, "and we'll begin."

Sunbright rubbed his nose to hide a grin. "You've a fine sword," he chided. "You and Blinddrum share it?"

"Yes," Thornwing answered simply, then made it swish in the air.

"A straight steel blade with a down-curved pommel ending in two lobes. Was that not forged in Remembrance, near Sunrest Mountain and the Glorifier? Yet in the past the Rengarth used only iron or bronze blades made at home. Is this some new tradition you introduced?"

Thornwing shrugged, and said, "We needed a stronger blade to teach swordsmanship in Scourge, so traded our old swords for this new one. Some new things are good, though it is well to recall old traditions."

"That's a shaman's job. To remind his people of who they are. To recount great deeds of the past, so we go forth into the future with sense, and without shame."

"Yet you fight," the woman snapped.

"Because I must. I'd rather talk and tell stories, but one must first cut a reindeer's throat to enjoy its haunch."

"Then pray," she said, "and fight."

Sunbright praised the Keeper of Law, and this time the crowd murmured with him, shouted "Praise!" at the finish, then cheered on the fighters.

Thornwing had seen Sunbright's limp, so immediately exploited it. Moving so fast her sword was a blur, she slung it across and over her shoulder, stamped toward Sunbright's bad leg, and let fly.

The shaman barely got Harvester back in time to deflect the blow. The skipping blade skinned his knuckles so they stung fiercely. Hooking the blade fast backward made Thornwing jump clear. He followed with a short thrust, but she spanked the heavy nose down and flicked steel at his face. Sunbright jerked back, but his bad leg hampered the jump. Thornwing's edge skinned his neck, and it bled freely.

Blinddrum had been reluctant to fight, he thought, while Thornwing was eager. She'd show a cub that the lioness was still boss.

Worried, Sunbright forced his throbbing leg forward, leaned on it—like driving a knife through his muscle—and hacked a rough circle before him, using his longer blade to advantage, but Thornwing slashed a figure eight while watching closely. Her blade flickered like a snake's tongue, and tagged the elbow Blinddrum had wounded yesterday. White fire shot up Sunbright's arm, so painful he hissed aloud. His enemy heard.

Leaping far to the left, Thornwing forced the shaman to swivel on his hurt leg. Before he turned completely, her tip slithered in to pink him over the kidneys. Now he was really in trouble, for to let an opponent strike behind meant imminent death. Chest heaving, Sunbright stamped on his good leg, thrust straight out, made the blow a feint, and jabbed high to snag her armpit. Thornwing jumped like a scalded cat when tagged. Blood ran down her ribs. "The cub remembers!" she said.

"Everything!" Sunbright hissed. Sweat in his eyes made him curse. That, and desperation.

Thornwing played a game of shuffling side to side. Sunbright had to weave like a snake before a hawk. Shuffling farther, again to his bad side, she ducked low, snapped up her blade tip, thumped his wounded elbow so steel cut to bone.

Pain lanced through Sunbright's frame, and made his muscles spasm and go limp, but fury and battle-lust flooded him too. Shouting "*Ra-vens!*", he leaped.

Again, Thornwing skipped backward, counting on speed to get out of range, but Sunbright's fury energized his muscles and shut off the pain. The swordswoman raised her blade to bat Harvester aside. Rather than be brushed off, Sunbright flexed his wrists and mighty arm and locked her blade hilt to hilt. For a second Thornwing hesitated as to which way to jump. In that instant, Sunbright drove both feet hard and crashed into her.

Bowled backward, the woman grunted. Sunbright shoved until she stumbled and crashed on her back. The shaman crashed atop her, and smashed both knees into her breadbasket to drive out her wind. Pressing the back of his thick blade, he mashed both swords to within a whisker of her throat. Thornwing lay very still lest she be sliced, and whispered, "Yield."

Sunbright climbed off wearily. Much of his strength had run out with blood, for he was slashed at elbow, neck, knuckles, wrist, kidneys, and elsewhere. Yesterday's thigh wound had split anew and soaked his bandage. Assessing the wounds, he didn't feel bad about using superior strength to beat Thornwing down. Idly he wondered: Would she have killed me?

The crowd stirred, watching Thornwing picked up and dusted off. She was almost as bloody as Sunbright, he noted with satisfaction, but that satisfaction didn't last long.

Tired, aching, raspy-throated from screaming, Sunbright gargled, "Who's tomorrow?"

"I," Magichunger, a broad-shouldered man with scruffy red hair and beard answered. "I'll use their sword also."

Sunbright was too spent to care. "Good luck," he muttered, and limped off.

* * * * *

"Magichunger's never liked me. I don't know why. It goes back to childhood. I think he was jealous of the shaman's son, born with powers, while he had none, hence his name. I may have failed in this, Knucklebones. I need that miracle."

They sat again on the rock overlooking the wasteland, watched the mountain shadow like a great sea wave eat the land. Tonight their roles were reversed, with Sunbright gloomy and Knucklebones oddly content. "Miracles come in many guises," she told him.

He squinted at her, but she gazed into the distance. "That sounds like shaman talk."

"I used to love one," she said, "so perhaps he rubbed off on me."

"Used to?"

Smiling, she turned his head and kissed him, but he broke off with a sigh, patted her thigh, and slid off the boulder. He was aching and stiff and slow, yet game. "Let's get on with it," he said, and the thief followed quietly.

* * * * *

Under many torches on long poles, the tribe bickered and wagered and argued. Off to one side, a clump of men and women drew in the sand and gestured wildly. Sunbright wondered what they drew. The crowd roared when they saw the fighter, and made way. Unsheathing Harvester, he kissed his mother, then his lover, and limped into the circle.

Magichunger had stripped off his short shirt to stand in breeches such as townsmen wore. With his bearded face and unkempt hair, he looked more city-dweller than tundra man. He carried the borrowed sword easily in one hand. The blade was polished silver-bright. It had hurt Sunbright's swollen and skinned hands just to hone Harvester. Grimly, the shaman planted his feet.

"Let's begin."

"A prayer!" The crowd's roar startled him. "The invocation! It's tradition!"

Stunned, Sunbright realized he'd forgotten. More than he, the tribe led a prayer to Amaunator. After, Magichunger flicked up his blade.

Sunbright swung Harvester to a defensive position. The familiar heft comforted him, but the heavy nose sagged. Plagued with wounds, he was worn down, in trouble already. He sent up a personal prayer to the Keeper of Law.

Magichunger knew his weakness and charged. Shouting his clan name, *"White Bears!"*, he swung two-handed as if chopping a tree. The shaman dodged on legs afire, and brought Harvester around to meet the blow. Their blades clanged fearfully, and Sunbright lost ground as he staggered sideways. Magichunger, a poor swordsman but strong, hastily drew back and swung again. Sunbright feinted to meet this new blow, then slipped his blade underneath and snapped his wrists. Harvester's hook creased Magichunger's ribs, spilling a web of blood down his sweaty, tanned hide. Shocked, the foe blundered out of range, then roared and charged anew. On leaden legs, Sunbright backed himself, pushed with Harvester flat on, and tried to trip his enemy. His tired foot didn't travel far enough, and he just ticked Magichunger's.

Sensing the touch, Magichunger flailed the sword backhand, even as he scrambled by. Sunbright jerked up Harvester, but too slow. The borrowed blade slammed his own aside, and razor-keen steel smacked his temple. Lights blinked in Sunbright's brain. Slashed to the bone, stunned, the shaman saw the crowd dim, then black out as if swallowed by fog.

He only passed out for a second, for he felt his head and shoulder strike sand. Feebly, he kicked to cup his hands and rise, but missed and flopped on his back. Harvester was an anchor and chain on one arm, pulling him down to drown. Blood ran over his face, pooled in his ear, trickled into his mouth so he spluttered. Fighting darkness, he forced his eyes open.

Standing over him, one boot planted on Harvester, blade poised to cleave his throat, waited Magichunger.

"I win!" he crowed. The crowd, rife with mixed emotions, gurgled rather than cheered.

"Concede," Sunbright croaked.

"No!" a voice shouted. "No, he must die!"

"No!" someone else yelled, though in agreement or denial no one could tell.

"A challenger can't concede! It is law!" yelled another.

"Is that true?"

Argument spun around and around.

Finally someone prevailed on old blind Iceborn, who guttered sadly, "It is true. A challenger cannot concede, only win or die. It is tradition."

"Finish him!" yelled a bloodthirsty soul.

"No, we need him!" snapped another.

"He must die!"

"Let him live!"

"*Hold!*" shrilled a voice above the tumult. "I claim right of combat!"

"What?" echoed dozens of voices. A burble of confusion filled the night sky. Even Sunbright was confused, until he saw someone step into the ring.

A small woman, stripped to leathers, barefoot, brass knuckledusters winking on both hands, called in a steady voice, "I am Knucklebones of Karsus. I have listened to the tales of your tribe, and the arguments over custom, but one rule is clear. A person too young or too old or too ailing to fight may choose a champion. I claim the right to fight for Sunbright!"

Tumult, bickering, squabbling. Someone argued, "He is none of those!"

Knucklebones answered, "He was ailing before he began the fight!"

"But she's not one of us!" came a cry.

"No matter!"

More noise, customs, and curses hurled back and forth.

Knucklebones cut to the chase, pointed her finger at Magichunger, and called, "Do you accept?"

"I do!" the man yelled before thinking.

"Then stand aside!"

Stooping, Knucklebones caught Sunbright's arm, levered him up, and passed him to Monkberry and a few willing hands. Sunbright finally found his voice. "You're a miracle . . . in disguise?"

"A gift from the gods," she quipped. She picked up his sword. "I said I'd help however I can."

Helpless, and knowing protest was useless, the shaman didn't argue. "You'll need a few years' practice to heft that sword," he said.

"This pig iron? This crowbar?" A brittle laugh. "I've all I need here."

Handing the sword past the ring, the tiny thief approached the towering Magichunger. He'd wrapped a hasty bandage around ribs, his only wound. The redhead sneered, "Sunbright sends a half-grown girl to fight?"

"I've seen forty summers, stripling!" the part-elf shot back. Sunbright blinked. He hadn't known she was that old! "And I talk with *this!*"

Stooping to a knife-fighting stance, she whipped out her long elven blade. Dark, casting no reflection, it seemed invisible in the night.

Magichunger watched as if hypnotized, a chicken staring down a hawk. He muttered, "T'will do you no good. If I kill you, Sunbright has to fight the next duel. If you kill me, t'will do no good either, for you must fight the rest."

"One battle at a time," cooed the veteran of a thousand duels. "First, I'll flay your stinking hide. See if you have a heart."

Despite his long sword, Magichunger gulped, but he grabbed the pommel two-handed, cocked it over a shoulder, and aimed to slice the thief in half. Knucklebones tensed.

"Hold again!" boomed a voice. "I stop this fight, and all others!"

Sagging in his mother's lap, Sunbright lifted his head at the new interruption. Monkberry wept tears of joy. "There," the old woman said, "is our miracle!"

Chapter 10

"Praise Jannath the Golden Goddess! It works! It works!"

Carried away, Candlemas whirled and grabbed the first person at hand, a wispy lesser mage named Jacinta. Two other mages laughed to see the chubby mage dance with the young woman, then laughed harder when he grabbed their hands and swung all three in a circle. Farm hands, gathered to witness the miracle, clapped their hands and hooted and stamped their feet.

The scene was a remote valley amidst steep hills covered with ash and elm trees, bottomed by a trio of jewel-like lakes. At the head of the valley was a small square keep of black stone and a few peasant cottages. The floor of the valley, split by a glistening stream, was not farmed in typically ancient meandering lots, but quartered with geometric precision and planted with every type of grain crop: wheat, barley, rye, spelt, oats, bran, timothy. . . . It was near a small bridge over the stream, at the sharp edge of the wheat field, that magicians capered like children.

"Whew!" Candlemas huffed to a halt. Two hundred and fifteen years old, he was still in his prime, but long hours and good food had slowed him down. Dressed in a plain brown smock and rope sandals, pudgy and bald with a bushy black beard, an observer would never know Candlemas was a leading mentalist of his time. In fact, hardly anyone in the Netherese Empire, archwizard or lowest peasant, knew where Candlemas was, or what he'd been attempting. And after three long years—

"I've done it! *We've* done it, for you've all helped, my friends! And you shall reap the rewards, and the ages shall sing praises to your names! But come, let us watch!"

With brown, work-worn hands, Candlemas parted wheat stalks and ran amidst them. Lifting his head high, he could see how, ahead in a wandering line, wheat was stained a bright red like rust. But when he brushed the stalks with his hands, the red dust was knocked free to shimmer down like fiery snow and disappear amidst the yellow stalks. Candlemas laughed at the sight.

"Oh, they will sing praises to my name, just as Sunbright prophesied!"

"Milord?" asked Jacinta, who was thin and colorless as wheat. "What prophecy is that?"

"Eh? Oh, it was—it's a long story," he said. "Never mind. Look ahead! The spell has jumped the line! It's working on the barley!" He let out another fierce howl that almost cracked his throat, then stopped running, and stood puffing and grinning.

"You see," Candlemas told the three gathered mages, "I knew, I mean, a shaman friend of mine . . . This rust, this crop blight, began—what was it—four years back? From the start I knew it was trouble. Lady Polaris brought it to my attention in Castle Delia, and ordered me to fix it—as if that were simple. The rust ate the heart of the wheat, hollowed the kernels into empty shells, then it spread to other grains, even jumped to apple trees and peaches, which made no sense. A disease stays with its host, usually. It doesn't attack everything living. I thought we'd never figure it out, but a friend of mine, a barbarian shaman if you can believe it, prophesied I would find a cure, and we have!"

The mage's voice trailed off as he remembered his enforced adventuring to the future. How frustrated he'd been as steward to the estates of Lady Polaris, when suddenly he was ripped up and transported to the future, where he witnessed the destruction of the empire.

And he remembered how, returned to his own time, he'd found a new goal in life, and succeeded. This morning, as the sun rose, he'd brought out a potion, one of thousands he'd experimented with. It contained brimstone and antimony, quicksilver and iron filings, fennel and cuckoo's pintel, and lungwort and foxglove. He'd chanted to Mystryl, Mother of Magic; and Jannath, Grain Goddess, She Who Shapes All. He'd invoked spells by the dozen: Prug's plant control, Anglin's wall, Fahren's glitterdust, Shan's web. Then, kneeling, almost weeping with exhaustion, he'd dumped the potion at the roots of the rust-ridden wheat that gleamed like blood in the dawn light.

And performed a miracle. For the earth bubbled and seethed where the potion spilled, and a soft green glow enwrapped the leaning stalks of wheat. Like a green fire, the spell whisked through the field. And where it touched, rust fell away like dust, leaving the young kernels green and healthy and growing, fit food for man and beast. Nor did the spell quit, but took strength from the land itself, and spread out in rippling waves, cleansing all the crops of the blight and moving on to purify more growth.

For the first time in decades, Candlemas looked out over his work and felt pride. The last successful spell he'd completed had been—when? When he'd jerked himself and Sunbright and Knucklebones back from the future. Yet that glow of pride, his second-greatest accomplishment after today's, still haunted him, for in that moment he'd lost the only woman he ever loved. She'd chosen to remain with her beloved city, and had died with it. Since then, Candlemas had been alone.

"I wish," he murmured aloud, "I wish Aquesita could see my triumph. That would make it perfect . . ."

"Perfection isn't for mortals," scratched a voice behind him. "It's for gods, and the dead. Such as am I."

Startled, Candlemas and his attendant mages whirled to confront—a monster.

The creature loomed over them like some scarecrow burned to cinders. Its mineral-glistening body was naked, without ears or eyelids, like nothing they'd ever seen. Yet, as Candlemas stared into the monster's bulging blue eyes, he found something familiar.

"*You!*" Candlemas shrieked. "Jergal get thee gone! I know you . . . by all the gods!"

"Yes!" From the slash of a mouth came a dry chuckle, "You know me. You helped give me this hideous form!"

Despite himself, Candlemas backed from the monster, but tripped in a tangle of wheat and fell on his fat rump. The lesser mages scattered through the grain. The farm folk were long gone.

Enjoying Candlemas's terror and surprise, the black monster casually raised claws to either side. With a whispered incantation, "*Worm food!*", twin bolts of dull brown lightning exploded from its palms.

Candlemas watched in horror as the bolts overtook his assistants, enfolded all three in brown carapaces like insects. Then the brown hulls split in a hundred places like old parchment. For an eyeblink, the mage saw all three standing frozen, as if unharmed. Then they fell apart.

First to drop off where their fingers, ears, noses. Their flesh split into thousands of long, wriggling tubes, like maggots or earthworms. The skin of their faces followed, leaving their skulls bare. Their brains boiled into writhing pink nests of worms, as did their organs. Within a minute, the humans were reduced to heaps of insect-like obscenities wriggling and boring through fresh white bones.

Candlemas was too stunned to look away, to fall down, to be sick. He just stared, until the monster rasped again, "Like that spell? I learned it in the deeps, dear Candlemas. I learned much in my own personal hell. Amusing, isn't it, when you think I *created* the place? That I couldn't *know* it?"

"What?" The pudgy mage craned up to the monster's staring blue eyes. "Your own . . . oh, by the Pitiless One."

"No pity," cooed the monster. "Only pain. I'd fashioned a pocket of hell to punish my enemies. You, among others, for you betrayed me. But Polaris, she who'll die most exquisitely, turned the tables on me. She stripped me of skin, remember that? Peeled me like a chicken so I'd feel the punishments with every nerve end. Then she hurled me into my own private hell for a year, that I might suffer for my disobedience. And how long ago was that, dear 'Mas?"

"Wh-What?" the mage stuttered. He couldn't look away, hypnotized like a bird before a serpent. "Uh, it was a-a year—"

"It *wasn't!*" the monster shrieked. The banshee wail stabbed into Candlemas's brain. "A year passed! And another! And a third! Years longer than my sentence, when every day, every minute was a seething torment of agony! Polaris *forgot* me!"

"But, but how—"

"I escaped! I grew this hide you see. I formed a whole skin from the rock walls that were my prison. I clad myself in stone, unpierceable, unstoppable. I became this hideous creature to escape the world of fiends, to enter the world of men, to get my *revenge!*"

"But you were—"

"Beautiful?" the flint monster thundered. "Ravishing! Gorgeous! Lusted after by men, envied by women! And look at me now!"

Candlemas remembered.

While he had been steward, responsible for the outbuildings and lands around Castle Delia, inside was another official, the castle chamberlain, responsible for the kitchens, dining halls, wine cellars, guest rooms, and great hall. A vibrant, brilliant, dashing mage with a cascade of beautiful red hair and glowing skin, a woman in love with herself, and the image in her mirror. A woman grown bored with her duties, who'd picked fights with Candlemas, plagued him at his work, and finally trapped him into ever-more dangerous and foolish bets, with the barbarian Sunbright as their pawn.

And all the while, the chamberlain had plotted to steal the seat of Lady Polaris, until the white-haired archwizard's iron hand clamped down, peeled the living skin from her chamberlain's flesh, and she cast her servant into hell—to be forgotten.

And driven insane. . . .

"Sysquemalyn, I . . ." Candlemas moaned. He didn't know whether to plead, or offer pity, or run for his life. "Sys, you must understand. I didn't know Polaris kept you locked there. I've been away from Castle Delia. I left years ago, and never looked back. I assumed Polaris—"

"You assumed *wrong!*" The hellspawn reared against the summer sky and hooked hands like eagle talons over him as she screamed, "You didn't care! And for that, you *die!*"

The pudgy mage just barely threw up Valdick's forcecage before sizzling chain lightning, some variant of Volhm's chaining, exploded around him. Electric bolts scorched the air, charging it with ozone. They struck Candlemas's shield so hard he was rocked to his knees, felt the charred earth blistering hot under him, felt the temperature rise within the cage by hundreds of degrees. He'd cook unless he dispelled the forcecage, but Sysquemalyn—she might as well be Shar, the Lady of Loss and Anger—loomed and waited. And prepared another spell, for she shrieked from a gash of a mouth like a cleft in broken rock.

"Like that, dear 'Mas? Wait until I set your bones afire to burn within you! Wait until I boil your eyes in their sockets, till I curdle your brain! You'll live three years of my pain in the longest seconds of your short life!"

Candlemas scrambled to his feet, and banged his head on an invisible section of forcecage. It was so hot it seared his bald pate and made him yelp. Yet he realized part of the cage was missing. She'd actually unconjured his spell!

Wondering at her awesome power, he stumbled backward over scorched earth, found wheat burning everywhere from the lightning. Smoke roiled to the sky at all hands. Vaguely he hoped his rust-cure spell, his precious work of three long years, escaped the havoc.

Then he prayed he'd escape alive. Sysquemalyn pouted and blew out cheeks like split rocks.

A stinking cloud of yellow-green gas enveloped Candlemas. Instantly he retched on the poison. His head wanted to explode for sneezing, his eyes watered, he gasped and gagged and choked for air. He flapped his arms, shambled left and right, but the cloud followed him like a harpy. Then he was breathing it, and vomiting at the same time, and choking on his vomit. He burned, for the cloud contained acid. His scalp and hands and nose and ears prickled, grew stippled with blood. To open his eyes would blind him. Already he felt pinpoints of acid in his eyes like the claws of tiny imps.

In his darkness came a grating laugh, "Like the smell? I lived with it for months at a time, when the air in hell was too foul to breath or burn! Taste it! Enjoy it!"

The mage's blundering feet left soil, squished in mud, and with tearful gratitude he splashed into the stream that cut the valley. Bathing his aching face and bleary eyeballs, he tried desperately to think of a spell—any spell—to drive Sysquemalyn away, or else cover his escape. A levitation spell might float him out of range, or a shadow door let him wriggle away. Even Undine's door, with no idea of his destination, would be enough. Perhaps he had a chance. He didn't hear her insane laughter.

Heat belched all around him. Brimstone bubbled just under his nose. He was afire. His smock ignited, as did the skin on his elbows and knees. He screamed at the sudden pain, and forced his eyes open to see this new attack, to get away.

The water was gone. Instead, the creek bed roiled with black, sticky tar. Huge gas pockets burped sulfur. Things charred and long dead floated on the surface. The tar was near boiling, and Candlemas was elbow- and hock-deep in it. It stuck to his face and neck, and burned where it touched. He wailed with fright and agony as he plucked himself free and grabbed for the shore.

The monster Sysquemalyn was there to meet him. He grabbed gummy grass near her craggy, twisted feet. "Hot, dear 'Mas?" the monster cooed. "Let me cool you."

A hand like a knot of thorns closed on his arm. He tried to yank free, but could not. The flint hand was powerful as a chain yoked to oxen, and it dragged him on tarry elbows and knees across burnt grass and ashes. At first Candlemas felt nothing, though the hand smoked on his upper arm. Then he saw it was not smoke, but ice mist. Frost dusted his bicep, then ice. The chill spread down his arm until it was numb. Steam rose where ice met hot tar, with Candlemas's flesh trapped between. He struggled to get his feet under him, to rise, but the monster dragged him like an anchor. When she let go, he collapsed onto the dirt path between smoldering crops. The whole sky was black now, or so it seemed to his seared eyeballs under tar-heavy brows.

"Sys, please . . ."

"No pleases, please," mocked the monster. She loomed against the sky like a lightning-killed pine. "Nothing can save you. You know you'll die, don't you? But not soon, not fast. A little at a time." She lifted her splayed foot and stamped down hard.

Candlemas couldn't move his numbed arm, and the foot crashed down like a boulder off a mountain. He heard fingers break and twist, felt the stamping vibration through the ground more than through his shoulder, which burned as if afire. Writhing, kicking gluey feet to roll away, he glanced at his arm and shuddered, almost sick. The flesh was not just chilled, it was frozen solid, dead forever. Broken in a dozen places, held together by skin.

"I bit your arm off once, remember?" From the scratchy throat issued—almost—the soft cooing wheedle the beautiful Sysquemalyn had employed years before, "Had it torn off by a yellow fiend, actually. That jolt will seem the gentlest caress after a day or two."

"Please," Candlemas wept with pain, "please, Sys. What do you want?"

"*Want?*" A mad shriek again. The claws flew high over the bald shining head. "Death, in all its forms, to all my foes!"

With a wildcat wail she stabbed down, fingertips sparkling. Candlemas was hoicked into the air, pulled in five directions as if by wild horses, and spun wildly. The world became a blur with dozens of flint monsters craning over him keening a death chant. He felt blood surge in his head, saw his vision cloud, saw blood squirt from his sundered arm. When Sysquemalyn suddenly shrieked a halt, the mage stopped so quickly his legs broke. Waves of pain and nausea rolled over, and suffocated him.

More frightening, Sysquemalyn vacillated between sane and insane, shrieking one minute, cooing the next as if playing her own games. She might torture him for days, heal him as needed, then continue. For years, even, her thirst for revenge unquenched.

A coo, "That's three limbs. What do to with the fourth? Smite the skin with exploding boils, perhaps?"

Hanging in mid-air, three limbs distorted, Candlemas knew he couldn't escape. He could only live and take it. To fight was useless.

At least in this form.

Biting his tongue, Candlemas reached for the only escape he could imagine outside death. Yet it was a form of death, for what he planned would leave him as something else. If he survived.

But pain tore at his mind, and soon he'd lose his reason. Become a babbling horror like Sysquemalyn, hung between the world and sanity.

Reaching deep inside, Candlemas conjured words to a spell he'd never attempted, wasn't even sure he remembered. It was long ago he'd read of it, but now it came back, like opening a cobwebbed drawer to find a diamond sparkling within. Or a scalpel.

Grinding his teeth against pain, he grunted the weird, twisted sounds of Quantoul's selfmorph.

The change was instant. An observer wouldn't have known if Candlemas truly changed, or merely swapped himself with some other-worldly horror. For the thing that suddenly hung in air was a purple granite cone taller than Sysquemalyn. Its bottom was hollow and ringed with savage teeth. Tentacles dangled and flapped. Two blind eyes like milky pearls started from its side.

And hating everything on this plane, the windghost attacked.

The flint monster never recoiled, or even ducked the hideous apparition. Its hate burned just as hot. Flint claws met granite cone, and for a few moments the air was filled with screams, scratching, and scrabbling. Then, quick as thought, the monster Sysquemalyn drove two hands like spears through the windghost's hide. Stone-hard organs and a many-chambered heart were rent like rocks in a crusher. Torn from its body, the tiny brain died.

Candlemas didn't die with it, for the mage's consciousness was gone, obliterated by the polymorph spell. For everything, including that keen brain, had changed with the spell.

Sysquemalyn was left with a stinking heap of purple rubble in a scorched field marred with tar and sulfur and blood. Yet even death could not satisfy her rage, and the gore-spattered monster slashed and stamped and tore at the ruined carcass, screaming, "I want to kill him again! I want him dead again! Again, *again!*"

All that remained to mark Candlemas's life and work was the blight-curing spell, quietly percolating at the edges of the valley, quietly dispelling the poisonous rust, then passing over the hill and jumping to other fields. And on and on, to the horizon and beyond.

* * * * *

"We halt this fight!" Thornwing crowed. Beside her, Blinddrum nodded. "And all others! There is no more need for battle!"

"What?"

"Are you mad?"

"Who made you chief?"

"Get out of the ring!"

Voices rose all around, a cacophony.

"Sunbright challenged every fighter! He—"

"He did, and he fought, and he defeated *us!*" the swordswoman shouted them down. "And by beating us, he has defeated the whole tribe!" More noise, objections, calls for quiet and dignity, questions of custom, but Thornwing plowed on. "Blinddrum and I are the best fighters in the tribe. None would dispute that. Yet Sunbright Steelshanks, son of Sevenhaunt and Monkberry of the Raven Clan, defeated us both. And by that act, he defeated all of us! So he need fight no more."

Grumbling, growling, cursing, yet many agreed with the logic while others pondered it, weighed it against tradition. Even old Iceborn admitted he'd never thought of a challenge in that light, but it made sense. To beat the best was to beat them all.

Magichunger kept one wary eye on Knucklebones as he bawled, "What of his sentence of death? Pronounced by Owldark?"

"Owldark is dead," rumbled Blinddrum, "and with him his sentence. I don't remember the reason for the sentence anyway."

"A vision!" crowed an elder woman. "Owldark saw Sunbright standing over us, a bloody sword in his hand and all of us dead. Smoke and fire filled the horizon, and even the reindeer were slaughtered, and the son of Sevenhaunt the cause of it all!"

Superstitious, Blinddrum deferred to the quicker-thinking Thornwing. She tossed back her horsetail, lifted her thin arm so sweat glistened in the firelight, and called, "Owldark had many visions, and he had brain madness! Yes, listen to me! We all know he blacked out, fell in the cookfires many times. In the end, he led us here, to misery. Then he wandered the wasteland, and was eaten by wild dogs. Owldark was a good man, but not all his visions rang true! And so I dismiss his vision of Sunbright."

"And we need a shaman, and have none," Blinddrum added. "The sacred fire is out, and we cannot council until our shaman reignites it."

"Sunbright himself stamped it out!" objected Magichunger.

The big swordmaster had no answer. Thornwing merely waved her hand in dismissal. Despite her attempt at severity, Knucklebones sniggered at Magichunger's indignant glare. She turned one good eye on Sunbright. The pale shaman swayed on his feet, but stood. Her heart swelled in her breast for such a man, who'd risk his own life and dignity to save these people, fickle and ungrateful though many were. Yet she wouldn't have wagered money on how this argument would end.

"If we can't council," objected Rattlewater, "then what are we doing now?"

"Talking! So shut up!" old Tulipgrace snapped. That drew a laugh.

"No!" countered Leafrebel. "If we only talk, not council, then nothing we decide matters! It's just wind off the sea."

There was more argument, much more, going on so long Magichunger let the borrowed sword point to the ground. Exhausted in body, Sunbright sat at his mother's feet like a child. Yet his spirit sang as his people debated, invoking custom after custom. Sniffing at Magichunger, Knucklebones sat primly by Sunbright and took his cold hand. Others built up the fire, and some fetched pipes with carefully hoarded sumac and willow bark to smoke, as if this were a proper council.

Forestvictory made a speech. She talked at length about similar earth-shaking arguments from the past. Other tribesfolk who'd been driven out decades or centuries ago. Some who'd returned and brought disaster, others who came empty-handed and furthered salvation. She talked a long time, lulling her audience with sonorous words. When she finished, there was long quiet. Children had nodded off, heads pillowed on parents' laps. Even Knucklebones yawned, and covered her mouth, inadvertently clicking her brass knuckledusters against her white teeth.

In the long silence, Thornwing stood up, steel sword in hand. She was framed by a yellowing sky, for the tribe had talked through the night, and when she flung it high, it flashed in dawn light. The swordwoman's raspy voice carried to everyone, mesmerizing them. "I say this! If Sunbright is driven out again, I shall follow him! He's disrupted our lives by returning, and that is good, for we were useless as seals on ice pack. Chosen by blood and by the gods, Sunbright has recalled what we live for, who we have been, and who we should be. If he goes, I go, as does Blinddrum. A tribe of three living the old ways is better than a herd marching off a cliff because they're too blind to see. I say this with *blood!*" And she slashed the sword across her palm and held up the dripping hand.

Without a word, Blinddrum took the sword, slashed his palm, and clasped Thornwing's. Forestvictory rose, laid flesh to sword, and clasped. Her lover, Starrabbit, followed. Then Archloft and Mightylaugh, and Goodbell, who carried her sleepy children forward, slit their fingers, and clutched them to her bosom. So many people joined they clasped in a mob. Rightdove joined. Old Iceborn was helped up and joined, though he had to slash his withered hands three times to draw blood. Then Tulipgrace. Rattlewater, Leafrebel, and many others, but not all.

Magichunger and three dozen tribesfolk remained outside the ring. Finally Thornwing called, "You'll not join us?"

"No. Not yet," Magichunger hedged. "But we'll abide by the majority."

Thornwing nodded in acceptance, lowered her gory hand, as did the rest. "Then it's decided" she said. "Sunbright is returned to the tribe, alive and under no sentence. And shaman, for we need one and he has the gift. Sunbright, welcome back. What need we do?"

Painfully, with help from his lover and his mother, Sunbright Steelshanks rose and faced them all, squinting in the now bright daylight. "Friends, I thank you," he said. "As you see, the gods send us a new day for a new beginning, but it is not my place, as shaman, to tell you what to do, but simply to read the signs and advise. To talk, we must council. So I shall gather the proper materials, say the chants, and light the sacred fire. Then, *together,* we'll decide our future."

Chapter 11

The common hut was empty and cool, and smelled of smoke, ash, and sweat. Sunbright used a chicken wing to sweep the fire pit radially. Knucklebones squatted on her heels and watched. "You're fussy as a nursemaid," she said.

The shaman smoothed dirt, moved tiny stones, and said, "The fire must be laid just so, with the lines matching the compass and the tip pointing to the Sled, our northernmost star. Shamans are fussy. Ask my mother, who lived with one."

The one-eyed thief frowned as he trickled grass in a triangular pattern, and gradually built a cone. "What I mean is, you take this shaman role seriously," she said. "I thought a shaman was just a priest. That you just went through the motions to keep the congregation happy."

"That's a cynical view," he muttered absently. He formed a tiny cone of twigs. "I wish we had blue sweet-grass and not just straw, but it must do."

"I'm not cynical!" she snapped. "Well, perhaps a little. But this mumbo-jumbo—you're just making it up, aren't you? To keep people occupied?"

He stopped, put down his collection of herbs and sticks. "Yes and no," he told her. "Yes, I'm making much of it up. I remember some of my father's invocations, saw a little of what Owldark did, but no, I never had real shaman training. But there's no one to teach me, so I perform as best I can, and improvise the rest. The gods don't mind as long as you're sincere."

Knucklebones cocked one pointed eyebrow, and said, "Isn't it presumptuous to speak for the gods?"

Sunbright sighed, and straightened his tiny fire cone with blunt fingers. "I don't claim to speak for the gods," he said. "If they send me visions and advice, I'll pass it on. I might make mistakes, but someone must be shaman, and I'm chosen by the blood of my forebears and by happenstance. And the gods know our tribe needs help."

"What about me?"

"Hunh?" Sunbright grunted, rocking back on his heels. Sunlight from the open doorway danced with dust motes from his sweeping. Knucklebones's face was hard to see in the shadows, but he knew she was unhappy. "What do you mean? You're my woman, I'm your man. We are together."

"Together with *your* tribe. I feel like an outsider. I *am* an outsider! I share no blood with these people, and now you're wrapped up in caring for your tribe, which is a giant family with old jokes and stories and songs I don't know."

Sunbright felt a pang at the hurt in her voice. "It's no different than when you had a tribe in the sewers," he said. "Mother and Ox and Rolon and them."

"They're dead, and the children scattered to the winds. My tribe was destroyed! How would you feel if that happened to you?"

Confused by her feminine switches in logic, Sunbright could only reach out and cuddle her close. He felt a tear on his bare shoulder, patted her back like a child's, and said, "I'd feel alone and sad, as I felt when my tribe was lost, but you were kind and stayed with me, even when I was bitter and afraid and angry."

"Yes, I did," she sniffled. "Because I love you."

"Yes, and I love you. Do you feel alone and afraid?"

"I don't . . ." She pulled back to see his face, held it in her small, calloused hands with the many scars, and told him, "I'm not lonely when I'm with you, but suddenly you're not *with* me. You're either arguing with your tribesfolk, or lost in dreamland. I'm alone."

The shaman hugged her, and she squeezed his ribs. "I love you, Knuckle' " he told her softly. "I must help my tribe, but I'll try to keep you close. That's the best I can offer."

"It's enough," she breathed in his ear. "Just don't forget me."

They were quiet a while, until, finally, Sunbright said, "I must start this fire. And I need you to leave."

Her single dark eye flashed at this new betrayal.

Sheepishly, he offered, "I must be alone for the ceremony. There are prayers to Jannath and Amaunator and such. And the fire must be lit at noon, and if the first spark doesn't take I need to wait another day. It's . . ."

"Fussy," the thief supplied. "Very well. I'll wait with your mother. She'll understand, having been a shaman's wife."

An hour later, Sunbright threw aside the rotted hide over the door, cupped his hands, and warbled an ancient cry: "To council! To council! All adults, to council!"

Knucklebones rose from the shade where she'd waited, and smiled at his grin. The shaman gestured with a sooty hand at folks converging from all around.

"Look!" Sunbright beamed. "They've waited all morning to council and talk. To discuss the future and what we should do. It's like zombies rising from their graves to find new life. There's just one thing, though—I need to find us a direction."

The thief squinted at his clouded face, and asked, "Direction for what?"

Sunbright moved aside to let villagers enter the common house. He cast his eyes over the rocky dunes, the brown mountainside, the shabby town in the distance, and the winking sea. "Where we should go," he answered. "No matter what, we can't stay here. I need to seek a vision."

Now the thief frowned. "Isn't that how you lost Whatshisname?" she asked. "Owlfluff?"

"Owldark. Yes. He went into the wasteland to find a new direction, and found only death. Yet I must follow, for we need the truth."

"Fine." Knucklebones shifted her belt on her hips, tugged her silver-wrapped pommel around, and said, "I'll go with you."

"No. A shaman always makes a vision quest alone. Dangerous or not. He needs to escape from distractions to hear the whispers of the gods . . ."

His vision grew distant as he stared at the Channel Mountains running off to the south. He didn't see Knucklebones reach into a flat pocket, slip on her brass knuckledusters, and ball her fists. She cooed, "Sunbright . . . If you can change and improvise customs, so can I."

And hauling back knotty arms, she slammed him in the breadbasket hard, four times in four seconds. Sunbright gasped, clasped his stomach, and doubled over retching.

Knucklebones cooed over his wheezing, "New rule. From now on, a shaman making a vision quest may take one companion to see he doesn't fall headfirst into a hole to be eaten by weasels. How's that sound?"

Sunbright couldn't straighten, but gasped, "I suppose . . . the gods . . . won't object . . ."

"Good." She kissed his horsetail and sashayed off, saying, "I'll go pack."

* * * * *

Dreaming, Sunbright flew.

He spiraled upward from the wastelands. Yellow rock and sand merged with green-brown mountains in the west, grasslands in the east and south, the silver-white sea in the north. His tribe's wretched camp was no more than an anthill, a smear of sticks amidst rocks. In a hollow of the Anchor, he saw broken shells in the nest of a bald eagle. Nimble chamois jumped along a sheer slope. A whale spouted in the sea, blew spray onto a boat with slanted sails. A mule train plodded across the plains, a small dog yapped after bounding antelope. Buzzards flapped lazily over Patrician Peak, riding the updrafts.

As he rose higher, he saw into the depths of the fetid Myconid Forest at the foot of the Channel Mountains, where fungusmen with stone spears tracked a lazy giant lizard across a swamp. He heard the dinosaur hoot in disdain. Beyond the mountains, in the Marsh of Simplicity, he saw fishermen spook ducks from the water with slapping sticks so the birds plowed into hidden nets and squawked. A girl caught a salmon from a rotting dock, and it almost yanked her into the water before she landed it. In a shipyard in Zenith, two fire giants caulked a careened boat with thunderous mauls. Orcs left the forest near the Nauseef Flow and crept toward a cabin where peasants tilled turnips. In the Columns of the Sky, two rams butted heads until one tumbled into a snowy crevasse. An elven couple made love in a glade near the head of the Gillan River. On the tundra, gaunt reindeer cropped moss along a glacier while the high sun sparkled on ice.

Sunbright saw all this and wondered. Was it real? Were these things true, and happening right now? Or did he merely imagine them? If all these events were true, then a human family would be slaughtered by marauding orcs along the Nauseef Flow, and that ram would starve to death in the icy crevasse. Yet he could do nothing about either threat. Visions could be a curse, he was learning.

But if the visions were not true, then did this dream mean anything, or were the images as worthless as marsh gas bubbling up in his brain? And why did he fly? Where was he bound?

Black flickered at the edge of his imagination. A black with a sheen of purple. A raven's wing. He flew as a raven, totem of his clan. Perhaps this was a true vision! Or perhaps it was just more brain-gas. Either way, he gave in and trusted the totem. He watched, and waited for truth, for falsehood, or for nothing at all.

Wings canted and the world banked from horizon to horizon. Sunbright's stomach lurched. The Channel Mountains passed underneath, then the floating enclave of Quagmire, then a grove of drooping birches along the Watercourse where he'd once stood with Knucklebones. The Watercourse was placid in late summer, still and empty, idly rippling instead of roaring as in spring when the tribes gathered to fish salmon. Then the river fell behind, a silver trickle near Sunbright's raven tail.

All was vaguely familiar, for the land turned to rolling grasslands dotted with horses, antelope, and deer. In a hollow between hills a mother mammoth and two yearlings lolled away the afternoon heat, their shaggy hair clotted with old mud and manure. More mammoths swayed and sauntered to the south, yanking up whole bushes with clever trunks and cramming them in their mouths. From a hill, a lone saber-toothed tiger crouched, only ear and eyes showing. Even flies settling on its rump couldn't elicit a twitch.

Sunbright knew this scene from his childhood, for once a year the tundra barbarians crossed the Narrow Sea and met their southern cousins to fish and fight and joke and carouse and flirt. But of these southern folk, the clans of Tortoise and Saber-Tooth and Hellbender, he saw no sign. No one in the tribe knew where they were, another link to the past gone missing.

The phantom raven flapped on. Or perhaps it was a real bird, and Sunbright only saw through its eyes. Gray lumps in the distance rolled higher to form the Barren Mountains, with the dense High Forest at their feet. Yellow grasslands met gray mountains, met green forest. The whole world was laid out like Jannath's Quilt. The shaman wondered about his destination, if any.

Then the picture turned half over, and he stared straight down. At the crux of three lands, grass, mountains and forest, stood the last mountain, Sanguine Mountain, so called because it bled red rust from a deep crevice in the rainy season. The phantom raven dived straight for the bloody crevice, until red-shot blackness filled his vision.

Faster they flew, and faster, until the world blurred and wind sizzled in the man's eyes and made them water. Gasping, mewling, pleading, he urged the bird to rise, to bank, to shy away, but the linked visionaries bored through air like an arrow. Soon only black loomed. Sunbright heard wind along a rocky ridge. There was no escape.

They struck, smashing in a bloody gobbet of feathers on granite.

"*Unnnhhh . . .*" Sunbright teetered and fell. He banged his shoulder, felt the world roll away, as if swept in an avalanche, then tumbled on his face, tearing skin off his forehead. Frantically, he clawed for a hold, broke fingernails on stone.

Something caught his waist, his leg, his arm. Strong hands like iron, but small, cool, and capable. He stopped falling.

Shivering, sweating, Sunbright opened his eyes, was stabbed by sunlight. Something blocked the sun. A hand. Knucklebones's.

"Are you all right? You were sitting on that mound, still as death, then you started groaning. I couldn't catch you before you fell," she said. "You're bleeding!"

Gently, the elf-woman eased him onto his back. She ran for a blanket, and wrapped him snugly to stop his shaking. From a canteen she tilted water on his face, wiped away sweat and blood.

Sunbright craned his head to see, to orient himself. Oh, yes. They were six or seven miles south of the village, in the worst of the wasteland. Three days ago Sunbright had drunk his last sip of water, eaten the last scrap of meat, and mounted a low mound that gave a view in all directions. Then he'd lowered his head, and prayed, and waited, while Knucklebones patiently tended camp and potted rats with a sling. Then, after three days of broiling in the sun and shivering by night, a vision had come.

"I know—I know where we're to go." Sunbright creaked. He could barely speak, for his tongue was swollen from thirst. Knucklebones cooed and trickled water in his mouth. But his thirst for knowledge was greater. "Sanguine Mountain, with a cleft like blood, where the grasslands end, and rise to mountain and forest."

"And what will we find there?" she asked, bandaging the scrape on his forehead.

"I've no idea," he rasped, then accepted more water. "It's the place. A raven showed me. Our fate lies there."

Knucklebones frowned, blew out her cheeks, combed his hair with her fingers, and said, "I believe you. I just hope you can convince the tribe."

* * * * *

Rengarth Barbarians were never easily convinced.

They argued for days until the shaky rafters of the common house rang. Smoke from sacred pipes was blown back and forth by shouts, accusations of cowardice and betrayal, threats and challenges, fistfights, scoldings, tears, pleas. . . . Talk went in circles and off on tangents. Stories were recounted and corrected. Prayers were offered.

Time and again, the argument came down to someone shouting, "We must go because we can't stay here! To live on foreign soil will be the death of our tribe!"

"All right," bellowed Magichunger, the loudest, "but why go the path Sunbright suggests? He's not a real shaman! He knows nothing! The gods wouldn't speak to him. We might as well follow a blind mole as go his route."

An angry chorus shouted him down while others agreed. More shouting went on outside where the walls of the common house had been removed. Anyone who'd killed an enemy or born a child could speak in council, and over three hundred barbarians gathered every night. Someone snatched the speaking stick from Magichunger and thrust it into Sunbright's hands.

"Tell them again!"

Reluctantly, Sunbright held up the speaking stick, just a plain stick with a skunk's skull atop. Yet when raised, only the wielder could speak. As if by magic, the council hushed. Sunbright suppressed a sigh. "I don't claim special knowledge," he said evenly, "but I made a vision quest, asking the gods for a destination. I was rewarded with a dream of Sanguine Mountain. The message—from the gods, not me—is clear. We should go there." He lowered the stick as if it were suddenly too heavy.

Someone amended, "And we can't stay here!"

"But how do we know?" someone hollered, and the wrangling ran around the circle again.

Sunbright slumped on the floor of the hut. Cross-legged, his knees toasted at the council fire, yet toes dug his kidneys. The room was packed, and steamy as a sauna with charged bodies. Knucklebones, who'd been silent for days, took his hand to rest on her knee. "How much longer will this go on?" she asked quietly.

"Forever, I fear," sighed the shaman. "You can't believe how hardheaded barbarians can be. My people don't remove rock slides from a trail, they just lower their heads and bash through."

"I believe it, but tell me . . ." the thief said, more loudly now because of the noise. ". . . that blood oath that Thornwing started that night. Most of the tribe swore with her, right? But what did they swear to do?"

"Hunh?" Sunbright grunted, rubbed his burning eyes, and cudgeled his brain. "Umm . . . They swore to . . . follow me if I were driven from the tribe."

"Then go."

Sunbright peered at her stupidly, as if she'd spoken a foreign tongue.

"Go." Her hand made a pushing motion. "Say you're packing and leaving tomorrow, and going to Sanguine Mountain. The ones who swore the oath must follow, mustn't they?"

The shaman juggled the new idea in his head: he had as much trouble accepting new customs as anyone. "They only swore that if I were driven out . . ."

"Driven out, walk out, there's little difference," Knucklebones said as she nudged him to his feet. "Just say it. Anything to stop this blather! We'll be rotted to skeletons before this bunch agrees on whether snow falls down or up!"

Sunbright untangled his legs to rise, mumbling, "On the tundra, it sometimes blows sideways—Ouch!" Knucklebones slapped his leg to keep his attention focussed.

The shaman stood a long time with his hand out, indicating he wished the speaking stick, but many people were heard before he got it. Finally grasping it high, he stated, "Come dawn I begin packing. The next dawn I leave for Sanguine Mountain. I ask those who took the blood oath to follow me to . . . follow me." He handed the stick to someone, and plunked down.

If Knucklebones expected that thunderclap to still the audience, she was disappointed. Shouting erupted louder than before. A dozen hands grabbed for the stick. Tears flowed. At some taunt, Magichunger whirled and punched a man. A brawl erupted among the hotheads. Folks cheered and booed.

Crawling around the fire, Sunbright spoke in Forestvictory's ear. The woman, big all over with forearms like hams, requested the speaking stick and got it. She held it high and shouted, and gradually the brawl subsided. Men and women untangled, rubbed bloody noses with skinned knuckles. In the hush, Forestvictory proclaimed, "Sunbright has suggested we need a trail chief to oversee the journey. I volunteer unless someone else wants the chore. No? Then I too will pack at dawn, and leave the next dawn. Anyone who goes with us must be ready."

She relinquished the speaking stick, and more people spoke, some passionately, some with anger, some calmly. There was wrangling whether the blood oath applied, but as more tribesfolk said their piece, it seemed the oath was enough to move them. Many agreed to go. A handful, led by Magichunger, held out, but when asked what they intended to do instead, gave no answer.

"Is the tribe to split then? Such a thing must not be!" a woman began to wail.

Sunbright gestured, took the stick, waited for silence. Finally he said, "So some will go, and some will stay. It makes my heart heavy to think the tribe may split, for together we are strong, singly we are weak. Yet I would ask one thing. The path we travel will be dangerous. We might meet orcs, renegade soldiers, bandits, marauding animals, monsters—anything. I think we should elect a war chief to oversee our defense. And for that task, a hard and thankless one, I suggest Magichunger."

For the first time, silence followed a proclamation. Big, broad Magichunger rubbed his nose, scratched blood from his red beard, glared at Sunbright across the smoky hut, and spat, "You don't fool me. It's a trick so I'll go along."

"No trick," said Sunbright. "You're our best fighter, after Blinddrum and Thornwing, and by tradition neither of them can be war chief. I know we've never been friends, and you resent my barging into the tribe, but most of us will leave. It would be a great boon if you helped. Certainly we can use your scrapping smarts and good right arm, and those of your friends."

The burly man looked for a trap, or some way to rebut the gentle request. "As war chief," he grumbled, "I lead the fighters in skirmishes? And when attacked, everyone must do as I say until the enemy is beaten off?"

Sunbright nodded, as did older folks recalling times of war. Magichunger turned, and muttered to his friends. They grumbled, fretted, and argued while the rest of the tribe waited. Finally Magichunger turned, rubbed his nose again as if embarrassed. "We'll go," he growled.

* * * * *

Walking hand-in-hand under desert-bright stars, Knucklebones said, "You were very clever in there, Sunbright."

"Not so clever," he said. "Just desperate to get my tribe off this ash heap. It reminds me of the worst corners of the hell I almost didn't escape, but at least then I left my enemies behind."

"What?" The part-elf looked up, but his hawk's face was only a silhouette against stars. "What do you mean, enemies?" she asked.

"Barbarians hold grudges forever, Knucklebones. From before birth even, for we're born into feuds going back to the day New Man rose from the ice. Some spend their lives plotting revenge, and will throw their lives away getting it. With us wild folk, the heart often overrules the head.

"Magichunger will always be my enemy. And his friends and family too. I must beware his knife in my back, awake and asleep. Many others don't like my new customs, or new twists to old ones, and for us to survive will take magic, I fear."

"Why fear?"

"Magic is taboo. A fear of magic runs strong."

"But you purified their drinking water! Everyone saw it, and appreciated it."

"I 'blessed' the water, I did not bewitch it. Not for my own gain, mocking the gods' power, but acting for the good of the people. That's why I said a shaman's no good without a tribe to work for.

"And now I'd have us cross our ancestral lands. I don't know . . . the grasslands—prairie—is stronger than the tundra, but the life drain happens there too. We may need magic to survive, and . . . I don't know what I'll do."

"You'll return to your mother's hut and sleep," the thief said, standing on tiptoes to kiss his cheek. "Then we rise and pack to embark on a new adventure!"

Chuckling, Sunbright hugged her off the ground and kissed her soundly.

Chapter 12

Toch swung his club backhanded and smashed Kab across the snout. Tumbling down the hillside, rolling in dust, the wounded orc sprawled to a halt, clutched a blood-spurting nose, and slobbered, "What that for?"

The larger orc wasn't finished. Toch crabbed down the slope, raised his obsidian-studded club, and thumped Kab repeatedly.

"No noise, I says! Quiet, I says! But you, you burp at wrong time and chase off game!"

Toch vented his anger with more blows. Other orcs squatted on their heels and picked at stones, or scratched lice, careful to avoid catching hell. Kab wailed and howled and screamed, thrashing limbs, as Toch beat and kicked every inch of the orc's gray, warty skin.

Finally Toch's arm tired, and he threw the club down in disgust. With filthy, cracked nails he scaled the slope again, plunked his tusked jaw atop the rise, and glared at the world. The goats had bounded up to higher slopes, out of reach. Toch was so hungry he could eat rocks. Perhaps he should beat Kab more, tenderize the meat, then eat it. It would teach the others to follow orders and maintain silence on the hunt. He hoped a female gave birth soon. Baby orcs made excellent stew, and he could keep it all to himself. That was one good reason for dragging along females. They were always pregnant.

Stomach growling, Toch stood on the hummock under an overcast sky, and tried to guess which way to go next. Like many Icebeast Orcs, he was tall, almost six feet, with long limbs and hands that could break bones. With the approach of winter, gray hair thickened on his hide like a mountain pony's. His head was a rat's nest of lank black hair, but he still wore a steel helmet and a tattered smock of stout gray wool that retained the faded sigil of the One King, a red hand with fingers splayed. The paint had mostly cracked off.

He remembered, vaguely, belonging to the One King's army. How the chief orcs had said they'd be well-fed, have huts and villages instead of wilderness and badlands, how they'd live among humans and share their wealth as long as they didn't kill anyone. Details were fuzzy, but he remembered fine food: fresh-killed beef, apples from orchards, wriggling eels from stocked ponds, even real bread such as orcs could never bake, and whole barrels of wine that made his head spin and his feet crazy. He licked gray lips at the memory. Life had been good under the One King. Lots of food, steel weapons, not much fighting, plenty of naps, fires under roofs at night.

Then it ended. They claimed the One King was dead, burned by a dragon, or overrun by enemies. Or that he'd gone to sleep in the catacombs. Or that he'd shunned the orcs because they didn't work and fight and kill enough to suit his bloodthirsty ways. Or that they were too quarrelsome for his ideas of peace. Memories were muddled in his dim brain, but the One King had been good.

Now he was chief of a troop in the Dementia Range, a hard life even for orcs. The land was difficult to cross, either naked rock or stunted cedars and heather and gorse, impossible tangles that forced the orcs to game trails or open spaces. The troop had done well raiding around Ascore and Sepulcher and Cantus. Too well. Men and dwarves banded together to root the orcs from the forest, even sending hated war dogs. Toch's troop retreated to the foothills of the Dementia, but found little game.

Goats were swift and bouncy, remorhaz and condors inedible, wolves and mammoths wary, humans nonexistent, and cave trolls considered orcs slave-fodder. So, after a frustrating summer in the north, Toch led his band out of the mountains, but the southern forests were infested with elves, and the prairie too open. Now where? West, into unknown lands? Or perhaps he should reduce the force, kill the older orcs and women, dry their meat, and whip the able fighters across the prairie to fat lands in the far south. They had to go somewhere, always roving as orcs had for centuries, wandering over the next hill, scrounging what they could.

He sighed like a bellows, licked Kab's blood off his fingers. It was hard being leader. . . .

"Uh! Look! There!" grunted an orc. "He comes! He comes!"

Toch whirled, and almost fell off the hill.

On a mount behind Toch stood the One King.

The king was human, but his skin had a yellow cast that denoted orcish blood, orcs always believed. The man was tall, black-haired and bearded, with a long, solemn face that was as cold and pitiless as a corpse's. He wore silvery robes with a splayed hand red as blood, and a silver crown studded with gems black as coal. The Hornet, people in Tinnainen had called him, like a black-yellow insect in man's form.

"Orcs, hear me," trumpeted the king. He kicked at his long hem, and walked down a trail through waist-high gorse. Two-score orcs fell back in awe and fear. Toch tripped down the slope. Dimly he remembered the etiquette beaten into him by orc chiefs. Picking up his studded club, he swatted the orcs to kneel, then knelt himself.

"My children," rolled the king's words. "Umm . . . My heart lifts at the sight of you again. I have returned to the world. As before, I, uh, come in peace for all the speaking races. Again there will be contentment and, uh, peace throughout the lands—"

"And food?" The words escaped Toch. He trembled, fearing death for interrupting the king.

"Uh, yes, food! Much food! Mead halls full of it. Tables groaning under the weight of golden turkeys stuffed with chestnuts and, uh, crusty brown bread! Wine by the gallon, rich and red as blood! And jam tarts with fluffy pastry, and fruits, such as melons . . ."

Murky eyes shining, the orcs slavered as the king rambled through a menu. Then he talked more of peace, and the good old times, but returned to food when their attention flagged. Finally, he summed up, ". . . but before there can be peace—or melons or figs or butter—we must take up arms, spread south, and attack the outposts of the Netherese Empire! As before, the Neth are our enemies! You, uh, what is your name? Toch? Toch, you are to lead your band south, cross the Barren Mountains to the Sanguine that flows red with rust, and punish the tall folk of the prairie! You will know them by their golden horsetails that shine in the sun! Find them, and make them suffer, for one of them assaulted your king in the old days!"

"Tall folk. Horsetails. A-salted." As trained years ago, Toch repeated the commands without fully comprehending them. He did understand that they should ambush blond people in the south. Clear enough. "Steel, majesty.

We need steel to kill. They have shining blades. . . ." He offered the obsidian-studded club as evidence.

As kings should, the One King anticipated his subjects' request. Gesturing the orcs to shuffle backward, the tall human sketched a door shape in the air, and a door appeared. Orcs *oohed* and *ahhed*. The king pulled the wooden handle. With a clatter and a clang, hand weapons cascaded out of nowhere: war axes, mattocks, cleavers, falchions, stabbing spears, all good steel sharpened and blackened against rust. Orcs scrambled for the treasure, but Toch kicked them aside. Stooping, he grabbed a short-handled war club of two lethal iron spikes shaped like buffalo horns. The tough hickory and heavy steel hefted nicely in his gnarled hand.

"Take them with my blessings, and go!" bellowed the king. "Go south and harry the tall ones with horsetails! You will meet others with my sigil."

Flicking a hand into the phantom closet, the king withdrew a silk roll, a paint brush, and a crock sealed with wax. Toch remembered this from the old days too. He shook out the silk, found it a cut-out pattern for the red hand such as decorated his faded tunic.

"Garb yourselves to show respect," the One King commanded. "Join others bearing my seal, and spread the word to all outcasts to punish our enemies! Do not disobey, else I visit you by night, and cut out your hearts."

Banging shut the magic-shifted cabinet, the king raised both hands in the air. The orcs cowered and whimpered, but the king only crossed his breast and disappeared like a soap bubble.

Orcs muttered and grunted, but with the king gone, their awe soon evaporated, and they squabbled over the weapons. Bloody-nosed Kab took a fancy to a cleaver clutched by a female. He picked up a rock, bashed in her skull, and snatched the weapon. "With this, I kill enemies! I become chief!" he said as he shook it high and cackled to the mountaintops.

From behind, Toch swung, buried an iron spike in Kab's temple. The orc dropped dead, and Toch wrenched loose his weapon, pleased at how well it killed. He kicked Kab's body hard several times, then spat on it.

To the rest of the tribe, he ordered, "Paint yourselves with the red hand like mine! We go south to kill horse-tails! But first," he kicked Kab's body again, "build a fire! I hunger!"

* * * * *

Far away, in a cave high in a mountaintop, the flinty Sysquemalyn touched the black glistening top of the scrying table. From this stronghold, out of reach of any-one without magic at his disposal, she smoothed the surface and spied on the world. And occasionally stepped into it disguised as the One King.

Using that legend, she chuckled, was brilliance on her part. As with all messiahs, the One King's death had mattered little, for rumors circulated that one day he'd return to lead his people to greater heights.

Of course, Sysquemalyn knew the original king had been a fake; a lich, a long-dead wizard with dreams of glory. Eventually, as always with such petty despots, the "One King" was exposed and killed, and his army fell apart.

Sysquemalyn herself had served in the king's court as a vagabond bard or freebooter named Ruellana. She forgot the details. She'd been keeping an eye on Sunbright, tweaking odds to win her bet with Candlemas. But she knew the One King's ways, had heard his insipid speeches, and remembered that he'd scared the hell out of the Neth. Memories of his short reign lived on, for scrying in nooks and crannies of forgotten lands, the monster-mage had often seen the faded red hand on the worn tunics of bandits, orcs, and other misfits.

So . . . employing a quick disguise, a flowery speech, many promises, a fistful of weapons, and threats of death, almost overnight Sysquemalyn had rejuvenated an army and aimed it like a fire arrow at her enemies. Even now, scores of bloodthirsty villains attacked outposts of the empire, especially the fields and orchards that fed Ioulaum and Specie, where Lady Polaris had homes, and the pastures and forests of Castle Delia, her country manor. Now she'd unleashed orcs upon the Rengarth Barbarians, whom she'd seen trekking across the prairie, bound for Sanguine Mountain, which would soon live up to its name.

"Sunbright will suffer when his people suffer. And Polaris will suffer, wounded in the purse. The whole empire—the whole *world*—will pay for what I've endured! And I, who was Sysquemalyn, will wait until my enemies' lowest ebb. Then shall I strike, and bathe in their blood!"

Cackling, she stroked the tilted black tabletop, located another wandering band of marauders and, donning the disguise of the One King, returned to work.

* * * * *

Having decided to leave the wasteland, the tribe did not depart in two days, or even a week.

In a flurry of activity, people flocked to kill wild game, barter for old cattle and sheep and jerk the meat; to slice hides into straps and pouches and boots; to hunt relatives in town and persuade them to rejoin the tribe; to fashion new weapons and baskets and clothes.

Some were convinced to come, and some dragged. Iceborn, blind and crippled, insisted he was too old to make the journey, wanted only to be left by the fire to die. Tulipgrace had sided with her husband. As shaman, Sunbright argued a whole day that both elders were the lifeblood of the tribe, living history books, indispensable. Sunbright pleaded he would carry both on his back if necessary, but to no avail. The stubborn old folks were tired, and would die soon anyway. So the shaman marched out, climbed a slope, cut down poplar trees with Harvester, dug up spruce roots and sliced rawhide, lashed together an extra-wide travois, and dragged it before the common hut. Entering the dim, round room, he picked up the two bundles of bones that were Iceborn and Tulipgrace and plunked them onto the travois. Standing on tiptoe, he yanked the roof thatch and rotted hides into the council fire so they ignited, and kicked the beams into the pyre. When the common house was consumed by roaring flames, he shouted at Iceborn, "Now will you go with us?"

The old man squinted at the fire, and spat drily, "I suppose, since it's the will of the gods. Or someone."

Finally, after many days, with precious little in hand, but nothing to hold them, the Rengarth Barbarians marched from the wastelands on a bright day in late summer. No one looked back.

By degrees they rounded Anchor Mountain, avoided Scourge and Lachery, and struck west along the Narrow Sea. Pilot whales spouted and leaped high in the water as if encouraging them. Gulls wheeled over their head, and terns flitted after, but finding no food, banked away.

Once, high up in the sky, they spotted a floating city like a man-of-war jellyfish on the clouds. Knucklebones guessed it was Sanctuary. The next morning it drifted south. Sunbright recalled there were pockets in the north so drained of magic that the enclaves could not overpass them, lest they fall. Such was the greed and waste of the Neth.

It took sixteen days to reach the Watercourse, the eastern boundary of the Rengarth's ancestral lands. The tribe camped for nine days to rest and fish, though they caught few. To mark the entrance to their homeland, Sunbright recalled the Victory Dance, which the tribe hadn't danced in years, and stomped the steps clumsily until Forestvictory put him right. The whole tribe rejoiced the night long, laughing for sheer joy even at mistakes.

Packing up, the barbarians marched northwest, never far from the dappled shore of the Narrow Sea, and with every mile, their feet grew lighter, for they walked familiar soil.

By day the tribe sprawled over a mile of grasslands, some four hundred thirty people and a handful of noisy dogs. Their woven baskets of cooking goods and blankets and tools were small, dragged by rawhide shoulder straps on travois, long sticks that striped the grass behind. The poplar poles acted as ridge poles for tents every evening. Rengarth Barbarians usually traveled with much bigger travois hauled by half-wild reindeer, but now they had none. In town they had captured brutish, garbage-eating dogs that they were beating into submission, or eating the untractable ones. Still, even in near-poverty, most of the tribe was glad to be moving again—doing something, anything, instead of rotting.

"So many people!" Knucklebones said once.

"More than I guessed," Sunbright agreed. He leaned into the straps of their travois. His mother marched on one side, his lover on the other. "But once we decided to go, they came from hill and dale. And from town, thank Lady Luck."

"Thank Sunbright," Monkberry put in. "Some would still be lost if you hadn't come and set us on the right path. They'd be rooted in town and on farms, cut off from their rightful heritage."

Sunbright smiled, and said, "I just hope we find a rightful home. This is a great mass of people to cross half a world on the dream of a half-baked shaman."

The women were silent, thinking of the burden Sunbright carried on his mind. Knucklebones said, "By the time we strike Sanguine Mountain, folks won't remember why they came, and they'll be too busy to fuss."

"There's always time for fussing," the shaman moaned, but he brushed any gloom aside and simply trudged on. Like everyone else, he was glad to be moving.

Still, he saw the division in the tribe, and hoped it could heal. Scanning the prairie, he saw that most of the barbarians were blond, but many brown and red heads dotted the plain. That was all right, for the tribe always needed new blood. Fighters wore the traditional warrior's roach and horsetail, non-fighters wore their hair tied back or else loose to their shoulders. All wore hide shirts and tall boots.

Except Magichunger's friends. Fifty or more, designated as guards by the new war chief, continued to wear long hair and beards and town-made shirts and breeches of cloth. The new apparel went against barbarian tradition, but Magichunger's crowd sported it proudly, for it set them apart. There wasn't much Sunbright could do about someone's clothing, so, for now, he ignored the division.

Their biggest problem was food. Twentyscore hardworking people could eat a farm valley to the soil. Here on the prairie grew only some roots and insects, minnows in streams, and the rare bird's nest. Everything big and edible outran them. Hunters armed with longbows and daubed with yellow mud crept far ahead of the tribe. When they could, they downed wily pronghorn antelope, skinny mule deer, and shaggy wild horses. The meat was tough and stringy, with hardly any fat so vitally needed, though the barbarians ate everything except the ears and hooves. Still, meat was scarce, and everyone hungered all the time.

Five days into the ancient lands, luck brought a rampaging mammoth driven insane by brain worms. Hunters and fighters surrounded and hacked at the thing with spears and swords. At the cost of three broken limbs and one death, they downed the beast and feasted for three days on blood, flesh, and organs. The children made a hidey-hole of the skull, and crawled in and out of eye slots giggling. By night, guards drove off skulking wolves and saber-toothed tigers that cried eerily like lost children.

Knucklebones was intrigued by the interconnected life of the tribe, so different from the complex and diverse life in the city. Once she asked, "What are the clans you speak of?"

"The clans?" Sunbright replied, still dragging the travois, the pole ends hissing in the grass. "Children are assigned to clans on their second birthday. They're picked randomly so the families are mixed up, so no family is pitted against another in a feud. It gives the children something to cling to as they grow, another circle besides parents and brothers and sisters. We have, let's see, eight clans: Raven, Elk, Griffon, White Bear, Beluga, Snow Tiger, Thunderbeast, and Gray Wolf. You draw wisdom and strength from your totem animal. In dire straits, I've been visited by ravens with advice."

"What's a beluga?"

"A big fish with a pointed snout."

"What's a thunderbeast?"

"A, uh, big lizard that . . . belches thunder," Sunbright improvised. "I don't really know."

"What can *it* teach you?"

Sunbright turned his head as he surged along. "Why so many questions?"

"I just want to know," Knucklebones said, gazing across the rolling sea of grass. "How does one become a member of the tribe?"

"Marry a member. Be born to it. Ask to join. Or just come in and stay. Some wander in and never leave. After a time, we accept them. Or you can be captured."

"Wife-stealing must make you unpopular with neighbors."

"What else can we do? We're a small tribe, and most related by blood. You can't marry a cousin, it's taboo. The elders would disallow it. So, if you need a wife, or husband, the best way is to hunt a stranger."

"Hunt?"

"Kidnap."

"How do you do it?"

"Oh . . . lie in wait by the side of a road or visit a town or marketplace, pick out someone you fancy, follow them home, stuff them in a hide sack, and carry them off. They're homesick for a while, but get over it eventually. Am I right, mother?"

"You're right, son." Monkberry smiled. "I went for a night swim and took off my shift. Your father must have seen something he liked, because he was waiting when I came out. I broke his nose the first night, but grew to like him, for he was kind. After my first child, I was allowed to visit my parents. Sevenhaunt gave them four wild horses. Considering how I plagued my parents with naughtiness, they thought it a bargain. 'Those horses aren't half as wild as that girl,' said my father. 'Good luck keeping a bridle on her.' " She laughed merrily.

Knucklebones drank in the lore. "Do newcomers get clan animals? Totems?" she asked.

"Their partners'," said Sunbright. "Or they can pick another. Which will you choose? The night owl? The sewer rat? How about the porcupine, because you're so bristly sometimes?"

Knucklebones hoisted her nose in the air and said, "Your totem beast must be the crocodile, with that big mouth. How are people married?"

Sunbright hitched the straps on his shoulder, squinted at the sun and their backtrail, tasted the wind for rain, all while Knucklebone stewed for an answer. Finally he teased, "Mother can tell you."

Knucklebones *tsked.* "Never mind. I don't care to

know," she lied, nose high, then she veered off to inspect an imaginary gully.

Monkberry teased, "I don't think you could stuff her in a hide sack. Though she'd make a fine catch."

"Watch where you step, Mother. You might fall down a hole."

Monkberry laughed.

* * * * *

The tribe walked on, singing and calling, breaking camp by dawn, snatching a quick breakfast, then packing the travois and swaying off. They halted when the sun was two hands above the horizon to assemble their meager camp, though there were only enough tents and blankets to cover the children and elders. They dug fire pits and gathered dry dung, brewed thin tea, heated what meat or bones they had, stewed groundnuts or artichokes they'd gathered, and soon fell asleep, hungry and exhausted.

But the precious hour between supper and slumber was the one Sunbright loved best, for then stories were told. At first only Sunbright related the old familiar tales. *How White Bear Lost His Tail. Why the Sky Burns Gold. How Dima and Nunki Tricked the Frost Giants. How Solenska Won the Heart of Ega.* Yellow firelight reflected from the faces of young and old attending stories funny and sad, romantic and courageous. Sunbright was glad, for those tales were more than entertainment. They taught truth and friendship and honor and love. The stories, more than anything else, formed the history of this proud northern race. Without them, the tribe would just be a collection of strangers.

Gradually, other storytellers arose to fill the starry sky with wonder. Forestvictory, so capable a trail chief, related *Why Whales Live in the Sea.* Crabbranch, quiet and shy, stammered through *The One-Eyed King and his Wife*. Old Iceborn, blind and half deaf, dredged from memory an ancient tale even he'd forgotten, a rousing saga of barbarians warring over *The Magic Spring*. Even Magichunger caught the fever, and hemmed and hawed through *The Two Brothers*.

There were still arguments every day, clashes and squabbles over details from how to hang a strap to how to end a romance, but Sunbright delighted in it, for people discussed, not despaired.

And one night, as Sunbright dozed off from a particularly long day, a voice made his ears perk. A cultured accent from the city. Knucklebones told a story new to the tribe, a long, sad romance about parted lovers who met again in death, a story she called *The Red Knight and the Blue Maiden*.

A short while later, people yawned and turned in. Lying on a bed of grass, Sunbright felt Knucklebones wriggle her spine against his chest for warmth, for they'd given their blankets away, and the autumn nights were chilly. Chuckling, he kissed her pointed ear, and whispered, "I liked your story."

"The tribe didn't." Hurt marred her voice. "They didn't understand it. They didn't get it."

The shaman nibbled her small ear, but she brushed him off. "I don't belong, Sunbright. I don't fit with your people. I never will."

Her wounded tone pained him, so he hugged her close. "Give it time," he told her softly. "People will ask for that story again, once they've thought about it. You're different, but you'll learn our ways—"

"What about *my* ways?" The woman spun in his arms and poked his chest. "I can't become a barbarian, not truly! And I like what I am: human and elf combined, and a damned clever thief to boot! I survived in the gutters of Karsus Enclave, but there's no place for me in this world, or this time. You have your tribe, and every day you grow closer to them. I'm left out in the cold."

"No, that's not . . ." Sunbright was hedging and knew it, so shut up. "You're right. I'm so worried about keeping the tribe together and reaching our destination safely that I forget you hail from the south. I don't know what to tell you. Perhaps in a few years, if the tribe is settled, you and I can travel, journey to cities like Ioulaum so you can feel at home."

"I doubt it." The part-elf nuzzled against his chest, tears betraying her voice. "You keep saying a shaman is no good without a tribe, and you were so fiercely homesick, you'll never leave. Not that I blame you. But what's to become of me?"

Sunbright had no answer, merely held her close, kissed her head, and whispered, "It'll be fine, Knuckle'. As long as we love each other. . . ."

Chapter 13

"Help! Oh, mercy!" wailed a mother. "They're gone! Taken!"

"Raiders!" shouted a guard. "East! Run east!"

The barbarian camp boiled from under blankets. Fighters grabbed swords, hunters bows and arrows, mothers and fathers their children. Dogs barked in a frenzy. Shouts rang all over.

With no other clues, Sunbright ran east. It was an hour before dawn, prime time for a raid. The tribe was not unprepared, for Magichunger posted guards at night and insisted everyone keep weapons at hand, even under blankets. It paid off as a dozen warriors dashed alongside Sunbright.

The rolling grasslands were broken by a meandering watercourse that sliced ravines jagged as lightning bolts. For days now the tribe had slid into each gully and surmounted the opposite bank. The terrain left them vulnerable, for the ravines were handy avenues for a skulking enemy.

"Where are they?" hollered Strongsea.

"Who are they?" shrilled Kindbloom.

"Just get to the first ravine!" Sunbright yelled. "The guards will tell us!" As if by magic, Knucklebones suddenly pelted alongside, running fleet as a deer despite her short legs and bare feet.

Magichunger had dropped into the first gully and scrambled up the other side. Dashing to the top of a hillock, he scanned, yelled, "It's orcs! They've got two children! Go north! Circle that next bend!"

"Orcs?" gasped Sunbright. That was queer. Orcs avoided the prairie, preferring to strike from forest and scrub with plenty of cover and ways to retreat. Snatching an arrow from his new quiver, he veered right to follow the ravine north. The thief turned with him. Far in the east he heard the signal of a scout spotting prey.

"How'd they steal children from under our noses?" Knucklebones panted.

"The brats snuck off, probably," Sunbright replied, "for a swim before we strike camp."

Up ahead, along the ravine, Firstfortune stamped to a halt, aimed her bow, and shot. By the time Sunbright and Knucklebones arrived, her plain arrow was stuck in a sand bank. Knucklebones called, "I'll follow the bottom!" and bounded down the slope like an antelope.

"Don't get shot!" her lover cried, and sped to catch the other archers.

Rounding a lazy bend in the stream, he glimpsed Magichunger in the ravine on a sandy bank. Trapping an orc in a pocket, the war chief flicked his heavy broadsword over his shoulder and cleaved the enemy's arm from its shoulder. He ran on before the orc fell. Spying Sunbright, he flung a blood-spattered arm and called out, "Here they come! Stand your ground and kill them!"

Sunbright and five others crouched in tall yellow grass, nocked arrows to longbows, and waited. Suddenly, like flushed quail, four gray-skinned orcs with war clubs and cleavers appeared above the grass, spun their heads to orient themselves, and died.

Arrows fletched with turkey feathers and pointed with iron skimmed the grass tops and slammed into their foes. Sunbright's arrow banged an orc's breastbone and knocked him flat.

"Go right! Get after the rest! Run!" Magichunger bellowed from the next ridge, waving a brawny arm. He tore over the landscape like a jackrabbit.

Ripping through waist-high grass, howling like banshees, Sunbright and Knucklebones and Crabbranch and Kindbloom and Strongsea boiled around the ridge, jumped into a sandy gully, and splashed in the rippling stream. Half a dozen orcs looked up in surprise, surrounded by a score of berserk barbarians. They gabbled and bawled and whipped up swords and war clubs and stabbing spears. In their midst crouched two blond, crying children, a boy and a girl.

The orcs died before they could kill their captives.

Knucklebones, clad in leathers and bare feet, poised at another edge of the ravine, took aim with her dark elven blade, snapped it hard, and pierced an orc in the kidney. The orc yelped and reached to grab the pommel. The thief landed behind it, light as a sand crane. Punching from below her waist, using the full power of her body, she slammed the orc's skull twice with her brass knuckledusters. Broken-necked, the orc pitched into the stream.

Sunbright dropped his bow and jerked Harvester over his shoulder. The hooked blade sizzled a glittering arc, bashed aside an arm and a club, then slammed into an orc's neck to the spine. The creature's beady eyes bugged as blood shot in an arc to stain the silver blade. The orc collapsed like a pile of leaves. The shaman wrenched his sword from the carcass, and whirled for another.

There were none. The orcs were bloody, smashed heaps on sand and water. Shining ripples carried away ribbons of blood that attracted minnows. Fighters raised gory weapons, cheered and hooted and huzzahed, except for Strongsea who bellowed, "The beggar's given me fleas!"

A chorus of laughs resounded, but was interrupted by—

"Look there! One's getting away!"

A thrum of unshod hooves shook the air. From a bend down the gully there exploded up a sandy slope a brown horse with a gray orc astride. A piebald pony, riderless, squealed and pelted alongside. The orc, clinging desperately, whipped the horse with a club, topped the slope, and bolted into the grass. Barbarians yelled and grabbed for bows. Strongsea flicked up his, shot, hit the riderless horse, and dropped it, but, whipped by the frantic orc, the other horse was gone.

"Bastards!" grumbled Kindbloom. "No one told us they rode horses!" Sunbright agreed it was news to him. He'd thought horses shied from orcs, if only from their stink.

A sniffling arrested Sunbright, and quickly he dodged to the children. Crabbranch already hugged the little boy close, and Sunbright wrapped his arm around the girl's shoulders. "You're safe," he cooed, "you're safe."

"I know," the girl sniffed, trying to rub her eyes without showing it. "I wanted to kill them too!"

"Then we'll get you a real sword, not a wooden one," said Sunbright. The child's smeared face lit up, terror forgotten. Patting her head, the shaman walked for the stream to swish blood off his blade—

—then stopped cold. He walked to a dead orc, and flipped it over with a boot toe. Slope-skulled and gray, hairy and knobby, the orc was clad in a faded smock gray with filth and campfire smoke. But the breast sported a bright sigil, a large red hand with fingers splayed. Freshly painted.

"Ugly as a rat's rump," spat Knucklebones, then noticed his face. "What?"

"This sigil," Sunbright mused, "brings back memories. The red hand is—or *was*—the blazon of the One King. A messiah king from the east, they said, who'd bring peace and prosperity, promote goodwill among the speaking races. We once met a party of orcs who invited us to tea! Their starry-eyed leader rambled all night of how wonderful the world would be once the One King ruled it. But when I was hauled before the king I, uh, lost my temper and tried to swipe his head off. I only dented his skin. He was a lich in disguise, an undead lord with big plans."

"And?" Knucklebones said. "Did you kill him, for Mystryl's sake?"

"Hunh? Oh, no. A red dragon tore down the wall and crisped him. Weren't even ashes left. I thought the king's crusade would die out, but later I met fools flocking to his banner. They wouldn't believe he was dead. And here's an orc with the symbol fresh-painted. And they carry steel weapons, and ride ahorse. Odd behavior for orcs . . ." The shaman shook his head and squeezed Knucklebones's shoulder. "Good fighting."

The part-elf beat her knuckledusters as if testing them. "I must be getting soft,"she complained. "I had to hit him twice."

The war party picked up the steel tools, left the orcs for the wolves and foxes, boosted one another up the sandy bank, and swished through tall grass, the rescued children in their midst. Someone ragged Magichunger about the two slipping past the guards to swim. "Pick guards who aren't blind this time!"

The war chief gestured obscenely, but grinned back, "Barbarian brats can slide under snakes! But we'll put you on point, Blackblossom." Laughter answered.

The tribe cheered the rescued and rescuers. The war party hooted back. Sunbright turned from the group to descend a defile. "They can have the glory. We'll take the dirty work."

Scrambling up the opposite bank, they helped Strongsea and Crabbranch skin the dead horse. It was a brown and white piebald growing a thick winter coat. Sunbright plied his belt knife to slice the mask from the long skull.

Knucklebones felt the coarse mane, clucked, "I'm glad for the meat, but this seems such a waste. You can ride horses, you know. I've never done it, but it would make more sense to work these beasts than just chop them up. From horseback, you could round up wild cattle and deer, even attack a mammoth, I should think."

"Naw," Strongsea said as he sliced raw liver, offered everyone a piece, and chewed bloodily. "Riding's a soft southern custom, for sissies. Barbarians walk. We only harness reindeer, and we ain't got none."

"We kayak," put in Crabbranch. "This hide would make a fine boat."

Sunbright agreed. "I've been ahorse a few times body-guarding pack trains. I bumped like a gutted deer and walked like a duck for days."

"I know it's an art," Knucklebones insisted, "and takes time to learn, but in Karsus we had parades with cavalry brought up from the ground, and those men and women rode like centaurs. The horses obeyed their every whim. Their helmets shone like the sun, and the horses wore blue coats with bells around the hem. They're such pretty animals." She sliced the tail intact from the rear of the hide, stroked it absently. "You'd never seen an orc ahorse before. Why not a barbarian?"

Strongsea and Crabbranch exchanged glances at this heresy, a break with tradition. Sunbright offered, "We get along fine walking." But inwardly, a germ of an idea took root. Something he'd have to think about. . . .

Returning to the war party with meat bundled in the piebald hide, Sunbright squeezed Knucklebones and steered for his mother's travois. Monkberry sat on their bundle like a round lump, smiled crinkly at her son and his tiny, exotic lover, but winced as she rose. "How much further must we go, son?" she asked.

The shaman stared at the western horizon, calculating, then said, "I'm not sure. The distance is almost double that from the Horn at the Channel Mountains to Oxbow Lake along the tundra. We've been out, uh, thirty-two days. Perhaps another twenty? Why ask, mother?"

"Oh," she puffed, "walking the world over is fine for young folks, but my poor feet are worn to the knee. It'll be good to find a rock to sit on."

Sunbright laughed, "You'll have rocks, mother, if I have to trudge to Northreach to fetch one."

"If we had horses," Knucklebones cooed, "we could build a bigger travois and you could ride."

Monkberry shook her head, and stated, "Barbarians walk. It's always been that way. I'm good for a few more leagues yet."

Shouldering the harness, now piled with thirty pounds of raw horse meat and hide, Sunbright leaned far forward to get started. "Come on, then. The sooner we walk, the sooner we arrive. I need to find my mother a rock."

* * * * *

The band passed deeper into the prairie, which now began to rise steadily, several feet in every mile. They saw no more ancient animals, mammoths or saber-tooths, and twice passed stands of poplar trees. Several times the tribe skirted ridges too steep to scale with leather soles. The mountains and forest were not far off.

With the good news came bad. Orc raids came more frequently. A woman gathering water was shot in the back by a crude arrow. The Rengarth beat the brush but never found the killer. One night three southmen, half-starved, bearing swords and scraps of armor, were caught rifling the food and were immediately cut down. Hunters found game clumsily butchered, so they paired up for protection. Once, at dawn, a pack of thirty or more orcs howled a battle challenge, hoping to stampede the tribe. When near two hundred fighters screamed back, the orcs melted into gullies. Two hunters were bushwhacked later, with only their heads recovered.

"I've never heard of orcs on the prairie, and suddenly they're thick as fleas," Sunbright mused. "Iceborn and Tulipgrace only recall it once, ages ago, when drought burned the highlands. What's got them on the prod?"

"The One King?" asked Knucklebones. "You saw the red hand on that big war party."

"The king's dead, and not coming back. I saw him blasted by dragon fire. Flagstones under his feet melted. Still . . ." Guessing got them nowhere, and they had to continue at any cost.

Then one afternoon a hunter pelted through the grass. From her empty hands, they concluded she'd routed an enemy. Magichunger hollered, "To arms! To arms!"

But this news was good. Panting, Firstfortune pointed wildly northwest, and gasped, "I-I've seen it! F-From a ridge top! Sanguine Mountain! Red as blood down a black cleft! Two days' walk. We're almost there—"

Cheering drowned out the rest. Sunbright grabbed Knucklebones and his creaky mother, and spun them both till they gasped. The tribe pushed on till dusk, threw up a hasty camp, then convened to discuss plans. Sunbright had little to say, instead listened to notions both fantastic and practical, glad his people had new ideas to share.

The next afternoon, the peak of Sanguine Mountain topped the grass. Two days later, they saw the whole mountain, and others beyond it, gray and solemn marching to the sky, while a counterpane of green shot with orange and gold and red cloaked their stony feet.

In the last mile, someone hollered and streaked forward. A child ran after, soon outstripped by two more youngsters. "A tree! First to touch a tree!" A flock of runners broke and ran headlong. The stragglers behind cheered the race.

The forest spilled from the hillside in long ragged arms of color to trickle amidst the yellow grass. Having reached the trees, someone shouted anew, and a race back to the tribe began. This time the runners carried leaves they'd snatched as proof of their triumph. Sharing their treasures, they were grabbed and kissed and jostled. Songs went up, and prayers of thanks.

Far at the rear of the wandering train, Sunbright stopped dragging their travois. Monkberry caught his wrist on one side, and Knucklebones the other. The small thief said, "You did it, Sunbright! You've brought them to safety! You pushed and pleaded and nagged, but they've arrived!"

"All the tribe," Monkberry added. "Every one."

Sunbright was quiet, for this place carried memories. It had been here, to the southern slopes of the Barren Mountains, that he'd first retreated when driven from the tribe years back. The mountains had proved bitter and barren, but the forest had sustained him.

"I hope it's safe," he sighed. "I hope this new soil receives my uprooted people. . . ."

* * * * *

The hillside swarmed with barbarians busy as beavers, each with a hundred tasks to do and each happy, for this new land promised great things.

While hunters slipped into the forest, men cut saplings with bronze and iron swords, dug holes to receive them, bent and lashed them with spruce roots, then moved on while women and children layered leafy branches to finish the wigwams. Days ago, Forestvictory had declared her task as trail chief ended with the trail, so Goodbell was appointed camp chief. Now the young woman, with twins slung on her back and a third swelling her belly, directed the laying out of wigwams and slit trenches for latrines, the packing with sticks and mud for a small dam to widen an errant stream, the digging of fire pits, and other tasks.

The tribe had chosen a wide vale with only a slight slope embraced on two sides by highlands of trees. Sanguine Mountain reared above the forest to the north like an orange-black beacon built by gods. The forest itself was edged by green-black spruces whose petticoats brushed the ground. Rising behind were bursts of yellow, orange, and red; tall, vase-shaped elms, round sugar maples, and thin, graceful birches. Sheltered on three sides, sloping to prairie, their camp looked like a harbor town verging on a yellow sea, and it was as busy as any seaport.

Sunbright left Monkberry and Knucklebones to house construction, and busied himself laying out a council ring. Sharpening a stick, he scraped away moss and grass and levered up rocks. He rolled them in a ring, careful that each touched its neighbors, then scraped off dirt for a seat. He whistled as he worked, happy, for they'd finished one odious chore, crossing the plains, and embarked on a new and promising one. Even the air was sweeter, rich with loam and pine and sparkling water, unlike the grainy dust smell of the prairie.

As he fiddled with stones, a tall barbarian named Wreathhonor approached, asked, "Goodbell asks how deep shall we dig the trenches? How long will we stay here?"

Sunbright scraped an imaginary crack. He'd dreaded and avoided this question for weeks, and had no answer now. Or rather, had an answer no one would like. "I think we'll be here a while. All winter, perhaps."

"All winter?" Wreathhonor scratched his head, and went away muttering, "Deep trenches."

It wasn't long before others came calling. Goodbell herself, with Wreathhonor trailing, and Magichunger and Mightylaugh, and even hobbling old Tulipgrace. Goodbell asked, "What's this about we're wintering over? I thought this was a temporary camp. Won't we return to the tundra after the first snowfall? We'll need to build dog sleds for seal season. . . ."

Weary in mind, Sunbright plumped on a rock. Gently, he offered, "The tundra can't support us over the winter. The land is sick . . ." He listed the bad signs, hoping they'd understand.

They didn't. Goodbell frowned. "But if we don't cross the tundra. . . ." she said. "Do you mean to stay through winter and into spring? What of the salmon run—"

"To arms!" From up the slope, the alarm-giver's voice broke, "To arms!"

Whirling, the impromptu council saw Firstfortune stumble down the slope. She dragged Lightrobin, an arrow jutting from her back. Not a barbarian arrow of plain wood, but a long, black arrow fletched with white. Firstfortune gave one more alarm, then was knocked sprawling by another arrow that slammed into her hip.

Magichunger howled to grab bows, parents shrieked for children, Goodbell yelled for non-fighters to take cover and ready bandages, Sunbright shouted for Knucklebones and his mother to duck behind trees. Even as they bolted in different directions, slow-thinking Wreathhonor caught an arrow in his lower belly. He collapsed, holding the shaft and crying like a child.

Sunbright left Goodbell to tend the wounded, and dodged from tree to tree up the slope to fetch his long-bow and quiver. He already wore Harvester on his back, indeed took it off only to sleep or bathe. By the time he reached the pocket they'd selected, Knucklebones had shoved Monkberry flat and flipped the flimsy travois over her. The thief had shucked to her leathers, loosened her dagger in its sheath, and hunted a dozen round rocks for her sling. Between two trunks with one eye she studied dark spruces thick as walls of thorns.

Sunbright grabbed his tackle and flopped on his belly beside her. As he hauled an arrow around to check the fletching he asked, "See anything?"

"Movement, very low, like rabbits creeping. Whoever they are, they're good. Silent, too."

"I'm not surprised. That was an elven arrow."

"Elven?" piped the woman with pointed ears.

"Very long, thin shaft, black. More a bird arrow than a war arrow." The shaman craned to see his tribe, most out of sight. Fighters with nocked bows crept up the slope. Sunbright touched his mother's shoulder, and said, "I'll cover you. Get down the slope toward the middle." Wasting no words, Monkberry scurried to the next tree.

In that instant, the attack broke.

Two spruces parted six feet in the air before Sunbright's eyes. Like a black panther, an elven warrior burst screaming from the green cover. The shaman glimpsed gleaming black armor, a shimmering green shirt, long, wild black hair and pointed ears, a black headband studded with white feathers, a curved bow and quiver. And swinging to meet the shaman, a sword with an ornate handle and a deadly, slim blade.

Before he was even sure of his target, Sunbright jumped to his feet and loosed. His broad arrowhead punched through the elf-woman's boiled-leather cuirass. Her screech cut off as her lung collapsed and her heart stopped. She'd bounded so close her dead body cannoned into the shaman's. He smelled wood smoke and sage, a painfully familiar perfume. The dying elf slumped, and Sunbright kicked her away with sudden, savage fury.

As he untangled his bow, another black ball exploded

from high between trees. Knucklebones shrieked her own cry—oddly, *"Kar-sus!"*—and slashed the air with her long knife. An elven warrior slapped his feet in a fighting stance, and grabbed his sword in two hands to swing and chop the thief in half. But Sunbright hopped over the dead elf, lurched in a long reach, and banged his bow against the warrior's sword to spoil his aim. The bowstring parted with a *twunk!*, the elf hesitated, and Knucklebones lunged. Sliding her dark dagger under the warrior's shirt, she slashed him behind the knee. Hamstrung, the leg collapsed, but he still slashed sidelong and almost parted Knucklebones's hair. As he fell, she twirled the blade and severed an artery. Bright, frothy blood skyrocketed. The elf dropped his sword to grab at the wound. Sunbright kicked his weapon away, kicking the elf's head to stun him. Lost blood and the blow laid him out, and he died in a pool of blood.

"Back!" Sunbright hollered. "Down the slope!"

Barefoot and nimble, the thief hopped backward in giant leaps like a hare's, knife out, ready to kill. Sunbright jigged and jogged, shuffling to keep his feet without tripping. They retreated, for a quick glance showed the elves weren't the only ones dying. The barbarians were attacked from three sides by dozens of black-wrapped, screaming elves.

Sunbright lurched, grabbed a tree for support, and skipped after Knucklebones to regain the ring of barbarians.

But inside he was stunned and heartsick. For he recognized these elves, their armor and weapons, their clothes, even the cut of their faces. He knew who they were.

Cormanthyran Elves of the High Forest.

Greenwillow's people!

ChapteR 14

The next attack came by night.

Barbarians were stripped to essentials. Sunbright wore only his shirt and wide belt and moosehide boots, and he'd even cut the iron rings off them. Harvester's scabbard was pulled tight to his back, for he carried the sword naked in his hand. Magichunger, Kindbloom, Blackblossom, Archloft, and a few others did the same.

The hunting party had returned to the forest in hopes of learning something—anything—about the enemy. The attack of three days before, where dozens of green- and black-clad elves had burst through the woods had ended almost before the barbarians could grab weapons. The elves had hit and run, killing two in the process before disappearing into the blue-black spruces. Whether that had been a warning, a testing of mettle, or a berserker raid, the humans didn't know. The only thing they knew was to retreat miles into the prairie and await the advice of the hunter scouts.

The hunters never returned. Six lost to the forest. Captured? Alive? Dead? Sacrificed? They had no hint. Another war party went out yesterday at dawn, saw nothing, but collected three arrows in their hides. Kingfeather was killed, and angry barbarians retreated farther into the prairie.

Now a group of volunteers went forth, by night, to seek the missing, or the elves' camp, or a whiff of campfire smoke, a trail, blazes on trees—any knowledge that might show how many they fought and how to fight back.

With superior night vision, Knucklebones the part-elf led the way up a shallow slope, from black tree bole to bole. Her pointed ears almost swivelled like a cat's to catch sound. She could barely hear the warriors tread silently behind.

Still, they were ambushed, for this forest belonged to the elves.

The first hint of danger was an arrow that punched Magichunger's thigh. Sunbright heard the sizzle of its flight, the smack as it struck flesh, and the thump as it slammed the earth beyond. Yet all he heard from Magichunger was a sharp gasp before the war chief hissed, "We're attacked! Take cover!"

Veteran of a hundred battles, Sunbright was already diving headlong, rolling as he hit the leafy loam, then twisting in a different direction lest he roll into someone's sights. The shaman thought again that, for all Magichunger threw his weight around to give orders, he took them too, and maintained the silence he'd demanded of everyone else. Yet their enemy were elves, the shaman knew, with ears sharp as foxes. Even brushing a leaf could bring a rush.

And they came, not screeching this time, but silent as owls swooping on mice.

Sunbright felt a faint thrum through the forest floor, rolled on his hams, and swung. Harvester slammed the trunk of a tree, cutting to heartwood. The wild swing never touched the elf, but it made him balk and lose the element of surprise. Snapping to a halt before the barrier of sharp steel, the dark figure ducked and stabbed with a long, slim blade at Sunbright's calf. The thrust missed, but only because, scrambling to gain his feet, the shaman slipped in hide-soled boots and flopped on his rump. A shadow and faint gleam on a blade was all he saw. He kicked at the gleam, hoping to break or bend the blade, but the fine steel only bowed under his kick, and, hastily withdrawn, sprang back straight.

Another stab would come next, he knew, a quick follow-up while he scrabbled to his feet. So he did the unexpected and attacked. Yanking hard on Harvester's pommel, he tugged himself up, wrenched the blade sideways to rip it loose of the maple, and threw himself after the momentum of the heavy blade. Harvester's razor edge cut a half-circle along crusty bark, then the heavy hooked nose thumped a boiled leather cuirass. The surprised elven warrior leaped backward at the touch like a skittish horse, but not before Sunbright kicked again. The elf's razor sword sliced the barbarian's boot tip, and passed between his toes with a bite like a vampire's kiss, but the sword cartwheeled into the dark forest. Sunbright shoved blindly, felt his own blade scratch leather—then the elf was gone. Fled, most likely, and weaponless.

He'd survived a bout, Sunbright thought, but couldn't even tell if his enemy were male or female. Night-blind humans shouldn't venture here, he cursed, but Magichunger had insisted they try. The gods knew they couldn't advance into the forest by day without being peppered with arrows like porcupine quills.

He heard a squeak like a rabbit's, hauled Harvester in a wide circle, belatedly recognized it, and swung high. His blade just missed cropping Knucklebones's hair. A star-bladed dagger thumped on turf as an elf retreated, winked away like a bubble. Knucklebones, watching over her lover, had sliced the elf's hand and saved Sunbright's back.

Their war chief reaped more punishment as an arrow again smacked flesh. Magichunger cursed in the darkness. Forgetting their orders, Archloft hollered as he chopped at a shadow with his cleaver. Sunbright heard the blade scuff in soil. An arrow aimed at the shout skimmed Archloft's back so he dropped flat. To the left, a blade spanked off another, then a human cried out. Sunbright couldn't tell who. He couldn't tell anything. "It's madness to come here!" he hissed.

"Down!"

Knucklebones grabbed his horsetail, jerked him to his knees like a balky reindeer. She slapped a hand on his broad back and vaulted him while slashing the air. Then she was gone like the full-blooded elves. It took an elf to kill an elf, he reflected bitterly.

Staying low, he hastily wiped Harvester on leaves, and thrust it into the back scabbard, dinging his own neck. Crawling like a demented tortoise, he recognized Magichunger by smell, groped to find him lying on his side. Certain the war chief still lived, Sunbright hauled the broad-chested man close. Sunbright butted his head into Magichunger's belly to wedge the war chief atop his shoulders. Harvester's tall pommel helped keep Magichunger in place. Slipping on leaves, the shaman strained to his knees, then feet. Magichunger swayed dangerously.

"Knuckle'!" he whispered. "Knuck—oh!"

The thief appeared under his chin, startling him. "Nightchild's dead," she whispered.

"Dead! *No!*" It was Archloft, Nightchild's blanket partner. "We need his body."

A bad omen, thought the shaman, for one so named to die out in the dark. "Leave him," he said, "or we're all bodies. Knuckle', lead us out!"

"Here!" she directed, but he couldn't see which way. She grabbed his arm and tugged, skipped to the others, and pointed them in the right direction. "I'll steer if you go wrong. Hurry!"

A one-eyed thief leading the blind, Sunbright thought inanely. His first step throbbed where his toes had been sliced. He spit out the pain and tramped, noisy as a wounded moose. He figured he'd probably stop a dozen arrows before he took five paces, but no barbs slammed into him, so he plodded on, lurching side to side as he jogged, for Magichunger was thick through the body. Knucklebones was a sparrow by comparison.

Tree trunks flicked by like pillars of smoke. Then cooler air blew in Sunbright's face, and he knew they'd reached the grassy slope. Darkness before his eyes was less intense. Prairie night. They were almost safe, for he doubted elves would leave the woods for open spaces for long. Perhaps, emboldened by darkness, they'd circle far ahead and lay a trap . . .

He jolted as Magichunger stirred, growled, and groaned, "What's—Who's—"

"Hush! I've got you!"

"Who? Sunbright? You're not—*ugh!*—strong enough to carry me!"

"You dream then." To gauge if the victim had lost too much blood, Sunbright gasped, "Still with us?"

"Uh! Yes! But you make a . . . damned poor . . . sled!"

The shaman hissed, "We'll drive buffalo ahead next time! You're beefy as one!"

"You just want . . . to cover your own back . . . with me as shield!"

"Don't be stupid," Sunbright growled. For some reason the quip irritated the shaman. "The tribe needs you."

"Don't see . . . why. I'm not . . . having much luck."

"Luck? You mean you're not learning something? No, we learned plenty."

"What—*ahh!*" Magichunger stifled a groan of pain. "What did we learn? First it's damned orcs, then it's elves. My son'll be war chief, and his son, and so forever at this rate—*aggh!*"

"Rest," Sunbright ordered. "We'll talk later."

Magichunger grew limp, which made him easier to carry, but Sunbright knew the war chief might die. The shaman sucked wind and jogged downhill, finally struck level earth, smelled tall grass, and heard it swish against his boots. The cleft between his toes throbbed, and blood squished in his boot, making it slippery.

"Need help?"

The whisper startled him. And fuddled him. Knucklebones had skipped alongside without his knowing.

Dropping to one knee, Sunbright wrestled Magichunger off his shoulder. Low down, the smell of grass made him feel safe. "Give me light!" he said.

"They'll see from the forest!" the thief objected.

"I need light, damn it! Crouch over it! No, better, light up his leg here! Give me your hand!"

Grabbing her small, cool hand, he directed it onto Magichunger's hot, wet leg. The rogue striped cold light from her fingertips. At the same time, she hunkered over the small glow to shield it from eyes in the forest.

After hours in the dark, the firefly light made Sunbright squint. He sucked his little finger, stuck it in an oozing hole, wiggled, felt it protrude past flesh out the other side. Quickly he bandaged the wound and tied it off. "Lucky?" he muttered. "Or maybe not. Magichunger would not faint from such a trifling . . . Oh, Moander's mirth!"

Exploring, his hands found a second arrow jutting from Magichunger's kidney. Then a third arrow standing from the point of his shoulder. "Shroud of Selûne!" Sunbright exclaimed. "I owe Magichunger an apology. He's tough as a shark's tooth. More light, please—Who comes?"

Knucklebones had already seen the shape, but the dark figure didn't move like an attacker.

"Blackblossom!" the barbarian woman whispered, not joking for once. "Need help?"

"No," Sunbright answered. "Stay out of the light! Get back to the tribe. We'll follow." The woman didn't waste words, but faded away.

Knucklebones plied minute strips of light to help Sunbright bandage the wound. The shaman decided to cut out the kidney arrow lest the barbs work deeper into vitals with every jostle. The thief eased her dark blade alongside the arrowhead, sliced damaged and swelling muscle, and withdrew the barb. Blood welled black until Sunbright plugged and wrapped it. The shoulder arrow he left embedded, but he found the shaft too tough to break.

"What *is* this wood?"

"Let me," Knucklebones whispered. By feel, the part-elf shaved hard splinters.

"If he lives, Magichunger will give orders from bed." With gallows humor, he added, "If he dies, we'll need a new war chief. You, perhaps."

"Not I. Did you—" The elf stopped short as she wiggled the arrow, then shaved more. No wood could resist an elven blade for long.

"Did I what?" Sunbright asked.

"Did you—kill anyone?"

A strange question in an odd tone, the shaman thought. "No," he told her. "Did you?"

"No. I don't—I don't want to kill anyone. Them."

"Elves, you mean?"

She nodded, forgetting he couldn't see the motion in the dark, then said, "Yes."

"Because they're elves?" Sunbright asked. He watched for anyone lurking or advancing. But wavy grass made a darker line against a dark sky, and nothing broke the line.

"More than that," she said, leaning on the arrow, then cursing under her breath. "They look like me."

"They do?" he asked, then the snap of the shaft ended the questions. "Douse this magic light."

"I can't," Knucklebones said, sounding oddly hurt. "Don't you know I can't dispel it? It fades on its own."

"Oh," he said awkwardly. "No, I never knew that."

There was much he didn't know about this part-elven thief from the future. Why didn't he? He'd known Greenwillow to her core, or thought he had. Then he was busy wrestling Magichunger onto his shoulders like a dead ox. Glancing around, he set off at a quick march.

"No! This way!" came the thief's whisper.

Flustered, Sunbright staggered after her voice. Normally he knew the compass with his eyes closed. He was rattled to mess up now. Rattled by Knucklebones's queer reticence about fighting, and killing, and not knowing magic, and much else that only a woman could know.

But one thing he knew: he didn't want to kill elves either. Not Greenwillow's kin.

Disgusted with his own maundering, he concentrated on lugging Magichunger to safety.

* * * * *

A glow silhouetted a grassy hummock to mark the main camp, though the barbarians were scattered along a five-mile line out in the prairie. Sunbright staggered toward the fire with his burden, Knucklebones dogging his heels. They didn't expect to be welcomed as heroes, but were unprepared for ugly wrath.

People spilled from the firelight to grab Magichunger, immediately shouting.

"Archloft says you left Nightchild's body to the wolves!" growled Mightylaugh.

"The Rengarth always bring out their dead!" shrilled Forestvictory. "Always!"

"You must go back for him!" yelled another.

"And who made Sunbright war chief if Magichunger falls? A shaman is never war chief! It's not allowed!" called a fourth.

Yet their shouts died as Rightdove pointed to the blue-white gleam on Magichunger's leg. "Witchlight!" Rightdove gasped. "Did you do this, Sunbright?"

"It smacks of magic!" said Forestvictory.

Knucklebones piped up, "That's my doing, a simple cantra. Everyone born to the empire can perform small magic—"

No one listened. "Magic is forbidden!" a voice shouted. "Taboo!"

"Hush, all!" Sunbright was exhausted in mind and body by the fight and panic, and drained of spirit. Taking Knucklebone's hand, he let others lug Magichunger to the fire, then asked, "What is there to eat?"

"Nothing!" Goodbell spat. She nursed a fidgety child by the fire, her face drawn and lined. "Our best hunters lie dead in the forest where the game must hide. The prairie offers nothing."

Sunbright plunked on grass by the fire. Dried dung smoked and wafted into his eyes. "I'll try tracking game at dawn," he promised.

"Better hunt that fight!" Mightylaugh said as he strode to the fire. "You learned nothing, Kindbloom tells us. You only got Magichunger shot full of arrows."

"We learned plenty," Sunbright snapped. "Use your brains instead of your mouth."

Magichunger's mother and sisters bandaged him, wrapped him in blankets, and rolled him near the fire. Fighters stood with empty hands, or swished swords in their anger. More barbarians came from the dark to hear the news and arguments. Mightylaugh demanded, "What did we learn?"

The shaman scrubbed aching temples, and said, "I'm

guessing, but think on this: I don't believe the elves mean us harm—"

"No harm!" scoffed several.

"I think they simply bar us from the forest. They can see in the dark. They shot Magichunger three times, recognizing he's war chief, and could have shot me a dozen times as I lugged him out, yet they didn't. So—"

"You're an elf friend!" someone bawled from the dark. "They wouldn't shoot *you!*"

Knucklebones's hand tightened on Sunbright's leg. The shaman refused to take the bait. "Look at the evidence," he demanded. "They could have killed us all, but instead they let us escape, and didn't pursue."

"They're afraid to fight us!" Kindbloom crowed. "They're cowards, and know we're better warriors!"

"Further," Sunbright plowed on, "if they intended war, they could slip out here and slit our throats while we sleep. They could slide through this grass like snakes, but don't."

"Get past our guards? Not likely!"

"Never! The prairie belongs to the Rengarth!"

"*And,*" hollered the shaman, "I don't think there are many elves. We're only attacked by three dozen at most. Their tribe must be small. Legends say elves are scarce."

"Legends say they turn invisible, and I don't see that!" argued Mightylaugh.

"If we could force them to fight here, we'd make mincemeat of 'em!" added Kindbloom. "No elf can stand against a barbarian!"

"They're cowards! Skulking like coyotes in the dark!" chimed Archloft. "We should burn the forest, drive them out like rats from grain!"

More threats, rants, hollering. Sunbright groaned at their illogic, and cursed himself too. His proud people refused to consider anything new, buried their heads in custom and tradition like a child burrowing under blankets. It was partly his own fault, for he'd recalled them to tradition, too well. Faced with a new problem, they could only ply old ways, lash out blindly instead of think.

Knucklebones huddled against Sunbright, and gripped his brawny arm with her small, strong hand. Over the belligerent bellowing, she murmured, "They call you elf-friend."

"They call me many names," he reassured her. "It's just wind."

"But you *are* an elf-friend, for my blood is shared with the Old Ones."

Sunbright squeezed her hands. "I love you, no matter what you are," he said.

Her hands jerked back, surprising him. One slanted eye glared, and she said, "You think it's evil to possess elven blood?"

"No!" he exclaimed. Shanks of Shar, thought Sunbright, was everyone mad? "No, I think ... Don't you turn against me too!"

In apology, Knucklebones laid her tousled dark head against his shoulder. "I won't," she promised, "but I honestly don't know what I am, Sunbright."

Tired, fuddled, the man hugged her close, kissed her curls. Around them, the frustrated war talk failed. The last question was, "So what now?"

"Try peace," offered Sunbright. Eyes turned: hostile, confused, angry. "Carry a flag of truce to the forest. See if the elves will talk. Explain we seek to camp and hunt and then move on. Perhaps they'll let us stay."

"You said we'd winter over into spring, not move on!" spat Goodbell. "Which is true?"

"Either," Sunbright hedged. "What's important is to talk. It can't hurt."

"They'd kill the messenger!"

"Let Sunbright carry the flag!" someone piped. "It's his idea!"

"I'm willing," he said. Though tired, the shaman stood. "Even collecting an arrow would be worth it, just to see the enemy's face. I'll go at dawn."

"I'll go with you," Knucklebones added.

"No, you won't!" Mightylaugh roared. When the crowd hushed, he barged on. "If we parade to beg a crust of bread and sip of water, they'll think us weak! We'll have lost the war! I say—"

"Who are you to contradict a council?" Sunbright snapped.

"This is no council!" Mightylaugh spat. The big man had earned his name for his jolly manner, but that had evaporated under the recent strain. The whole tribe was wrought up. "The council rules in peace. This is war, and the war chief decides! Magichunger is hurt, so as second, I become war chief, and I say we attack at dawn when the rogues are tired from watching through the night. We attack with every fighter, and slay every pointy-eared bastard in the forest!"

The tribes' battle cry shook the starry night. Screaming and whooping ran up and down the line of campfires. Sunbright spat in disgust. That challenge would alert every elf from the Barren to the Purple Mountains. And the mountains wouldn't be barren, but drenched in blood. He groused to Knucklebones, "Ravens and foxes and maggots will rejoice at this choice."

"We don't expect you to join us, Sunbright!" sneered Mightylaugh. "You or your pointy-eared friend."

"We'll fight," the shaman returned. "If nothing else, I can fetch wounded. That'll keep me plenty busy. But be warned . . ." Standing tall against the small fire and dark horizon, he reached over his shoulder, and hauled out Harvester of Blood with a low moan. The long blade flashed yellow in the firelight. "The next time someone mentions the ears of the woman I love, or doubts her loyalty, I'll cut off his ears and feed them to him."

The shaman stalked into the night.

Knucklebones matched his long strides by half-skipping, clinging to his elbow. Her spirit sang at Sunbright's public proclamation of love. Yet she sorrowed, too. For deep in her heart, she doubted her own loyalty.

* * * * *

As the sun rose blood-red on the eastern horizon, the Rengarth Barbarians roared a challenge and charged the forested slopes, their shadows running ahead.

Straight into disaster.

Slim black arrows flew from the forest like dragonflies, and every one of them found a target. A dozen barbarians, howling and waving their bronze and iron swords, fell before they reached the woods. More arrows whistled from close blue spruces before the tribe broke through, then they were barging under the canopy of maple and ash leaves. Dark ghosts flitted amidst trunks, elusive shapes that infuriated the screaming barbarians and faded like morning dreams. Still, like magic, arrows sped amidst the barbarians and slammed backs, buttocks, bellies, and biceps. The woods were a bedlam of noise and pain.

Sunbright and Knucklebones had hung back from the initial charge. They'd shown loyalty in joining the tribe, but were reluctant to run mad against the dark ones defending their homeland. The pair ran up the slope after stragglers, past wounded and dead, until they reached the trees and green dawn light.

"What now?" the thief panted. "Which way?"

Human screams and the elven shrills resounded like thunder before rain. Sunbright shook Harvester in rage. "I don't know! We shouldn't even be here!"

"Then why—"

From the ground, a shower of leaves exploded upward. Dark forms camouflaged with greenery and berry juice stabbed with slim swords. Sunbright had a moment's thought: Now we know how they disappear so quickly. Then he fought for his life.

He lunged backward from a blade stabbing for his face, and batted wildly. He trod on Knucklebones's foot and lurched. The elf's blade kissed his neck, then flicked back to skewer his heart. The shaman knocked the steel aside just in time, lashed to kick the elf away, but the slim female warrior was too quick. Amidst berry stains and hair black as Greenwillow's, her black eyes raged. With a deft snap of her wrist, she sliced Sunbright's thigh, parting his long, faded shirt, then skin and muscle. Instantly the leg felt weak. When Sunbright snatched it back, it trembled.

With no other defense, he lunged at the elf-woman. She dodged easily. He stumbled and twisted, too late, felt steel pink his kidney. He cannoned into a tree to avoid the blade. Behind, Knucklebones gasped and cursed, but before Sunbright could swing Harvester into play, steel slashed his forearm. Then the elf's point flickered at his eyes. He might as well fight the wind.

The shaman wrenched Harvester up as an awkward shield, but his heart despaired. Barring a miracle, they'd both be dead in seconds.

The wild-eyed, wild-haired elf stepped back, and braced her foot for a killing blow. Sunbright swung his huge blade—

—and a warhammer flew from the trees behind.

The hammer smashed the elf's jaw, and knocked her sprawling. A cleaver flung from a different direction, and smacked aside the blade of the elf pressing Knucklebones.

Sunbright gaped. The warhammer on the turf was battered, nicked, the handle sweat-stained. And familiar. He'd carried it for years.

He turned to see who'd thrown it, and finally found his breath.

"Drigor!"

Chapter 15

Not wasting words, the old dwarf dropped a hand like a vise on Sunbright's forearm. The shaman was towed as if chained to oxen. More dwarves swarmed, even bulled through blue spruces where Sunbright couldn't pass. The elf attacking Knucklebones was clubbed down with axe and mattock handles. The thief was hoisted bodily over two heads, and toted down the slope like a reindeer carcass in a game dance.

Dragged along, Sunbright tried to quell his amazement. Drigor looked the same: face wrinkled as a winter apple, bushy white beard with six silver rings braided into his mustache, queer leather tunic with shaggy hump, stained goat hide kilt, and rusty, pitchy boots. The dwarf was hung like a peddler with satchels, rope, blanket, axe, warhammer, backpack, pouches, and tools. Seven more dwarves, all younger than Drigor, thudded through the woods in heavy boots. Knucklebones squawked to be set down, but no one listened.

They burst free of the trees and down the slope. The dwarves neither panted nor sweated, but jogged like clockwork engines. Sunbright felt like a child in the iron grip of Drigor, son of Yasur, father of Dorlas, of the Sons of Baltar of the Iron Mountains.

The barbarian attack had been broken. Survivors limped down the slope for the prairie. Some sported black arrows, and several helped wounded companions. Sunbright demanded Drigor let go. Disregarding his own wounds, the shaman sheathed Harvester, and tended the wounded on the slopes. The dead he let lie: over a dozen in sight. Wives and husbands streamed up the slope, wailing and sobbing when they found relatives. Sunbright hoisted Peacefinger, a small red-haired woman, across one shoulder, and with Drigor's help, shouldered Darkname across the other. At Drigor's direction, dwarves carried others. Before long, all the Rengarth Barbarians, living, dead, and in between, retreated from the slope.

"What madness is this?" asked Drigor. He lugged Hammerlove across his backpack. The man's white head lolled, neck broken. "Who ordered such a foolish attack?"

"A fool," Sunbright answered. "We've a tradition of foolhardiness going back centuries." His bitter irony was lost on the dwarf. Sunbright needed breath to carry, but needed answers more. "Are you real, Drigor, or a dream? I left you half a world away. On the other side of the empire."

"We are real," stated the literal dwarf. "We needed to find you. To warn you . . . to settle our debt."

Debt? the shaman wondered. Oh, yes, returning Dorlas's warhammer. Dwarves took promises seriously. Sunbright sucked wind as they swished through prairie grass, waist-deep on the dwarves.

"Warn me of what?"

"A monster hunts you. Like nothing I've ever seen. Tall, thin as a sword, with a hide like ice-worn granite. And more spells than fill a grimoire. It followed you and attacked us, crying for revenge."

Sunbright almost dropped two carcasses. "A what? A monster? After me? Arms of Targus!" he swore. *"Why?"*

The old weaponsmith shrugged under his grisly burden and said, "You made a powerful enemy somewhere. Mighty queer you don't know it, though. I recall enemies better than friends."

Sunbright asked a dozen questions, learned the gory tale of the tentacles of doom and the shrieking fiend, but knew even less when he'd finished. A monster clad in flint? How was that possible? And why hate him? None of it made sense.

Plodding toward camp with morning sun in his eyes, Sunbright asked, "How did you find me?"

Old, crinkly eyes squinted to guard a secret. "Dwarves know the earth," Drigor answered vaguely. "We listened for your tread."

A lie, Sunbright knew, mystic mumbo jumbo. Many folks had seen the barbarians enter the prairie, bound west. Hundreds of marchers left a wide track. He didn't press. His mind whirled with enough questions.

The sun was fully up, bright in the huge, deep sky. But a chill stained the air, a painful reminder that winter was not far off. Having failed to win a foothold on the forest, Sunbright's tribe might be trapped on the prairie without food or shelter or fuel. Was there no place for them, now that the tundra had died?

Which reminded him. "Thank you for saving our lives," he said to the dwarf. "Our debt must be repaid in spades. Or do I owe you?"

"You owe me doubly," the dwarf calculated. "Cholena, who had been my wife, was killed by your monster, blasted to flinders before my eyes. And three other sons of the mountain. You brought the monster upon us, and now we've saved your life and hers,"—he nodded at Knucklebones, still being carried aloft—"as we once saved you from yak-men in White Owl Pass.

"My warning of the monster extinguished your debt

of returning the hammer. But let's not quibble. You can, perhaps, balance the bargain."

Quibble? thought Sunbright. The old miser attached prices to everything, with Sunbright sinking in debt by the minute. Wearily he asked, "Balance how?"

Drigor stumped along, staring at the horizon, or something inside his head. "Not now," he said. "I'll tell you when 'tis time."

"Fine," the shaman said. "I owe you."

Sunbright let it go. Probably he'd be dead of starvation before spring anyway, providing his tribe didn't stone or burn him to death first. . . .

* * * * *

Sunbright dreamed.

Greenwillow tripped from the night, dainty as a deer. Tall, black-haired, shining green and black like a lizard, ornate silver pommel swaying at her hip. As shadows crept up her frame, her face was revealed. Dour, eyebrows puckered, mouth pursed.

That expression Sunbright recognized. Greenwillow had often been angry at him in life, but never in dreams. He asked, "What is it?" though she'd never spoken in dreams.

"You slay my people!" Her lithe hand fell to her sword pommel.

"They slay mine!" Sunbright protested. "They insist on war! We only seek a home!"

"My people inhabited these woods when yours had tails!"

"We don't seek to usurp them!" Even in a dream, Sunbright's voice whined. "There's no reason—"

"You must not slay my people!" The phantom drew her sword with a hiss. The silver blade winked and flashed in moonlight. "Kill them and you kill me!"

The blade seemed coated with frost, and Sunbright

felt its chill. Greenwillow, and her sword, never looked so real. Was it because he lay sleeping near her forest homeland? The keen steel whisked near his neck, seeking blood.

"All right, I shan't harm them!" Sunbright made more promises, more to break. "I wouldn't harm anyone if I could help it! But I can't speak—"

Surprising him, Greenwillow lunged forward, caught his shirt, and kissed him hard. Her lips were icy, but his body stirred at her touch. She was so like Knucklebones, so vital and vibrant, yet so different, as an eagle is from a kingfisher. How were they so alike, yet so different? Who understood women, or dreams?

When Greenwillow pulled back from the chilly kiss, one eye winked, then stayed oddly closed as she retreated. "I'll be seeing you," she said, then she ran into the black forest of death, or limbo, or wherever she dwelt. As she ran, she grew shorter, slighter, smaller.

Clumsy too. No longer silent as a white-tailed deer, her feet pounded the ground. Thumps made his bones thrum. Harder came the blows, until the dream shattered.

Someone kicked him awake. Mightylaugh in big boots laced to his knee. "Wake up!" the big man grunted. "We council!

"About you!"

* * * * *

". . . *his* idea we come here! And he's brought nothing but death to the clans, widows and orphans who weep the night . . ."

". . . befriended an *elf*, not of our tribe, nor our race. And now we find elves here, hungry to kill us, in the very spot *he* directed us . . ."

". . . how many have fallen to the Shadow Folk? Yet *he* goes unharmed amidst the elves! How can this be, unless he works with them . . . !"

Speaker after speaker took the talking stick and heaped the tribe's woes at Sunbright's feet. Accusations flew, wilder and wilder: he'd led them into the jaws of orcs and elves; pretended visions of these woods; murdered Owldark in the desert to become shaman; consorted with one elf and colluded with more elves to sacrifice his own tribe; practiced magic with cold light and healing; run like a coward from battle, suffering no wounds; opposed plans for the last battle, then informed the elves ahead of time; coveted the position of war chief and so plotted to have Magichunger slain; and on and on.

Sunbright Steelshanks sat like a stone and stared at the council fire as his name was blackened. Some speakers defended him, but not many, nor was he surprised. When a tribe suffered, they needed someone to blame, usually the shaman, who should know the will of the gods and the future. And he had led them here. Monkberry sat beside her son, holding a big hand in her gnarled one. Knucklebones held the other hand, hers cool and strong. Tears silently spilled down both women's cheeks.

Long into the night the council dragged. Finally it was quiet. Mightylaugh offered the stick, saying, "Would anyone else speak? Sunbright Steelshanks, will you?"

The shaman didn't look up from the fire, only shook his head.

"Damn it, *I* will!" Knucklebones spat, leaped to her feet and, quick as a jackdaw, snatched the baton. "*I'll* speak!"

She stood defiant, clutching the stick like a fighting knife, as if to kill with it. Objections rang out: "She is not of our tribe!"

"She is an elf!"

"She is Sunbright's friend!"

But croaking Iceborn cut through the tumult.

"Whoever has slain an enemy or born a child may

speak in council. There is no custom against an outsider speaking. Long ago, when Heatherhill was chief, a man from the city came—"

"Thank you!" Knucklebones interrupted, stamping her foot. The tribe crowded around the council fire on the open prairie. An early morning wind damp with rain hissed in the grass tops. The fire guttered as if ashamed to see its creator laid low. The thief shook the stick as she spat her words. "You miserable lot of ingrates! If you had the honor of garbage-eating dogs, you'd be ashamed! Sunbright saved all your worthless lives by his actions and sacrifices! He sat three days without food or water in the broiling sun to find the vision of this place! You wallowed in your own dung on a pile of rocks near the ash heaps of a town scorned throughout the empire, but Sunbright made you listen! To make you listen, he challenged the lot of you to combat, when there isn't one man or woman here worth his little finger!

"When he fought, and nearly died, you finally saw sense, and crawled off your rubbish dump to a land and sky clean and free! Sunbright recalled your traditions, promised to carry Iceborn on his own back to keep your pitiful customs alive. He fought beside you against your enemies. Look at his arms, his forehead, his knee: count his wounds! He slaved night and day, fetching water, carrying children, butchering sheep—every dirty task in camp, and never complained once, because he was glad to be *home!*

"And when you got here, to this verdant land that could be a paradise, he asked only to seek truce with the elves, that no blood be shed, and you might gain a foothold. But you wouldn't listen! And now, you lousy, stinking, pus-eating, maggoty gutter rats, you'd condemn *him?* Condemn *yourselves,* for being lazy cowards, hardheaded and hardhearted—"

With an oath, Mightylaugh tore the speaking stick from Knucklebones's hand, and slapped as if to break her neck. Quick as a terrier, she ducked, whipped out a knife, and carved a stripe up his arm from wrist to armpit. Bleeding, the war chief rocked back in shock.

"She draws blood in council! It is forbidden!" shouted an onlooker.

"Mightylaugh tore the stick away! *That* is forbidden by our most ancient laws!" countered another.

"She had no right to speak! And insult us when we suffer!"

"Sunbright's suffered a hundred times!"

"No truce! No cowardice!"

"No magic!"

Words turned to shouts, to a babble of noise. Fists flew. Men and women tussled, knocked each other down.

Worried, Monkberry yanked on Sunbright's hand and said, "Son, get up! Come quickly!"

Knucklebones hoisted Sunbright by the hand. He seemed half-dead, or frozen, slow as a crippled snake. Standing, he tottered, grabbed his forehead and squeezed. The thief bawled, "Wake up! What's wrong with you?"

"Drag him!" Monkberry yelled. Knucklebones helped, but Sunbright's feet plodded clumsily, as if made of wood. No one helped or came near them. Open prairie beckoned, a slate-black sky overhead, but a red glow lighting the east. The mother repeated, "Hurry!"

"Why? What's—*Ow!*"

A fist-sized stone bounced off Knucklebones's back. Another stone sailed by and thumped on grass. Risking a glance, Knucklebones saw tribesfolk flocking to a rock pile at the hillock. Men, women, and children hurled rocks. Another struck Knucklebones on the back of the thigh, and she grunted. One knocked Monkberry to her knees. Several hit Sunbright with painful thuds, but though the shaman staggered, he made no sound.

Desperate, the thief yanked Monkberry up, dragged

mother and son. Stones whistled. Then one clipped Sunbright's scalp so he crashed like a falling tree, almost trapped Knucklebones under his great frame.

The elf-woman wept for frustration as stones pelted the ground like hail. Monkberry struggled to rise. Clambering, the thief tried to shield both with her small body. More stones hit Sunbright, and one banged Knucklebone's forehead. Woozy, she fought to keep conscious. To collapse was to die. Another stone struck her shoulder, lamed her arm. She cried unashamedly with fury and sorrow.

"*Hold!*" boomed a voice. "The next to throw dies!"

Like a passing storm, the stones stopped. Feet thudded all around. Meaty hands like bear paws grabbed Knucklebones, Sunbright, and Monkberry, and towed them toward the dawn. The shaman's toes dragged in the grass, marking a double trail from the dappled stones.

Their rescuers were Drigor and his seven dwarves. The old leader leveled a crossbow at the tribe, and loosed a sizzling bolt that shattered on rocks to drive them back. Barbarians jeered, "Coward! Betrayer!" But gradually the taunts and curses died as the dogged dwarves carried all three victims far out of range, then out of sight. Four dwarves carried Sunbright spread-eagled like a sacrifice. Monkberry was toted across two shoulders like a log.

With help, Knucklebones found her feet, though her head throbbed. Laying a small hand on a dwarf's shoulder, she murmured, "Thank you again. Again we owe you our lives."

"Chalk it against the next life. You'll never repay in this one." Drigor's dwarven humor came straight-faced. "Cappi, swing north. We'll circle the camp."

"Where are we bound?" asked Knucklebones, glad someone else took charge.

"Barren Mountains."

Knucklebones swooned at the thought of all that

marching, but bit her lip and trudged, supported by a dwarf she realized was female. She hadn't seen the dwarves since they arrived. After the rescue in the forest, Sunbright had told them what little he knew of the surrounding land. Drigor had said, "We shall be back," and the lot marched off. Knucklebones hated to think of the consequences if they hadn't returned.

"What's wrong with Sunbright?" she asked. "Why so slow, as if dead drunk?"

"I have seen it before, in dwarves and humans." Drigor marched at the head, parting grass like a boat. He carried the famous warhammer, stout enough to fell an ox, in his hand. "These barbarians follow hearts as much as heads, and your friend has lost heart. His tribe has cast him out, but kept his soul. He is empty, dead inside. A tree uprooted. Do you understand?"

"I—I think so." Pain and fear and despair made Knucklebones sob, just once, then she swallowed the lump in her throat and said, "Cut off from his people, he loses part of himself."

"*Most* of himself" Drigor corrected. "So with dwarves."

Knucklebones murmured, "So with all of us . . ."

* * * * *

Ground down by exhaustion, fear, and worry, Knucklebones collapsed hours later. It mattered little to the dwarves. Drigor draped her across his backpack like a dead deer and marched on. Dusk was near when he called a halt.

A tilted canteen and rough hand gently washed Knucklebones's face. She spluttered awake, grabbed for her knife, but the rough hand pinned hers, and a guttural voice cooed, "Rest. . . ." The dwarven woman stepped back to give the thief room.

Knucklebones was chagrined and disgusted that she'd fainted, then awakened so slowly. Yet moving her head sent a jolt through her whole body, made her groan aloud. A fist-sized lump throbbed above her eye patch. For a second, panic made her stomach flip. Had the stone hit her one eye, she'd be blind. Breathing slowly, she let the fear go, and forgave herself for weakness. Careful with her tender head, she looked about.

They sat high on a mountainside, higher than the tallest elms of the forest. Sinking sun on autumn leaves made a forest-fire glow. To the east the prairie burned gold, but the long shadow of night rushed across it like a storm cloud. She lay on an irregular shelf of rock. Monkberry lay nearby, head pillowed on someone's white leather pack. A fire crackled in a crevice, and meat skewered on sticks sizzled and dripped. Dwarves perched on rocks like gargoyles and stolidly munched their meal. Behind them, an overhang formed a shallow cave. Sunbright sat with his back against rock, eyes closed, unmoving.

Close to tears, the thief took in the wide-sweeping vista, the quiet camp with crackling fire, the stunning sunset. In the time she'd been asleep, the world turned from a violent, self-consumed hell to a haven of peace. Part of her wished to stop the sun, to stay like this forever.

But another part blazed with anger at the barbarians' blind, stubborn stupidity. Fear and despair had bred a cold rage. Crawling to wobbly feet, she clutched her head and croaked to Drigor, "What—*Ow!*—what are your plans?"

The dwarf bit a bone in half with yellow teeth, and sucked marrow before saying, "We shall explore."

Knucklebones peered at the gathering gloom. The mountain chain rose like stairs to snowy peaks in the distance. "All these mountains?" she asked.

Drigor pitched bones on the fire, nodded.

"What about us?"

A shrug. "You may come with us, if you can keep up," the dwarf said. "Or stay here."

Knucklebones stifled a groan. Here was a lovely spot,

but she was no mountain goat. Teetering on her wobbly legs, she staggered to Sunbright, and creaked down beside him. "Sunbright? Are you awake?"

He nodded without opening his eyes. He was pale as a corpse, and as still. A cracked scab marred his neck where a stone had struck. He bore many bruises, but his silence most bothered the thief.

"Are you all right? Open your eyes."

He did, but stared at the twilight without seeing. Knucklebones was reminded of Wulgreth of the Dire Woods, with eyes dead as stone. Staring into those hopeless eyes, she couldn't think what to ask.

"Um, the dwarves . . . Do you have any hope of . . . where to go?"

The shaman only shook his head, like a scarecrow in the wind.

Suddenly chilled, Knucklebones shuddered, and drew her leather vest tight across her bosom. They'd been driven from camp with nothing but her elven blade and Harvester of Blood. High overhead, stars sparkled, forecasting a chilly night.

"We can't . . . I . . . Sunbright, what can we do?"

The shaman reached a dirty, blood-stained hand to rub his temple, but had no answer. When she repeated her request, he sighed, "I don't know, Knuckle'. I've nothing behind me, and nothing ahead. I'm worthless."

"You're worth something to me!" she yelled. The thief's cold anger sought an outlet, but blaming Sunbright for their troubles would make her no better than the fickle tribesfolk. Swallowing her fury, she growled, "We can't just sit in a crack in a mountainside."

Sunbright waved at half a world. "Pick a direction," he said, then closed his eyes again.

His heart was truly gone, Knucklebones saw. His tribe held it hostage down there on the prairie. Bitterly she recalled how sad and lonely and homesick he'd sought his tribe, how happy he'd been to find them, even when abused and accused and harried and carped at. And now, with that link broken, he was broken too. Perhaps, in time, he'd recover, find another goal in life, but perhaps not. What was that legendary bird, she wondered, that when captured and caged always died? Could Sunbright survive being cut off forever from his tribe, any more than a finger could survive being severed from the hand?

"Hallooooo!"

The caroling call rose from below like a lark's warble. The sound perked up the dwarves, who dropped food to grab crossbows and axes. Whispering, skidding on hobnail boots, they scuttled into corners and crevices as if melting into the rock. In seconds, the shelf was bare except for Knucklebones and Sunbright, and the sleeping Monkberry.

Creeping forward on bare feet, the thief scattered the meager fire with a stick. Darkness enfolded them. The call came again, a singing, like a babbling brook. "Hallooo! We wish to talk!"

No dwarves answered, or even poked up their noses. Unsure, Knucklebones minced to the edge of the shelf. Her cat's-eye vision made out broken rocks, scrub and gorse in cracks, and a line of black, stunted trees a long stone's throw down. No people. For lack of a better plan, she went along. "Come ahead! Empty-handed!"

Something left the tree line. Three white blobs. Faces. A few paces later, Knucklebones made out dark, slim forms, a smooth, high-stepping walk like deer, black, curved lines behind heads of black hair.

Why, she marveled, did *they* come?

When the trio closed to scale the last slope to the shelf, Knucklebones barked, "I said empty-handed! Two dozen crossbows can sweep this rock!"

In answer, six white palms rose. Still, the surefooted trio scaled the rock. So graceful and strong, they made Knucklebones feel crippled and clumsy. She backed from the edge and almost turned her ankle in the fire pit.

Standing on gray-white rock, framed against black sky, three elves waited patiently with hands in the air. Knucklebones imagined that they were the same elves who'd tried to kill her many times these past days. Wild black hair banded with headbands, smooth faces without war paint, boiled black armor and green shirts, and small slippers. Ornate swords swung at their hips. At their back hung quivers of black arrows and short, curved bows.

Hoping the dwarves were still present, not slipped over the next mountain, Knucklebones demanded, "What do you wish?"

"We come in peace," said the middle, an elf woman, one of two. They were all the same height, within inches. "We sue for peace."

"Peace? With whom?"

"You. The dwarves. The horse-tailed clan on the grasslands," the elf said. "We know their shaman is here."

"How do you know—*Oh!*" Knucklebones jumped as Sunbright stepped up. Absorbed in the terrible beauty of the elves, the music of their voices, their aura of ancient dignity, she'd failed to hear him.

His voice was flat as he said, "Sunbright Steelshanks am I, but no longer shaman of the Rengarth."

The elves looked at one another. The middle one said, "We need you to negotiate a truce with your people. Orcs swarm into our forest from north and east, more every day, vast hordes. We cannot fight barbarians and orcs too. You must tell them—"

"I can tell them nothing," Sunbright interrupted. "They will not listen."

Again the elves exchanged glances, and Knucklebones thought a sigh of exasperation escaped the spokesperson, as if dealing with thick-witted humans were a chore.

"They *must* listen," the elf woman said. "You must talk to them. Failure to talk will have dire consequences for all our peoples. Mortal consequences."

Chapter 16

Everywhere on the outskirts of the Netherese Empire, fire and sword and steel reigned supreme.

Zenith was attacked by pirates swarming from the Marsh of Simplicity and sacked, the gates breached and torn down, the marketplace and city hall burned. Near Earsome, orcs massacred religious pilgrims and heaved their bodies into Kraal Brook until the rapids overflowed their banks. The muscular mining community of Bandor Village was overrun by bandits that burned scaffolds and sluices and hoppers, but worse, introduced a throat-rotting plague that claimed four thousand lives. Angardt Barbarians took revenge on Thiefsward, long suspected of cheating them, and crucified the city elders and dozens more on the high wooden gates. Kobolds and goblins dragged ballistae and catapults and siege towers from Blister and laid siege to Frothwater. The noise awoke a jacinth dragon, rarest of beasts, that swooped upon the remnants of both armies. Trolls rose from the ground near Coniferia and burned their own forests, so smoke blackened the sky for days and ash smothered winter crops. Even Seventon, birthplace of the Empire of Netheril, was overrun by orcs of the Eastern Forest.

More than the people, the land suffered. Already strained by the life-drain of the Phaerimm, the fields of the empire felt the axe, the torch, the scythe, and the spade. Rampaging armies burned ripe grain, chopped down orchards, slashed vineyards, slaughtered cattle and hogs and fowl. Half the harvest was lost. Food shortages became so acute even the highborn Neth looked up from their gaming tables and decided to take action.

What they saw were not petty raids, but concerted action by many scattered factions of humans and monsters. Most wore the bloody red hand of the One King. The empire roused their army: young, battle-hardened, scarred veterans under officers with twenty or more years' experience, fitted with the finest armor and honed steel.

But the empire had grown complacent in decades past, had cut back the army to save money, and the current forces were stretched to the limit. Sometimes they conquered, sometimes they were overwhelmed. Yet the raids increased, and in the wake of marauders flowed other horrors: wyverns, tanar'ri, plagues, elementals, dragon-kin, swarms of magebane and kalin, and more.

Then, a call for truce.

Messengers of the One King, unarmed and carrying a banner with a bright red hand, approached Ioulaum, oldest of cities, and delivered a dispatch. The One King would meet a negotiator for the empire atop Widowmaker Mountain at the next new moon. But the king insisted on choosing the envoy. He would address only the strongest, most brilliant, most capable archwizard of the entire empire.

Lady Polaris.

* * * * *

Widowmaker Mountain stood alone in a vast plain of dead grassland rapidly turning desert. Nine airboats skimmed the air in approach: wooden peapod hulls topped by horizontal masts and metal foils to catch the sun's rays. For this occasion, each boat was painted black and white, the ambassador's colors, and black banners marked by an ornate white **P** snapped in the wind. Six boats took station around the mountaintop, which was artificially flattened and the size of a large pasture, while three boats touched down. The small navy crew dropped gangplanks, and twenty of the empire's soldiers in black and white tunics and shining helmets stepped out smartly, ornamental silver-headed maces held diagonally across their breasts. More soldiers tramped from the other two ships to form a line of protection halfway around the top. After them came a dozen minor officials and clerks, all in black and white. Six mages then departed the ship and trotted the perimeter of the mountaintop. Finding no traps, magical or mechanical, they skipped to the ship to report.

Finally, out marched Lady Polaris.

The archwizard upheld her reputation as a crown jewel of the empire. Silver-haired, golden-skinned, serene and poised, so achingly beautiful men beholding her thought they dreamed. Her rich black robe shimmered like the northern night sky, silver embroidered thread glistened, silver fur that hemmed it riffled in the wind. From her shoulders hung a black cape fastened at her shoulder by a diamond brooch large as a child's fist. If anyone could sweet-talk a human king into submission, the envoys knew, it was Polaris. More majestic than a queen, she swept across the barren rock toward her opposite.

By comparison, the One King was unimpressive. Exposed to direct autumn sunlight, his skin was sallow, almost as yellow as a hornet's stripes. His black hair hung like rotten straw, his silver crown needed polishing, the big red hand on his faded tunic needed repainting. His attendants were only a dozen sturdy orcs in gray wool, carrying pikes, whereas a king should boast hundreds in his entourage. King and party stood on bare rock: no table, no treaty, no gifts, no tea service.

Lady Polaris withheld a sniff from the sickly, greasy king. This corpse animated armies beyond counting? Well, who knew what the lowborn thought, any more than cows? Her mission was clear. Size up this One King, promise anything while studying his weaknesses, and learn how the empire might destroy him and his patchwork army.

So Polaris plied etiquette, cooing, "Your Majesty, good day. May I congratulate you on the success of your enterprises? You've gained the attention of the most-high of the Netherese Empire. Very few enemies can boast so."

"Lady Polaris." The voice was dry, as if the mouth contained no saliva. As if the king were dead as a stuffed bear. "You do me honor. How was your trip?"

"My trip?" Polaris went along with the empty pleasantries, saying, "Fair. Airboats are a smooth ride, but there are air pockets. One needs to wear a lap belt, which wrinkles the clothing. How is your majesty's health?"

"Fair," the king croaked. "Considering I rose from the dead."

Polaris swallowed the odd comment, pressed on, "So we heard. You ruled some city to the east, suffered a disagreement with a red dragon, goes the tale. But you recovered nicely. So glad."

"Nothing like a sojourn in hell to make one appreciate life," rambled the king. "How are your lands? Your estates?"

"My lands prosper," the archwizard lied nobly. "I employ only the most clever stewards to oversee them.

Losses to, uh, vagabonds are minimal. As to my estates, my chamberlains strive impeccably. My many homes are a pinnacle of taste and comfort that others only aspire to."

"Chamberlains . . ." mused the king. His black-eyed, stony face hid his thoughts. "Yes. Even in my distant land, my household mentions your country home, Castle Delia, and how ably it runs. At one time, you employed a woman named Sysquemalyn. Recall her?"

"Vaguely," she mumbled. Lady Polaris stole a glance at her attendants: soldiers and clerks and court officials to present the truce details. They listened curiously, but looked at ease. Yet to Polaris, the mountaintop seemed suddenly chilly. "Red-haired, as I recall, with a temper to match. Flashy, a fancy for sailors, but competent, so I tolerated her audacity and vulgarities."

"And what became of this Sysquemalyn?" creaked the king. "Might I hire her away? I plan to maintain many homes myself once my conquest is complete."

"Oh, I don't think so . . . What did I do with her?" Polaris wasn't even listening to herself, only killing time to fathom this madman's desires and so exploit them. "I discharged her, I believe. No, wait . . ."

"You condemned her to hell, did you not? Her own personal hell, copied and crafted from the nine known levels. You even stripped her skin to make her suffering more acute, her tortures unimaginable."

"Yes, I remember now. One needs to punish servants fully to keep the others from getting airs. But how did you know—"

"Condemned for a year, correct?" The dry voice picked up speed like a sword on a grinding stone. "After which time, you would fetch her out, her punishment complete? Yet how long since you imposed that sentence worse than death?"

Without thinking, Polaris stepped back. The frozen face and dead eyes of the One King looked lethal as a cobra's. She raised a hand to shuffle soldiers before her. "Your Majesty, let not emotion overtake the proceedings. We needs talk—"

"*Three* years! Three long years!" rasped the king. He leaned forward as it to bite Polaris. "Three years when every day, every hour and every minute was the most exquisite torture! And had Sysquemalyn not escaped, she'd languish there still! Because you didn't care to retrieve her from hell! You *forgot* her!"

Feet pattered as everyone moved. Soldiers tramped in time to bar the king from the archwizard. Courtiers surrounded Polaris. Sailors readied the gangplanks of three ships for quick retreat. More hopped out with cutlasses in hand. An admiral in silver braid ordered flags to signal the six hovering ships to land.

Yet the dozen orcs and their One King never stirred. Only now did the king sink black nails into the skin at his temples.

"You forgot Sysquemalyn, Polaris! But *she* did not forget *you!*"

With a screech, the disguised Sysquemalyn tore magical flesh from her face to reveal the bald, flinty monster she'd become. Eyes of bitter blue bulged, and the lipless slash of a mouth creaked like a bear trap. "Flashy?" Sysquemalyn shrieked. "Vulgar! I'll make *you* look like this!"

Polaris snapped spells while courtiers screamed, sailors bawled, and soldiers charged. Sysquemalyn raised clawed arms and brought hell to the mountaintop.

Imperial soldiers swung clubs high to batter the fiend. Sysquemalyn gabbled a conjuration like a curse, stabbed fingers at the ground. Instantly it split, a hundred cracks radiating from her scaly feet. From every crack oozed gallons of black muck that stank like sea mud at low tide. The vile stuff clung to the soldiers' boots, burned through leather like acid. Even steel hobnails melted under the hellish stuff, which climbed like

poisonous tentacles. As their boots leaked, the putrid
gunk burned men and women's flesh like molten lead.
Soldiers howled, jumped, landed in the slop so it
splashed legs and hands, eating cloth and flesh. Shouts
turned to screams. People saw their own bones daubed
with blackness as it seared meat. Panicking, some batted at it, found their fingers rotting. Others tried to run,
but tortured feet betrayed them and they splashed face-
down. Ooze filled mouths, eye sockets, noses, and cor-
roded flesh like melting candle wax.

Caught in the hellish tide were the dozen orcs who'd
guarded the One King, their lord and master. They died
writhing, seared by acid, suffering inside, knowing
they'd been betrayed.

Courtiers stumbled and ran, pushing the ambassador
Polaris toward the flying ships. But the lady stood firm.
She was horrified and outraged by this base deception.
Now she remembered how Sysquemalyn had coveted
her power, beauty, and position, and plotted to gain it
any way possible. How Sysquemalyn had insulted her
mistress behind her back, then laughed at her own cleverness. That arrogance and presumption had driven
Polaris to consign her chamberlain to hell. But now the
archwizard saw that she'd made a mistake. Better to
have killed Sysquemalyn outright, than let her harness
the cabalistic conjurations of hell.

She'd remedy that mistake immediately. A fiend from
hell would hate the cold. Polaris shrilled, "By Veridon,
feast on this, *traitor!*"

The air around the monster shimmered, thickened, and
frosted, sucking moisture from the air. In seconds the spell
formed a block of ice as big as a house around
Sysquemalyn. Dead and dying soldiers were crushed as the
ice mass solidified and settled, pressing them deeper into
the black ooze. A grinding like icebergs colliding resounded
as ice cracked and refroze. The flint monster was obscured
behind an ice wall until she looked like a shadow.

But the ice block didn't last long. The shadow within flitted like a fish under a frozen river. Then, from the depths, a hole bored through the ice, then flashed hellfire that scalded ice to steam. The weeping hole was matched by a second, then a third, until the ice block was shot through, fragile as spun glass. With a shriek, the trapped flint monster shattered the block. Chunks of ice tumbled, threw sprays of water, spun crazily. Revealed—dripping wet, dark and dangerous as a storm-lashed mountain—was Sysquemalyn.

The monster-mage unleashed more hellfire as if hurling hatred from her heart. Snapping an arm, Sysquemalyn flung a flaming gobbet at Polaris that sizzled like a meteor. Only the archwizard's personal shield stopped it a foot from her face. Polaris even flinched as hellfire engulfed her, and raised the temperature inside the shield enough to wilt her silver-white hair.

The pool of black ooze, now studded with bones and helmets, caught fire at Sysquemalyn's feet, snapping and gouting around her skinny waist. But a fiend who'd endured real hellfire could ignore this pale imitation. With a curse, the monster raised her hands to spread pain and terror and death.

People had panicked at the first sign of trouble, their first impulse to quit the mountaintop. Soldiers and courtiers stampeded aboard the three landed ships. The six hovering ships, unsure how to help, dropped to pick up anyone they could. Sysquemalyn aimed to destroy them all.

Screeching, she windmilled her arm until it caught fire, convulsed in a giant fireball that burned to her armpit. With an oath, she whipped the arm and let the fireball fly. It struck the middle ship's gangway where people mashed to get in. Screams erupted as the hellfire ignited hair, clothes, leather, and parchment. The boat caught fire, paint and wood blistering and smoking. Sailors recoiling from the heat screamed and toppled from the upper decks, some crashing their heads on stone, others falling scores of feet down the mountainside. As the fire consumed the magical ship, it lifted, a floating coffin of charred dead and dying that sagged in the air. Its stern crunched on rocks. Flaming, smoking, it tilted, then plunged over the mountainside. A rending crash bespoke death on an outcrop far below.

The fiend struck again and again. Airboats battered by flaming gobbets burned immediately. Neither water hurled on the fires nor beaten blankets could extinguish it. Any attempt to put it out only spread it further. Two ships tried to rise but crashed. A third, burning from end to end, with flaming sailors spilling like ants, collided with its neighbor and turned that one into a torch as well.

Blinking sweat in her eyes, Lady Polaris cast about, saw only dead as attendants, and sucked wind. Rarely had she seen such power, and never directed at her. She'd better unleash some awful spell, and soon, or she might actually be harmed. Racking her brain, she mumbled words to a spell read long ago but never uttered, even as her fingers and thumbs, inverted, formed a square to box the monster.

Sysquemalyn spun two fireballs on her arms, the flames flickering eerily on her granite, mineral-shot hide. Now the monster chirped as a square of blackness appeared under her feet. No, nothingness. A portal to a negative energy plane. It gaped under her splayed, horny feet like an open trapdoor that could drop her back into hell.

Yet Sysquemalyn had been to hell, and the portal did nothing but rob her feet of dweomer. With a harsh croak, she shook off the fireballs, and called to Polaris. "I can withstand anything, you pathetic *bitch!* Can you say the same?"

And stepping off the gaping void, she planted her foot against the hole's edge and kicked.

Lady Polaris balked as the fearsome portal skidded across the ground like a dinner plate, aimed straight at her. She barely jigged aside before the cavity sailed by, revolving slowly. Near the edge of the cliff, soldiers racing for an intact ship failed to see the rocketing threat. The portal clipped off their feet as neatly as a spinning saw blade. Men and women fell shrieking and spilling blood. Those who fell on the portal were sucked within, some disappearing, some cut in half to tumble across rocks in red chunks. Traveling on, the portal reached the cliff and winked out.

Lady Polaris stared in disbelief. Sysquemalyn gargled a laugh. "Fool! Taste this!"

Forking clawed fingers, the fiend hurled a spray like hard water at the archwizard, a whirlwind of steel like a flying buzz saw. Polaris brushed it aside, so it sped on and disappeared over a cliff. But in the meantime, Sysquemalyn invoked a spell by whistling and keening like a shrike's call.

Lady Polaris's first inkling of danger was a crinkling, crackling noise. She turned, found a crystalline structure towering over her, reaching with diamond claws. The giant insect tilted to one side like a malformed scorpion. Its body was indistinct, a moving column of jewels. Blue dots like multi-faceted eyes fixed her with sapphire brilliance: for a second, the greedy archwizard wondered if they really were sapphires. Then triple jagged, glittering claws snapped. Polaris's diamond brooch, the clasp fastening her cloak, was torn off. Her cape slithered off her shoulders and crumpled behind her.

Polaris burbled, retreating in shock. The creature had penetrated her personal shields, something an ogre's arrow couldn't pierce! The gem beast must be an elemental, an earth spirit, but not of this plane. And coming from another plane, it could stab through her shields in this plane! And now the jewel claws weaved, bobbed, and grasped at her robe. It wanted her silver embroidery!

Bleating, Polaris staggered backward, tripped on her fallen cape, and almost fell. The elemental shifted its massive bulk, sunlight glistening in its diamond depths, and crunched after her.

Laughing at the archwizard's discomfit, Sysquemalyn glanced at Polaris's entourage. At the cliff, the last two ships gathered frantic passengers. One lifted with the gangplank still down and people still clinging to it. The fiend's mind was crowded by a thousand evil spells, but one amused her. With wry humor, she pointed at individuals on the escaping ship with a finger like a stone stalactite.

"Befriend! Befriend! Befriend!"

Immediately, the people pointed out changed, distorted. Eyes blazed hatred, mouths gaped in a rictus, hands clenched. They ground their teeth, bit their own tongues so blood flowed. And, battle-mad, berserk, attacked everyone within reach. Drawing knives or swords, or plying their bare hands, they stabbed, slashed, tore, bit, battered. A screaming clerk grabbed his neighbor's hair and bit the man's ear off. A soldier jammed her sword through her comrade's belly, then twisted and shoved to spill his guts in a gory pile. A third stamped on the fingers of a woman clinging to the gangplank. Broken-fingered, the woman plunged to her death. One berserker was pushed bodily over the side by three men, but the mad one yanked a victim to tumble along with him. Sysquemalyn cursed others with berserk rage, hoping one would chop or loosen ropes and so drop the sail, make the ship veer into the mountainside, but the cursed folk savaged humans, not a wooden ship. They ran punching, kicking, biting, strangling.

Finally the flint monster shrugged, balled her fist, then blew it open. A wind vortex gathered strength, engulfed the ship, knocked the hull at a steep angle so people pitched overboard, and shredded the metal foil sail. Stricken, the ship sank. But Sysquemalyn knew that safety devices might kick in and bring the ship to a safe, though ungainly landing. She needed more destruction.

Pointing fingers that chilled, she flicked them. Icicles six feet long sailed like arrows and thudded into the ship. They punctured wood and people, sheared rigging, crunched gunwales to splinters, and exploded deep inside like giant ballistae. Something broke, for the listing ship dropped from the sky like a shot goose. No safety devices spared it from hitting the desert floor.

Lady Polaris had outrun the crysmal elemental, for the thing was slow. Yet her gown was torn at the hem, slashed on one sleeve, and she was actually bleeding from a razor-slice on her shoulder. Her gorgeous hair was disheveled, spilling around her golden face, a novel sight for Sysquemalyn. The monster laughed like rocks splitting in frost. "A simple elemental, Polaris?" the monster-mage chided. "You can't stop that? How about this? The best for last!"

Polaris panted spells, but nothing worked. Her anger was gone, washed away by terror. Never had she fought anyone so fearsome. She might even be killed! And now, cornered on this mountaintop, rattled so badly she couldn't think straight, her repeated shift spell failed too. Somehow, without anyone suspecting, even those idiot mages employed to spot traps, Sysquemalyn had ringed the mountaintop with an anti-shifting sphere such as protected floating enclaves. Polaris despaired, ready to run for the first time in her life, but couldn't! And now—

She shrieked as something warm and wet slithered down her back. It tingled and burned as it touched her skin, and for a second she feared the black ooze. Then tentacles slimed her neck. Grasping, screaming, she caught the slippery pod in both hands and yanked. The thing clung to her skin. She glimpsed it, a bright golden color, and instantly knew it. A laraken, a swamp parasite that fed on magical energy. And Polaris was charged with magic like a mythallar engine!

Sight of the parasite blotted out as a squirming tentacle covered her eyes. A tentacle tip bored into her ear like a slimy tongue. Another slid down her shorn gown, and oozed between her breasts to fasten on the skin over her heart. The thing would suck her dry of magic and life like a golden leech. She shrieked, voice cracking, "Get it-t o-off! Get it *off!*"

"You didn't say please!" crowed Sysquemalyn. The archfiend laughed so hard she almost fell. In three years of suffering hell, she'd imagined this revenge a million times, but reality was far sweeter than any dream. To have Polaris scream and beg for mercy was utterly delicious!

From the corner of a bulging eye she caught movement. The last ship yanked its gangplank to lift off. Its commander was either incredibly brave or incredibly stupid, for he'd waited to scoop up everyone still living. Sysquemalyn fixed that.

She clapped stony hands, arched the fingers to a point, and thrust toward the ship. Before her, a dent creased rock. Like an invisible knife, the crease enlarged as it slashed stone like cheese. The phantom plow was nine feet wide when it struck the ship. Wood splintered, copper-riveted boards split and sprung loose. People were either chopped in half or pulped with bone-crushing force. Screams echoed within as the magic cleaver chopped the keel, a curve of oak fourteen inches thick, and broke the back of the ship. As the ship died, so did the magic. The shorn hull fetched on a spur of rock, then, with a grinding roar, slid down the mountainside on a path of blood before tumbling out of sight.

The fiend from hell surveyed her work. In a black pool fragments of soldiers dissolved. The stone mountaintop was furrowed as if by giant carpenter tools, yet pools of ice water remained, and someone had drowned face down. Two burning hulks gave off greasy smoke from charred flesh. Blood, shorn limbs, dropped weapons, and splinters littered the ground. A hole showed where the elemental crysmal had burrowed away.

A frenzied squirming and mewling was the only action left. Lady Polaris lay on her back and wrestled with the laraken. Thriving on her personal dweomer, the parasite had expanded as large as a wolf, and now engulfed Polaris's torso like a giant ball of snot. Tentacles flailed for her arms and legs like some grotesque dance. Voice broken, she whimpered pitifully.

Plucking thorny feet from black ooze, Sysquemalyn loomed over Polaris. The archwizard's beautiful face was scratched, sweaty, scraped. Her hair was dirtied and dull, her eyes wild and bloodshot with fright.

"That's better," cooed the monster in a rasp like a file. "No longer high and mighty? Afraid? Suffering? Worried about dying? Oh, believe me, Great White Cow, Greasy White Sow, Gorgeous White Mistake, there are worse things than dying. Much, much worse. Having your skin peeled from your body, for one. Would you like that?"

A claw like an iron nail lovingly touched Polaris's cheek. She recoiled, but the throbbing laraken pinned her tight. With ease, Sysquemalyn drove the nail through Polaris's cheek. The archwizard screamed, but a thumb and finger like pliers snagged her tongue, pierced it, yanked. Polaris had to spit out blood or choke.

"We could do this all day. We might yet," crooned the fiend. "But I want you whole, to feel the touch of your pet." With a snaky hand, she caressed the laraken. It perked up, sensing more mystic energy, but Sysquemalyn flicked aside a questing tentacle. "Stone skin has advantages, see? I'll tell you what's going to happen. This laraken grows by consuming your dweomer. You'll weaken to a shell, utterly helpless. Then the laraken will move to its next task. You see, they don't mate, but reproduce themselves when they find plentiful magic. You'll serve nicely. The laraken will open a cavity in your body, plant an egg, and wait while it hatches. It will keep you alive while the offspring grows inside you, feeding off you. Slowly. Over months, or years. Oh my, I expect it'll hurt terribly! You'll feel yourself consumed from within! That almost pays us back, dear Lady Polaris, but come with me."

Grabbing the archwizard's white hair, Sysquemalyn dragged her to the black cavity left by the departed crysmal. She tipped Polaris and the laraken at the edge. Even in near-mindless fright, Polaris felt a bitter wind blow from the hole. The crysmal had bored back to its own plane. This drop would take her far from anything she'd ever known. Better to die—but would she die?

"This little friend will devour you," Sysquemalyn cooed, "but you needn't watch. Lie in darkness, deep in this mountain, never to see light again. And while you lie there, and shrivel, eaten alive, dream of revenge. As I did."

And the monster tipped parasite and prey over the edge.

Dazed, in shock, Polaris barely felt her head strike stone, her face rasp as they slid down the corkscrew hole. Too, the plump laraken absorbed some blows as they tumbled and rolled. Horror overtook Polaris, and she wished to find death quickly.

Yet part of her native intelligence fought back, calculating, though fear almost drowned out reason. For Sysquemalyn had made a mistake.

By her words, the monster assumed the hole simply dropped into the mountain like a mine shaft. But Polaris had felt the alien breeze, knew it traveled to another plane where she'd never survive. If so, there'd be an instant crossing of border to the next plane. And at the junction, the anti-shifting sphere around the mountaintop would end.

And so, despite grinding, pitching, and rolling, Polaris repeated her shifting spell over and over. Blackness wrapped her, the laraken strangled, rocks bruised, she grew dizzy, would soon black out—

—then the spell took hold.

* * * * *

Sunlight dazzled Lady Polaris. Or twilight, for the sun glared on the western horizon. Feebly she shielded her eyes, and found her hand free.

She was aching, and stiff with blood and slime. Sand clung to her face, clotted in blood at her punctured cheek. Her clothes were shredded, every inch of skin burned or scraped. Thirst throbbed as if she'd swallowed fire. Crawling, rolling over, she fought to locate herself.

Thin yellow grass clumped around, and she parted it to see. Through bloodshot eyes, she recognized a gray lump lit by dusky fire. Widowmaker Mountain belched smoke, spilled yellow-red lava down cracked sides, whirled ash into the air for miles. Sysquemalyn had turned the mountain into a blazing torch to celebrate her victory.

Polaris fell back, sucked dry of magic by battle and the laraken, but her final spell had worked. She'd shifted and left the parasite behind. She was alive, and whole in body.

But her spirit was shattered. The twilit sky seemed too big, the land too wide, the world too large. An overpowering ache possessed her, homesickness, the desire to snuggle in a dark apartment to eat, and drink cool wine, and rest.

Polaris, one of the highest mages the empire boasted, was surprised not to lust for revenge. Sysquemalyn and her hell-spawned powers were too great. Let others, a conclave of great wizards, punish the fiend. Lady Polaris only wanted to get home, take a bath, eat, and rest.

Yes, she'd stay home from now on.

Chapter 17

"Orcs!"

"Kill 'em all!"

The canny orcs chose a perfect spot for an ambush. This deep defile, almost a canyon, was the only pass through this stretch of the Barren Mountains. They'd hidden on ledges shrouded by gorse, hurled rocks onto travelers to stun and panic both horses and humans, then rushed from above like falcons. Unfortunately, orcs didn't plan far enough ahead or post a rear guard, so as the orcs battled the travelers, Sunbright and Knucklebones, and glory-hungry dwarves, tore into the orcs.

Knucklebones ran right while the shaman dashed and cocked Harvester of Blood over his shoulder. A pair of orcs bludgeoned a woman, holding her hair while her children screamed. Everyone shouted in the rock-strewn canyon, but Sunbright hollered *"Ra-vens!"* loud enough to make the orcs turn from their victim.

The first thug died instantly. Harvester of Blood

swung in a whistling arc for the orc's elbow. As Sunbright expected, the cowardly creature ducked and flinched. The heavy blade clove into the orc's scrawny forearm, and slammed its slack-jawed head. Lopped off clean, wrist and hand flipped away while Harvester bit deep the orc's temple and snapped its neck with a heart-stopping crunch. The orc dropped like a log, pulling Harvester down. Sunbright's blood boiled with a battle-high. Flexing his thick wrists, he ripped the blade free, wary because he was temporarily unarmed.

He needn't have worried. The second orc had abandoned the attack to run. Sunbright took a long step, flicked the blade, and snagged the orc's ankle with Harvester's hook. Blood spurted as razor-sharp steel cut skin and tendons. Crippled, the orc collapsed on its own cleaver. It blubbered and cried for mercy, but the barbarian took another step, planted a heavy boot on the orc's back, and stabbed straight down as if gigging fish. Harvester's keen tip cleft the orc's spine, and the creature stopped wriggling.

The big barbarian whirled to appraise the battle. The travelers were twenty people, two or three families with many horses, more than twenty beasts. Tied head to head on long leads, the horses plunged and kicked and screamed so orcs and fighters ducked flying hooves. Humans grappled with orcs—there were nearly sixty villains—or else crouched behind packs and panniers dumped from the horses. Charging into this milling melee, dwarves with mattocks and warhammers chopped at orcs, hollering the names of their ancient gods and ancestors.

Knucklebones, not much taller than the mountain men, used the dwarves as shields, darting from behind to ply her dark elven blade. Even as Sunbright watched, she hung onto Cappi's belt to alert him that she was there and a friend. Working as a team with Pullor, the two dwarves carved into orcs that they had backed into a pocket of rock. Sunbright thought that action foolish, since even orcs would fight when cornered. Better to give them room to flee, then kill them from behind, but the dwarves were hot to destroy ancient enemies and win glory. One orc broke from the pack by hurling a spear at Cappi's face and bolting.

As the dwarf staggered, Knucklebones zipped around him and poised her blade. The orc ran right into it. Black steel sliced its guts just above the naked hipbone, slid out its back, and was ripped out its side by the thief's deft twist. The orc ran a dozen paces before shock and pain dropped it.

At Sunbright's feet, two dark-haired children, a girl and boy perhaps eight and six, hunkered behind wicker baskets and howled at their mother, fallen and masked in blood.

Sunbright shifted Harvester and cuffed both across the heads. "Stop that!" the shaman said. "Help, don't squall! Here!"

He grabbed the boy's tattered smock and ripped it off his body, and left him standing in a loincloth, so surprised he stopped crying. Stooping, the shaman cradled the woman's head and wrapped the rag around her head and neck wound. That they still bled showed she was alive. Sunbright snatched the boy's hand, and pressed it atop the crude bandage. "Hold this and don't let go or your mother will die," he said bluntly. "You, little sister, dig in these packs for blankets, wrap her tight, and keep her warm. And feed her water, understand?" The teary-eyed girl nodded and jerked at the ties on a pannier. Sunbright called, "Good work!" and raced off, Harvester winking in the early winter sunlight.

Dashing around a knot of tangled, kicking horses, the shaman ran smack into three orcs, looting. Their hands overflowed with tin canteens, horse bridles, a knitted shawl, and other junk. One had even laid down his war club to dig in a saddlebag.

Sunbright didn't holler, just sucked wind for a stronger blow. He went for the armed orcs first. A big one, fast on its feet, held a war club of hickory and iron spikes—damned well-armed for orcs, the shaman noted—but few humans could stand up to a Rengarth Barbarian, and Sunbright was fitted with the finest sword his tribe ever knew.

Swung wide, Harvester didn't break the club's hickory handle, but snagged and ripped it from the orc's grasp. The big orc ducked the sweeping steel, but Sunbright stamped for balance, chopped his blade backhanded, and crushed the orc's collarbone. Yanking the leather-wrapped pommel past its ribs, Sunbright hooked the smashed shoulder into gray meat. Jerked like a pike on a line, the orc toppled at Sunbright's feet. The warrior-shaman kicked the gray head of lank hair, and stepped to kill the other two. The middle orc froze in fear, and Sunbright pierced its breadbasket, then twisted the hook to carve a hole that spilled guts. Leaving that one to die, the fighter lunged for the third, who ran.

Harvester's keen tip kissed the orc's shoulder, slashing muscle to white bone. Grabbing the spurting wound, the orc tripped over its own flying feet and crashed to earth. Sunbright scanned, found the gutted orc falling slowly. He batted it backward, then stabbed the prone orc behind the ear, snuffing the light in its sunken eyes.

Battle-lust sang in his veins as Sunbright Steelshanks whirled to find more enemies, to drown his sorrows in an orgy of blood. It was hard to see now, for the horses had kicked up dust, but the action had died down. Most of the orcs had fled or been killed.

A scratching by his feet caught his attention. The big orc with the crushed shoulder struggled for the hilt of its spiked war club. Sunbright hooked a toe and flipped the orc like a turtle. Despite grinding pain from a bleeding shoulder, the creature still craned for its weapon. Sunbright stamped on its breastbone.

Harvester poised above the orc's throat, Sunbright growled, "What's your name, beast?"

The dying orc focussed yellow eyes and sputtered, "To-Toch."

"Tell your gods you died game."

And Sunbright plunged the blade into the gray, dirty throat. Blood welled like a red fountain, then trickled away. Sunbright wiped his blade clean on his foe's tunic: gray wool with a freshly-painted red hand. "Symbol of the One King again . . ." the shaman mused.

Stooping, he picked up the war club. The long hickory handle gave a good heft, balanced, not nose-heavy, reminding him of Dorlas's warhammer. Chaffing the handle with dust to swab off blood, he slid it into his belt.

"Was that necessary?" Knucklebones asked. She stood nearby, small chest heaving, and buffed her brass knuckledusters on her lion skin jacket. The mane formed a curious hood. "He was dying anyway."

"I've left too many enemies alive."

Battle-lust passing, Sunbright was shaky and tired. He wore a brown bearskin vest but no hat, and never seemed cold.

"And I've paid for that mistake too many times," he continued. "It's a weakness, and I cannot afford to be weak. Besides, you never leave a throat uncut. Are you growing soft?"

The part-elf only polished her shiny knuckles. Raised to be ruthless, she couldn't argue, but one of Sunbright's major attractions had been his gentle kindness. Now, cut off from his people forever, he'd turned bitter, and she wondered if he'd ever be kind or gentle again.

Yet he sheathed Harvester to tend the bludgeoned woman, saw to her wounds while crooning to her children. His heart was still true, the thief knew. Only his mind was bitter. But his curt words, or lack of words, were a bugbear to endure.

Four dwarves joked and swapped boasts as they cleaned weapons and touched blades to whetstones. By contrast, the travelers grimly counted their dead, four lost out of twenty. A short, thickset man with massive, hairy arms jogged to Sunbright. Hugging his cowed children, he gasped, "How is she?"

"To tell the truth," the shaman told him. "I'm not sure." Sunbright knelt with the woman's head in his lap. The children had stanched her bleeding with rags and bundled her in blankets. Sunbright plied his belt knife to shave her scalp around a seeping wound. He rolled the woman's eyelids, examined her pupils, found them the same size. Nor did they bulge, as can happen with a severe head wound. "She may take the day to awaken, or three days. Or not at all."

The thick man gulped. All the travelers wore the same outfit. Canvas vests, thick knitted sweaters without sleeves, trousers of leather, knee-high boots wrapped with rawhide, leather caps with bills. Most had thick forearms and thighs, Sunbright noted, and wondered why. The man said, "I—we thank you for our rescue. We hoped to escape such troubles by fleeing the empire. But even here you're overrun."

Sunbright sliced up a skirt, and wrapped neat bandages around the patient's skull. "What troubles?" he asked. "We've heard naught."

Thick-fingered hands waggled helplessly as the man told him, "These orcs with the red hand raid everywhere, all around the compass. The emperor's soldiers wear themselves to a nub fighting, but they're like grass fires in drought. And they carry disease. Men partake in raids too. Bandits and pirates loot whole cities and torch them. Cities and towns shut the gates and admit no one, not even their own peasants. Markets and fairs languish. We journeyed to Zenith for the Festival of the Harvest Moon and found naught but empty fields. We've met no buyers, no one with cash, yet everyone wants our horses. The bandits are bloodthirsty, but imperial troops are just as bad. Twice we met small armies that threatened to take the horses in the empire's name, and give us nothing but wooden chits . . ."

Talk of rampant raids and chaos intrigued Sunbright, the dwarves, and Knucklebones. While the horse traders untangled their mounts and picked up and packed, and Sunbright stitched wounds, the dwarves brewed rose hip tea and unwrapped oak cakes. With the hostlers' permission, they butchered a dead horse and sliced the red meat into long strips. The dwarves cut wood and scraped a fire pit as the short winter day ended and brittle stars winked. Everyone feasted on horse meat and liver and brains that steamed in the frosty air like their breath. The hostlers unfolded curious shaggy ponchos with slits that left their bare arms free.

The hostlers' news was patchy and shaded by personal escapes, but it was clear the empire was inundated by the One King's ravagers. Rumor said Lady Polaris had discussed truce with the One King, but they'd warred instead and blown the top off Widowmaker Mountain. No one knew who controlled what territories. Orcish and imperial armies alike splintered into raiding parties. All strangers were foes, and no place was safe. The hostlers, honest traders once welcome throughout the empire, were war refugees, as were many other folk.

Sunbright went quiet as Hilel, the leader of this horse-trading clan, spoke of meeting "tall men with horsetails like yours." Stranded on the grasslands, the Rengarth Barbarians had dug sod houses into low hills. They foraged game from the grasslands, ventured into the forests for food and firewood, but many were waylaid by orcs, and the surviving barbarians were a morose lot, Hilel claimed, starving and haunted-eyed. He'd feared a massacre and the theft of their horses, but the barbarians let them pass without even asking the news. Some mothers and fathers had begged food for their children, who shivered with hunger.

Late in the night, Hilel asked for directions north-west. The brooding Sunbright didn't answer, so Knucklebones explained. "You can't go on. We've explored with the dwarves. This canyon rises too steeply for horses to mount, and cave bears are big as your horses. They'd eat you and your animals like blue-berries.

"Nor can you pass south of the mountains, for the elves kill interlopers. Were it spring, I'd recommend you swing around Vandal Station and follow the Bay of Ascore to the Waterbourne River. But in winter, that'll be frozen. So there really is no way northwest except through the Cold Forest.

"Perhaps they can advise you better at Bandor Village."

The negative news disheartened the hostlers, who quietly posted guards. Rolling in blankets, Sunbright, Knucklebones, and the dwarves curled by the fire.

But Sunbright didn't sleep.

In the morning, the hostlers buried their dead. Diota, Hilel's wounded wife, had not awakened, so they rigged a travois to ferry her. Thoughts of travois and traveling deepened Sunbright's gloom. With final thanks, the refugees tramped down the canyon. The dwarves, toting hides of horse meat, mounted stone slopes for their base camp. The headquarters was a high, stair-stepping cave that overlooked the High Forest: a place where, by standing on a jutting spire and leaning far out, Sunbright could just see the yellow grasslands where his people huddled in starvation and misery.

While winter closed in, the dwarves had spent weeks exploring the Barren Mountains, which is how they'd stumbled on the orc raid. They crawled into every cave and cleft as if looking to buy the mountains, and indeed, Drigor finally admitted, that's what he intended. The distant Iron Mountains were played out, food and iron ore exhausted, and the encroaching yak-men were too numerous to withstand. So the old dwarf's mission had been two-fold: to warn Sunbright of the flint monster (this, the barbarian still didn't understand), and to seek a new homeland for the Sons of Baltar. With nothing better to do, and safety in numbers, Sunbright and Knucklebones helped, figuring to winter with the dwarves before moving on in spring. They didn't discuss where to go then, for the subject pained Sunbright too deeply. As did the word "homeland."

But today's return offered a surprise. For as they passed the base camp's guard, she whispered, "Them elves are back."

* * * * *

"We ask again that you speak to your people about truce."

The same three elves on the same mission. They stood, not sat, in the lowermost cave.

From a broad ledge outside, a crack in the mountain only waist-high gave entrance to a squat chamber hardly head-high. The floor then slanted upward where dwarves had built ladders of tree branches to access the various splintered caves within the mountain. The damp cleft reeked of brown bears, the former inhabitants, and eye-watering smoke, the method that had evicted them. Outside, winter light glittered on frost.

"I cannot approach my people," Sunbright explained patiently. With him were Drigor, Knucklebones, and Monkberry. "I am no longer a member of their tribe."

"They are less a nuisance now," said the elven woman, "but we must still guard, and shoot those who trespass. We would rather you humans stay out, so we might better repel the orcs who stream over the mountains in hordes."

Sunbright was aware of the orc problem. Lately, orcs were thick as ants in spring.

"I'm sorry my people forage for food and wood in your forest." Sunbright said, tired and ironic. "Yet there's nothing—*eh?*"

A tug on his belt. Monkberry's wrinkled face was thoughtful. "Son," she said. "I must talk to you."

"Now? Can't it wait?"

Monkberry caught Sunbright's ear and towed him toward the cave entrance. Bent almost double, the barbarian hobbled after.

Outside, in glittering cold and bitter wind, Sunbright rubbed his ear while Monkberry clasped arthritic hands and glared up at her son.

"I've thought about our troubles, Sunbright. A lot. You've been away and busy while I've tended the fire, and watching flames always gives one ideas. I have one for you. You must convey this truce offer to our tribe."

"Not I," he said, annoyed. "I couldn't walk within arrow range of the Rengarth."

Monkberry ignored his objections. "Our tribe needs help," she insisted. "They'll die on the prairie in winter. Already the children hunger, you tell me. They need help, and only you can give it. So you shall."

"What help?" Warriors were not to be scolded by their mothers, yet he fidgeted like a boy caught stealing apples.

"I don't know. I'm only an old woman who's outlived her usefulness. But you're shaman, because you're blessed—cursed, too—with imagination. You can't lounge around a drafty cave and mope."

"Mother," the man drawled, "if I go near them, I'll be killed!"

"So be it," she said. "Go anyway."

"Hunh?" Sunbright started as if his mother had pulled a knife.

Monkberry took her son's calloused hands in her twisted

ones. "Son, we mustn't question the will of the gods. Our job is to endure. Suffer sometimes, but endure. You've been selected as shaman by blood and birth, by the gods and the tribe. And by your father and myself. Your destiny was laid before you were born." Her voice grew softer and she said, "I have only one son. If I lose you, I have nothing. Then would I walk into the first snowstorm and lie down to pass into the next world. But I'll sacrifice you, and myself if need be, to save the Rengarth. For our people must endure. Do you understand?"

Tears in her eyes spoke louder than words. Sunbright Steelshanks of the Raven Clan hugged his mother, and said thickly, "Yes, mother, I understand. Thank you for reminding me."

The mother pushed her son away, wiped her wrinkled face, and said, "Now. What shall you propose? Those elves inside might help us. And the dwarves. And what you think up. You're clever when you don't mope. What shall we try?"

Sunbright sighed, scratched his head, fiddled with the thongs of his horsetail. "Well . . ." he said. "I had the germ of an idea, but it's probably stupid and won't work. Drigor's blather about a homeland planted a seed in my brain. And those hostlers we met, with the horses, made me wonder. . . .

"But come inside, Mother. It's chilly."

He steered the old woman into the cave. "You know, to claim you've outlived your usefulness is foolish talk," he told her. "Almost as foolish as mine . . ."

* * * * *

Icy wind howled on the prairie. It bit through Sunbright's bearskin vest, stung his face so hard that ice particles drew blood, numbed his huge hands, and made his eyes water so he couldn't see. Dead grass crunched underfoot, frozen solid. Behind him trudged

Knucklebones, huddled in her lion skin. She'd insisted on coming, but shivered continuously.

In the long winter night, Sunbright worried they'd miss the barbarian camp, but then he whiffed smoke. Rounding a ridge no higher than his shoulder, he spotted crude sod houses. Only half a dozen, for the tribe had scattered over miles to hug behind ridges, pitiful shelter from man-killing wind.

Sunbright staggered to the biggest sod hut, perhaps twenty feet across and knee-high, put his mouth to the smoke hole, and shouted, "Meet me outside!"

His small party shivered while sods were unpacked from a hole in the hut's side. Finally, hunched and dirty as moles, a few barbarians crept out with bronze swords in blue fists. They were so filthy, with hair grown in and thick beards on men, it took Sunbright a moment to recognize Forestvictory, no longer fat, and Strongsea, who resembled his long-dead father, Farmyouth.

At sight of the shaman, Strongsea hefted his sword. Sunbright stepped aside to reveal his companions. Three elves in black capes and armor, pale as vampires, not shivering. Two dwarves bundled in bearskin and horsehide.

The shaman warned, "Don't!"

"What do you want?" asked Forestvictory. The former trail chief's eyes were pouchy.

"You're invited to council!" Sunbright had to shout above the wind. "With the elves and dwarves and me. Don't protest, just shut up and listen. We can hammer out our differences, and get you off this benighted plain, if you'll listen. Tell the others, the whole tribe, to come to the vale where we camped. You'll be unharmed if you keep swords in sheathes, and there'll be food. The elves and dwarves will feed you while we council. Bring the children, if only for that. Tell the rest. Tomorrow!"

"It could be a trap!" Strongsea wheezed.

Forestvictory stared as if her brain were frozen. "What if we refuse?" she asked.

"Then keep your pride and die! It's nothing to me!" Sunbright lied. "I'm no longer Rengarth. Tell the others. Tomorrow."

Without waiting for an answer, he let the wind push him and his guards back toward the forest and the mountains.

* * * * *

"They killed Darkname! And Lightrobin! Shall we take blood money, and stain our name?"

"How do we know they won't kill us in our sleep? Lure us with kind words, and a knife behind their backs!"

"Aye, or poison the food?"

"I'd take orcs over these soulless monsters! An enemy you know is better than an unknown!"

"Elves eat babies! And suck the goodness out of food so there's nothing left to sustain a body!"

"I say we turn back for Scourge! We were happy there!"

Wrangling rang round the amphitheater. The barbarians had come, of course, lured by food. Sunbright and his protective elves and dwarves met them on the ill-fated camp between the sheltering highlands, then led the straggling band into the dark forest for nearly three miles. Here the barbarians found a natural amphitheater sunk into the ground below trees and wind. Ancient stones covered with moss ringed the circle, and at the bottom, a blazing bonfire consumed entire trees. Shivering, starved, dirty barbarians crept into the bowl so close to the fire their eyebrows singed. Set on stones were elven winter rations and fresh game: oat cakes with salt and maple syrup, dried herring, hunks of deer and bear and bison, even barrels of ale and a trough of spring water. The hungry barbarians fell on the meat barehanded and ate it raw.

During this orgy of warmth and food, Sunbright sat with his personal bodyguard: Knucklebones and Monkberry, three elven archers named Gladejoy, Deerspirit, and Lionmoon, and the two dwarves, Cappi and Pullor. They occupied a stone midway between the barbarians, the chief elven negotiators, and Drigor's band in shaggy winter hides.

The elven contingent was a vision from a dream. Thirty of them were led by a tall elven woman with cascading white hair. They were mostly dressed alike, in soft green shirts and fine boots and armor, with some differences in rank. The leader, Pleasantwalk, wore no boiled breastplate, instead a pair of black epaulets on a harness, gem-studded black gloves, and a black helmet adorned with black leaves. She sat on a throne of blond wood ornately carved with birds and animals, worn smooth by ages of monarchs. The throne had been toted through the forest on the shoulders of courtiers, who were armed with curved black bows and sheaves of slim, black arrows. Sunbright had not spoken to this elven queen (if such she was), but only to Tamechild, her chancellor, who conveyed the shaman's messages to the queen only twelve feet away.

For the first time in a long time, Sunbright wore no sword. Harvester's baldric and scabbard hung from a peg on a tree above the amphitheater. The barbarians had also left all weapons at the upper rim, while protesting they were being rounded up for slaughter. But the elves' calm poise, and the lure of heat and meat had finally spilled them over the edge like lemmings.

Now, with hunger and thirst and cold sated, the Rengarth Barbarians counseled—for Sunbright had added prayers and offerings to the elves' bonfire. As barbarian bodies warmed, so did tempers and grudges. Some humans hurled accusations and threats, hinted darkly of treachery and collusion between Sunbright and the Shadow Walkers. But most barbarians recognized that the elves were their hosts, had fed and warmed them, and so held their tongues. Sunbright was proud of them, but his heart was stricken as he counted their numbers. Just under three hundred arrived, while they'd enter the ancestral grasslands with over four hundred thirty. Still, Tamechild murmured, it showed the barbarians' toughness to survive this long on winter prairie.

Finally, after the stupid and stubborn aired their empty heads, Sunbright dusted his seat and walked to a small dais that each ring of the theater sported. He raised both hands and waited for silence, which meant from the barbarians, for the elves were quiet as graveyard ghouls.

"Rengarth!" Sunbright called. "You know who I am. Sunbright Steelshanks, son of Sevenhaunt and Monkberry of the Raven Clan."—Someone booed, yelled, "Not any more!" but was slapped quiet—"Know that I did not invite you! 'Twas our gracious hosts, the Moon Elves of the Far Forest, cousins to the High Elves of Cormanthyr in the west. They wished to council, not I. I am merely the mouthpiece between you."

The barbarians stirred, watched the silent elves with new interest, and listened.

"I don't need to tell you," Sunbright went on, "how harsh the world has grown. All lands suffer, their magic drained by forces unknown. Thin crops and scarcer game drive many peoples to move, including ourselves. In addition, the One King again leads armies to ravage both cities and hinterlands. So it proves here, for orcs and other vermin flow over the Barren Mountains like rats fleeing a fire. The elves doubled and tripled their efforts to keep the orcs out, and then we, the Rengarth, arrived. Since we invaded their forest, they worked to keep us out too."

Over shouts, he continued, "Now, I could talk all night, and we shall, but I'll lay out a simple plan to consider. Simply this. That Moon Elves, the Sons of Baltar, and the Rengarth Barbarians forget grudges, and declare peace! That the dwarves fortify the Barren Mountains. That the Moon Elves guard the Far Forest. And the Rengarth guard the prairie—"

A howl of protest went up, that the tribe would die, that they couldn't last the winter, that—

Sunbright plowed on, "Yes, yes, yes! True! And since the prairie can't support so many, the Moon Elves generously offer us the fringe of the forest for a depth of two leagues. From the grasslands, into the forest for six miles, to a river called the Delimbiyr. An escort will show you this boundary. A six-mile band, free, to use as we wish. In return, you must promise to guard the prairie from outside attack, and keep faith with elves and dwarves, and work together for the good of all. So elves may call on barbarians if needed, and humans might retreat to the dwarven mountains in an attack, or into the elven forest.

"In short," Sunbright droned to a mesmerized audience, "you will swear—by blood oath—to harm neither elf nor dwarf, but aid all to keep out the orcs and other villains. In short, we build an alliance of people secure on their own turf—prairie, forest, and mountain—with secure borders. A mighty triangle that can withstand any force, from any direction!"

Sunbright let his words die in the air, then shouted, "Children of the Rengarth, do you agree?"

Barbarians muttered, questioned, buzzed, and argued. Over the babble Forestvictory called, "We can cut trees to build huts? Shoot game and set snares? And we only need keep out raiders?"

Sunbright smiled. For the question gave the answer.

Chapter 18

Deep in the Barren Mountains. . . .

With oil lamps and pickaxes, Oredola and Hachne explored a tall cave from which rust water trickled. Rust meant iron. But not far in they gagged on a gut-wrenching stink. A hashed coyote carcass writhed with maggots on the cave floor. The skull had been crushed as if by a stone, then gnawed by strong, dull teeth. Without a word, the dwarves pulled back.

Too late.

From the dark rustled something twice as tall as the dwarves, mottled green and scabrous black in the lamplight. Empty eye sockets drilled into their souls.

"Trolls!"

The dwarves whirled and ran on stumpy legs.

But the trolls were quick as spiders. Crud-caked claws tore at the dwarves' backpacks, ripping stiff ox hide like paper. The dwarves shucked their packs and ran faster, breath sobbing in their lungs, hobnailed boots ringing on stone and splashing in rusty water. As they reached the dim sheen of twilight, they screeched, "Help! Trolls! Help!"

Oredola felt a claw tick the back of her neck and draw blood. Without turning, she whipped her pickaxe behind, heard it thud on stony flesh, gained a second's respite, then charged into flat winter light that was overcast but blinding after the dark cave. Hachne stampeded down the narrow canyon, shouting for help.

With a screech, the trolls erupted from the cave behind. Scaly feet skittered on rock while a curious kitten's mewling whined in their throats—a sound of hunger and rage. Then Oredola heard a gasp like a death rattle at her ear. Covering the back of her neck, she threw herself flat on rough stone.

And help arrived.

Slim black arrows zipped from the sky like ospreys after fish. The shafts slammed into trolls' empty eye sockets, stabbed deep into dim brains, and hurled them backward to crash like dead men cut from the gallows.

The hideous creatures didn't die, only thrashed and pulled at the wood jammed in their skulls. Their undying thrashing was the most hideous sight of all.

Oredola rolled to her feet, grabbed up a rock hammer, and pounded the nearest troll. She knew that any limbs that she might hack off the thing would only regrow, but the dwarf hoped that *breaking* limbs would slow the monsters down. Having heard the zip of arrows, Hachne returned to smash his pickaxe again and again into a troll, crunching joints and mauling the thing's throat.

Soon, an elf in green and black, with long, wild black hair and a pale face joined them. Darting from her high guardpost, she'd fetched an armful of sticks and branches and feathers and fluff: an old condor's nest. Flinging the mess over the trolls, she called, "Only fire will kill them! Spill your oil!"

Swiftly the dwarves smashed lanterns atop the pyre.

Ancient dried wood and downy fluff caught immediately. The trolls gasped and sobbed horribly as the flames curled around them. Dwarves and the elf retreated down the canyon to avoid the stink.

"Well!" Oredola said as she mopped her brow with a shaking hand, slurped water from a canteen, then offered some to the elf, who took it. "I guess we'll mark that cave as 'occupied!' "

"Not any more!" Hachne laughed at the weak jest. The elf smiled.

They congratulated themselves on their cooperation and the success of the elven/dwarven/barbarian alliance. Here the dwarves explored the mountains and flushed out monsters while keen-eyed elves guarded the work details from on high.

Flames crackled down the canyon and the pyre quit heaving. The elf said, "I shall return to my post."

"Yes," Oredola said. "And we thank you." She held out her craggy paw, as did Hachne. Bemused, the elf stared, then, for the first time in her life, shook hands.

* * * * *

In the Far Forest. . . .

Blackblossom and Kindbloom knelt at a small stream off the merry Delimbiyr River. Behind them, in the six mile stripe allotted to the barbarians, axes rang and chinked. The two warriors pulled axes from the stream and wiped them dry. They'd soaked the hafts overnight so the wood would swell and make a tighter, safer fit. The new broad-axes were dwarven-made, for Drigor had built a forge near an iron deposit at the foot of Sanguine Mountain.

They'd shouldered the axes when Kindbloom suddenly grabbed Blackblossom's arm.

"Listen! What's that?"

Blackblossom tossed back her horsetail, and cupped

her ear. "It's—coyotes yapping," she said. "From across the river."

"Too deep for coyotes," Kindbloom whispered. "Something bigger."

Blackblossom, tall and willowy and decisive, hefted her axe and yanked the sash of her sheepskin coat. "We better go see," she said.

"We're not supposed to cross the river," stated Kindbloom, who was surly and quick to cite rules.

The barbarian warrior didn't answer, only tripped across a new log bridge and into the winter forest. Rather than miss a fight, Kindbloom followed.

Leafless brush was still thick and tangled along the riverbank, forcing them to take the path, though they went warily, with axes foremost. Undergrowth gave way to open forest where wide-spaced white oaks allowed easy walking. Only sunlit glades sported brush. They turned north off the trail toward the yapping. Gradually they made out a familiar sound. Orcs. But happy and raucous. What could it mean?

Silent in moosehide boots, the two women skirted a glade, spotted flickering movement, and picked from trunk to trunk. Five orcs gamboled around a tree, hooting and laughing like dogs barking, hurling rocks and sticks into the branches. In the tree something like a big kingfisher, painted black and green, ducked and dodged.

"They've treed an elf!" breathed Blackblossom.

"Good enough," snapped Kindbloom. "One of the bastards shot Darkname. Let 'em suffer!"

"Go left," Blackblossom whispered, ignoring the snipe. "I'll go right opposite. When I shout, charge in, screaming your head off. They'll probably run."

Kindbloom stared, whispered, "I won't risk my life for a vampire."

"Risk it for mine then," Blackblossom said. "I swore by blood to uphold the alliance."

Blackblossom slid off right to circle another glade. A minute later, the clan cry *"Be-lu-ga!"* split the woods. Bashing through brush, swinging a shining pole axe, a tall, thin barbarian woman flew screaming from the forest. Seconds later, from the opposite side, another woman roared, *"Snow cats!"* and exploded among the orcs.

The villains dropped their swords and shields to scatter. One orc stood its ground, but its upraised war club was battered aside, then a heavy axe head crushed its breast. A fleeing orc was tripped to crash in loam and leaves, had its head smashed by an axe.

The other orcs were long gone. The two women scanned the woods, panting, axes poised, but there was no counterattack.

An elf dropped from the wide limbs of the oak, and picked up his fallen knife and hat. He was tall, but looked Blackblossom in the eye. "I thank you," the elf said. "I am Starvalley."

Deliberately withholding their names, Kindbloom instead sniped, "How were you taken, elf?"

The elf's pale face colored.

"I was drinking at the river while thinking of a poem. Not paying attention. I got separated from my bow and had to run."

Kindbloom sniffed, "You were quick enough to shoot our people in the back when hiding in the forest!"

The elf drew up straight and said, "Such was I obligated by duty. Whether I liked to kill or not wasn't asked of me."

"And anyway," Blackblossom breezed, "that's in the past. We're allies now. Come, comrade." With a short nod and hint of a smile, she sashayed off.

"Wait!" called the poet. "What are your names?"

Kindbloom marched on, but Blackblossom turned back, teased, "Oh no, Sir Elf. We've heard that if an elf learns your name, he gains power over your soul. You'll just have to guess our names—Starvalley!"

Back at the log bridge, Kindbloom groused, "Consorting with elves, bah! Darkname and Firstfortune and Lightrobin must writhe in their graves!"

Blackblossom only mused, "Starvalley . . . And he favors poetry. These elven men are not uncomely, you know. Not big and sturdy like our breed, but spry like willows. Even . . . tingly."

"*Tingly?*" Kindbloom almost fell off the bridge as she said, "And comely? Are you mad?"

Blackblossom only whistled as they crossed the bridge.

* * * * *

Later that day, along the river. . . .

A boy and a girl, Greatreeve and Meadowbear, squabbled as they overturned a rotten log and kicked at red-brown punk. Grubs and wood lice spilled loose, legs windmilling to escape the light. The pair scooped dozens of insects into a birch bark cup.

"I still say it's a waste of time!" Meadowbear stated. "We tried these bugs, and the fish won't bite!"

"What else is there?" demanded Greatreeve. "There aren't any worms. The dirt's too rocky."

"Quiet!" the girl shushed, though she was just as loud. "They'll hear us!" The two had sneaked away from their chores to try their luck with the rainbow-speckled fish in the river Delimbiyr. They'd never seen such fish before, but they looked succulent. And fussy, for the creatures rose to no bait the children offered. "And elves live in these—*Aah!*"

The children jumped so high their birch bark cup flew in the air. Bugs flitted across winter leaves. An elf, tall and green and black and wild-haired, had stepped from behind a tree as if invisible.

"Don't be frightened," the elf said. Calm and kind words belied the elf's fierce appearance. "I see you seek the *shalass* but lack luck."

"The what?" asked Meadowbear. "Oh, the fish? Is that what you call 'em?"

"How do you catch 'em?" asked Greatreeve.

The elf smiled, face lighting up. He pointed at the rotten log. "Not with those," he said. "The best bait is the grub of the mayfly in spring, when the shalass is hungriest, but there are none now. Rather, try here . . ." The elf crooked a finger and walked away smiling.

"What d'ya think?" Meadowbear hissed to her partner.

"Elves eat babies, my papa says," whispered the boy. "But we're not babies . . . And he *lives* here—"

"So he knows how to catch fish!" finished Meadowbear.

Together, the barbarian children picked on silent feet after the elf. The tall archer climbed into a tree with thick branches still adorned with dark green leaves. Jumping free of the trunk, the elf bent a branch for the children to reach. "Pick a few nuts," he told them. "Not too many."

Wondering, the children plucked a handful of dark green nuts like olives. Releasing the branch, the elf drew a wicked curved knife that made the children step back. The woods-dweller smiled as he peeled a green husk. Revealed was a nut white as chalk. Quartering the nut, the elf handed each child a white curl.

"The shalass is delicious but dim. Bait your hook with this nut and jig the line ever so gently, and Sir Shalass will mistake it for a mayfly grub. Trust me, it works."

The erstwhile fisherfolk looked at the nut hunks with awe. "My thanks . . ." said Meadowbear. Remembering her manners, she added, "But what do I owe you? Rengarth Barbarians always pay their debts."

The elf nodded and said, "Fair enough. Know you the names of the two women who entered the forest this morning? They came after axes soaking in yon stream.

One was middling-high and dark, but the other was tall and graceful as a sandhill crane—"

"You mean Blackblossom?" blurted Greatreeve. Meadowbear jabbed him with an elbow, too late.

"Blackblossom." The elf tasted the name. "Apt, for one so rare and fair . . . My thanks, fishers. Our debt is square. Good luck!"

Swinging bow and sword hilt, the elf melted into the forest.

"Big mouth!" snarled the girl. "You blabbed Blackblossom's name. Now he'll get power over her soul!"

"I wonder why he wants it," said Greatreeve. "I hope he doesn't hurt her. . . ."

* * * * *

On the slope between forest and prairie. . . .

Strongsea threw down his axe in disgust. It bounced off a log and flipped over. "Gah!" he spat. "Next to useless!"

"Don't be silly," Graysky said as he patiently hammered the back of his axe with a wooden maul to split a log. "Just because you can't sharpen an axe—"

"It's not something you can learn. Either you're born knowing how to sharpen a blade, or you're not, and I'm not! And I'm damned to walk all the way to the mountain just to have a dwarf sharpen it for me! I hate walking as much as I hate sharpening."

The bigger man flopped down on a stump. There were stumps everywhere, scores of them, for the barbarians had labored to cut back the forest and build homes for the winter. Already a dozen longhouses striped the hillside and sent smoke curling into the blue-white sky. Stacks of cordwood and piles of burnable slash ran higgledy-piggledy up the slope.

"Everyone's busy," Graysky said as he hammered his

maul a last time to divide the log, then leaned back and wiped his brow. "The dwarves are too busy forging tools to come sharpen them, so we needs—Hello! What are *you?*"

"A fairy!" Strongsea hopped off his stump to grab his fallen axe.

"No, sir, I'm not! Please don't hurt us!"

The barbarian men stared at the tiny being. Barely thigh-high, she was stooped and thin with a narrow head dominated by a bulbous nose and lank brown hair. She wore rags of red and blue once cut for humans, much too large. Huddled behind her legs were two tinier creatures, all noses and eyes.

"We're gnomes," explained the female. "Kin to dwarves, but city-dwellers. Or we were until the troubles. My husband was killed by a mob, so we fled with only our tools and the clothes on our backs. We heard this land still knew peace, and trekked across the tall grass—"

"Yes, yes, we know," Graysky said, shaking his head as he regarded the trio, mother and children, who'd appeared from the nearby woods. The barbarian had heard of gnomes, but had never seen one. These days all sorts of refugees streamed into this mighty triangle framed by prairie and forest and mountains, for the barbarian/elf/dwarf alliance kept at bay the wars and riots and plagues that raged elsewhere. "You're not the first, nor the last. I imagine you're hungry."

The gnomes' bright eyes glittered, but Strongsea ventured, "Don't feed 'em! It'll just encourage 'em to stick around like stray cats."

"I'll remember that when next you belly up to the trough," returned Graysky. He unwrapped an oilskin containing acorn bread and smoked elk meat. The gnomish mother saw that her two children ate before she wolfed down her own portion. Strongsea sighed in disgust.

Graysky sat on a stump and studied the gnome. Her hands were overlarge for her pipe stem arms, but long-fingered and clever. She wore a belt with many pouches of thin tools that jutted every which way. The barbarian asked, "Kin to dwarves, eh? What can you do with this?" Strongsea objected when Graysky plucked away his axe.

The gnome *tsked* at the dull edge, hastily wiped her mouth, then propped the axe in a cleft of a log. Selecting a short file of jagged crystal from her belt, she worked on the edge, almost pressing her big nose against the hardy tool as she stroked quickly and methodically. Within a few minutes, she handed the tool to Graysky, who passed it to Strongsea.

"Humph. Never saw a file like that. Can't be much— *Whoa!*" The bigger barbarian touched a thumb to the edge and cut his flesh. Swearing, he sucked his thumb. Then light dawned. Laying the axe down, he leaped up so fast the gnomes recoiled in fright. Yet Strongsea caught them all in a gigantic bear hug.

"Welcome, brethren!"

* * * * *

Out on the prairie. . . .

Two dwarves, Cappi and Pullor, stopped at an invisible line anchored by distant horsemen. The riders waved "All clear."

Cappi huffed, "I guess we part here. Thank you."

"No bother," said Magichunger. "I like to get out, see what stirs on our border. Though these days our scouts do the job."

Dwarves and men gazed over the prairie. There wasn't much to see. Rolling grass, winter white, marched to the horizon. A pair of vultures soared idly. Behind, the tip of Sanguine Mountain just showed to the tallest men. The barbarians considered that landmark the border of their new country.

The war chief and five fighters accompanied the two dwarves. Laden like donkeys with satchels and weapons, Cappi and Pullor journeyed to the distant Iron Mountains to tell the Sons of Baltar of the promise in the Barren Mountains. Through his message-bearers, Drigor hoped the entire tribe would relocate. The dwarves shook hands, were wished good luck, and stepped off on their thousand mile journey. The barbarians would see them out of sight, but the sudden thrum of thunder underfoot set both teams staring north.

The outriding scout pounded across the prairie on a half-wild horse. Knots lumped her bare arms as she wrestled the horse to a standstill, and jerked her leather-billed cap square. "Tracks!" she shouted. "Many of them! Entering our lands!"

"Show us!" commanded the war chief, and the party trotted after the scampering horse.

A mile on, the rider pointed to crushed grass, a path meandering north. Magichunger stooped, and rolled bruised stalks between his fingers. The trail was only a day old. Without a word, men and dwarves turned north at a trot flanked by the tall rider. Soon the trail wended west into barbarian territory.

Hours on, the rider dismounted, and waited for the war party to catch up. Where the land folded, Magichunger and the rest smelled smoke. Splitting up, they crept forward. Strange voices carried on the wind. Edging to a creek bed, they peered down.

A mix of scruffy soldiers, men and half-orcs, and even two half-ogres, hunkered around a small fire. No one ate, for their haversacks lay flat. They only watched an iron pot boil in hopes of weak tea. Their dirty clothing was mixed, but pale gold predominated in tunics. Weapons lay by every hand.

Magichunger pulled back, consulted with Cappi and Crabbranch, then signaled fighters forward silently. When everyone was posted, Magichunger reared to his feet with bow at full draw.

The hungry soldiers jumped, yelped, grabbed, but the

burly barbarian hollered, "Touch them and die! You're ringed by arrows!"

The soldiers cursed, but stayed still. At the war chief's command, they backed with hands on heads against the sand bank. Most shivered, fearing to be shot. A barbarian and dwarf slid into the ravine to toss swords, war axes, spears, and clubs up on the grass. One older man rasped, "We're to be left defenseless on this godsforsaken plain?"

"You're lucky to be alive," Magichunger told them. "You trespass the lands of the Rengarth Barbarians. We claim all territory to the west and kill raiders. For such you look to me: deserters from the empire's army hunting easy prey." The renegades squirmed.

"Yet we value peace and never kill unless provoked," Magichunger continued. "So I suggest you turn for Northreach to find honest work. Follow the Sled by night. Keep your belt knives, and set snares on the way: these hills swarm with rabbits. On your way. To linger is to die."

Grumbling, but relieved to be safe, the soldiers grabbed meager packs, filed along the ravine, mounted to the grass, and stepped off northeast. The barbarians watched them out of sight, the half-ogres disappearing last.

Then the war party laughed with relief. Magichunger said to the dwarves, "You'd best be off afore nightfall."

Agreeing, the dwarves hitched their packs. But Cappi gazed northeast after the departed soldiers. "I wish the lands we must cross were as safe as this corner of the empire has become," he said wistfully.

"Then hop to!" Magichunger chuckled. "Fetch your tribe home and it'll be even safer!"

Everyone laughed and waved as the dwarves marched with the long evening sun shining on their packs.

* * * * *

Where the craggy feet of Sanguine Mountain rived the earth, Hilel and his horse-traders had selected a brushy, steep-sided ravine and blocked the ends with stumps and slash. This makeshift corral contained forty wild and half-tame horses, some brought by Hilel initially, others captured on the prairie.

Sunbright walked the ravine's edge and studied the milling animals as Hilel and his clan cut out individuals with horsehair lariats. The stocky horse-traders in their sleeveless sweaters and canvas vests and leather caps looked much alike, so Sunbright had difficulty telling them apart.

He more watched how they worked. The riders moved with a clever ease that belied skill. Men and women and children of the clan could plunge amidst a hurtling maelstrom of spooked animals to whip a snug noose around a neck while dodging flailing hooves, then somehow jerk the recalcitrant beast out of the herd and pacify it within a few minutes. Such skill bespoke years, generations of practice.

Outside the ravine, Hilel had snubbed a large roan stallion's forehoof against its chest to sling a saddle across its back. Timing just right, he hooked a boot, bounded to the saddle, and hauled the reins to keep his seat and teach the animal a lesson. Nudging, cooing, occasionally swatting, he forced the huge red mount to limp a tight circle.

Lazily, yet watching everywhere, Sunbright paced alongside and called questions: How many times must you mount before he'll accept you? Do horses ever strike when your back is turned? How smart are they? Are they loyal? How far can you ride one in a day? How much can they carry comfortably? What precautions are needed at night to protect them? And dozens more.

Hilel answered questions as he worked, puffing but

patient, for his clan owed Sunbright a favor. First, the shaman and dwarves had rescued the entire clan from destruction by orcs early in the winter, then given clear directions for travel northwestward. But the traveling horse-traders had found chaos and danger in every path, for themselves and their beasts, so had returned to beg sanctuary of Sunbright. The shaman had spoken to the joint council, arguing that the riders could scout, haul supplies, run messages, locate herds of livestock, and perform other useful and unique tasks. So the clan camped, and set to culling wild horses from the plains.

Finally the exasperated trader asked, "Why so many questions, my friend? You pester me as if you'd buy the entire herd. Yet I know your people do not ride, but walk—they declaim it often enough—and view horses as nothing but steaks and sweetbreads on the hoof. So why all these questions?"

"No reason, just curious," Sunbright lied. "I admire how well your family rides, and wonder whether it's a skill that can be learned by anyone."

"Such as yourself? Steady!" Hilel cooed to the horse pacing on three legs. "Would you become a mounted barbarian? A dragoon or lancer, perhaps? Or a carter hauling loads of shoes and ale?" He laughed out loud.

"No, not I," Sunbright smiled. "I just wonder . . . Never mind. Who comes?"

At a trot clipped Hilel's oldest son, a brawny young man named Micah. His canvas vest was laced tight yet bulged. When he reined in, he dug in his vest, withdrew a flat rock, and handed it to Sunbright.

The shaman studied the black rock, which was polished on one side and delicately etched with an odd design. Brushing off dirt, Sunbright saw two thin elves with high-pointed ears who talked amidst unrecognizable glyphs. "Where did you get this?" he asked.

"A dwarf found it," Micah explained. "They enlarged the area around Drigor's forge and turned up this stone.

It was the only black one. What shall we do with it?"

"Give it to the elves," Sunbright ordered. "It may be important to them."

"Oh. Could—could you return it?" Micah made a face. "I don't fancy riding into the woods. I'm leery of elves. Too many stories of how they drink blood and steal babies—"

"Forget those," Sunbright cut him off waving a hand. "Everyone's heard such rumors, but no one's ever suffered such. Just ride up the vale into the woods, and call across the river. Give it to any elf. 'Twill benefit all of us. They'll be grateful we value their artifacts and make efforts to return them, and your family will prosper from their good will."

"How?" asked the boy doubtfully.

"Just do it," Hilel ordered. "The shaman speaks true. An unexpected favor is returned doubly, our ancestors say. And the gods chalk them against your name. Now get along, or you'll be late for supper."

Frowning, Micah obeyed, clucking and thumping his heels to aim the horse for the barbarian camp. The men watched him go.

Hilel huffed, "You have some scheme up your sleeve, friend Sunbright. I thought I was a cagey trader, and always got the best of a deal, but you're a master. I only wish I could fathom your scheme and somehow profit by it." He added a laugh to pull any sting of accusation.

Sunbright laughed also. "You praise me highly, friend Hilel," he said. "I'm just a simple shaman seeing after the welfare of my people, and hardly good at it, but I do have some simple ideas, and if they pan out . . ." His words ran out as he gazed along the ravine toward the distant prairie. Something turned over in his mind so he finished aloud, ". . . But if not, even the gods may be powerless to aid us."

Chapter 19

"Aaaaarrrggghhhh!!!"

The monster Sysquemalyn hefted the black scrying table and hurled it against the cave wall. It shattered into a thousand fragments. The flint creature raged, smashed stalactites with iron fists, blew fire like a dragon, and shot frost from her fingertips. The cave grew murky with smoke and steam and rock dust.

Nothing, she raged, neither scrying device nor spell could penetrate the depths of an elven forest. Damn all ancient peoples and their unfathomable defenses! Yet Sunbright must be hiding among elves, for she couldn't locate him anywhere else.

"He hides because he fears me!" she ranted. "Because I've killed all my enemies and wounded an empire! Candlemas is deader than dead, his soul expunged from the spheres! Polaris, the screaming, putrid cow, was reduced to blubbering terror before I pitched her into the blackest of holes! But Sunbright, a simple, stupid barbarian, eludes me! I should visit him in person, tear his lungs out, blind him—"

An idea struck. Why not seek him out? Her work here was done. By donning the guise of the One King, she'd stirred up hordes of orcs and other villains, wounded the Netherese Empire sorely, butchered thousands of innocents, and lured Lady Polaris to a horrible quasi-life. But she needed the One King no longer. She could turn her attentions to—

"*Sunbright!*" The stony creature raised wicked claws. "Prepare yourself! I come in person to bring you agony and slow, painful death!"

And crossing scarecrow arms, she vanished.

* * * * *

Sunbright indeed walked the High Forest of the Moon Elves. But not to hide. To seek.

An elf named Blessedseed guided him and Knucklebones through the forest. A good thing, for these woods were enchanted and Sunbright knew he'd lose his way alone.

He'd seen many forests, but this one was magical. Even in winter the oaks and birches and maples seemed alive, not dormant, glowing and vibrant with health. The sun shone brighter through their branches, as if through ice crystals, yet the earth felt warm to the touch, for snow never lingered long. Despite a chill, the air possessed a sweet tang, as in maple-sugaring season, and deer and foxes and even shaggy wood-bisons watched them pass, showing neither fear nor interest. How could that be? Sunbright wondered, when the elves killed game like anyone else?

More incredibly, how had he once passed through this forest without seeing its otherworldly beauty? For as a boy, banished from this tribe, he'd crossed the Barren Mountains and cut through this forest toward the heart of the empire. But on that journey he'd seen no elves, and sensed no magic. Was it true what men said, that an elven wood wasn't part of a man's world, but rather a shadow realm that existed side by side, unseen unless the inhabitants wanted it to show? If so, where were they now? Sunbright shook his head as if to dislodge idle ramblings. He needed to concentrate on his mission.

If the elves had a city, or town center, or if that elven queen owned a castle or mead hall, Sunbright never saw it. Blessedseed led them over rill and vale along narrow and ancient trails. In some places the paths were worn knee-deep. Where they crossed oak roots, soft elven soles had polished inches deep into tough wood. Occasionally they passed wigwams of branches, or glimpsed tree huts high up, or saw paths wending toward caves trickling smoke. Sunbright guessed these elves didn't have proper homes, only sleeping hollows and nests like birds and badgers. Perhaps they simply lived outside year round. When he asked the guide, Blessedseed only smiled, so Sunbright gave up wondering. He had more important questions.

"There."

In the silent forest, the elf's quiet word startled him. The archer pointed out a trail to a hogback ridge. Sunbright peered. There seemed only tangled rhododendron atop the ridge. Then he saw a dark slit, hardly wide enough for a fox, and he asked, "That's her home?"

"Yes," said the elf. "I shall wait here."

"We might be a while," the shaman warned.

"I shall wait here." Blessedseed leaned against a tree, folded his arms, and scanned the sky as if reading a book.

Shaking his head over these queer and muzzy-headed fairies, Sunbright strode up the trail. He had almost forgotten Knucklebones followed, looking out of place in her lion skin coat. Her voice startled him.

"Are you sure you want what you might find?"

"What?" The shaman turned, fuddled, and said, "Of course I want to know! I've wanted to know since forever. Years, now."

Knucklebones's one eye stared at the ground. "I hope the answer makes you happy."

Sunbright didn't understand her comment, nor her reticence. Grabbing her hand for clumsy comfort, he towed her to the slit in the tangled bracken, and squeezed through.

The cramped chamber looked like the inside of a wicker basket, dark and smoke-stained, though without fire. In the chilly dimness, Sunbright thought the hovel deserted. Then he noticed a white glow illuminated by leaks of light through brush, and feared the owner had died, it was so cold in here.

"M-Milady Brookdweller?"

"Eh?" the old elf woman cracked, startled from sleep. "Who is there? Ah, I see. Come in, come in."

Her dark clothes rustled as she edged to a tiny fire pit. Without flint or steel, she struck a fire in a handful of twigs. There was barely enough tinder to fill a pipe, yet it instantly warmed the hut. Somehow, the shaman sensed, this ancient elven priestess drew more heat from wood than a human could draw. The warmth brought to life scents of exotic herbs.

"A human," croaked the priestess. "I don't see many of those. And a creature of our blood. Nice to have company. I am so old, I spend more time in the next world than this one. So 'tis well to commune with the young. Your names?"

Sunbright gave their names, added that the queen's chancellor, Tamechild, had told Sunbright of Brookdweller's wisdom.

"My grandchild. One of many," the elder rambled. "May I take your hand, my dear?"

Even sitting cross-legged, Sunbright ducked his head under the brush roof. He offered his hand, but found it was Knucklebones the priestess addressed. The small thief sat on her heels, her single eye shining under a mop of tousled black curls—hair as wild and free as these elves'.

"Who are your people, dear?" The priestess spread Knucklebones's hand in both her own as if reading a book.

"I—I don't know," stammered the part-elf. "I was born, or will be born, in the city of Karsus. I was hurled into the gutter, grew up in the sewers, never knew my mother."

"Father."

"Eh?" Knucklebones was so startled she jerked back her hand.

Carefully, Brookdweller took it again, saying, "Your father was an Old One. Your mother a New One."

"My *father* was elven, and my *mother* human?" the thief breathed so fast Sunbright thought she'd pass out. "I—I always thought it the other way around. I don't know why. . . ."

"Of the High Forest," Brookdweller continued. She closed her sunken eyes as she stroked the thief's hand. "Not a Moon Elf, not Illefarni, not of the forest . . . Eaerlanni, most ancient of the Shadow Folk . . . A sad folk, beaten and blaming themselves, given to wandering . . . But, but . . ."

Human and part-elf strained forward, barely breathing, as the priestess hissed, " . . . But *also* Moon Elf, *also* Illefarni! The signs are jumbled, many streams flowing to one river, and the river running backward. Blood creating blood, and flowing through time . . . I—I—"

She stopped as Knucklebones yanked her hand free. The small thief shivered and rubbed the limb. Brookdweller opened her eyes slowly, fed twigs to the fire, though the first ones had barely burned.

"I understand, dear. Second sight is a frightening power. Many who possess it wish they did not, eh?"

The last was addressed to Sunbright, and he nodded. "Visions are a blessing, and a curse, my mother told me. It was years before I understood why."

The old woman nodded as if they discussed the weather. Straightening her back, she asked, "And what do you seek, northman?"

"An elf. A—a friend. One Greenwillow, who was lost, killed . . ."

Quickly, Sunbright told of Sysquemalyn's pocket hell. How, as the floor crumbled, Greenwillow confessed her love, and shoved Sunbright to safety. How the barbarian had turned to find only a gaping chasm roiling with hellfire. "Her death," he finished, "if she's truly dead, haunts me. And if dead, I fear her soul is trapped in those awful depths, unable to escape. I've searched for years, by magic and other means, but learned nothing. Can you—"

"She is dead." Seeing the pronouncement jolt the human, the priestess explained, "We People of the Woods are charged with magic, as a fish is charged with water. Yet no elf could survive hellfire. No living thing can. So the question is to Greenwillow's soul. And that is no question, for souls have no bounds. They come and go, or linger forever, as they wish. Even ghosts damned to walk the earth do so of their own will, though they deny it. Nothing can trap a soul; Greenwillow has indeed walked on."

"Where?" Sunbright blurted. "Do you know where?"

The priestess closed her eyes, pondering, but snapped them open when Knucklebones added, "Yes, please! Tell us where! I must know!"

"*You?*" Sunbright stared at his small lover. "Why should you—"

"Because I'm tired of hearing about Greenwillow!" she blurted. Sudden tears spilled down the thief's cheek from one good eye. Knucklebones wiped them frantically, fearing to look weak. "I'm tired of you talking of her! I'm tired of living in her shadow! These Moon Elves are beautiful and slender and tall and graceful. Not short and homely and scarred and starved and one-eyed like me! Compared to Greenwillow's memory, I'm nothing but a louse, a bastard half-breed pitched in the gutter to die because my own mother couldn't bear the sight of me! But even if I am only a sewer rat, I love you, Sunbright, and want you to myself. I can't compete with a noble half-goddess who's dead, so I can't even confront her!"

The small woman sobbed, covering her face. Stunned by her outburst, Sunbright touched her shoulder, but she shook him off. In the meantime, Brookdweller had closed her eyes to rock back and forth, crooning aimlessly like an idiot. Had the whole world gone mad? the shaman wondered.

"Knucklebones. Knuckle'." Sunbright struggled for words. "I love you. Please don't think otherwise. And I don't compare you to Greenwillow. She was sweet and lovely, true, but so are you. You've a kind heart and gentle core that I admire so. I don't care about your origins. Mine are no better. And despite your hard life, you've kept your heart pure—*Wait!*"

He grabbed, but the thief slipped away like an eel, slithered out of the brush hut, and vanished down the trail. Fuddled as a hammer-struck cow, Sunbright clambered up, banged his head on brush and fetched up Harvester's pommel, almost tore the hut down.

At that moment, Brookdweller broke from her dream. "It clears! I see the links!" the old woman cried. "I know where Greenwillow's soul has gone!"

* * * * *

Far down the trail, sobbing for breath, blinded by tears, Knucklebones ran helter-skelter past fork after fork, not caring where she ended up. The part-elf stumbled far off the beaten trail, reached the end of a path, and kept going, bulling into rushes in a swamp. Dimly she perceived her feet splashed in brackish water, but she didn't care. If she drowned, her sorrows would end. For no matter how long she followed Sunbright, nor how deeply she loved with all her heart, he'd always compare her to the slender, beautiful Greenwillow, and Knucklebones couldn't live as his second-best love. And without Sunbright, with no links to the past and her future lost, she had nothing and had nowhere to go. Any place was as bad as the next, and death no worse than life.

And too, she felt so queer lately, her guts churning all the time, her emotions running hot and cold, as if she were two people fighting for control. She'd never felt this way, and couldn't explain it. And right now, she didn't care.

Saw grass tore at her hands, cut her red cheeks, stabbed her clothing. The water to her knees slowed her. And her breath tore for crying. Soon, part of her mind knew, she'd collapse, and cold and the short winter night would claim her—

Strangled, she jerked to a halt. A tree branch had snagged her throat, but it snapped shut like a mink trap and cut off her wind.

Suddenly Knucklebones didn't want to die.

Lashing out, her fists struck stone, not wood. Gasping for wind, she forced open her one eye, swollen from crying.

And beheld a monster.

Inches from her face leered a bald head of stone. No eyelids, no ears, no hair. Bulging blue eyes shot with red bored into her face. A gash of a mouth hissed like a volcano pit.

Knucklebones was hoicked from the swamp water. Her neck popped and creaked at the strain, her vision dimmed. Windmilling her legs only banged her toes on a stony body. Punching scraped skin like a rasp. Slapping her belt, the thief whipped up her dark elven knife, jabbed at the bulging eyes, the stony mouth and skin. The knife tip didn't even scratch the stone hide. A claw flicked the knife away.

The helpless thief writhed like a rat in a trap.

"You," hissed Sysquemalyn, "I can use."

* * * * *

"Where the in the nine hells can she *be?*"

Sunbright was disheveled, sweaty, and pale. He and Blessedseed had tracked Knucklebones's flight through the forest and into the swamp, and found where her footprints disappeared in churned mud and saw grass. Other prints, long and clawed, marked the spot. Elves had joined the search, and turned up her dark elven knife, but no other trace. Old Brookdweller closed her eyes and stated that the thief was vanished from the forest. Charging from the enchanted wood, Sunbright had run to his mother's hut in the valley, asked outriders on the prairie, and finally bolted to Drigor's forge. The old dwarf had seen everything.

"Mud churned by long feet with claws, eh? I'm afraid to name the culprit. It must be that monster that attacked us in the Iron Mountains."

"Monster!" Sunbright slapped his forehead. "By the Wild Fire, I'd forgotten that! But why does this fiend pursue me? And why take Knuck—Oh, *no!*"

"The monster punishes you by seizing your little lady. That's plain enough."

The dwarf fiddled with a five-pound hammer, flipping it end over end without realizing it. Others stood around helplessly: Monkberry, Magichunger the war chief, Forestvictory, a handful of other barbarians, the elven guide Blessedseed. With the sun directly behind the mountain, shadows gathered around the forge, the air was so chilly their breath steamed.

Drigor's forge lay below the wide streak of rust that

named Sanguine Mountain. The dark soil was black volcanic ash mixed with red ore, folded like a rumpled blanket around the mountain's foot. Rich soil made grass grow head-high, and fed many stands of poplar trees that shivered in a breeze. To the east, a crazed dropoff overlooked rolling prairie. A bubbling cascade that spilled down the mountain had been deepened into a pool that would someday power a water mill. Drigor's workshop was logs and bark with a brush roof. The forge was made of dry-laid rocks. A flat slab served as anvil.

Drigor flipped his hammer while his two helpers, Agler and Erig, worried a lumpy hunk of iron with mauls. Life and death might teeter around, but dwarves kept working. Over their regular bangs, Drigor called, "It strikes me queer you don't know your enemy. It's got a powerful hatred of you."

"I don't know!" Sunbright's hands windmilled, plucked at his shirt and straps in his frenzy. "I'd remember if a giant, stone-hided monster tried to kill me, wouldn't I?"

"I'm not criticizing your memory, lad." The old dwarf said, flipped the hammer again, and Sunbright ripped it from his hand. "Oh, sorry. I just say, fathom its craving for revenge and you'll know how to combat it. So think."

"I've thought till my brain aches!" the shaman said. "Until it's caught fire! There's nothing—"

"*Look!*" hollered Magichunger.

Standing at the cracked dropoff, a half-bowshot away, the monster clasped Knucklebones in its claws. In the gathering gloom the fiend was black except for bulging blue eyes like lamps. Held by her throat, the exhausted thief hung as if dead. Yet a glimpse of Sunbright revitalized her. Gasping for air, she scratched and pulled with bloody fingernails at the monster's claws, solid as iron bars.

People stared, hollered, and reached for weapons. Sunbright charged.

To attack with Knucklebones helpless was not smart, but the shaman warrior wasn't thinking. Hauling Harvester over his shoulder with a shriek, he crossed the space in seconds, slung the fearsome sword behind—

—and crashed into an invisible wall.

He struck so violently that his neck snapped, his nose spurted blood, his jaw almost dislocated, and his knees folded. Harvester fell from numbed fingers onto red-black dirt. The shaman slumped to a heap holding his bruised face. But immediately he grabbed up his sword, and stuck out a hand to explore the shield wall. Its bounds extended above his reach and far past the dropoff. He growled like a rabid dog, for the monster and its victim were only five feet away. Poor suffering Knucklebones watched him with fear-haunted eyes, pleading for rescue, but also begging he not die foolishly.

The flint monster chortled, a gurgling like lava bubbling, then spoke: "As with Candlemas, as with Polaris, so you, the easiest of all. There, at dawn." A claw pointed to the prairie. "I'll bury you in your ancestral land, and throw your poppet atop your corpse!"

Shaking Knucklebones like a doll in Sunbright's face, the fiend vanished.

With it went the magic wall, and Sunbright's hand touched only empty air. With a curse, the barbarian slung Harvester far back, then hurled it through the space the monster had vacated. The glittering sword pinwheeled over the dropoff. Fists furled, Sunbright screamed rage at the sky, damned every god he knew for rendering him useless.

By and by, a hand like a bear paw clamped his shoulder. Sunbright slumped on his knees, a ball of misery and anger and helplessness. By the light of birch torches, he saw Drigor and many others gathered: dwarves returned from exploring, elves from the forest, barbarians with tools and weapons in hand.

Erig offered Harvester pommel-first. Slowly Sunbright climbed to his feet and took the sword, though it hung limp in his hands, point trailing in dirt, something he'd never done before.

"So you must fight the monster," drawled Drigor, as if proposing a horse race. " 'Pears to me you need help."

Sunbright mopped his face. He was exhausted, wrung out mentally and physically, too weak to wrestle a kitten, and despondent. "Yes," he said quietly. "Dig my grave and carve a tombstone. 'Here lies Sunbright, who failed *both* the women he loved.' "

"Now, now," rasped the old dwarf. "It's not as bad as all that. We've talked, the elves and us, and we've got an idea. Show him, 'Seed."

Across Blessedseed's palms lay a strip of white metal as long as a man's arm, but no wider than a thumb. Sunbright couldn't imagine what it was.

Drigor took the strip reverently as a king's crown. "This is elven truesteel. Magic steel such as only elves make, such as I've seen only thrice in my many years. They fetched it from the forest. For you."

Dully, Sunbright croaked, "And what do I do with it?"

"Not you. Me and my helpers," the dwarf said. He stood only breast-high to the crowd, but was clearly in command. "With luck, and help from these pointy-eared blokes, we'll weld this strip to Harvester of Blood's edge. With our mumbling, and their enchantments, you'll gain a sword that'll cut anything—*anything*. A magic sword from a legend. A sword such as no dwarf or elf could ever create alone, but together. . . ."

"Tarry a minute!" Magichunger called, then shouldered to the front of the crowd. A war axe big as a shovel hung in his belt, and his shaggy head still sported the full beard and unshaved temples of town men. "Our tribe don't hold with magic. It's taboo." The gruff man hesitated.

"I'm sorry, Sunbright, but enchanting is disallowed.

We'll help you fight the fiend. The lot of us ganging up will bring it down, same as killing a mammoth."

Drigor turned angry eyes on the war chief. Wiping his big nose, he rasped, "What flavor of fool do you be? He needs a *king's* sword! And never before have elves and dwarves collaborated to make one! This monster killed three dwarves, and tied up the rest without hardly lifting a finger. It killed Lady Polaris, no less than one of the empire's archwizards. It blew the top off a mountain and started a volcano!"

"And killed Candlemas," Sunbright almost whispered. Only now did he recall the creature's boast. Poor, fat Candlemas, who worked so hard at the wrong things, but saved Sunbright and Knucklebones when the empire fell.

Magichunger, no great thinker, only shook his head stubbornly and grumbled, "I'll help any way I can. We all will,but anyone practicin' magic is cast out! It's tradition!"

Cursing, Drigor turned to Sunbright. "Well, which shall it be? Will you accept our magic, or not? You don't stand a chance without it!"

Sunbright surveyed the crowd, saw his mother quietly urging him on. For she knew, as did he. Sucking air, Sunbright announced in a strong voice, "Always I needs make the hard choice. Yet this one is easy. I need magic to rescue Knucklebones, yet magic-using would banish me. Thus I must choose between my love, and my people. Hear this. Twice my tribe banished me, so a third time can't hurt much. Yet in all my trials, Knucklebones stood steadfast by my side with narry a complaint. And so I choose: Love over loyalty!"

Frowning and grumbling, his tribesfolk filtered away, until the only one left was Sunbright's mother, with tears in her eyes. Sunbright extended Harvester of Blood to Drigor pommel-first. "Fire your forge," he said.

Chapter 20

Dwarves and elves crowded around Drigor's workshop to witness a new event in the long, long histories of both races: the combination of elven and dwarven magic to fashion a sword fit for a hero. Hammers big and small rang and pinged. Elves slipped from the darkness bearing magic herbs and potions. Drigor bellowed for more charcoal. Musical elven voices rose above dwarvish growling. Forest folk related ancient tales of other swords, other heroes, other crises, their whispering like the rustle of poplars. Dwarves whooped when a spell took, howled when it failed. Arguments sailed back and forth, for both races were loathe to reveal their secrets and enchantments, yet heads of long black hair bumped scruffy mops over the stone anvil.

Not far off, poised at the dropoff where Knucklebones had disappeared, outlined by winter stars and night sky, Sunbright sat with his legs crossed, only dimly aware of the hubbub. The lack of Harvester hanging at his back made him feel light, insubstantial, weak. The lack of Knucklebones by his side made him cold. His only support was his mother, for Monkberry sat nearby to watch over her son. Her quiet presence gave him strength.

But his heart was heavy. Sunbright had sat most of the night, trying to meditate, striving to summon shamanistic powers from the earth underneath, the sky above, and the other worlds beyond less obvious veils. He eschewed the traditional trappings of shamans: the spiral-carved stick, the circle of stones, the pyramids of crystals, and other gewgaws. Sunbright knew a shaman's greatest tool was his mind.

For hours the young shaman concentrated, especially on his ancestors, shamans all, who stretched through history to before there was a tribe called Rengarth. He vied to pull ancestors from the depths of time. Past Sevenhaunt, his father. Past Shortdawn, his grandfather. Past Waterfly, his great-grandmother. Past Crystalfair, mother of Waterfly. And other shamans such as brain-crazed Owldark and crusty old Deertree, many more, until in his half-dream Sunbright was crowded by shamans so thick he could smell fur and musk and sweat and hair.

They all possessed powers. Sevenhaunt could talk with the dead. Waterfly could fly the polar night. Shortdawn could fashion walls with his mind: walls of ice, fog, light, or noises of beasts. Crystalfair could shapeshift to swim with seals or run with wolves. Deertree could wear horns of wisdom granted by Mother Reindeer.

May I have a power? asked Sunbright in his mind. *Just a little. To save Knucklebones, whom I love. It seems a small thing to ask.*

Any power would help. Sunbright prayed to his ancestors for the power of the Thunderbeast, that his skin might boil and curdle and harden, and his footfalls crash like thunder. Or the wind wings of Sky Pony. Or the ferocity of Red Tiger, or the quickness of Gray Wolf, or the mad fury of Blue Bear. Even the roar of the Black Lion would aid him.

But his ancestors stood silent as mountains, cold as glaciers. They did not condemn, nor did they aid, but only seemed to wait with the eternal patience of the dead. Why? Did they disapprove of Sunbright's begging? Jealously horde their spells? Or resent his lack of concentration?

For his mind kept drifting. Fear for Knucklebones ached in Sunbright's heart, and threatened to choke him. Idly, he wondered what the battle would bring. He was willing to die if Knucklebones could live, but there were no guarantees. Most likely he would battle the monster and die, and Knucklebones would die soon after. Monkberry would wander the prairie for the last time. Perhaps Sunbright had been wrong to contact his ancestors across time, for compared to their turmoil and sufferings, and all the pains and glories of history, he amounted to little. Given enough time, nothing much mattered.

The dead waited, as did their descendants. Sunbright was missing something obvious, he felt. Or perhaps even these ghosts were powerless to help him. After all, when it came time for battle, he must leave all others behind, and walk onto the field alone. So perhaps the dead could only offer him their quiet comfort. He couldn't tell.

With nothing more to say, Sunbright's ancestors turned to fog and melted away.

Sunbright opened his eyes to night darkness, and the lumpy shape of his mother sitting on a rock.

"I'm a poor shaman," the man croaked to his mother. "I've let down my lover, and my people, my ancestors, and myself."

"No." Monkberry caught her son's face, pulled it down to kiss his forehead, then whispered, "You've let no one down, for you've tried your best."

From the forge came a babble, a roar, then a cry: "Get him! Get the bright one! He must draw the blade from the fire!" Fifty voices picked up the cheer.

Dark shapes clustered around Sunbright. Elven hands, long and supple and cool, and dwarven paws, craggy and hot from the forge, hustled him to the workshop. Nudged gently through the low door, he saw Drigor standing in a spark-spattered apron and enormous horse hide gloves. The forge was piled of dry rocks, long enough to hold a plow blade. Harvester's pommel jutted from a flare that smarted Sunbright's tired eyes.

"Take it. Take it!" the dwarf commanded. "That's it . . . draw it out slow, now . . . slow!"

Sunbright laid hold of the long pommel, which was bare steel, the leather and wire having been unwound. Touching steel sent a tingle through his arm. It was only warm, not red hot, but the blade seemed alive, as if he'd caught a dragon's tail. Under Drigor's direction, he pulled the blade free of the flames.

Harvester of Blood flared in the night. Polished like a mirror, it made Sunbright squint. The strip of elven truesteel was forged so tightly to Harvester's old edge he couldn't see the juncture. The long edge retained its original curve, yet that curve suggested power like a cresting wave. The barbed hook behind the nose was cruel as an eagle's beak. The edge, once razor-sharp, was now invisible, fine ground to atoms. And the blade had a new balance, so it bobbed in his hand, light as a fishing pole, as if it matched his muscles, learned from them, helped them. He could wield this new-old weapon all day and never tire.

Dwarves and elves hurrahed for the hero and his legendary blade. Moving close, Drigor took it, gently as a baby, laid it on a stone table, felt the edge and flat, tested by striking a beard hair against the edge. So clean it cut, the hair seemed to evaporate. Chuckling at his cleverness, the dwarf polished the glistening blade with a chamois, and lovingly wrapped new leather and silver wire around the pommel. "Now," the dwarf said, "for the real test!"

Surging outside with the crowd, the dwarf hunted under a torch for the right rock, found one black and speckled with silver flecks—a rock not unlike the monster's flinty hide. Holding the sword blade up, he dropped the rock against the lowest part of the cutting edge. The rock dropped straight to the ground, but landed in two pieces. The crowd *oohed* as Drigor held up one chunk of granite. One side was smooth as glass.

"It's ready."

"One more thing," said an elf. "Actually, many small things."

From the darkness, elves approached Sunbright to surround him. They said nothing, but touched him in a dozen places with tiny things Sunbright supposed were charms or talismans. Slim elven fingers tucked a four-leaf clover into his sleeve. An elven woman tied a bead to the rawhide binding his hair. A young lad stooped and fastened a silver heart to an iron ring on his boot. A woman pinned a striped feather to his bosom. Other charms were laid on him. Finally old Brookdweller shuffled forward on twisted feet. Raising a withered fern, she brushed Sunbright from head to toe, back and front, even signaling to raise his arms to brush underneath, all the while she crooned a song like a lark's trill. Brushing his hands, she and the other elves drew back.

Sunbright thought to say thank you for whatever they'd done, but they'd been silent and so he answered the same way. His mind was elsewhere anyway, already fighting the battle, or already dead, as if he moved in a dream world.

Polishing, polishing, Drigor inverted Harvester and offered it to Sunbright.

But the barbarian gazed east, out over the prairie, where a band of yellow light filled the horizon.

"Almost dawn," he said absently. Reaching, he caught Harvester's pommel and slid the enchanted sword home over his shoulder. The weight at his back made him stand taller.

Then he marched toward the sunrise.

* * * * *

One minute's walk, and Sunbright was alone on the rolling grasslands. Elves and dwarves stopped at the first grass as if lining an arena. Barbarians came too, drawn by the sun, and stopped to watch their tribesman stride out alone.

Then, from thin air before him, stood the monster. Its black flint hide sparkled with minerals in the rising sun. Knucklebones hung limp from one claw, her strength gone but her single eye alive. The little thief watched Sunbright approach with a mixture of love, hope, and fear.

Sunbright stopped a dozen feet from the monster, hands on hips, and studied it for the first time. The bald head, thick skin of stone, fierce claws, mismatched, mighty arms, long, splayed feet, all suggested a creature fashioned for killing. But the bulging blue eyes this morning looked familiar.

Raising a long arm, the monster hoisted Knucklebones in the air, and flung her like a rag doll. The thief pinwheeled across the tops of the grass like a skipped stone, and came to a gentle, dizzy landing three hundred feet away. Croaked the monster, "She's nothing to me."

"She's everything to me," replied Sunbright. "Will you tell me your name?"

"You know it. Knew it." The voice was painful to hear, like a man strangling on poison. "In life I was called Sysquemalyn."

"Sys—" Sunbright's brow clouded. "I don't recall—"

"You know me!" the fiend screeched. "I was chamberlain to Polaris, whom I've beaten and banished beyond hell! I was competitor to Candlemas, whom I transfigured into a horror, then tore to shreds!"

"Aaaaah!" Sunbright nodded. "A beautiful woman, tall and striking, with red hair."

The barbarian's denseness annoyed the former mage. "The *most* beautiful!"

"Beautiful, yes. You posed as Ruellana to seduce me. And as a courtier to the One King. You played some game, a wager with Candlemas. I never wholly understood it, but—"

"But why seek revenge? Why come I to kill you?" Sysquemalyn raised curved claws and slashed the air. Sunbright's calm befuddlement, rather than stark fear, made her squirm. The mortal should beg for his life, not pose idle questions. She shrieked at him, "Look at me! Look at the horror I've become! Think on the suffering I endured in my own personal hell, trapped for three years when every second was torture!"

Sunbright, awake all night, poised for battle-madness, was yet cursed with curiosity, so struggled to understand. "Why hate me?" he asked. "I spared your life in hell, when that big winged hell-king ordered I behead you, and I did nothing to imprison you."

The monster's gashed mouth champed in frustration. Where was the fear, the cowering, begging, and whimpering?

"You were *there!* You helped condemn me, did nothing to prevent it! For this I will kill you, and all you hold dear!"

"Vengeance?" Sunbright scratched his horsetail as he said, "Revenge rings hollow, I've found. I planned to avenge myself on my tribe for years, too, but when I finally found them, they were helpless as baby birds. I was needed, so pitched in to help them survive. My mother insisted. Revenge would have killed us all. It's foolish."

"Foolish?" Sysquemalyn stamped forward, lowered her head like a bull about to charge, and hissed like a snake, "It's foolish to beg for your life, for this morning you die!"

"I don't beg, and won't," he said. Sunbright squinted with sun in his eyes. Sysquemalyn didn't listen well, for she was mad. And dangerous. Stepping backward through knee-high grass, the shaman said, "I'll ask one question, if you please. Tell me why, with the powerful magic at your disposal, you hare about gaining revenge? Why not use your power to restore your beauty?"

For a second, the idea so stunned the monster, it froze her in her tracks. Never once since crawling from hell had she considered regaining her beauty. She'd been too bent on revenge. On her enemies, such as the barbarian before her. Who enraged her with calm words and awkward thoughts.

"You'd *pity* me?"

With a shriek that shriveled grass, the monster charged.

Sunbright was staggered by the ferocity of the attack. And slow from fatigue and worry. He wasn't really prepared for this fight, didn't want it. Lately, battling raiders and monsters and even his own tribe, he'd fought enough for a lifetime.

Yet if his mind was distracted, instinct saved him.

Without thinking, Sunbright stepped back on his left foot, body following, and cocked Harvester over his right shoulder. Before he knew it, the sword sliced a path of death through the bright winter sky.

Sysquemalyn bellowed in rage, and slashed to deflect the blade with a stony wrist. Yet as the sword, swung with all Sunbright's strength, clanged off her arm, a tiny chip of stone flew free. In a blind fury, the monster didn't see or feel the wound, but the shaman did, and took note, and heart.

Then the fiend was on him like a pack of wildcats. "I'll flay your flesh from your bones!" she screamed.

A long-fingered hand clamped atop Sunbright's head. Flexing claws like broken glass dug in, punctured his shaven temples and scalp. Sunbright felt blood start, and his skull ached. Yet something, he sensed, kept his skull from collapsing. An elf had tied a bead to his horsetail thong, he recalled. Did that protect him?

Howsoever, he could strike back. Retaliating, he shot the pommel of the sword straight at the monster's skull face. The heavy steel end banged and skidded off. Sysquemalyn chuckled and twisted the claws fastened to his head. Pain shot through Sunbright's skull and down his neck. He had to get free, even if he ripped his own flesh, but the monster's other hand snatched at his throat. When he made to grab it, fearsome claws closed around his wrist and squeezed. The shaman groaned as bones ground together, but the mighty claws didn't crush him, and again he sensed protection. The four-leaf clover tucked in his sleeve? Could these piddling charms protect against such evil?

But it was idiotic, Sunbright thought, to fight bare-handed when he possessed a magic sword. With a gasp, he flailed his right hand to flip Harvester and chop at Sysquemalyn's head, but the sword only wobbled in the trapped hand. To drop it was to die, but he couldn't engage. Nor think, for pain exploded in his head like northern lights. Finally, he simply dropped his whole body.

His great weight tore skin from his head, but he got free of the monster's claws. His left hand was also free, though the right was trapped. As the monster swiped to claw him anew, he calculated, timed, pried open his right hand, and dropped the sword.

A miss would sever his hand, but he caught Harvester's pommel in his left, bobbled the sword, and hung on. Then he poised, aimed, and stabbed for the creature's armpit.

The enchanted blade lodged in a hollow against skin turned stone, then bit like a miner's drill. Encouraged, Sunbright shoved harder, saw the point chip another pebble away. Sysquemalyn dropped her free hand to his shoulder, and guttered, "First hand, then arm. I'll break both, but not tear them off. I want you alive to *suffer!*"

Grunting with effort, resisting a howl from his trapped arm, Sunbright bunched his arm, sucked wind, and redoubled his shoving. He saw his blade twist in stony flesh, bite, and sink almost to the barb.

A caw like a crow's startled him. Sysquemalyn was surprised by pain. Hopping back, she let go of his aching right arm.

Rising to a crouch, Sunbright waggled his crushed wrist, found it serviceable, and flipped Harvester to his fighting hand. " 'Twas enchanted by elves and dwarves working together . . ." he said, panting. He shook his head, for the blood trickling into his ears tickled. ". . . for the first time in history. Just for you!"

"Worm food!" the archwizard retorted. Hanging out of sword's reach, she flicked both hands while hissing like a dragon.

A tingling possessed Sunbright. An itch like severe sunburn crawled over his skin. At his inner elbow, tanned skin curdled like birch bark in a fire, split and broke and bled and itched abominably. He felt it elsewhere, under his chin, behind his knees, in his groin, between his toes. A skin curdling spell? Was this her worst threat? Or did more elven charms, feathers and lace and owl bones, stop the worst effects?

Nor did Sunbright ponder long. He didn't trust his right hand to keep the sword, so used two hands to hoist Harvester high, and charged across the winter grass.

The monster fell back, and raised a long, crooked arm to block the blow. When the truesteel struck with an awful shattering noise, Sysquemalyn suffered a slice in her forearm long as a man's little finger. Sunbright didn't hesitate, but caught the sword on the backswing, and hauled it through the arc and around to strike again. Another fearful clang, and a chip like obsidian spun from a clawed hand. Sunbright cut again, and again, and each time the monster fell back. But the hero was too winded to deliver another blow. They were almost useless anyway. He'd spend his strength and only whittle off chips like sawdust. Sobbing for air, the warrior tried to think what to do.

And thought of nothing. He had no battle plan, no strategy, and little hope. Deep down, he'd never expected to survive this long, let alone win. The monster was too powerful, and he was, after all, only a man.

As if reading his mind, Sysquemalyn planted her dark, splayed feet like condor claws, and gargled. "I know every spell of every creature in the nine hells, for I conquered them all! Taste *this!*"

From one hooked palm, there spat a fan of liquid, a flood of putrid rain stinking of sulfur. The spray spattered Sunbright from head to foot, filled the air, and rained on the prairie grass, which shriveled and curled black. Some spots puffed into flame. Sunbright felt afire himself, for the acid burned on his cuts and bruises. His eyes smarted, he gagged on the stink, he smelled leather and wool, and even his own hair corroding. Yet native strength and elven charm protected him, and so he attacked.

But as he slung Harvester sidelong for a rib shot, the fiend's hand soared in an arc. Sunbright smashed a ringing blow on her gaunt ribs, then felt heat all around. His boots squished in something soft that wasn't grass.

The prairie cracked in a hundred places to ooze foul black tar that bubbled and boiled. Within seconds, Sunbright was ankle-deep in gunk. He sniffed burning moosehide. Unable to see clearly for sweat and blood and heat waves, he ignored the threat. Some curse would kill him eventually, but until then he'd fight. With a different attack, if possible.

Waving Harvester high, he spun his hands in midair, took a new grip, slammed the blade down. Enchanted steel crashed on Sysquemalyn's shoulder and grazed the stone ridge. The barbarian heaved the blade sideways and yanked. The barbed tip of Harvester snagged her scrawny spine behind the bald head. The barb had also been welded with truesteel, for it bit, and hung on.

Sysquemalyn staggered, thrown off-balance, and almost toppled into the shaman. Sunbright jerked his feet free of boiling tar, danced sideways, and yanked again. By hanging on and levering, he could steer the fiend where he willed. Now he wanted her down in her own foul mess. "Down, damn you!" he screamed. "Go *down!*"

The monster sliced the air, dug claws into seeping wounds on Sunbright's arms, clenched, and held. The hero felt his warm blood spurt. The foes were locked. Then Sysquemalyn leaned her great weight, as great as any boulder's, to drag him down.

Sagging, Sunbright crashed on one knee, felt a sear of hot tar, smelled crisped flesh, but the charms of the generous elves still worked, for otherwise his flesh would have split and caught fire, crumbled in chunks to leave scorched bone. Taking advantage of his new stance, Sunbright levered an elbow against his knee and pulled until his muscles cracked and jumped. He could do nothing more, and prayed it was enough.

Sysquemalyn sagged with him. Bubbling tar grew deeper around them, as if they'd blundered into a tar pit. Sunbright was spattered with the stuff, as was she.

The sword pained her, bit the nape of her neck like a vampire, and she couldn't reach to dislodge the hook. She'd have to kill the man first. Dragging up a tarry hand, the monster aimed a palm at Sunbright's straining face.

Chain lightning erupted from the palm, and splashed over Sunbright. The barbarian flinched, ducked his head. Lightning that could shatter a tree only sparkled on his skin, made his horsetail friz, and lit rings and buckles on his clothing with curious fire. Ignoring the tingles, he levered harder on his sword.

Keening outrage, Sysquemalyn spat a bolt of dark energy, negative force that should have bored through the human like a auger. Sunbright shook off the blow like a mammoth shaking off a spear. Screeching, Sysquemalyn unleashed an icicle storm, then a pocket tornado, then a whirlwind of steel. Ice stung the shaman's cheeks and drew blood. The tornado ripped hair from his horsetail. Phantom steel shredded his shirt and blistered his skin.

Yet, grim as a statue, he hung onto the sword and pressed harder, and slowly crushed Sysquemalyn into the tar until she propped on one hand and attacked with the other. She gargled in his face, "What protects you?"

Straining, grunting, grinding, Sunbright had no breath to spare, but answered anyway: *"Love!"*

Her snort puffed his hair. Twisting against his stinging blade, she dug into his thigh with a clawed hand, inched to his belt, then his torn shirt, and finally snagged his chin. She would gouge out his eyes, render him blind and helpless.

But Sunbright hissed, "It's nothing you know! You live for hate and revenge and death. I live for love! I've the strength of a thousand folk who stand behind me. I've the love of a good woman, the respect of my people, the wisdom of my ancestors, the guidance of my mother, the friendship of people from forest and mountain. What have *you* to live for?"

A strangled hiss answered. At the end of her arm, the monster inched a hand across his cheek, flicked a claw—and hooked his eye socket. Sunbright shuddered with pain, fright, and pure agony as the flint dagger bit his eyeball.

Dimly, he heard the monster's command, "Release me!"

Growling, Sunbright tried to jerk his head back, but his neck was strained to the limit. His hands jumped and shuddered as he pried at Harvester. He was slowly rising as Sysquemalyn sank into the tar. Her deadly hand ground in his face like a stone spider. The jagged digit pressed harder on his eye. He'd only save his sight by letting go.

But he didn't let go. He groaned, "I'd give my life to save Knucklebones and my people. I'll gladly give an eye to stop *you!*"

With a roar like the ocean crashing on his head, he felt the claw puncture his eyeball. He rasped in pain but shoved harder downward. Blood spilled down his cheek and down the monster's arm like a river.

Sysquemalyn's stone chin touched tar. For the first time, she felt fear. Sunbright held her trapped by the fearsome hook, then stepped on her back to drown her in the hellish tar she'd summoned. Stretched as if on a rack, Sysquemalyn couldn't wriggle free, nor could spells free her. Only the volcano spell, to turn prairie into inferno, would loose the hero, but she'd die too. From her own death, she drew back.

And so lost. For she knew Sunbright was right. She had hate and revenge and the powers of hell to drive her. He had more: the love of a woman and community, a love that made a person sacrifice all. She couldn't defeat him, she could only lose.

Strange, came an errant thought, she never used magic to restore her beauty. Or even considered it.

Bubbling tar filled her gashed mouth, seared her bulging blue eyes. Lacking eyelids, she had no protection against the hellish stuff, and felt it burn deep, as Sunbright's ruined eye must pain him. But he was atop while she was pressed into tar like a dying saber-tooth.

Then Sysquemalyn felt his foot shift, and both sticky feet crush her back. Tar engulfed her, but she'd already given up the fight. If she couldn't get revenge, she got nothing. Was nothing.

Grunting, shaking all over, weakening from loss of blood, the mighty barbarian twisted Harvester's enchanted blade into the gaping wound he'd inflicted on his enemy. Stabbing the thing was as difficult as prying open a mountain with a chisel, but the enchanted blade cut, and his native strength of arm and spirit bore down.

With a final heave, he slammed the sword through Sysquemalyn's spine. The tarry flint-hided monster writhed once, then lay still.

Weaving, Sunbright let go the blade. The monster didn't move. Sysquemalyn, a self-made monster, was dead.

Finished with his grisly task, bleeding in a hundred places, scorched, seared, and exhausted, Sunbright had a sudden, dim vision.

Long ago, the Shaman Owldark dreamed of Sunbright standing with bloody sword while smoke and fire filled the horizon. The reindeer were slaughtered, the tribe was shattered and defeated.

Was this that vision?

Then he toppled like a felled tree, and crashed on his back in roiling tar.

Chapter 21

Sunbright awoke in a strange place.

Beams and planks stretched overhead, reaching a point at the top. A familiar ceiling, like the hide yurts of his childhood. Sunlight slanted through a doorway. His vision was oddly flat and tilted to the right.

"Where am I?"

"Uh!" Knucklebones grunted, startled. She had sat by his side, head on her knees, napping. "You're awake!"

"Yes," he croaked. "Water, please."

Gently, the small thief lifted his head and helped him sip from a gourd. The tiny trickle extinguished a fire in his throat. A drink of water when you're dry, he concluded, was the richest gift of the gods.

Sipping, he studied his lover's face. She was pale and worn with bright scabs on both cheeks. Her hair was disordered and lank, and burned short in patches. Her normally nimble hands were clumsy with bandages.

Questions bubbled in his mind.

"How long. . . ?"

"Three days. The elves helped with healing spells, and the dwarves brought a dark bread that gives strength, though we had to mash it to gruel to feed you."

"Your hands?"

"Burned them pulling you from the tar. I thought— we thought—you were dead."

Sunbright laid his head back. "I almost was," he told her softly, "but I had a lot to tell you, so I needed to survive. I had more than the monster. She had nothing."

"She?"

"Sysquemalyn. Just a woman who'd suffered and craved revenge on the world. She wasted the powers of a goddess. Revenge is not cool and sweet. It's a fire that burns you inside, and leaves a hollow shell."

Knucklebones wondered if he remembered his own brooding before he found his people. To change the subject, she spooned venison broth to his lips from a wooden bowl.

"What did you want to tell me?"

"Eh? Oh," he stammered. "That I love you."

Tired, she yet smiled, and leaned close to kiss his forehead. He smelled her perfume: sweat and spice and wood smoke, and a breath of wildflowers. "I knew that," she said.

"No. Not just that." He reared to his elbows and spoke intensely, "That I love *you,* Knucklebones, not anyone else, not the memory of poor, dead Greenwillow. I love what you are, a small sweet woman with a good heart. When I look at you, I don't think of another woman, or anything else. Just wonderful you." He flopped back, exhausted, and said, "Which is funny, in a way."

His kind words made tears stain her scabby cheek, but her mouth turned down. "Funny how?" she asked.

"Something else I needed to tell you. The elven priestess, Brookdweller, touched your hand and read your soul. She learned that your father was Eaerlanni, but you were also a Moon Elf, of the Illefarni. I may have the names wrong, but that's the idea. The clues confused her for a while, and you ran off. How the gods must laugh at us . . . !"

His voice trailed off as he nodded. Knucklebones touched his shoulder. "What?" she asked. "Please, tell me. What of my ancestry?"

"Hunh!" He blinked awake, and said, "After all my foolish chasing of Greenwillow's ghost, it turns out you *are* Greenwillow."

"What?" she breathed. The thief's mouth hung open, her single eye stared.

"Reincarnated . . ." Sunbright fought sleep to relate the vital news, "You were born in the future, three hundred years from now, but all things return to their roots. Brookdweller read your past lives. A recent one was Greenwillow. That's why you called me country mouse. It's why I confused you and Greenwillow in dreams. It's why we were attracted in the first place, because I was hunting Greenwillow. Fate brought us together, but I ignored you to find Greenwillow, when you were both by my side all the time. . . ."

He blacked out. Knucklebones laid her tousled head on his chest, listened to his heart thump, and sighed with contentment.

When next Sunbright awoke, the sun was gone, and cool night air bathed his face while a nearby fire warmed him.

"He's awake."

Sunbright shook his aching head, tried to focus, but still found the world curiously flat. An audience knelt around his pallet. Many elves in green and black, bristling with arrows and bows and knives, all strangers, yet oddly familiar. One was small and wore a green eye patch. With a jolt, the shaman recognized Knucklebones. She smiled shyly.

"Sunbright, I'd like you to meet some people who've

journeyed from the Star Mounts in the High Forest. My—family." To his dazed look, the thief explained, "They're kin to Greenwillow. They heard of my ancestry from Brookdweller and came to meet me. Fashioned new clothes for me, too."

She made a small curtsy, the first Sunbright had ever seen. Cleaned and rested, in shining elven clothes of soft green and deep black leather, Knucklebones looked like a princess. The shaman sighed, "You're beautiful."

Awkwardly, the part-elf made introductions. "My father, Marshwind. My mother, Pinemagic. My sisters Gracewealth, Butterfly, Earthstork, and my brother, Fullshrub."

Solemnly the elves nodded in turn, and Sunbright knew why they looked so familiar. They resembled Greenwillow. He chuckled, "I'm happy to meet Knucklebones's family. She's wanted one all her life. Pardon me if I don't rise."

The elves smiled. A tall woman with Greenwillow's eyes laid a hand on his chest and said, "We go. Rest. We'll have much to discuss with our new brother-in-law." Silent as cats, they padded from the room.

Knucklebones lingered. Sunbright shook his head again, still couldn't clear his vision. When he pawed at his face, she caught his hand. "Don't, please," she said. "It's gone."

"Gone?"—then he understood—"My eye. The monster gouged it out."

"The elves healed the infected socket, but there was nothing to save." She smiled weakly when she said, "You'll need an eye patch, like mine. I'll embroider you one."

Sunbright lay still. He felt no sorrow. One-eyed was better than dead. Suddenly he smiled at her.

"We'd best stick together, to have one good pair of eyes between us, but our children will think anyone outside the family strange . . . with two orbs."

Chuckling, the transformed Knucklebones kissed his forehead. "Rest," she said, and Sunbright blacked out.

A day later he could sit up, propped by a wicker backrest. His mother fed him strips of meat, bread soaked in beer, and apple slices.

"Your father would be proud. Your sacrifices have brought the tribe safety and prosperity. But I'm glad you lost an eye, for now you must leave fighting to others. I don't want to lose my only son."

Sunbright smiled, munched, and teased, "Why the only? You're still young and attractive, mother. Why not get married again, have another brood?" His mother tweaked his nose.

With permission from Monkberry, Magichunger came to visit. Sunbright hardly recognized the war chief, for he'd finally shaved his scruffy beard and temples, reclaiming the traditional haircut of a Rengarth warrior. The blocky man rubbed his chin as if it itched, or he were embarrassed.

He hemmed and hawed so much that Sunbright asked a neutral question to ease his mind, "What is this building?"

"Hunh? Oh, this." The war chief looked around and said, "We finally finished the common house. Just dropped other tasks and fell to until it was built. We've kept the council fire alive, too. It's the same one you started. We figured there'd be lots of . . ."

He scratched his white temples, scuffed his foot. "We've, uh, talked," Magichunger finally said. "For five days now. And the tribe's decided you aren't banished for using magic. Shamans use spirit magic anyway, and you needed that enchanted sword—That was some fierce battle, Sunbright! I've never seen its like! You two clashed like mammoths, like *gods!* And you wouldn't quit, even when she jabbed your—Uh, well, anyway . . . That was braver than I could be. And another thing. I want to, uh, thank you for bringing us here, and together . . ."

Sunbright raised a hand that quaked, for he was still weak. Bemused, Magichunger shook. The shaman said, "I did nothing but recall who we are. The tribe decided to come here, and together came to safety, with a great amount of your help. I thank you for that."

"Oh . . ." The war chief actually blushed. He said, "Bashing orcs in the head, that was nothing."

Sunbright asked for news, and the war chief gladly changed the subject. Refugees and raiders still drifted into the territory, but under control. Magichunger and Mightylaugh had arranged a warning system with Hilel's horse clan.

"Any decent folk we let stay, as long as they promise to work as hard as we do. Raiders we disarm and turn back. We've had to kill a few, but it's been pretty peaceful. More than the empire can boast. Stragglers tell us there's famine, and the One King's orcs are still raiding while the empire's army is splintered and looting. People in the floating cities squabble over who should run the empire so much they're assassinating each other. It's a mess."

"Yes, I know," Sunbright said. He had visited the future, had seen the ingrown shambles the empire would become, before Karsus finally destroyed it. "I've known for a while, and fear the empire's collapse might harm our people. That's why I must announce the rest of my plan."

"Plan?" Slow-thinking Magichunger frowned. "What plan? You're not going to meddle with tradition again, are you?"

"Yes and no," he said. Sunbright smiled at his oblique answer. He wasn't done fighting yet, not with the future at stake. "Hand me my sword, please?"

"Eh?" The war chief took Sunbright's scabbard from a peg on the wall and said, "Who will you bash now? I can't imagine a fair fight. This enchanted sword is a dragon killer!"

"True. Too much sword for me. Can you summon Drigor, please?"

A fuddled Magichunger left while Sunbright nodded off.

"What is it?" A gruff tone woke him. Drigor stood in his stained apron, gnarled hands bunched at his hips and said, "I hope this's important. With new folk streaming in and a mighty heap of weapons to turn into tools, I'm busy night and day."

Sunbright smiled at the crusty dwarf and said, "And you're happiest when busiest. So I've another task, if you will. Take my sword please. Take Harvester of Blood back to the forge."

"To the forge?" Drigor asked. Stunned, the dwarf propped the sword beside him, tall as himself. "What shall I do there?"

Slowly, Sunbright gave instructions. Before he finished, the dwarf was hopping in place, face red as an apoplectic fit. "Are you *mad?*" Drigor growled. "Stark, staring *crazy?* This sword is a legend! It's history! It's—it's never been done before, dwarves sharing secrets with elves to forge this—a blade fit for a king! An emperor! A conqueror!"

"But I'm none of those," Sunbright returned mildly. "Just a simple shaman trying to guide his people. And they won't listen unless they see me sacrifice as much as they do. Please, do it."

Grumbling, cursing, stamping pitchy boots, the dwarf dragged the sword as he stalked out. Over his shoulder he bawled, "I don't expect *humans* to make sensible decisions!"

"Neither do I."

Sunbright snuggled down to sleep in carefree warmth.

* * * * *

Three nights later, Sunbright was strong enough to leave the council hut.

"But mind," Monkberry warned, "there'll be a few surprises."

"Did everyone move away while I was asleep?" Sunbright joked.

He limped, stiff, bruised, raddled with scabs that itched and cracked, clumsy with one eye, and muzzy from a bandage swaddling his skull. Monkberry propped one side, Knucklebones the other. Then he jumped, startled.

For as Sunbright appeared at the lodge's door, a thunderous cheer exploded in the frosty winter sky. Humans, elves, and dwarves hooted, applauded, sang, hollered, and laughed. Sunbright just stared, stunned, while the cheering rang on and on. He shook his head like an old man chiding children, but with a smile.

Slowly, he was eased into a wicker chair at the council fire pit. Sunbright breathed slowly to clear his head, then looked around. Stretching into the darkness, hundreds of barbarians packed the hollow around the council ring. Salted amidst them were elves like bright green flowers, including Knucklebones's new family, and Drigor's dwarves, hunched like stones. There were many strangers, mostly humans, but also gnomes and even half-ogres, all refugees who'd found safety in this pacified pocket of a chaotic empire. Among them were Hilel's horse wranglers in wool shirts and leather trousers and caps.

When the crowd grew silent, Sunbright talked. He greeted many by name, thanked all for coming to council, and talked of the weather and how peaceful and beautiful the land looked from their hard work. The crowd strained to hear his weak voice. Finally, he got to his main point.

"My friends, I've bad news, but also a hope. We know the tundra is dying, and may be dead entirely. All the empire's lands suffer, and the most fragile die first. So we are banished from our ancestral hunting grounds, cut off from the old way of life. So my bad news is, we must change again."

A rustle shook the crowd, but a minor one. Everyone knew the truth. Their question was: What next?

Sunbright told them, "We've prospered here, on the edge of the forest that the elves graciously lent us. And the dwarves revel in the mountains, now almost clear of monsters and renegades. And, too, our ancestral prairie lands beckon, though they too suffer a shortage of game.

"Lacking the tundra, I propose we stay put for now: elves in the forest, dwarves in the mountains, barbarians on the plain. We work well together. Our mighty triangle can stave off threats from any direction in wartime. Peacetime will be even better. From this triangle, we can cross the plains to link with coastal towns and the Narrow Sea and the south, establish trade routes through the forest in the west, build bridges over the northern mountains. Everyone, every race, can benefit by the alliance, and everyone can eat well."

He let the words sink in. There were no objections, for already combined parties of humans, dwarves, and elves had spoken of building trading posts, arranging caravans, cutting roads and bridges. And Sunbright saw other alliances being formed, for the barbarian Blackblossom held the hand of elven Starvalley.

He went on, "But for our own, personal change. We Rengarth Barbarians cannot subsist on six miles of trees and a day's walk of grasslands. We'd scrimp all our lives just to eat, always be poorer cousins of prosperous ones around us. Yet if we can't trek the tundra after herds of reindeer, can't spear the seal through the ice, can't smoke the white bear from his cave, can't trap salmon in weirs, how shall we live? I've thought on this a long time, and have a proposal. I only ask you consider it. Drigor, the bag, please."

Hundreds of barbarians and friends watched the stumpy dwarf set a large leather bag by Sunbright's feet, for the shaman was still too weak to hold it. With clumsy fingers Sunbright untied the leather while hundreds held their breath. Yet when he finally plucked something from the bag, a puzzled buzz arose.

Sunbright held up two large rings joined loosely by a metal bar. He jingled the steel to catch the firelight. Then he flung the object across the circle. Hilel, the refugee hostler, jumped as it landed in his lap. The shaman called, "Hilel, what is it?"

The horse wrangler held it up. "A horse bit. You put it in the nag's mouth to attach a bridle."

"It's that, and our new way of life."

Over the rising buzz, Sunbright explained, "Barbarians don't ride horses, I know. I've heard it a hundred times. They walk, and follow reindeer. Such is tradition. But the reindeer are gone while horses run wild on the plains. And who here hasn't mounted a reindeer as a child and taken a ride?" His smile brought chuckles, but most faces bore mixed emotions: curiosity, fear of change, hope, doubt.

"Always the Rengarth roamed the tundra. Now I would amend that. Now we can roam the plains on horseback. There are antelope to round up, and cattle, and bison, and deer. By learning to ride, the Rengarth could journey all over our ancestral plains—not just a day's walk out and back, but a hundred miles in a week! We'd not be penned to this six-mile strip of forest, but have all the grasslands under our feet and hooves!"

He called in a confident tone over the babble, "I know 'twill take time to learn new skills, to learn to ride and rope and drive livestock, but it's worth it! And we have good teachers, for Hilel's family has run horses for generations. Now, who's willing to try this new style of roaming?" Sunbright reached into the bag, pulled out another jingling horse bit.

"Wait!" Magichunger scratched his shorn temple. "Where'd you get all those—what'd you call them—horse bits?"

"Ah," Sunbright said and leaned back, tired but happy. His work was almost done. "Drigor's doing. I gave him my sword, Harvester of Blood, you see, and he cut it up, reforged it into twenty-odd horse bits."

A chorus of protests welled, barbarians stunned at the news. That legendary sword, a sword of kings, chopped into scrap metal? Sunbright cut off the protests by jingling the steel bit.

"We needed steel for our new way of life, so I gave up my enchanted sword. I hope some enchantment lingers in these new tools. Harvester of Blood has become many Harvesters of Horses! Now, who wants one?"

A rush like wind in the trees swept the audience. Above the noise, Blackblossom let go Starvalley's hand. "I'll take one!" she called.

"Good!" Sunbright flung the glittering metal over the crowd.

The elf Starvalley raised an elegant hand and called, "I, too, please."

"Elves join us in riding!" Sunbright crowed, and flung another horse bit.

"Hang on!" bellowed Magichunger. "I want one! I can watch better from atop a horse!" Metal pinwheeled by firelight.

Then most everyone wanted one. The dwarf Hachne yelled he'd learn to ride a pony. Goodbell would teach her children to ride. Mightylaugh needed to stay close to Magichunger. Firstfortune and other hunters could track and hunt from horseback. And so it went, people flinging up hands and grabbing for flying steel, until Sunbright's bag was empty and he slumped, exhausted.

He hollered, "Drigor, you might switch to making horse tackle. You won't lack for customers! Oh, I'm so tired!"

Knucklebones left her new family to join her lover. Kneeling, she kissed his cold hand and said, "I'm so proud of you, Sunbright. You've done so much for so many. But you sacrificed your beautiful sword!"

"That suits me fine," he said, and squeezed her hand. "I've had enough fighting to last a lifetime. From now on, I'll work to heal, and keep peace. We've many warriors, but only one shaman, and I'll be busy. And happy. But will you be?"

The thief smiled and kissed his cheek. "I couldn't be more happy, Sunbright. I've a new family. I'm back in the thick of busyness, just like in Karsus, and it'll be busier from now on. We'll be a city before long! And—"

Warmed by the fire, wrung out by healing wounds, Sunbright nodded, but jerked awake.

"And what?"

"And—" Knucklebones blushed. "And I'll be busy tending our first child."

"Our first . . ." Suddenly awake, Sunbright hugged her till she squeaked. "Oh, Knuckle'! The first of many, we hope. Some to ride the plains, and some to walk the woods. Others to work the mountains, or follow trade routes."

"And one child to become shaman," Knucklebones added.

"Shaman?" Sunbright slumped again. "Oh, no. It's such a burden, I wouldn't wish it on any child. But I suppose. . . ."

"It will be so," Knucklebones smiled. "It's tradition."

Epilogue

The tundra never did heal, for the empire lands, drained of life by the alien Phaerimm and exhausted by the greed of the archwizards, declined slowly like a forest of dying redwoods. After the End of the End, the last vestiges of the Netherese Empire were swallowed by sand to become Anauroch, the Great Desert. The Narrow Sea dried year by year, eventually disappearing, so the High Ice and Sunbright's tundra receded into a rocky wasteland.

With the tundra died the Rengarth Barbarians' way of life, but under the guidance of Sunbright and Knucklebones, and their descendants, the Rengarth lived on, though they eventually changed into—

But that's another story. . . .

The Netheril Trilogy by **Clayton Emery** began in . . .

Sword Play

Sunbright, banished from his home, finds himself the unwitting pawn of two of the Empire of Netheril's powerful archwizards. Their game sends him across the empire, and to hell itself!

. . . continued in . . .

Dangerous Games

Pulled through time by Karsus, the greatest archwizard Netheril has ever seen, Sunbright and Candlemas fight to survive the greatest catastrophe in the history of Faerûn!

. . . both available now from TSR!

For more adventures involving the legendary past of the FORGOTTEN REALMS world, look for:

Elminster in Myth Drannor

Faerûn's greatest mage in Cormanthyr's greatest city, as only **Ed Greenwood** can tell it! Available now in hardcover!

Realms of the Arcane

An all new anthology by your favorite FORGOTTEN REALMS authors takes you into the misty beginnings of TSR's most popular setting! Available now!